Murder Backstairs

A
James "Bonnie" Dundee Mystery

By Anne Austin

Originally published in 1930

Murder Backstairs

© 2015 Resurrected Press
www.ResurrectedPress.com

Published by Resurrected Press

This classic book was handcrafted by Resurrected Press. Resurrected Press is dedicated to bringing high quality classic books back to the readers who enjoy them. These are not scanned versions of the originals, but, rather, quality checked and edited books meant to be enjoyed!

Please visit ResurrectedPress.com to view our entire catalogue!

For updates on future releases, LIKE us on Facebook:
http://www.Facebook.com/ResurrectedPress

ISBN 13: 978-1-937022-95-2

Printed in the United States of America

MORE MYSTERIES BY ANNE AUSTIN

Murder at Bridge

When an afternoon bridge party attended by some of Hamilton's leading citizens ends with the hostess being murdered in her boudoir, Special Investigator Dundee of the District Attorney's office is called in. But which one of the attendees is guilty? There are plenty of suspects: the victim's former lover, her current suitor, the retired judge who is being blackmailed, the victim's maid who had been horribly disfigured accidentally by the murdered woman, or any of the women who's husbands had flirted with the victim. Or was she murdered by an outsider whose motive had nothing to do with the town of Hamilton. Find the answer in . . . Murder at Bridge

One Drop of Blood

When Dr. Koenig, head of Mayfield Sanitarium is murdered, the District Attorney's Special Investigator, "Bonnie" Dundee must go undercover to find the killer. Were any of the inmates of the asylum insane enough to have committed the crime? Or, was it one of the staff, motivated by jealousy? And what was is the secret in the murdered man's past. Find the answer in . . . One Drop of Blood

The Black Pigeon

There were plenty of reasons for "Handsome Harry" Borden to be murdered. After all, he had cost numerous investors their life savings with questionable securities. And he had left his wife for a string of actresses and dancers, only to shed each in turn for a new flame. And the office boy that he had bullied. Not to mention the jealous boyfriend of his secretary to whom he had made unwanted advances. So there were plenty of suspects when was found dead of a gunshot wound in his office. The question is, which of them actually committed the crime?

Resurrected Press Books in A. E. Fielding's *The Chief Inspector Pointer Mystery* Series

RESURRECTED PRESS CLASSIC MYSTERY CATALOGUE

J. S. Fletcher

The Herapath Property
The Rayner-Slade Amalgamation
The Chestermarke Instinct
The Paradise Mystery
Dead Men's Money
The Middle of Things
Ravensdene Court
Scarhaven Keep
The Orange-Yellow Diamond
The Middle Temple Murder
The Tallyrand Maxim
The Borough Treasurer
In the Mayor's Parlour
The Saftey Pin

R. Austin Freeman

The Mystery of 31 New Inn from the Dr. Thorndyke Series
John Thorndyke's Cases from the Dr. Thorndyke Series
The Red Thumb Mark from The Dr. Thorndyke Series
The Eye of Osiris from The Dr. Thorndyke Series
A Silent Witness from the Dr. John Thorndyke Series
The Cat's Eye from the Dr. John Thorndyke Series
Helen Vardon's Confession: A Dr. John Thorndyke Story
As a Thief in the Night: A Dr. John Thorndyke Story
Mr. Pottermack's Oversight: A Dr. John Thorndyke Story
Dr. Thorndyke Intervenes: A Dr. John Thorndyke Story
The Singing Bone: The Adventures of Dr. Thorndyke
The Stoneware Monkey: A Dr. John Thorndyke Story
The Great Portrait Mystery, and Other Stories: A Collection of Dr. John Thorndyke and Other Stories
The Penrose Mystery: A Dr. John Thorndyke Story

The Uttermost Farthing: A Savant's Vendetta

Arthur Griffiths
The Passenger From Calais
The Rome Express

Fergus Hume
The Mystery of a Hansom Cab
The Green Mummy
The Silent House
The Secret Passage

Edgar Jepson
The Loudwater Mystery

A. E. W. Mason
At the Villa Rose

A. A. Milne
The Red House Mystery

Baroness Emma Orczy
The Old Man in the Corner

Edgar Allan Poe
The Detective Stories of Edgar Allan Poe

Arthur J. Rees
The Hampstead Mystery
The Shrieking Pit
The Hand In The Dark
The Moon Rock
The Mystery of the Downs

Mary Roberts Rinehart
Sight Unseen and The Confession

Dorothy L. Sayers

FOREWORD

Anne Austin began her career as an author writing romance stories in the mid 1920's, but soon switched to the mystery genre. Several of her early mysteries first appeared in serial format, a form that was popular with the newspapers and magazines of the period.

Detective fiction was evolving in a number of directions at the time. In Britain it was the "Golden Age" where writers such as Agatha Christie and Dorothy L. Sayers were documenting the exploits of such stylish sleuths as Hercule Poirot and Lord Peter Wimsey. In America the homegrown domestic mysteries of Mary Roberts Rinehart and Carolyn Wells was being joined by the first of the hard-boiled stories and novels of writers such as Dashiell Hammett and Raymond Chandler. Such was the state of the mystery novel when Anne Austin began writing in the genre.

Her first mystery, *The Black Pigeon,* is similar in many ways to Carolyn Wells' *The Man Who Fell Through the Earth.* Both deal with a murder that takes place in an office building and both involve young women who are forced to assume the role of detective. For her next mystery, though, *The Avenging Parrot,* she was to switch to a male character, the detective James "Bonnie" Dundee, as she sought to find her own unique style. Dundee was to appear in a number of mysteries in the 1930's through *Murdered But Not Dead,* which was published in 1939.

Dundee is something of a hybrid character. Though he is college educated, he works within the official system, first as a detective on the Hamilton Police's Homicide Squad, and then as Special Investigator for the District Attorney's Office beginning in the book *Murder at Bridge.* Yet, despite his official position he operates with a great deal of independence, almost as if he was one of the British sleuths. Unlike these, however, his method of operation depends not so much on brilliant deduction as on traditional police work, the finding of evidence and tracking down the details of the suspects past. And at each step of the way he must deal with Captain Strawn, chief of the Homicide Squad, who is always quick to jump at a theory, and is by turns Dundee's boss, friend, colleague and nemesis.

Though it takes place in the Midwest town of Hamilton, *Murder Backstairs* takes the form of a British country house mystery. A number of guests including Dundee are spending the weekend at the estate of Mr. and Mrs. George Berkeley where the occasion is the announcement of the engagement of the Berkeley's eldest daughter. The weekend is interrupted when the body of one of the maids is found in a lake on the estate, the victim of a murder. Suspicion falls on the chauffeur, the butler, the fiancé, and various members of the Berkeley family as the details of various events in the past come to light and the relationships between the characters unfold, and ultimately it is Dundee's ability to understand these which leads to the solution of the crime.

Subsequent mysteries involving Bonnie Dundee were to take on a grittier, darker edge, though they never approached the true hard-boiled tone of Hammett or Chandler. Dundee remains at heart an optimist with a positive view of humanity even as he is aware of the foibles and flaws of those he is forced to investigate. As an author of detective fiction, Anne Austin walks a middle ground between the slick and the rough, successfully putting together mysteries that are both engaging and with depth.

Despite the fact that she wrote a dozen or more novels and her work appeared in serial form in a number of newspapers, Anne Austin is today one of those obscure mystery writers of the 1930's who is little known and whose work has not been readily available. It is with pleasure, then, that Resurrected Press offers its readers this new edition of *Murder Backstairs*.

About the Author

Born in 1895, Anne Austin began by writing romance novels about young women in the mid 1920's but soon turned her talents to producing a string of mysteries through the 1930's, some of which appeared as serials in newspapers.. Many of these mysteries feature as the detective "Bonnie" Dundee, Special Investigator for the District Attorney, including *Murder Backstairs*, *The Avenging Parrot*, *Murder at Bridge*, and *One Drop of Blood*. Several of her mysteries were translated into French, including *Le Pigeon Noir* and *Le Crime Parfume*. Despite her success as a novelist, Anne Austin disappears from the public record after the 1930's.

Greg Fowlkes
Editor-In-Chief
Resurrected Press
www.ResurrectedPress.com
www.Facebook.com/ResurrectedPress

I.

"Λ note for you, Mr. Dundee. Delivered by the Berkeleys' chauffeur in a limousine and a plum-colored uniform," Mrs. Caroline Rhodes announced, when admitted to the bedroom of her favorite boarder. "I hope it's not another warning that a murder is to be committed, though if that note is from Abbie Berkeley I wouldn't be a bit surprised to hear she's yelling for help—and I can't say I'd be sorry, either!" she added grimly.

"Whew! You *are* bloodthirsty!" the novice detective grinned at his landlady. "Sorry to disappoint you, Mother Rhodes, but this is nothing more exciting than a written confirmation of an invitation to spend a week-end at Hillcrest, which, I take it, is the name of the Berkeley feudal castle. I ran into young Dick Berkeley on the street to-day and he urged me to lend him the moral support of my presence over a week-end which he seems rather to dread. . . . But do you know Mrs. Berkeley?"

"Know her?" Mrs. Rhodes snorted. "I went to high school with Abbie Berkeley when she was plain Abbie Smith and didn't have three whole dresses or a real friend to her name, and now she stares at me through a pair of specs on a handle like I was a strange kind of insect she hadn't happened to run across before."

"Not an uncommon result of a 'rags-to-riches' romance, is it?" Dundee suggested.

"Well, if there's anything I can't abide, it's a nobody putting on airs like she was the Queen of Roumania," Mrs. Rhodes went on acidly. "Spent a year in Europe with her oldest daughter, Clorinda, and then come trotting home in August with a penniless "high-society" woman from New York for a social secretary, all primed to take Hamilton's social citadel by storm."

"How poetic you are, Mother Rhodes!" Dundee grinned at her delightedly. "Has Hamilton a 'social citadel,' really?"

"I'm only quoting the society editress if *The Morning News*," his landlady defended herself. "She used those very words in her write-up of the big dinner-and-dance Abbie Berkeley is giving to-morrow night. 'To meet Mr. Seymour Crosby, of New York, Palm Beach and Newport,'" she quoted further, in a mincing voice. "Believe me, Bonnie Dundee, if Hamilton's Big Bugs *have* lowered themselves to accept one of Abbie Berkeley's invitations, it was out of curiosity to see this Mrs. Lambert and because she's managed to get a real swell like Seymour Crosby roped in to help Abbie's game along."

"Just who *is* Mrs. Lambert?" Dundee asked cheerfully, as he set about packing his dressing-case for the week-end.

"Mrs. Letitia Lambert, of course. I guess everybody that can read has heard of the Lambert family," Mrs. Rhodes informed him scornfully. "Real society people since before the Revolution. This Mrs. Lambert was the beautiful Letitia Cavendish, who refused the hands of a prince and of an earl to marry, Van Rensselaer Lambert—"

"As well she might, if he had a name like that," Dundee chuckled. "Still quoting the society editress, I suppose?"

"Well, if I am, I suppose she knows what she's talking about," Mrs. Rhodes retorted. "She had a big write-up of Mrs. Lambert when Abbie Berkeley and Clorinda brought her home with them from Europe, like a prize dog on a leash."

"Poor Mrs. Lambert," Dundee sympathized. "Now, Mother Rhodes, be a lamb and help me check this junk to see if I have enough glad rags to last me over a Berkeley week-end."

Mrs. Rhodes bent over the dressing-case. "Tennis flannels. That's right. They've got a court. . . . Golf plus-fours, woolen stockings, sports shirts. . . . They'll be dragging you over to the Country Club to play golf and I'll bet my new fall hat Abbie'll apologize because their own private golf course ain't laid out yet! . . . What's this? Just a Tuxedo? Haven't you got a swallow-tail coat? I told you the big blow-out to-morrow night is to be formal. . . . Well, if you haven't you haven't, and I guess they ought to be glad to have you, even if you wore overalls."

"What about a little low comedy to liven things up to-morrow evening? I might pin my detective badge on my evening waistcoat and flash it nonchalantly," Dundee suggested, his blue eyes wicked with amusement at his landlady's horror.

"Abbie Berkeley'd have her butler throw you out and then she'd disinherit Dick Berkeley for having invited such low life scum," Mrs. Rhodes assured him. "You didn't let on to Dick that you're a detective now, did you?"

"No," Dundee admitted, "but a crook disguised as a lady or a gentleman might pinch the fair Abbie's pearls and it would come in handy top have a detective on the scene. . . . After all, I'll have to give Captain Strawn *some* excuse for being off duty for a whole week-end. . . . Not that anything every happens in this town, since Dan Griffin was removed from circulation," he added gloomily. "Not a single, honest-to-God murder mystery in two and a half months. I've a good notion to move to Chicago!"

"Now who's bloodthirsty?"Mrs. Rhodes mocked. "And where's your bathing suit? . . . Give it to me! There's a natural lake at Hillcrest that's been deepened and enlarged, and if the temperature ain't below zero Abbie Berkeley will make you all try out her swimming pool if she has to push you in."

"You *do* love Abbie, don't you?" Dundee grinned. "I take it she must be rather poisonous. Perhaps if her guests or her family feel as you do about her, my week-

end won't be wasted—speaking from a professional
standpoint."

"When you see—and *hear!*—Abbie Berkeley I guess
you'll understand," Mrs. Rhodes assured him grimly.
"But where did you know Dick Berkeley? At college I
suppose?"

"Right!" Dundee agreed, as he snapped the lock of the
dressing-case. "He was a freshman when I was a senior
at Yale. I didn't know him very well, but naturally we
greeted each other like chums when he bumped into me
on Grand Street to-day."

"Did he tell you he got expelled from Yale for drinking
and girl-chasing?" Mrs. Rhodes demanded from the door.
"The papers said he'd left college on account of illness, but
it didn't take long for the true story to get around."

Dundee grinned, but said nothing. He was
remembering the shamefaced bravado with which young
Dick had confessed: "Kicked out in my sophomore year.
Drunk and disorderly. Particularly disorderly. It turned
out she *was* a 'nice girl'—just as she claimed to be!"

"Well, I'll be going, if there's nothing more I can do for
you," Mrs. Rhodes said. Then she added, her lips
quivering: "I suppose you think I'm nothing but a loose-
tongued old gossip—"

"You know I think nothing of the sort," Dundee
protested. "I appreciate your giving me an informal
introduction to my hostess, and to prove it I'm going to
ask you to tell me something more: Have the papers
hinted at the real reason for Seymour Crosby's visit to the
Berkeleys?"

"The society editress said in the paper this morning 'A
little bird tells me that a very interesting announcement
may be expected at the formal dinner-dance on Saturday
evening. Mr. Crosby, who was a fellow-passenger of Mrs.
Berkeley and Miss Clorinda Berkeley when they returned
from Europe on the Mauretania in August, is said to have
been markedly attentive to the beautiful young heiress.' .
. . She might just as well have come out and said that

Seymour Crosby is marrying Clorinda for her money. And it beats me that a fine man like George Berkeley will stand for it."

"I wonder," Dundee remarked, carefully casual, "if the well-informed society editress said anything else particularly enlightening about Mr. Seymour Crosby?"

"There! I knew there was a nigger in the woodpile!" Mrs. Rhodes cried triumphantly. "I'll bet you your next week's board bill it wasn't till Dick Berkeley mentioned Seymour Crosby that you agreed to fritter away a week-end playing society! *Maybe you'd better put that badge in your suitcase!*"

"I'm afraid I'll have to pay my next week's board bill as usual," Dundee confirmed her suspicions obliquely. And he took her suggestion—pinning the silver star securely inside a cretonne pocket of the case.

"The society editress didn't *dare* say anything about— *that!*" Mrs. Rhodes nodded her severely coiffed gray head emphatically, as her eyes narrowed. The annoyance chased away the look of mystery. "Oh, there's that Tilda! She stands right in the middle of the downstairs hall and *bawls* when she wants me. . . . I do hope you'll have a nice time, Mr. Dundee—*and get what you're going after!* Don't worry about your parrot. I'll feed him myself, and come up as often as I can to keep him company. We've got our own secrets, haven't we, Cap'n?"

The parrot, which had belonged to Mrs. Emma Hogarth, one of the victims in the first murder case "Bonnie" Dundee had solved after joining the Homicide Squad of the Hamilton Detective Bureau, and which had been of very real assistance in bringing her murder to justice, now stirred on his perch, flapped his green-and-yellow wings, and obligingly rewarded Mrs. Rhodes with a hollow cackle of mirth for her exit line.

"I hate to leave you, 'my dear Watson,'" Dundee told the parrot, reaching into the cage to scratch the brilliant plumage.

The parrot cocked his head, then slowly drooped a paperish white eyelid.

"Eh? What's that?" the detective demanded. "You mean to imply that we shan't be separated so long as I think? That I may be sending for 'my dear Watson'? Let's hope not, but I assure you that if business looks up at Hillcrest this particular Sherlock could not get along without his Watson. . . . So long, old top. I've got to rush to get there in time for dinner. And I rather wish I had time to look into a newspaper file of some eighteen months ago—or that I had as good a memory as my astute landlady."

If the "society editress" in her much-quoted story had referred to to Hillcrest as "palatial." The adjective was not ill-advised. For the house was a huge, three-story affair of rough-hewn white stone, with gables and turrets in profusion, and a respectably imposing tower at one corner. Encircling the thirty acres of the estate was a high wrought-iron fence, but the pair of stately gates was not locked, nor had the Berkeleys yet achieved the dignity of a gatekeeper.

As his taxi swept around the curved drive Dundee caught a glimpse of the lake. The setting sun turned it into a broad pool of molten gold, and for the first time since he had accepted the urgent invitation from Dick Berkeley, the young detective felt a thrill of anticipation not at all connected with his profession. Certainly this week-end would afford a welcome change from the clamor and friendly familiarity of the boarding house. And he had not played for rather too long, considering how young he was and how much he liked to play.

His taxi driver was holding open the door. Dundee hesitated before descending. Had Mrs. Rhodes frightened him? That was absurd, of course. He was not here to ingratiate himself with Mr. George Berkeley. He was here to make a keen, close study of Mr. Seymour Crosby for certain reasons of his own. . . .

But any qualms he felt as to the warmth of his welcome in that impressive house were quickly dispelled. Indeed, the young detective, whose official connection with the Homicide Squad was known to only a very limited number of trusted people, found himself embarrassed by his hostess' effusiveness when, with Dick Berkeley, he made his first appearance in the drawing room at the dinner hour that Friday evening.

Short, stout, rigidly corseted, and swathed in fluttering draperies of violet chiffon, whose color warred with the orange rouge on her puffy face, with the pale blue of her prominent eyes, and with the harsh henna of her mechanically waved hair, Mrs. George Berkeley bore down upon him.

"*Dear* Mr. Dundee! You don't know how delighted I am that my darling Dick has found a congenial spirit in this ghastly little town!" she caroled, offering him both her heavily ringed hands. "The poor boy has been simply starved for intellectual companionship. Simply starved! Dick tells me that since you graduated from Yale you have been studying in Europe. You lucky boy! But now don't you find America frightfully crude, *bourgeois.* Somehow *metallic,* if you know what I mean?"

"Aw, lay off, Mother!" Dick begged, his weakly handsome young face red with embarrassment. "Dundee's a regular—Oh, hello, Dad! I want you to know Mr. Dundee, a friend of mine at Yale."

And then Dundee shook hands with the handsomest man of middle age that he had ever set eyes upon. If Clorinda Berkeley, by the grace of God, resembled this tall, dark, kingly man, instead of "taking after" her pigeon-breasted, gushing mother, then heaven protect him, for he was due to fall in love again. . . .

"He's in a towering rage about something," Dundee mused, after the conventional greetings. "And I rather think I know what that something is. Looks as if he's just found out exactly whom his wife has roped in for a son-in-law."

"Oh, dear! Wickett is hovering and looking reproachful," Mrs. Berkeley fluttered, with a self-conscious trill of laughter as she cast her eyes toward the butler who had appeared for an instant and then vanished. "I wonder where every one is. *Have* you seen Clorinda, George? And I do wonder where Mrs. Lambert and Mr. Crosby are. . . . Of course, a distinguished guest like Mr. Crosby—" She paused, with an arch, confidential smile at Dundee, then went on in a lowered voice: "But one *would* think that a *paid* social secretary, what*ever* her former position in society, would *rah*-ther make a point of being on time for dinner. . . Oh, there you are!" she caroled, in the imitation-Oxford accent she frequently remembered to assume, her voice rising to draw in the woman who hesitated in the wide, arched doorway.

"*Dear* Mrs. Lambert!" she gushed affectionately. "How very charming you look! I always say a woman with that silvery-white hair looks loveliest in black. I wish *my* hair would turn white, though of course I'm too young—Not that *you* aren't prematurely gray yourself, dear Mrs. Lambert! . . . But do forgive me! You look such a picture that you've made me forget my duties as a hostess. . . . This is Mr. Dundee, Dick's chum from Yale. . . . And Mr. Dundee, may I present Mrs. Lambert, *the* Mrs. Van Rensselaer Lambert of New York and Newport, you know," she added triumphantly, and Dundee, as he bowed, remembered Mrs. Rhodes trite simile—"like a prize dog on a leash."

A tiny smile flickered in the depths of blue-gray eyes as Mrs. Lambert murmured an acknowledgement of the atrocious introduction. But not a vestige of added color in the delicately beautiful face of the social secretary betrayed resentment or annoyance.

She was perhaps forty-five years old, but in spite of her white hair she looked younger. Her graciously mature body looked slenderer than it was in its sheath of black velvet. Dundee's eyes clung to her, grateful for the contrast her quiet elegance and serenity made with the flamboyance and vulgarity of his hostess. She moved lightly toward him, and the smile extended to the thin, sensitive mouth. Dundee felt that she had accepted him at face value, and he was glad. . . .

"What was your class, Mr. Dundee? . . . '26? Then did you by any chance know my young nephew, Tommy Cavendish?"

The two were still talking of the popular and redoubtable Tommy when a miniature storm broke.

"Hi, Dad! 'Lo, Abbie! Am I feahfully late, old thing? . . . Whoops, Dickie! Who manhandled that tie of yours? It's a holy mess! Let me fix it for you. . . . Hullo, Tish darling! You look stunning, and I think you rate a kiss!"

And to Dundee's amazement the small whirlwind, with pale-green chiffon skirts whipping about slim legs, flung herself upon Mrs. Lambert and kissed her soundly. And Mrs. Lambert seemed vastly pleased. . . .

"Gigi! I mean *Georgina!*" Mrs. Berkeley cried despairingly. "How many times have I told you *not* to call me 'Abbie' and not to address Mrs. Lambert as 'Tish'? . . . And if you don't drop your ridiculous imitation of an English accent—"

"Rilly, old thing," the child drawled impudently, "I thought you'd be feahfully pleased, doncha know? 'Subdeb follows in mother's footsteps'—all that rot! . . . No! Let's be brutally frank!" she cried with sudden fierceness. "I do it sole to wise you up to how God-awful it sounds. Abbie! We've got phony furniture and phony culture and a phony family tree. All we've got that isn't phony is *money*, and I guess if the truth were told, that is all Mr. Seymour Crosby is interested in! But I can't bear to have him laugh at us for a phony English accent, on top of everything else—"

"George! *Are* you going to stand there and let that awful child talk to me like that?" Mrs. Berkeley moaned, but the words sounded almost automatic. Dundee was sure it was an ancient, futile plea. "Do you know where your sister is, Gigi?" she added, as if the amazing scene had not taken place.

"She's holding an impassioned telephone conversation in the library," Gigi obliged. "I listened, but I couldn't make out a word. . . . Now may I meet this adorable man? I know he isn't the fascinating *fiancé*, because he hasn't a mustache—"

It was George Berkeley who performed the introduction.

"This is my younger daughter, Gigi, or rather Georgina, Mr. Dundee. . . . A friend of Dick's, from Yale," he added to his daughter, his dark face flushing as he mentioned the college which had not found his son good enough."

"Forget the 'Georgina,' Mr. Dundee," Gigi commanded, thrusting out a tanned little paw. "It's only for official records. I find 'Gigi' an awful useful nickname. Not even Abbie can shout 'Gigi' and sound real sore. . . . Oh, here's Clorinda! Exit little Gigi from the spotlight. Isn't she gorgeous, Mr. Dundee? . . . Rather like an Italian 'old master.' Don't you think? And yet that sophisticated modern touch—"

"Shut up, Gigi!" her father commanded, but he rumpled her short, fire-tipped brown curls with a fond hand.

Dundee scarcely heard the flurry of words with which Mrs. Berkeley introduced her daughter, Clorinda, for his attention was wholly on the tall, dark, arrogant beauty, dressed in a period gown of wine-red velvet. His blue eyes eagerly met the somber, slanting, brown ones, but he had an uncomfortable conviction that Clorinda Berkeley did not see him at all. She bowed slightly, but did not speak. . . .

"Mr. and Mrs. Benjamin—Smith," Wickett announced, and Dundee chuckled to himself as he noted the faint hesitancy and distaste with which the butler pronounced the plebian name.

But perhaps his distaste was for the couple themselves, Dundee decided, as the Benjamin Smiths hurried nervously into the drawing room and had themselves introduced by Mrs. Berkeley as "my brother and his wife." While the detective was guessing that George Berkeley had made a moderately rich man of his brother-in-law out of the kindness of his heart or in self-defense, Mrs. Smith was twittering to him.

"And are *you* Mr. Seymour Crosby? We've been simply dying to meet Clo's young man, and of course we've *read* all the newspaper stories—Even before we knew you'd ever be in the family, Ben and I said to each other we just knew you weren't guilty—"

"Don't be an idiot, Lily!" Mrs. Berkeley cut in sharply. "This is Mr. Dundee, a college friend of Dick's. Mr. Crosby hasn't come down yet and if you *dare* refer to— Oh!" She broke off, as Gigi kicked her. Startled, she glanced toward the wide arch leading into the grand hall. In an instant she had control of herself. She glowered, she beamed, she adored, she fluttered.

Hurrying to meet her honor guest, she brushed aside his low-spoken apologies. "No, silly, *dear* Mr. Crosby! You're not at all late. I *do* hope you found your rooms comfortable, and Johnson not *too* fearful a valet. Mr. Berkeley simply refuses most ridiculously to have a 'man' for himself and Dick, and Johnson is the best dear Mrs. Lambert could do for you locally. . . . But I mustn't monopolize your, must I? I'm afraid you'll find us a dull little family party to-night. We're *rather* saving our energy for the big affair of to-morrow night—"

And thus Detective Dundee met a man whom he would have traveled may miles to look upon, curiously, speculatively. For Dundee was a born detective, and the true story of Seymour Crosby and a certain tragedy in London was one of a score of famous mysteries he would have sacrificed much to solve. . . .

II.

Before Wickett, the butler, had removed the soup plates Detective Dundee had a fair idea that the dinner party, considered from the standpoint of entertainment, was going to be a painful failure. But the food and the wines were superb.

He was rather sorry for Mrs. Berkeley, regardless of his sudden and profound dislike for the hostess. For George Berkeley, brooding somberly at the foot of the table, did not help her at all. When forced to do so, he talked briefly and always well, but during the entire course of the elaborate dinner he did not address a single remark to the honor guest of the evening. But when his black eyes flashed a covert, measuring glance toward Seymour Crosby, the nature of his thoughts might easily be guessed by the tightening of his lips and the flaring of his nostrils.

As for the Benjamin Smiths, they were thorns in the flesh of their hostess, for they were alternately overawed into silence and mysteriously compelled to brief little spurts of embarrassing gayety.

Clorinda Berkeley, coldly arrogant, held herself as aloof as if she were dining alone in a place she did not particularly like. She was, apparently, as determined to ignore her reputed *fiancé* as was her father.

And Dick Berkeley was worse than useless to his mother. His sole interest seemed to be in the various wines which correctly accompanied each course.

During the first ten minutes of the meal Gigi frankly devoted herself to appeasing hunger, so that Dundee, seated between the child and Mrs. Lambert, was free to join the social secretary and Seymour Crosby in a gallant effort to save a party which was already doomed.

Those two were wonderful. Between them, they seemed to have been everywhere, seen everything, heard the best music, read the best books, known all of the most interesting people; but they did not flaunt their knowledge to their advantage. They merely used them or tried to use them to help their hostess. And toward Crosby, Mrs. Berkeley was embarrassingly grateful, drawing him out eagerly; but it was easy for the detective to see that she was not at all pleased with her secretary.

And for all her ease and quiet charm Mrs. Lambert was suffering under the strain. Once when Dundee turned to address her he was amazed to see that one of her beautiful, thin hands was clenched in her lap, although she was listening with an eager smile to one of the few remarks which George Berkeley could bring himself to toss into the conversational pool.

Again, during one of those hate-charged glances which Berkeley sent down the table to Crosby, Dundee's eyes swept from his host's face to the social secretary's and saw there an expression which baffled and startled him.

"Poor thing!" the detective commiserated silently. "I suppose she's simply afraid of losing her job as punishment for having introduced Crosby to Clorinda." But the explanation did not wholly satisfy him. . . .

"Whew! I was hungry! A ride with Dad before breakfast, two hours of tennis with Dick this morning, and eighteen holes of golf this afternoon with Dad—But I'm ready to talk now," Gigi announced to Dundee, when Wickett was removing her entrée plate. "Oh, Lord! There's Abbie after you again! Aren't I every going to have a chance?"

He grinned down at her, then subjected himself as gracefully as possible to another barrage of questions, flattery, and comments upon "bourgeois" Hamilton from his hostess.

"I really can't see, *dear* Mr. Dundee, what a man of your evident culture and social gifts can find to interest him in a provincial little town like Hamilton," his hostess concluded.

"Considering that the 'provincial little town' made us so lousy rich, I think you might lay off it, Abbie," Gigi suggested in her strident young voice. "If you really think all those nasty things—"

"Gig!" her father cut in sternly, and the girl slumped dejectedly into her magnificent chair besides Dundee's.

But she was not crushed for long. In a low, eager voice she challenged her dinner partner, when he had completed his brief defense of Hamilton: "I bet you agree with me, don't you, Mr. Dundee? You're the only thrillingly handsome man I ever saw, besides Dad, who looked as if he had sense."

"Thank you, Gigi," Dundee said gravely.

"You're Scotch-Irish, aren't you? We're English 'way back on Dad's side, and 'pore white trash' on Mother's. That wouldn't be bad at all—might be a lot of fun, in fact, if Abbie weren't trying so damned hard to be 'society.' . . . Of course Dad's a born gentleman. Isn't he precious? Even Mrs. Lambert, who's been friends with royalty, says Dad is the finest type of American thoroughbred. . . . And isn't he gorgeous to look at? I'm nuts about Dad, and it makes Abbie simply wild because I can wind him around my little finger—and she can't."

"I should think you'd be rather expert at winding any male around your most adorable little finger," Dundee assured her gallantly but sincerely.

"Do you really think so?" Gigi was pathetically earnest. "It's terrible to be only fifteen, and not to *know* whether you have sex appeal or not. But I do think I'm going to have quite a lot, don't you? I've only tried it out on Arnold—that's the chauffeur—and he's so disgustingly in love with Doris, the lady's maid—"

Dundee did not laugh. "*I* am completely bowled over—if that helps!"

"Oh, it does, for I've been trying to sex-appeal you all evening," she assured him shamelessly. "You see, it's rather hard with Clorinda around. She's so absolutely gorgeous, and I'm just a sun-burned, leggy kid. . . . What do you think of Mr. Seymour Crosby?" she demanded suddenly, her childish eyes of a clear topaz blazing up at Dundee. "I saw you making up your mind about all the rest of us, but Mother interrupted before you got around to Mr. Crosby."

"You *are* a little devil!" he laughed, flushing.

But he obediently raised his blue eyes and studied Seymour Crosby, Clorinda's *fiancé* being engaged in conversation with Mrs. Berkeley at the moment. And suddenly it came to him, with a little shock, that Crosby and Clorinda looked enough alike to be too closely related for their marriage to be legal. Both were tall and slender and very dark as to hair and eyes. Both looked like thoroughbreds, the product of centuries of blue-blooded ancestors. But where Clorinda Berkeley was arrogant, Seymour Crosby merely had that indefinable air of pride in birth and position.

"If he were not so young, I believe I should characterize Mr. Crosby as 'a gentleman of the old school'—and I mean that in the most complimentary sense," Dundee answered Gigi, in all sincerity. Looking at Crosby, those dark speculations upon the mystery with which he was connected seemed impertinent, even absurd. Still—

"*So young?*" Gigi echoed. "He's thirty-four! Dad's simply *furious* to-night, and nobody will tell me a word of what it's all about—"

To Dundee's relief the child broke off to listen gleefully as her mother called insistently, with increasing shrillness: "Clorinda! Clorinda! . . . What *is* the child brooding over, to make her so deaf? . . . Ca-lo-rin-*da!*"

Gigi giggled and leaned close to Dundee. "Listen to Abbie! Doesn't she sound exactly like one of the bugle horns on a car? Ta-ta-ta-*ta!*"

"You little fiend!" Dundee chided her, but he laughed as hard as he dared. And then he looked at Clorinda Berkeley.

"I'm sorry, Mother," she was saying stiffly. "What is it?"

"Your Aunt Lily has been trying for ages to attract your attention, darling," her mother soothed her.

"Oh, it's really nothing, Clorinda," Mrs. Benjamin Smith twittered apologetically. "I was just wondering if you knew John Maxwell is in town. You remember John, don't you? . . . But how silly I am! If anyone in Hamilton remembers John Maxwell, it must be you, Clorinda. Every one was sure you were going to marry him—"

"Don't be an idiot, Lilly!" Mrs. Berkeley interrupted sharply, with a venomous glance at her sister-in-law. "Clorinda was never engaged to John Maxwell. It was simply one of those boy-and-girl crushes, wasn't it, Clorinda darling?"

"It was not!" Clorinda retorted clearly, curtly, her nostrils quivering and her black eyes blazing briefly upon her mother.

Not for the first time that evening Mrs. Lambert, with exquisite tact and ready wit, saved the dinner party from becoming a family battle.

"Isn't she precious?" Gigi whispered softly to Dundee. "I simply adore her. When she first came I tried to be exactly like her, but of course I'm not really a lady and never can be, so it was a no go, and Tish told me to go right on being myself. She says that in real 'society' you can be as frank and eccentric as you want to be, 'specially if you're a member of the younger generation, and it's just considered a swell line."

"Do you want to go into 'society'?" Dundee led her on.

"I suppose I'll have to," Gigi replied gloomily. "For years they've been shooting the works to me—in ritzy schools and camps. I can ride and shoot and swim and hunt, play tennis and golf, but—I can't spit a curve in the wind," she added with mock grief. "Say, would you dope it out that Clorinda and Mr. Crosby are in love with each other? They don't *look* it, though Mr. Crosby is the most chivalrous-acting man I ever saw. But if there's one of those electric currents vibrating between him and Clo, like you read about in novels *I* can't feel it!"

To himself Dundee admitted: "Neither can I," but Mrs. Smith's tactless remark about John Maxwell explained at least half of the puzzling situation. And, undoubtedly, the Berkeley millions quite fully explained Seymour Crosby's desire to marry Clorinda. An explanation which Dundee was loath to accept, for he could not help liking and admiring that tall aristocrat, with the sad, gentle brown eyes. *Gentle?* That might be a strange word to apply to Seymour Crosby, if certain whispered suspicions were true. . . .

The butler, at an imperious signal from his mistress, was advancing from the sideboard, with the napkin-wrapped champagne bottle in his hands, when Dundee was surprised to see George Berkeley countermand his wife's order with a stern and unmistakable gesture. Wickett hesitated and involuntarily looked toward Mrs. Lambert for guidance. Dundee switched puzzled eyes to the social secretary and saw her move her silver-crowned head slightly in the negative. Perhaps Mrs. Berkeley had failed to see her husband's gesture; at any rate, it was upon Mrs. Lambert that she poured the flood of her easy wrath.

"Obey me instantly, Wickett! Fill up the champagne glasses all around. And kindly remember in the future that I, and *not* Mrs. Lambert am mistress in this house! . . . Of course I realize, *dear* Mrs. Lambert that it may be natural for Wickett to forget that you are no longer his employer, but I really must ask *you* not to forget again!"

"Oh, I hate us all!" Gigi whispered fiercely to Dundee. "How Mother dares speak like that to Mrs. Lambert! I know the poor darling would leave in a minute if she weren't so poverty-poor— And Wickett would walk right out, too, if it weren't that he adores Tisk. He was her butler for years before she lost all her money, you know. . . . Oh, this is a terrible party, and something tells me it's going to be worse before it's over!"

And Bonnie Dundee silently agreed with her.

III.

"Run along, Gigi," Dick Berkeley commanded, slumping to the couch besides Dundee as Wickett was serving coffee in the drawing room. "You've probably handed Dundee so many shocks already that he's as groggy as I am. Go cheer up Mrs. Lambert. She's looking rather low, and no wonder. . . . Thanks, no coffee for me, Wickett. I don't want to take the edge off this jag I'm conscientiously acquiring," and he appropriated two of the tiny glasses filled with a golden liqueur.

"I'll bet Mr. Dundee would rather I'd do the shocking than *you!*" Gigi retorted, thrusting out her tongue at her brother. But she obeyed, winging her way across the long drawing room to where the social secretary sat quite alone.

"Funny kid, Gigi," Dick commented, after he had gulped the thick sweet brandy which should have been sipped slowly. "She's the best of the lot, of course. Half-baked yes, and disgustingly frank, but heart of gold, and all that sort of thing. I *like* Gigi!" He was on the verge of becoming maudlin.

"So do I!" Dundee agreed cheerfully, his eyes taking in with pleasure the picture which the golden-brown child and the beautiful white-haired woman made as they sat together in a distant window seat.

"This stuff is too damned sweet," Dick decided suddenly. "Got to have something to take the taste out of my mouth." And he plunged, not too steadily, toward the dining room.

As he was returning his father intercepted him, saying something sternly emphatic in a low voice. The older man strode determinedly into the dining room.

"Poor Dad! He had a hard time trying to keep the inebriates of this family from making holy shows of themselves," Dick told Dundee, as he slumped again upon the couch. "But in case you're feeling dry, old man, I had the happy thought of filling my pocket flask on that trip."

"Thanks. I've had more than enough," Dundee replied absently. He was wondering just how many "inebriates" the Berkeley family was cursed with, and just who they were.

"Rather Sir Galahadish, aren't you?" young Berkeley almost sneered. "So is Dad. He unlocks his pre-war cellar only when Mother browbeats him into it, to celebrate some such auspicious occasion as this. Happy-looking love birds, aren't they?" and his sneer was unmistakable as his glance brooded upon his sister Clorinda and Seymour Crosby, who sat silently in an ornate love seat, each handsome face somber with brooding. "God! I've got to do something to liven up this party!"

A minute later Dick's half-blind fumbling with the dials of an enormous radio cabinet released a flood of jazz music.

"Come on, Lily!" he shouted to his aunt. "Let's show these corpses how to do the 'Breakaway! . . . Breakaway! Get hot and break away!'"

"Dance with me, Mr. Dundee?" Gigi cried at the top of her voice, as she slithered across the floor. "Dad, you make Tish dance! . . . Come on! Get hot!" she challenged Dundee, and he willingly held out his arms.

Three other couples obeyed the compelling syncopation, Dick harangued and scolded his giggling aunt; Clorinda and Crosby, their steps matched perfectly, proved that dancing was a fine art; and Mr. Berkeley guided the slender, gracious figure of Mrs. Lambert with surprising expertness.

"Don't they look simply too marvelous together?" Gigi whispered after she had blown a kiss to her adored "Tish." Who looked really happy for the first time that evening. "Look at poor Abbie grinning like a Chessy cat. Oh dear! *Can't* some one invent a new simile for that? Anyway, she thinks the party's going swell at last, and she's happy."

"Shall I ask her to dance?" Dundee smiled down into the vivid brown face with its topaz eyes and babyishly round white teeth.

"Ask her, of course. She'll be pleased, but she'll make an excuse. The bitter truth is that poor Abbie has arthritic knees that creak so loudly they drown out the music. . . . Whew! You're a wow of a dance, Bonnie Dundee!"

"So you've found out my nickname!" Dundee groaned. "I suppose Dick let the cat out of the bag, to use another mossy simile?"

"And I thought I was so clever—thinking that up all by myself!" Gigi mourned. "I've been trying to quote that Burns poem ever since I met you, though it is about a river, not a man, isn't it? But you *are* 'Bonnie'—Oh, tha-a-a-t's all!" she mocked the tootle of the saxophone disgustedly.

Dundee was chivalrously devoting himself to his hostess during the lull in the music when Seymour Crosby joined them, apologizing for the interruption with a jerky little Continental bow.

"I've just remembered that I have a present for you, Mrs. Berkeley, and since I'm rather keen to see how you like it, will you pardon me while I run upstairs to get it?"

Mrs. Berkeley watched him leave the room, a pleasant simper on her broad, peasant-like, over-rouged face. "Isn't he the most perfect expression of a dying era, Mr. Dundee?" she gushed. "So suave, so—so gentle, so *polished,* if you know what I mean! Darling Clorinda is a very lucky girl. Aren't you, Clorinda?" she called teasingly, but her daughter either did not hear of did not want to answer, for the tall, splendid beauty continued her restless, almost feline prowling about the room.

"Dundee murmured a polite answer, and his hostess' caroling voice gushed on.

"I do hope my bad little Gigi hasn't given you a false impression of me, dear Mr. Dundee. The child is incorrigible, and her father aids and abets her in all her impertinences. But she's a dear little thing at heart— really adores me. *Dear* Mrs. Lambert assures me that Gigi will be a great success socially. Of course she will make her debut in New York, sponsored by the Seymour Crosbys, though I am afraid Gigi is still not properly impressed with what her big sister will be able to do for her—Oh, you dear *man!*" she broke off to exclaim with a cry of delight, as Seymour Crosby again presented himself before her.

"What is it?" Gigi shouted, taking long, skating steps across the highly polished floor. But when her own eyes answered her question, Dundee was amazed to see them widen with something remarkably like horror.

"Oh, *no!*" she cried, then, with a queer side glance towards Mrs. Lambert she clapped a hand upon her mouth.

There was certainly nothing in the exquisite cut-crystal flask which Mrs. Berkeley was seizing with curious avidity to inspire horror in the child, Dundee thought, his brows knitted in a puzzled frown.

"Let me smell!" Gigi demanded shrilly, snatching the heavy crystal bottle from her mother's hands, even as they tightened convulsively upon it. A little brown finger and thumb wrenched out the big carved stopper, and before anyone could stop her, Gigi had poured the overpoweringly strong perfume into her cupped palm and was dashing wildly from person to person, sprinkling dinner coats and evening frocks with terrible prodigality.

"Stop, Gigi!   Stop, I tell you!" Mrs. Berkeley commanded frantically.   "Do you realize what you're doing?   That's *Fleur d'Amour,* and it costs thirty-two dollars an ounce! George! Stop her! She'll waste it all!"

But the mad outpouring continued. Even Wickett the butler did not escape a dash of the costly scent.

"You've waste at least an ounce of my lovely perfume, you wicked child!" Mrs. Berkeley sobbed, as she panted after the flying Gigi.

What happened in the next minute Bonnie Dundee would have given much not to have witnessed, and, later, a great deal more to have been able to forget. For Mrs. Berkeley cornered her younger daughter, and, even as Gigi laughed impudently up into her mother's rage-reddened face, lifted a broad hand and slapped her cheek resoundingly.

"Oh!" Gigi gasped incredulously. And she made no resistance when her mother snatched the crystal flask from her suddenly relaxed little hand, before it could drop and shatter. Then she looked at her mother, and Dundee thought he had never seen such contemptuous hatred as paled the puckish little brown face and distended the no longer childish topaz eyes.

In another moment George Berkeley was at his wife's side, and he was saying in a low voice of concentrated fury, that was perfectly audible in the hushed room:

"Don't do that again, Abbie! Never again, do you hear me?—or—"

At that moment the recuperated orchestra, miles away, broke into *The Pagan Love Song*, and the room was filled with languorous melody, superimposed upon quivering waves of anger, fear, and hatred.

As the paralysis lifted, Dundee, still dazed, still seeing red, was aware that Dick Berkeley was lunging drunkenly toward the wide-arched doorway that led into the front hall. Gigi, who had been cornered near the doorway, backed blindly a few steps, then turned and ran, her rasping sobs loud above the music.

Uncertainly, Dundee glanced about, saw the still white misery in Mrs. Lambert's delicate face, the contemptuous shrug with which Clorinda was trying to dismiss the incident, and the shocked amazement and disgust on the aristocratic face of Seymour Crosby.

"Will you excuse me for a moment? I wish to speak to Dick," Dundee mumbled to George Berkeley, who gave no sign that he heard.

It was no desire to speak to Dick Berkeley, however, which took Dundee out of the room. It was an urgent impulse to telephone Captain Strawn of the Hamilton Homicide Squad.

The wide front hall of the Berkeley mansion extended beyond the immense circular staircase of white marble, which wound upward to the third floor, with a broad landing on the second. A few feet behind the staircase the hall ended in a wall, with an ordinary-sized door opening into what Dundee knew must be the mysterious regions of "backstairs." Devoted to butler's pantry, back hall, servants' sitting and dining room, and kitchen.

Now that door stood slightly ajar. And from it came sounds which caused Dundee to abandon, temporarily, his search for the library and its telephone.

"Please, Mr. Dick! Let me go! If Gene saw us—No, no! I shan't dance with you!"

It was a girl's voice, high, sweet, flurried, unmistakably British. And the only answer to that frantic plea was a tipsy, exultant laugh.

"Oh, Lord! Dick up to his old tricks!" Dundee shrugged disgustedly, and, on impulse, jerked open the door and plunged into the narrower backstairs hall.

The detective's first impression of the girl was that she was fairy-small and slight and blonde. Pale gold hair curled about her delicately flushed little face, and was knotted in a shining bun on the nape of her slender neck. Her blue eyes were wide with genuine fear as her black-clad body strained to release itself from the embrace of the drunken son of her mistress. But Dick, his reddish brown hair falling in dank wisps across his forehead snatched the girl closer and forced her to follow his shambling dance steps. The languorous notes of *The Pagan Love Song* from the radio penetrated sufficiently to animate his groggy legs.

"Say you'll meet me when that beastly crew in there's gone to bed, and I'll let you go—"

"Hello, Dick!" Dundee sang out from the threshold, as he pulled the door to. "Sorry to intrude, but will you tell me where I can find a telephone?"

"Sure! Butler's pantry. First door on your left." Dick Berkeley answered, his feet halting but his arms holding the straining girl more closely against his breast. "Jus' a minute, old man! Wan' you to meet pretties' girl in Hamilton—Miss Doris Matthews. Ladies' maid to Abbie and Clorinda. 'At's funny, ain't it? *'Ladies' maid'—*"

"You're drunk, Dick, and you'd better go to bed," Dundee interrupted quietly. "If you'll let Doris show me where the telephone is—"

"Not on your life! I'm on to your game! Wanta date up my sweetie yourself, don't you? . . . Listen, Doris! Don't you fall for my old pal, Dundee. He's a heartbreaker—'at's what he is—"

"Please let me go, Mr. Dick!" Doris pleaded, her little hands pressing frantically against his breast.

"If you'll promise to meet me when and where I said," Dick bargained with tipsy solemnity.

"Very well!" the girl capitulated suddenly, but the blue eyes shot a glance at Dundee, which told him that she had no intention of keeping the promise. "Oh!" she wailed softly, as young Berkeley released her. "Look! You've quite spoiled my apron!" And she tried ineffectively to smooth the wrinkles from the crushed scrap of lace and lawn. "The telephone's right in here— Oh! Mr. Wickett!" she gasped, the lovely face going almost white as the crumpled apron, before she turned and fled up the backstairs.

"Listening in, Wickett? Good show, wasn't it? But listen, Stone-Face, you'd better mind your own business—

see?" And Dick Berkeley lurched toward the butler who stood in the door of his pantry.

"Yes, sir." Wickett answered, but his eyes spoke so black a hate that a shudder rippled along Dundee's already overwrought nerves. "You wish to use the telephone, Mr. Dundee? I'll show you to the library, sir."

"Thank you, Wickett," and the detective rather sheepishly followed the butler from the back hall to the library. A fair-sized room overlooking the west lawn, and directly opposite the wide-arched doorway leading into the drawing room.

Rather to his surprise, Dundee found the library remarkably well stocked with books of all kinds, most of which looked as if they had been read. Which of the Berkeleys was a bookworm, he wondered. Gigi? Probably. But the shabbiest books were not the sort to appeal to a fifteen-year-old girl. George Berkeley? Most likely. Rather curiously Dundee selected a novel by Henry James, and found pasted on its flyleaf an impression from a wood-block bookplate—"Ex libris George Berkeley"—and below it, in faded ink, a date of ten years before. And the book had been read not once but many times.

"I knew I liked George Berkeley," he grinned to himself, as he lifted the receiver from the hook of the telephone on the broad desk set in the middle of the room.

A minute later: "Captain Strawn, please. Dundee speaking. . . . Hello, chief. Dundee reporting."

"Hello, boy!" came Captain Strawn's heavy voice. "Having a good time with the swells?"

"A good time? That rates a laugh!" Dundee retorted. "Listen, chief! Can you send one of the boys over to *The Morning News* to get me a complete file of the Crosby case? Although it happened in London I rather imagine every city in the United States carried a leased wire report of the affair and the inquest, the Crosbys being who they were. . . . About eighteen months ago, I believe. . . . Thanks! And have it mailed in a plain envelope."

"What's up, boy?" Captain Strawn asked curiously.

"Probably nothing, but—I've got a funny prickling of the scalp. If I were a woman I'd say I have a premonition. . . . 'Night, sir."

When he returned to the drawing room, where the air was heavy with the perfume Gigi had so foolishly wasted, Dundee found that Dick had not rejoined the party, and the George Berkeley had left it, temporarily, at least. A new tune, something about tiptoeing through the tulips, was throbbing from the radio cabinet, and Clorinda and her *fiancé* were dancing alone, with grave perfection.

With almost sick distaste, but obedient to his promise to the absent and disgraced Gigi, Dundee crossed the big room to where Mrs. Berkeley sat on a couch beside Mrs. Lambert.

"All right! I promise! Though I must say—Oh, there you are, dear Mr. Dundee!" Mrs. Berkeley broke off a sulkily indignant remark to her social secretary and turned with obvious relief to her son's friend.

With her hennaed head cocked coyly, she listened to his request to dance. "Thank you so much, you dear man! But I'm saving all my strength for the big party to-morrow night. And the music is just stopping, too. To-morrow night, remember!" She raised her voice: "Won't someone turn off the radio, please? . . . Oh, there's George again! . . . I suppose—: she lowered her voice, as if to make a confidence, then changed her mind and called shrilly: "George, darling! Turn off the radio. My sweet girl—" stretching out both hands towards Crosby and Clorinda, "mustn't get herself all tired out, must she, Mr. Crosby?"

"Rather not!" Crosby agreed stiffly, The fine fabric of his tact was wearing a bit thin, obviously.

"What *is* the matter, darling?" Mrs. Berkeley demanded of her daughter with intense solicitude. "I pray you not going to be ill—"

"Just a headache," Clorinda answered curtly. "That ghastly perfume Gigi sprinkled all over us."

"Why, I adore it!" Mrs. Berkeley hastened to declare, fearful that Crosby's feelings might be ruffled. "Of course, some people are very sensitive to heavy scents. My maid, Doris, for instance, positively gets a sick headache if she so much as catches a whiff of perfume, which makes it ridiculously awkward—"

"Doris?" Crosby interrupted eagerly. "Surely you don't mean little Doris Matthews?" and he turned toward Mrs. Lambert, a queer expression quivering across his thin, aristocratic face.

"Didn't I write you that I had had Doris come on to me with Mrs. Berkeley and Clorinda?" Mrs. Lambert replied. "But I'm quite sure I did, Seymour. I hope you don't mind, but she was looking for a place—came to see me when I stopped off in New York on my return from France—" She hesitated, and Dundee was sure that there was a real anxiety in her lovely, soft voice.

"Mind?" Crosby echoed. "I shall be delighted to see Doris again. How is she?"

"Still adorably pretty," Mrs. Lambert smiled, "and quite happy. She has just become engaged to the chauffeur, Eugene Arnold. A splendid young man, I believe."

"I'm going to bed," Clorinda announced abruptly. "Good-night, everyone."

"Why, it's not eleven yet, darling," Mrs. Berkeley protested, but as her daughter left the room without replying she added: "I'm really glad the dear child is being sensible. To-morrow will be such a heavy day."

"We'd better be going, too, Ben," Mrs. Smith twittered. "I wonder if we may borrow your car and chauffeur, Abbie. Our car's out of order, and we came by taxi."

"Certainly," Mrs. Berkeley replied, but she frowned slightly. "Oh, George! Have Wickett telephone to the garage for Arnold to bring the car around immediately."

But it was fully ten minutes before Wickett announced the car to the waiting Benjamin Smiths, who had already said their good-nights twice around and who

now repeated their mendacious assurances to Mrs.
Berkeley that "we had a simply wonderful time, Abbie!"

"I'd like to talk with you in the library before you go
upstairs, Abbie," George Berkeley halted his wife, as she,
Mrs. Lambert and Seymour Crosby were moving toward
the marble staircase.

Dundee, who had already reached the second-floor
landing of the stairs, heard the stern but low-spoken
words very clearly, and again his scalp had that odd,
premonitory prickling.

IV.

The room to which Dundee had been assigned was on the third floor of the Berkeley mansion. Dick Berkeley, ushering him into it upon his arrival that Friday evening, had explained:

"Nobody but the servants and me up here. I chose my quarters for privacy. Sorry, but you'll have to use my bath, old man. Your room is really what Mother calls my 'den,' but the couch is comfortable. Mother wanted you to have one of the lordly guest chambers on the second floor, but I thought you might enjoy a little bachelor peace and quiet. The ballroom's on the east, extending the length of the house; otherwise there's nothing clear across the front but my rooms. I don't think you'll mind the servants. They turn in fairly early, all except old Wickett, the butler, and use the backstairs."

Now, as Dundee plodded rather wearily up the great, winding marble staircase, his mind was a jumble of half-formed forebodings of he knew not what, snatches of strange conversations; distorted pictures. A queer, mad evening. A nightmare reaching its crescendo in that terrible moment when Mrs. Berkeley's broad palm had left its mark upon Gigi's cheek. Funny, brazen, impudent little Gigi! But she had not deserved that!

His hand, slipping along the cold marble balustrade, suddenly encountered something soft and living and warm—a small brown hand.

"Gigi!" he whispered, and bent over to stare at a forlorn little figure in incongruously gay pajamas, crouching against the stairhead.

"I've been waiting for you to come up," she whispered, her voice catching on a sob. "Dick's not in his room, and I wanted somebody to pet me and tell me what an awful little beast I am. I couldn't sleep," she confessed miserably.

Dundee rounded the stairhead and, protected from the sight of anyone below by the high marble balustrade, crouched beside her, cuddling the twisted little brown hands against his dinner coat.

"You do smell sicky-sweet!" she giggled faintly. "Did you think I was terrible, wasting Abbie's perfume like that? Well, I wasn't! I was just—" She broke off the confidence abruptly, however; began on a new tack, her topaz eyes glowing like a cat's in the dim light from the third-floor hall bracket. "I wasn't just being mean *then*, but afterwards—after Abbie—slapped me—Oh, I did something perfectly dreadful! And now I'm so frightened I can't sleep!"

"Poor little, dear little Gigi!" he crooned tenderly, and lifted the small hands to his lips. "You can't have done anything 'perfectly dreadful,' and of course you're going to trot off to bed right now."

"O-oh!" she breathed softly, solemnly. "You kissed my hands, Bonnie Dundee! Just as if I were a grown-up young lady like Clorinda! I—listen!" she pleaded wistfully, "if you'll kiss my eyelids I bet I *will* go to sleep!"

He kissed the ecstatically fluttering lids very gently, but, though he was sorely tempted, he did not kiss the soft, childish lips that quivered expectantly. After all, she was only fifteen. . . .

She waited there, crouched against the stairs, until he had gone into his room and closed the door.

Switching on the lights he found that a chambermaid had converted the couch into a beautifully made-up bed, and had left a thermos bottle of ice water and a napkin covered plate of tiny sandwiches on the bedside table. Munching one of the dainty triangles, he went into the bathroom, tried the door leading into Dick's bedroom, and found it unlocked. He knocked, had no answer, then entered. The lights were on, but Gigi had been right. Dick Berkeley was not in his room, but he had been there very recently, for a thin blue layer of smoke still hung over an armchair, and an ash tray beside it held half a dozen cigarette stubs, deposited there since the chambermaid had turned down the covers of the bed. And in the room was a heavy odor of whiskey and perfume.

"He can't have got far," Dundee said to himself, and frowned thoughtfully.

Suddenly, his mind was made up. Regardless of the fact that Dick was his host, and that his host's love affairs were none of his concern, Dundee knew that if he could prevent it Dick Berkeley should not further annoy Doris Matthews that night. The girl feared him, despised him, and he was more than half-drunk. There was his empty pocket flask. . . .

Without forming any definite plan, Dundee hurried out into the hall. Yes, thank heaven, Gigi had gone to bed! He plunged down the stairs, his steps inaudible on the thick velvet runner.

In the ten minutes or so since he had gone up, the house had apparently settled down for the night. In all the big front hall there was only one dim light burning, but as Dundee was crossing noiselessly to the drawing room there came the faint sound of a door opening, immediately followed by an angry, implacable voice.

"And that's my last word on the subject, Abbie! There'll be no engagement announced here to-morrow night! I'll not have *my* daughter marrying a wife murderer!"

"Shut that door, George Berkeley!" Dundee heard Mrs. Berkeley's voice shrilling in the library. "Do you want Wickett to hear you? Now you listen to *my* last word—"

The library door closed, and Dundee was temporarily saved from the charge of eavesdropping. He hesitated, his plan to interfere with Dick Berkeley's amorous pursuits forgotten for the moment.

So George Berkeley suspected, too! Or did he more than suspect? Had he ferreted out, with the aid of private detectives, something that had not appeared at the strangely perfunctory inquest some eighteen months ago in London? But wait! Perhaps he had had no need of private detectives! Right here in the house was Doris Matthews, Mrs. Crosby's personal maid, whose testimony had figured so prominently in the inquest! Just what had she testified? Dundee knit his brows in an effort to remember clearly.

Then he shrugged. To-morrow he would have the newspaper file of the case which Strawn had promised to mail that night. The Dick matter was the more pressing now. And he stepped softly into the dark drawing room. His goal was the buffet in the dining room. If Dick wasn't there, he probably wasn't in the house at all. Halfway across the drawing room a light from the dining room made the going easier.

Wickett, the butler, stood at the big sideboard, counting silver spoons into a velvet-lined chest. He wheeled at some faint sound the detective had made, and peered frowningly.

"I was looking for Mr. Dick Berkeley, Wickett," Dundee declared himself.

"He is not here, sir. The wine was returned to the cellar some time ago, sir."

"Right, Wickett!" Dundee grinned, then protested as the butler was advancing dutifully to turn on the drawing room lights. "Don't bother! I can see well enough. But if you do see Mr. Dick, I wish you would tell him I very much want to speak to him before I turn in."

The butler, with a "Very well, sir," returned to his work, and Dundee threaded his way through the dimly lit drawing room. He was just about to step out into the hall when a faint, muffled cough warned him that some one was descending the stairs. Not relishing the idea of again explaining his presence on the darkened lower floor, he shrank back against the heavy silk brocade hangings, then, because he was a detective, and because that active sixth sense of his warned him that the person stealing down the stairs was anxious to be unobserved as he was himself, he quite shamelessly peeped.

It was Clorinda Berkeley. Even in the dim light her tall, slender body was unmistakable. And she was going out— stealing out—for she was wearing, over the wine-red velvet evening dress, a cape of gold metal cloth, trimmed with dark fur. His eyes quite accustomed by now to the dim light, Dundee could even distinguish the modernistic pattern of the batik scarf she was nervously pulling through her fingers as she tiptoed down the hall toward the last steps of the stairs.

He waited, scarcely breathing, for he thought she must pass very close to him on her way to the front door. But she did not leave by that way. She rounded the stairs, listened for a moment to the muffled clash of voices within the library, then tiptoed down the hall toward the backstairs regions.

Dundee heard the door open very softly; did not hear it close. Apparently Clorinda was guarding her return, that it might be as noiseless as possible. After a minute of hesitation, Dundee followed her to that door, and listened. Very faintly came the sound of a chain being rattled, then still more faintly the sound of a bolt being shot back. Clorinda had left the house by the back door, which Wickett had already made fast for the night.

So Dick Berkeley was not the only member of that family who stole out to keep secret appointments! Whom was Clorinda meeting? Seymour Crosby? After all, they were engaged to be married, and their first evening together after weeks of separation had not been a signal success. But —they had not looked at each other like lovers ardently desiring to be alone.

Half an hour later—a quarter to twelve—when Dundee had had a tepid bath to induce sleep, young Dick, at least, had not returned from his rendezvous. Dundee shrugged wearily as he got into bed. Apparently the lovely little Doris had been quite willing to meet her mistress' son clandestinely, in spite of her seeming reluctance. Still—she certainly hadn't looked like "that kind of girl." And hadn't Mrs. Lambert told Crosby that Doris was very happy in her engagement to Arnold, the chauffeur?

The next questions Dundee asked were spoken aloud; "Who's there? What is it?"

It was broad daylight and some one was pounding on his door and calling his name.

"Did I frighten you?" Gigi laughed joyously when Dundee opened his door, showing tousled black hair and startled blue eyes. "You look exactly as if you were expecting to hear that the millionaire master of Hillcrest had been discovered foully murdered in his library, with the doors and windows securely locked on the inside. Sorry to disappoint you, but Dad is in his room and has just sworn roundly at his favorite daughter for waking him up so early—in the middle of the night, as he called it, though it's nearly seven o'clock."

"I feel like swearing roundly myself," Dundee growled at her. "What's the big idea, young woman?"

"Woke up early with a headache—that terrible perfume, I suppose," Gigi elucidated. "Thrust my aching brow out the window, discovered it's a heavenly morn, dew-pearled, God-in-His-heaven, etc., and that it has turned divinely warm. So—" and she flung open her silk Happi coat to display a brief bathing suit of tigerishly striped brown-and-orange jersey. "Wake Dick up, lamb darling, and meet me at the lake in not more than ten minutes. I've got to bang up Clorinda and Mr. Crosby now. Do you suppose I'll ever get around to calling Clo's lordly *fiancé* by his first name? . . . By the way, didn't you hear me pounding on Dick's door? He wouldn't answer, but you can roust him out. Tell him a sunrise swim will be good for that hang-over of his."

And, after reaching up to tug his tousled black hair impudently, she was off down the grerat marble staircase, her golden-brown curls bobbing merrily as she bounced lightly on rubber-soled sneakers.

"Ugh!" Dundee shivered as he thought of how cold the lake must be, in spite of the unseasonable warmth of the new morning. But he had no intention of disobeying. Grinning a little at the realization that Gigi was rapidly reducing him to the wax-like state in which she kept her adoring father, the detective padded into the bathroom and knocked at the door leading into Dick Berkeley's bedroom. There was no answer, and he turned the knob, calling:

"Wake up, Dick! Gigi has decreed a sunrise swim!"

But he was talking to an untenanted room. The bed had not been slept in, and the light in the floor lamp beside the armchair glowed yellowy in the morning brightness.

"A fine host you are!" Dundee apostrophized the missing young man. "Invite a guest for the week-end, then spend the night out on a bender."

Underneath his surface disgust, however, there was a growing uneasiness. Doris Matthews most decidedly had not looked like "that kind of girl," and yet what other explanation of Dick's all-night absence could there be?

"Well, what shall I do?" Dundee asked himself gloomily, as he returned to the bathroom and prepared to take a cold shower. "Alarm the family? It's early yet. The young rake may come sneaking back in time for breakfast and be properly indignant at my interference. Yes, I guess I'd better give him a little more time—and quite a large piece of my mind when he does turn up!"

After the biting cold of the shower, followed by a vigorous toweling, he felt fit to cope with any lake. And by the time he had pulled on his dark-blue swimming suit he was even whistling in a sudden surge of animal spirits. His scalp-prickling premonitions of the night before were temporarily forgotten.

In the front hall he found Wickett awaiting him, a tray laden with four tall glasses of orange juice in his hands.

"Miss Gigi has just gone to the lake, sir. It lies to the east of the house. Is Mr. Dick not swimming, sir?"

"I rather think not, Wickett," Dundee answered evasively, as he took the orange juice the butler offered.

Wickett, whose middle-aged face seemed old and tired this morning, was about to ask another question, but the faint sound of a door opening on the second floor deterred him. He set the tray upon a little table in the hall, and gravely opened the front door for Dundee.

It was a glorious September morning—"dew-pearled," as Gigi had said: a young, fragrant, joyous morning. Suddenly Dundee broke into a run, his dressing gown flapping gaily about his bare legs. It was good to be alive, good to be up with the birds, good to be running to meet an orange-and-brown little hoyden capering with mad abandon upon the edge of a rose-and-silver lake.

"Isn't it gorgeous? Aren't you glad you came?" Gigi cried, running to meet her new friend, her arms spread like wings.

For a long minute they stood swinging their clasped hands joyously, while Gigi's topaz eyes shown at him. "You look about fifteen yourself this morning, my Bonnie Dundee!" she decided, an oddly deep not under her strident young soprano. "Bonnie, bonnie!—with your black hair all wet-curly, and your eyes as blue as a baby's. . . . I wonder," she added frankly, "if I'm falling in love with you. Just this minute I had the funniest roller-coaster feeling in my tummy when I looked up at you— Oh, damn! Here come the grown-up lovers, and you'll have to pretend to be grown-up, too. . . . Where's Dick? Couldn't you get him up?"

But she did not wait for a reply, for which Dundee was grateful. She went skipping across the close-cut grass to greet and badger her sister and Seymour Crosby.

"Slow-pokes!" she gibed shrilly. "Or did you two pause on the gr-rand marble staircase for a posh embrace? Race you to the lake, Mr. Crosby!"

And Dundee had not realized how much he could like Seymour Crosby until that slim aristocrat had flung off his dressing gown and dashed wholeheartedly after the flying child, catching her, for his long legs were swift, two yards short of the springboard.

Clorinda followed slowly, her beautiful face dark with sulky resentment.

"Mad at me?" Gigi challenged her sister impishly. "Did wicked little sister cheat booful big sister out of her beauty sleep? . . . Say!" she discovered suddenly, "You look as if you haven't slept at all, Clo! You've got awful circles under your eyes. Why didn't you tell me to go to the devil, then turn over and go to sleep again? Gigi's sorry—honest!"

"Oh, leave me alone!" Clorinda commanded sharply. "I'm all right, but I don't think I shall swim, after all. That water must be icy," and she shivered and turned her back upon the lake.

"Don't be a spoil-sport, Clo!" Gigi begged, hopping upon the springboard. "You'd only be cold a teeny minute, and then—Goodness!" she broke off suddenly, and raised her short little nose to sniff, as a sudden breeze from the south rippled the surface of the lake. "*Fleur d'Amour!* Can't you smell it, everybody? It must have soaked clear through to our bones, to keep on stinking like this!"

"Don't be an idiot, Gigi!" Clorinda commanded angrily, as the little orange-and-brown figure darted from one to another, sniffing like an eager puppy. "It's just your imagination—"

"I do smell *Fleur d'Amour!*" Gigi insisted. "But come on! Let's swim! Bet I can dive farther than you can, in a racing dive, Bonnie Dundee! One for the money, two for the show—come on, Bonnie! Let's show 'em some real diving!—three makes ready, and four we go!" And on the last word she released her new playmate's hand and ran, executing as pretty a racing dive from the edge of the lake as the athletic young detective had ever seen.

Her dive took her far into the lake, or rather far to the west side of the lake, alarmingly near the little circular summerhouse upon the very edge or the water.

"Swell dive!" he sang out, as the wet curls emerged. Then, because there was a queer expression on her dripping face, he shouted anxiously: "What's the matter, Gigi? Did you hurt yourself?"

"Hurt myself?" she echoed, her voice queerly muffled and trembly. "Of course not! But—" and she began to swim rapidly toward the springboard on which he stood. "I think—I—think I saw a—a mermaid down there!"

"A *mermaid?*" Dundee stooped to give her a hand and she clambered upon the board, shivering violently.

"Don't pay any attention to the little idiot!" Clorinda commanded with contemptuous anger. "I told you it was too cold for swimming, Gigi. Come back to the house."

But Gigi had drawn up her goose-fleshed knees and had dropped her head upon them. She was trembling more violently than ever, and suddenly Dundee knew it was not from the cold. She had gone to camp in New Hampshire, she had told him the night before, and had swum every sunrise in a icy lake—

The hair stirred on his scalp, with that horrible prickling he had experienced twice the night before. Without another moment of hesitation his long legs climbed over the huddled, shivering little figure, and stepped to the edge of the springboard.

"No, don't!" Gigi cried, when she realized his purpose, but only a mighty splash answered her.

His dive took him many feet short of the spot where Gigi had gone under, but when he had risen and got his bearings he plunged again. . . .

When the detective rose the second time, after a long minute under water, his face was a ghastly gray-white.

But he did not speak until powerful, overhand strokes had brought him swiftly to the springboard.

Gigi stared up at him, dumb with horror, and he comforted her with a hard grip of her shaking shoulder before he addressed Clorinda Berkeley:

"Take your sister to the house immediately, Miss Berkeley! . . . Crosby, I'll need your help."

V.

"Murder!" Bonnie Dundee replied curtly to Seymour Crosby's question, but he spoke in a low voice so that the dreadful word should not reach the ears of the two girls who were on their way to the house.

Gigi had held back at first, hysterically asserting her right to stay since she had already seen "it," but Clorinda had jerked her small sister roughly to her feet and had dragged her away. Oddly, Clorinda had not asked a single question. Now Gigi had broken into a blind zigzag run, one hand pressed against her eyes which had seen a sight they would never forget. . . .

"*Murder?*" Crosby repeated incredulously. "Who?"

"Please go into the summer house, Crosby, and wait for me there, but I warn you not to touch anything," Dundee instructed sternly, ignoring the older man's question, rather as if he thought Seymour Crosby already knew the answer, and there was no need to waste time or words.

An angry flush replaced the dead pallor of Crosby's cheeks. He parted his lips to speak, then thought better of it and turned away, running toward the summerhouse in a jog trot. In his black bathing suit—he had discarded his dressing gown upon the lake's edge—he looked like a distance runner in an early morning workout. Although he was slender his tall body was well-muscled, potentially powerful. . . .

Dundee stared after the running man with narrowed eyes, then, taking a deep breath and clamping his mouth in a grim line, he plunged into the lake again. Once more he came to the surface many feet short of the spot where his dreadful work was to be done. Treading water, he glanced toward the little summerhouse. Seymour Crosby stood on the first of the three narrow steps leading down into the water, a trembling hand shading his eyes from the sun.

"A rather terrible form of third degree for him, if—" Dundee said to himself, as he executed a surface dive that carried him to the spot directly in front of the summerhouse, where Gigi had discovered her "mermaid."

After nearly a minute of frantic work under water, the young detective rose again, his agonized lungs demanding great, deep draughts of air. As his chest heaved hurtingly, Dundee glanced upward toward Crosby again. The New Yorker had apparently not moved a muscle, except in that trembling hand that still shielded his eyes.

"Just a few seconds more down there, thank God!" Dundee called to Crosby, and dived again.

When he arose once more he was towing a burden by the hair—an inert burden which could offer no hampering resistance, except that of weight, and now that he had done his gruesome work below water, the weight Dundee towed was pitifully light. . . .

"Lend a hand, Crosby!" he panted.

But for a moment Seymour Crosby seemed too frozen with horror to obey. The hand which had been shielding his eyes from the sun now pressed frantically against them, to shut out the dreadful sight.

"I'd rather not try to manage alone, Crosby!" Dundee called sternly. "I don't want to bruise—her. Kneel down on the bottom step and lift her by the shoulders, please."

Seymour Crosby came out of his trance of horror sufficiently to kneel as commanded, and his white lips began to babble:

"Why, it's—Doris! *Doris!* I thought at first it was Letitia—Mrs. Lambert—"

"Did you?" Dundee grunted noncommittally. But he told himself that if Crosby's horrified astonishment was assumed, he was doing it rather well. . . . "That's right! Not very heavy, is she, poor girl?" . . . Careful! Don't knock her head against the bench. . . . Now!"

And between them they laid the body of Doris Matthews, lady's maid, upon the wide bench that encircled the round floor of the summerhouse. The pale gold hair, which Dundee had admired the night before when he had seen it curling about the flushed, beautiful little face and knotted in a shining bun on the nape of the white neck, hung below the hard bench now in long, dripping strands, the color of white sand. The slender body was clad in the plain black silk uniform she had been wearing when Dick Berkeley had forced her to dance, importuning her tipsily to meet him. But her little white apron of lace and lawn was missing, and the full skirt of her dress was bound about her knees with a clumsily tied silk scarf of many colors.

"Couldn't it be—suicide?" Crosby stammered, his teeth chattering against each other.

"If you had seen me untying that scarf to take out the rocks with which the body was weighed down, you wouldn't ask that," Dundee retorted. "I left them piled together on the floor of the lake, to be retrieved and examined by the police—"

"The police?" Crosby repeated, and Dundee saw his face grow even more bleak and gray. And Dundee knew that this new horror was reminiscent. "But of course—" he conceded jerkily.

"Of course!" Dundee agreed harshly. "Didn't I tell you it's murder? Look at that gash across the top of her head! . . . No, don't touch her! We've done all we can do until the police arrive. Please step outside and wait till they come. I'm going to telephone, myself." He glanced toward the house, saw a man emerging from the back door. "Wickett—and heading this way. Coming to see what's up I suppose. I'll wait for him," he added to Crosby, who had staggered blindly out of the summerhouse.

Dundee remained inside. One of his senses had been telegraphing an insistent message to his brain and now he had time to take it in. *Fleur d'Amour!* The little open-

sided, circular arbor was reeking with the perfume which
Seymour Crosby had presented to Mrs. Berkeley the
night before and which Gigi had madly splashed upon
every person in the room.

Kneeling so that his nose almost touched the floor the
detective confirmed his instinctive suspicion.
Undoubtedly the crystal flask had been broken here, for
in one of the broad cracks of the flooring he found a sliver
of glass, as bright as a diamond in the sun.

Still crouching, he let his eyes rove over the floor, and
across that part of the circular bench not occupied by the
body. Yes, the blow that had killed or stunned Doris
Matthews had been struck here, for the murderer's hand
had hastily, clumsily swabbed a section of the floor and of
the bench. Very near the bench, to the left of the steps
leading into the water, there was a faintly brownish
stain, which the hasty swabbing had not been able
entirely to obliterate. Blood!

He was about to rise when his eyes caught sight of
something several feet away, on the floor against the
three-foot wall which formed a back for the circular
bench. He was about to pick it up when he remembered
the necessity for preserving fingerprints. He let it lie.

It was the big crystal stopper from the perfume flask.

"Has there been an—accident, sir?" Wickett called, his
voice quavering like an old man's.

"No, Wickett! Not an accident. Murder!" Dundee
answered with brutal directness, for there was no time
now to spare feelings. "I am going to telephone to the
police, and I think you and Mr. Crosby had better remain
where you are. By no means go into the summerhouse,
and let no one else enter it until the police arrive. Have
you spread the word that there's been an 'accident'?" he
added, ignoring the butler's horrified quavering.

"No, s-sir. I s-saw Miss Gigi and Miss Clorinda
returning. They seemed upset, but Miss Clorinda would
not let Miss Gigi explain. I—I thought one of you
gentlemen had been hurt, sir."

But before the butler had finished his explanation Dundee was sprinting for his dressing gown, discarded at the springboard. Struggling into it, he cut across to the cement walk which led directly from the summerhouse diagonally across the lawn to the driveway that curved about the back of the house. IIis trained mind automatically made note of the fact that the murderer's feet, if the murder had come from the Berkeley house, need not have left the hard, unbetraying surface of cement whether the exit from the house had been made by front door or rear. For the broad driveway completely encircled the house. But the shortest route to the summerhouse was, of course, from the rear door.

To his own knowledge, Clorinda Berkeley had stolen out last night by the back door. And it was *her* modernistically patterned batik scarf with which the stone weighted skirts of the maid had been tied!

But Dick Berkeley had also stolen out of the house, to keep a rendezvous with the girl who was now dead. And Dick Berkeley was missing, or had been missing as late as half an hour ago. Two suspects already. . . .

The back door was not latched. The detective entered and strode swiftly but quietly toward the butler's pantry, which had a telephone, he knew. As he passed an open door on the opposite side of the hall he heard a flat, indignant female voice declaring:

"No, ma'am, she ain't in her room! Her bed ain't been slept in, I tell you Mrs. Ryan! A fine howdy-ye-do, I must say, even if she is engaged! Staying out all night—I never did trust that uppity little English snip—"

The servants' sitting room. Probably the cook and a chambermaid mulling, with relish, what they thought was a nasty bit of backstairs scandal.

Reaching the butler's pantry unheard, Dundee found the telephone and gave the number of Police Headquarters.

"Hello! Dundee speaking. . . . Connect me with Captain Strawn's home, please." A minute or two later, after his chief's sleepy growl had come over the wire, Dundee recounted the discovery of Doris Matthews' murder in as few words as possible.

"*Murder* at Hillcrest?" Strawn interrupted early in the recital. "You didn't get bored with nothing to do, and kill the girl yourself, did you, Bonnie?"

But when the brief story was finished Captain Strawn was not in a jocular mood. He issued orders grimly; "Get back on the scene of the crime immediately, and don't let Crosby out of your sight till I arrive. You say the butler's with him now? Good? See that nothing's touched, and for God's sake, don't spread the alarm through the house. . . . And say, lie low, Bonnie! Don't give yourself away as a detective. As a guest in the house, forcibly detained there by the police, you may be a lot of help, just as you were in the Rhodes House murders."

Dundee grinned faintly as he "Yes-ed" every order of his chief. "A lot of help" in the Rhodes House murders, indeed! He'd solved that case practically single-handed, hadn't he? And Lieutenant Strawn had become Captain as a result! But what did credit and promotion matter? It was the game itself that he loved. . . .

As he obeyed his chief and returned directly to the summer house, Dundee realized, a little shamefacedly, that his horror over Doris's brutal murder was already giving way to the thrill of the chase to run down her murderer. He still felt sick at the thought of such beauty being foully blotted out, but perhaps the thrill of eagerness to be up and doing about the business of avenging her death would be more welcome to the dead girl, if she could look on, than all the tears that would undoubtedly be shed backstairs for her to-day.

But tears for Doris had already begun to flow, Dundee discovered, as he neared the summerhouse. Wickett was dabbing at his eyes with a folded handkerchief, and Crosby wheeled, whipping out his own handkerchief from his retrieved gown, when he saw his fellow-guest approaching.

"The police will be here immediately," Dundee announced. "Captain Strawn in charge."

"Mr. Crosby and I have been talking about the poor girl in there, sir," Wickett explained tremulously. "You saw her for a moment last night yourself, sir. I'm sure you will agree with us that she was a— a little darling, sir."

The expression fell strangely from the usually austere lips of the butler, and Dundee was touched to the heart. Here was sincere grief.

"Yes, she was a very beautiful girl," Dundee answered huskily. "You knew her, too, Mr. Crosby? I believe I heard you talking about her with Mrs. Lambert last night."

Seymour Crosby pocketed his handkerchief as he answered unsteadily: "Yes, I knew her very well indeed. She was my—wife's maid for several years. Phyllis—Mrs. Crosby—was extremely fond of little Doris, and so was I. But—if you'll forgive me, Mr. Dundee—I don't believe I can talk about her—yet." And he turned sharply away, to stare at the placid, silvery surface of the lake which had been Doris's very temporary grave.

"I understand," Dundee answered sympathetically, in the character of fellow-guest.

"Pardon me, sir," Wickett spoke. "I see a special delivery boy coming up the driveway. Perhaps I'd better go and sign for the letter, sir—"

"I'll go," Dundee interrupted. "I'm expecting a special-delivery letter myself."

Luckily he reached the back door before the boy had dismounted from his bicycle. As he had expected, the long, thick envelope was addressed to himself. He signed the slip, and was eagerly scanning the first of the newspaper clippings which the envelope contained before the boy was well away.

No time to read them all now, although he was keen to refresh his memory of the briefly sensational "Crosby case." Strawn and his men might arrive any minute, and

his chief must not catch him disobeying orders. He thrust
the envelope into the pocket of his dressing gown, wished
heartily for trousers, and walked slowly back to the
summerhouse. If only he could get to work, make a
thorough search of the summerhouse and the lake's edge
for clues! But of course Strawn was right. As a guest in
the Berkeley home, his profession unsuspected, he could
be of infinite value to the police. He did manage,
however, without being noticed by Crosby and the butler,
who were talking together, to retrieve the crystal stopper,
picking it up with his handkerchief, in which he wrapped
it carefully before putting it into the pocket of his
dressing gown.

It was dreary waiting, with that still, wet body on the
bench, and the sickening odor of *Fleur d'Amour* pouring
over them with every gust of the now brisk south wind.
But at last the ordeal was ended. Three cars, with the
initials "P.D" on their doors, swept up the driveway and
curved round the house to the east. Climbing out of the
first car, Captain Strawn apparently gave orders to his
police retinue to sit tight and await further orders, for he
was alone as he strode across the clipped green lawn.

"Well, the law is upon us and I imagine I am in for the
first grilling," Dundee said to Crosby, and, with a well-
assumed air of resignation, went to meet his chief.

His fellow-guest and the butler saw Dundee and the
uniformed captain of detectives shake hands, but could
not hear the low-toned conversation that took place on
the lawn.

"Well, boy, what's the lay?" Strawn asked. "Any facts
you didn't tell me over the phone?"

Briefly, but omitting no essential detail, Dundee told
of seeing Clorinda Berkeley steal out of the house the
night before; of Dick Berkeley's proposed rendezvous with
the murdered girl, and of Dick's absence from his room
throughout the night.

"Hmm!" Strawn considered, frowning. "Wonder if
those two facts are connected? Suppose Clorinda knew,

in some way, of the affair between her brother and the maid, had the same bright idea you did of preventing another meeting and a possibly messy scandal on the eve of the announcement of her engagement to the society swell, sneaked out to argue with the girl and killed her during the quarrel that followed—her brother being present and then beating it in a panic?"

"Perhaps," Dundee conceded respectfully, "but—*how did the flask of perfume get mixed up in it?* Clorinda wasn't carrying it. I'm sure of that. Not in her hands, at least, for she had nothing in them but the scarf with which Doris's skirts were bound. And she was wearing one of those evening capes which don't have capacious pockets, I believe. Although the light was dim, I had a pretty clear picture of her as she descended the stairs and I could swear the cape wasn't weighted down at all— floated about her, in fact."

"Maybe the maid, Doris, had stolen the perfume," Strawn offered.

"I heard Mrs. Berkeley say last night that Doris hated perfume, that it gave her a sick headache to smell it," Dundee objected. "And although the stuff was expensive—worth thirty-two dollars an ounce, according to Mrs. Berkeley—and the crystal flask was valuable in itself, I can't somehow see Doris as a petty thief. Also, why should she take it with her on a rendezvous with her mistress' son?"

"By me!" Strawn shrugged. "But you yourself say she was killed with the perfume flask, or at least stunned with a blow which broke the flask before she was dumped into the lake. It'll be up to the coroner to determine the cause of death, and he's on his way. . . . Now, one other thing. Young Berkeley hasn't returned yet, I suppose?"

"Not that I know of. I haven't been upstairs since the murder was discovered. You told me to stay on the scene of the crime."

"Right!" Strawn agreed. "But now at the risk of Crosby's thinking you are too thick with the police, I want

you to go and have another look in his room. Take care
not to spread the alarm, however, and if young Berkeley's
there, have him come to the summerhouse immediately. .
. . By the way, whose idea was the swimming party,
anyway?"

"Georgina Berkeley's," Dundee answered curtly. "They
call her Gigi. She's only a kid—fifteen."

"Then I suppose that lets her out," Strawn conceded.
"She'd hardly invite a party down to see what she'd done,
then obligingly discover the body herself. Unless there's
something in that old saying about a criminal returning
to the scene of the crime. . . . Hey, boy! But in a case like
this you've got to think of everything. Now get along with
you!"

VI.

As Dundee let himself into the house by the front door, hoping to evade the hysterical questions of the servants, who must have noted the arrival of the police cars, the door leading into the backstairs quarters was torn open and a young man in chauffeur's uniform lunged toward him, pausing only long enough to slam the door in the face of a maid who was pressing forward inquisitively.

"Excuse me, sir!" the chauffeur panted. "But will you tell me what's up? What are the police doing here? Della, the upstairs maid, told me Doris—Mrs. Berkeley's maid—didn't sleep in her room last night. It's not true, is it? Nothing's happened to Doris! The police aren't here about her, are they, sir?"

He was almost sobbing, and one big, freckled hand kept running distractedly through his curly, dark-red hair.

When Dundee hesitated to answer, the chauffeur so far forgot himself as to seize the guest's arm and shake it frenziedly. "For God's sake, sir, why won't you tell me? I'm Arnold—Eugene Arnold, the Berkeley chauffeur, and I'm engaged to be married to Doris. I have a *right* to ask if anything's happened to her—"

"I'm sorry, Arnold," Dundee said slowly, "but I can't speak for the police. Will you please wait as quietly as possible in the servant's sitting room until Captain Strawn calls for you? And I think it would be wise for you not to talk—"

"Then it *is* Doris!" Arnold interrupted, his voice going heavy and dull with despair. Then apparently realization swept over him. His freckled, pleasant young face flamed with anger. "Did she elope with Dick Berkeley, sir? Is that what the row's about? For God's sake, tell me!"

"Sorry, but I'm afraid I can't tell you anything Arnold," Dundee said quietly, and started up the stairs.

"Gone! With that drunken rotter!" Arnold groaned, and lurched blindly toward the back-hall door. But before he disappeared Dundee heard him vow, with terrible intensity: "I'll find him and kill him if I have to hunt all over the world for him!"

"A violent young man," Dundee commented wearily to himself, as he plodded upstairs.

He hoped to gain the third floor without further interruption, but as he reached the second-floor landing Clorinda Berkeley stepped forward. She had changed from bathing suit to a morning dress of dark-green jersey, a color that made her pallor quite ghastly.

"Why didn't you tell him that Doris had committed suicide?" she demanded coldly. "I imagine he would rather have had the news from you than from a policeman."

"Because I don't know that Doris committed suicide," Dundee answered, watching the beautiful, somber face keenly.

"Don't quibble with me!" she retorted. "Gigi confessed to me on the way to the house that she recognized the 'mermaid' in the lake, and I watched from my window as you dived for the body and took it into the summerhouse."

"Where is Gigi now? Why aren't you with her?" Dundee asked sharply.

"You don't like me, do you?" Clorinda asked, with amazing irrelevance. "So few people do! . . . Gigi preferred to be consoled by Mrs. Lambert, as I was busy being rather sick at my stomach. Doris was one of the few people who liked me, and—I was very fond of Doris. I can't imagine why she would commit suicide, unless—"

She broke off abruptly, and Dundee was a flicker of quickly controlled fear in her magnificent black eyes.

"I'm rather anxious to get into my clothes," Dundee excused himself curtly. Not for him, in the character of house guest in Clorinda's home, to probe the meaning of that unless" . . . "By the way, Miss Berkeley, do your father and mother know yet?"

"No. I didn't fancy the task," Clorinda retorted cooly. "There's nothing Mother enjoys so much as a good fit of hysterics, and Father and I are not on confidential terms just now," she added, with bitter humor. "I see the police have arrived. They'll probably enjoy the sensation. I would."

Without being stopped again Dundee went to his own room, thence, by way of the bathroom, to Dick Berkeley's. As he had expected and feared, the missing man had not returned. For the first time he tried the door leading into the hall. It was locked. Doubtless Dick had pocketed the key, to prevent his absence being discovered by anyone but Dundee, who had heard him make the rendezvous with Doris and who, he must have thought, could be depended upon not to give him away. But now, Dundee reflected grimly, it was no longer a question of shielding a friend engaged in an intrigue with a pretty servant. Doris Matthews had been murdered, and the hounds of the law would have to be set upon Dick Berkeley's trail.

Ten minutes later, decently clothed and sketchily shaved, Dundee sped down the backstairs and out of the house. A frightened cook and a housemaid had peeped out at him, but he had given them no time to question him.

The machinery of the law had been set in motion during his absence. Captain Strawn and the coroner, Dr. Price, whom he had met during the investigation into the Rhodes House murders, were bending over the body of the dead girl, still stretched upon the curving bench of the summerhouse. The fingerprint expert, Carraway, was already busy with his black powder and camera. Wickett, the butler, still stood outside the little arbor, but Seymour Crosby was missing from the gruesome picture. A knot of uniformed policemen and plainclothes detectives stood on the lake's edge, awaiting instructions from the chief of the Homicide Squad.

"Dick Berkeley has not returned," Dundee reported to Strawn in a voice so low that Wickett could not hear. "Since he's still in dinner clothes—they're not in his closet—I don't think he could have got far without being noticed."

Strawn turned his back on the corpse, and jerked his head toward the immobile butler. "Got any reason to think the old boy's mixed up in this?" he whispered.

"None whatever!" Dundee answered sincerely.

"Then don't you think it might be a good idea to let him in on the secret of your official connection with the police?" Strawn suggested. "If this thing isn't quickly cleared up by a confession from Dick Berkeley and develops into a first-class mystery, we'll need Wickett as an ally. No one knows as much about a family like this as its butler, and besides, he can keep the coast clear of other servants while you snoop around in the bedrooms and such—"

"Just a minute, chief!" Dundee interrupted, flushing. "I agree with you that I might be of infinitely more value as a trusted guest, rather than as a detective, but—hang it all, Captain Strawn, I *am* a guest here, and I simply can't do it—snoop around in the bedrooms as you suggest—"

"Resigning from the force, because a friend of yours is mixed up in this, Dundee?" Strawn asked, a sneer twisting his broad, thin mouth.

"I don't think you mean that, Captain Strawn," Dundee answered quietly. "I want to be on the case, but I'd rather be open and aboveboard about it."

"And jeopardize your future usefulness on the Homicide Squad?" Your uncle, the police commissioner, and I agreed after the Rhodes House murders that you could serve us best by not getting yourself tagged as what the people call a 'common detective.' With the education and social advantages you've had you can move in circles not open to the rest of us—"

"I know the argument, and I've been willing to be of service in any way possible," Dundee interrupted, "but in this instance I can't bring myself to abuse hospitality so flagrantly. There's another thing, too; as a guest, presumably under police surveillance as much as any other person in the house, I should have little chance to be of any real use to you. I couldn't be secreted behind screens while you were conducting your investigation, as I was at the Rhodes House, and not even Wickett's connivance could long cover my snooping from servants or members of the family. But if you want my official connection with the Homicide Squad to be kept dark, I have a suggestion to make."

"Well?" Strawn growled. "Shoot! We've got to get busy."

"You can give out that I am an amateur criminologist, engaged in research work preparatory to writing books on the subject—which is strictly true, by the way; that I have studied Scotland Yard methods, and that I was able to render you valuable aid in solving the Rhodes House murders. . . . Otherwise, chief, I'll have to resign now—with deep regret."

An angry retort trembled on Strawn's lips, but he bit it back, and considered scowlingly. At last he capitulated grumpily:

"All right, Dundee! You know I need you, but I'm warning you now that *I'm* in charge of this case, and I won't have you getting too big for your breeches. . . . Wickett!"

With dignity, unhurriedly, the butler obeyed Captain Strawn's summons, but halted just before setting foot on the first of the two steps leading from the cement walk into the little summerhouse, his sad eyes involuntarily flinching from further sight of the slim, rigid body laid out on the bench.

Strawn and Dundee descended the steps together. Strawn spoke, his voice curt but not unkind.

"Wickett, does young Berkeley drive his own car?"

The butler appeared startled. "Why, yes, sir. There are four cars, sir. The family limousine, Miss Clorinda's coupe, Mr. Dick's sports car—a two-passenger, that is; and the service truck."

"Thanks. . . . Come here, Payne!" Strawn called to one of the group of uniformed policemen and plainclothes detectives awaiting orders a short distance away on the lawn. "Dash down to the garages and check up on the cars you find there. Should be four. I particularly want to know if a two-passenger sports car is missing. That's the garage, isn't it, Wickett?" and he pointed to a wide, narrow stone building which lay several hundred feet behind and slightly to the west of the Berkeley house.

"Yes, sir. Arnold—Eugene Arnold—is the chauffeur, but he's probably at breakfast now in the servants' dining room. He sleeps over the garage, sir, and has doubtless opened it for the day."

"Get along, Payne, and make it snappy!" Strawn ordered. "Now, Wickett, before I go into the house and notify the family that murder's been committed out here, I want you to answer a few questions. . . . First, do you know anything at all about this bad business?"

"No, sir," the butler answered, after the faintest hesitation.

"Any suspicions, Wickett?" Strawn pounced.

"I—no, sir!"

"Wickett," Dundee interrupted, "I've already told Captain Strawn that you, as well as I, overheard Mr. Dick Berkeley urging Doris to meet him outside last night, after the family were in bed. You know, Wickett, that I am Mr. Dick's guest here, his friend, but at a time like this everything we know must be told. I am sure you want to see poor little Doris avenged, and as speedily as possible."

"That I do, sir!" the butler agreed huskily. "I did overhear, quite by accident, the conversation you refer to and I thought it my duty to speak to Doris when Mr. Dick had left her. It was in the back hall, sir," he explained to

Strawn. "The poor child assured me she had no intention of keeping her promise to Mr. Dick. She said she had already arranged to meet Arnold for a stroll around the lake—"

"Arnold, the chauffeur?" Strawn interrupted sharply.

"Yes. Sir. They are—Doris and Arnold were engaged to be married, sir; had become engaged a few days ago," the butler explained. "I might add that we were all very much pleased, sir—"

"Well! A new suspect and a new motive!" Strawn ejaculated. "Jealousy, eh?" and he raised his eyebrows triumphantly at Dundee.

The butler coughed deprecatingly. "If you'll pardon me, sir. . . . Thank you, sir. . . . The chauffeur and the limousine were required at about eleven, sir, to drive Mr. and Mrs. Benjamin Smith, Mrs. Berkeley's brother and sister-in-law, to their home in Westview."

"Westview, eh?" Strawn frowned. "That's about fifteen miles from Hillcrest, Dundee. . . . did you hear Arnold return, Wickett?"

"No, sir," the butler answered readily. "But I feel sure he did not make any effort to see Doris, sir."

"Why?" Strawn snapped.

"Because, sir, when he brought the car around to the front door, I admitted him, sir, and he asked me to give Doris a note, in which, as he told me, he had explained why he could not meet her last night. I intended to hand her the note, but my duties kept me constantly downstairs, and I placed it on a little table in the back hall. I knew she would find it there on her way out to meet Arnold, if I did not have an opportunity to give it to her before."

"And you left the note there?"

"Yes, sir. In fact I am ashamed to confess that I forgot about it. It had been a heavy day, preparing for the big party which was planned for to-night—"

"And which won't come off now!" Dundee interrupted with a certain grim satisfaction. At least the ordeal of another of Abbie Berkeley's terrible parties would be spared him!

"Yes, sir," Wickett agreed gravely, and Dundee suspected that Wickett shared his feelings on the subject of Mrs. Berkeley's parties.

"Well, Wickett, get along with your story!" Strawn commanded impatiently. "Did you see the girl again? After she told you she wasn't going to meet young Berkeley, I mean."

"No sir. She said she was going up to her room, to finish a letter to her sister in England, about her engagement to Arnold, sir. She also said that Mrs. Berkeley had told her it was not necessary for her to wait up for either herself or Miss Clorinda."

"Did Mrs. Berkeley know of the date Doris had with Arnold?" Strawn asked.

"No, sir! Doris remarked that she hoped Mrs. Berkeley would not find it out," the butler answered.

"Why?" Strawn shot at him.

The butler flushed slightly and his eyelids flickered, but he did not answer.

"How did Mrs. Berkeley and Doris hit it off? Not so good, eh?" Strawn probed.

"Doris was an excellent lady's maid, sir—sweet-tempered and efficient," Wickett answered. that husky note of grief in his voice again.

"But Mrs. Berkeley—not so sweet-tempered, eh, Wickett?" Strawn dug at him relentlessly.

"If you'll pardon me, sir—" Wickett pleaded.

"I guess I'm answered," Strawn concluded, with satisfaction. "All right now: what about the note? You forgot about it last night, you said. Did you see it this morning?"

"No, sir. It was not on the little table where I had left it."

"Then Doris must have found it on her way out to meet Arnold, eh?" Strawn deduced, glancing toward Dundee.

"But if she found the note, calling the date off, I'm wondering why she left the house at all," Dundee objected.

"That's easy!" Strawn laughed drily. "With Arnold safely out of the way, she could keep her promise to meet Dick Berkeley!"

"No, sir!" Wickett spoke with positiveness starling in its contrast with his former respectful mildness. "Not Doris, sir! She was not that sort of girl."

"Perhaps you don't know, Wickett, that Dick Berkeley sneaked out of the house last night to keep that date with Doris, and is still missing. Or did you see him go out?"

"No, sir," the butler answered, but for an instant there was in his eyes that same black rage with which he had looked at Dick Berkeley the night before.

At that moment Detective Payne came loping up, breathless, apologetic. "All four cars in the garage, sir. Sorry to be so long, but I had to go to the house and get the keys from the chauffeur. And say, chief, that guy, Arnold, is in an awful stew. Tried to get me to tell him what's up, but I kept my mouth shut. It seemed to give him an awful jolt when he saw that the sports car was sitting pretty—"

"All right, Payne!" Strawn interrupted. "Take three of the boys and scour the estate for Dick Berkeley—a young man in dinner clothes. Any place he could hide that you know of, Wickett?"

"There are several buildings in the estate, including a gardener's cottage which is not in use now, and Miss Gigi's little playhouse—also not often in use now, sir," Wickett answered.

"All right, Payne! Hop to it! Search everything, even if you have to bust down doors," Strawn ordered. "And you, Wickett, you can go to the house and get along with the family's breakfast, but don't serve it until I give you the word. And don't talk—understand?" he cautioned sternly. Then: "Wait a minute! What time did you go up to bed last night?"

"At eleven-fifteen, sir."

"After everyone else had gone to bed?"

"Mr. and Mrs. Berkeley were still talking in the library, sir, but Mr. Berkeley told me to go to bed. I had already locked up."

"Did anyone, to you knowledge, leave the house last night, after the Smiths had gone?"

"No, sir. I did not see or hear anyone leave the house."

"After you went up to your room, did you see or hear anything that might have any bearing on the murder?"

"Nothing, sir. I was very tired, and went to sleep almost immediately."

As the butler, dismissed again, moved away with mournful dignity, Strawn commented: "There's one guy would like to jerk the rope himself if Dick Berkeley killed the girl. . . . Well, doc, what's the verdict?" he asked, as he and Dundee reentered the summerhouse, where Dr. Price, the coroner, was awaiting the,, whiling away the time by watching Carraway, the fingerprint expert, at his work. "Death by a blow to the head or by drowning? And when did she die?"

VII.

Dr. Price shook his white head. "Sorry, Captain Strawn, but I can't answer either of those questions now—definitely. Only an autopsy can tell whether the blow killed her or whether she was only stunned, and died by drowning. As to the time death took place, that will be hard to fix accurately, even after the autopsy. Unofficially, however, I'll say now that she has been dead between eight and nine hours—that opinion subject to revision, of course."

"Hmm. . . . That places the murder between eleven o'clock and midnight, if you're right—and you usually are. Good enough for a starter, at any rate. . . . By the way, doc, in examining the body did you find a letter or note?"

"No—nothing of the sort. There's only one pocket—on the blouse of her uniform, and you can see for yourself it's empty. I rolled the stockings down to look for bruises, and can assure you that no note was concealed in them. The stockings, by the way, have snags and runs in the back of them."

"Runs? Funny that a pretty girl like that—" the chief of the Homicide Squad began.

"There were no runs in her stockings when Dick Berkeley was forcing her to dance with him last night," Dundee interrupted. "I distinctly remember noticing how pretty her legs were in her sheer black silk stockings. But I think I know what is responsible for those runs," and he pointed to the rough edge of the flooring which extended slightly over the flight of three narrow steps leading down into the lake. "See! Here's a tiny thread of the stocking silk, caught in a splinter. The body was dragged down to the steps—"

"Dragged!" Strawn repeated. "Then it couldn't have been a very strong person—"

"Remember the rocks with which the body was weighted," Dundee reminded him. "I told you over the phone that I untied the scarf that bound the skirt together about her knees and removed the rocks, piling them together on the bottom of the lake. The water's quite deep almost to the very edge here—about eight feet, I'd say."

"And whoever dumped the girl in knew the lake pretty well—knew the water was deep enough here to hide the body, provided it was weighted down so it couldn't rise and float," Strawn pointed out. "Temporarily, at least, that counts Crosby out, unless he was so panicky he had to take a chance. . . . How far out was the body?"

"Very near the steps—not more than five or six feet," Dundee answered. "Here's how I visualize the crime— and by the way, I think it was an impromptu murder, one growing out of sudden anger, or fear. The use of the perfume flask as a weapon certainly points that way—"

"How do you know it was the weapon?" Strawn objected.

"Three reasons: first, your nose tells you that perfume has been spilled here. Lots of it! Second, there's a glass splinter in that crack between the boards. Third—" and he drew from his pocket the handkerchief-wrapped stopper of the crystal flask. "I found this under the bench, overlooked by the murderer. I suppose you'll want Carraway to look it over for fingerprints, but I doubt that he finds any. It's so intricately carved that there's practically no smooth surface to take a print."

When Carraway had accepted the stopper, shaking his head dubiously, Strawn burst out:

"But how the devil did the perfume flask get out here?"

"If we knew the answer to that question, I think we would know everything," Dundee replied. "Frankly, it stumps me. But it is certainly obvious that nobody but a maniac would choose a crystal flask of extremely concentrated perfume with which to clout anyone over the head—with premeditatedly murderous intentions, I mean. Therefore I say the crime was impromptu, the weapon the first and only one at hand. The deeply cut crystal flask broke with the first blow, of course, and the perfume spilled on the floor. I've sniffed with my nose to the floor, and I'm pretty sure it didn't spatter much; therefore, it's rather obvious either that Doris was sitting on the bench, or that she had slipped from the bench to her knees, to plead with her assailant. The latter, I think, since that would bring her head closer to the floor, to account for the fact that the perfume did not splash all over the place."

"Poor little thing!" And Captain Strawn, who regarded himself as very much hardened to murder, shuddered with horror and pity.

"Whether that assailant meant to murder her or not we can't know yet, of course," Dundee went on. "But granted that the blow only stunned the girl, the person who had hit her thought she was dead, or desperately feared the consequences if she regained consciousness and told what had happened. In any case, that person had only one thought—to conceal the body. And here was the lake—a made-to-order grave. The girl's disappearance would cause excitement, of course, but it might be days before it occurred to anyone to suspect suicide or murder, and to drag the lake. The swimming season was over. No one could have foreseen that this morning would be so unseasonably warm that Gigi Berkeley would get up a swimming party. . . . Poor Gigi!" he added compassionately.

"You like the kid?" Strawn asked, grinning.

"Very much!" Dundee answered curtly. "But to get along with the story, as I see it. The murderer was panic-stricken, but the instinct for self-preservation was strong. The body mustn't rise to the surface before he had a chance to escape, as naturally as possible. Therefore it must be weighted. And the means for that too were at hand. An artistic border of rocks is all along the lake's edge, and right up to the very steps that lead down into the lake. . . . Look!" and he drew Strawn to the top step and pointed. "There's where he got the stones. Didn't even have to leave the steps. Stooped and gathered them in—three from the right side of the steps, two from the left."

"Hey! Wait a minute!" Strawn protested. "How could the murderer see to do all this, unless he had been thoughtful enough to provide himself with a flashlight? I happen to know there wasn't any moon last night."

"There again circumstances played into the murderers hand," Dundee said. "No moon, but light where it was needed. There are wire-covered electric lights placed among the rocks, all along the lake's edge, at intervals— sufficient to light up the lake and the interior of the summerhouse. Dick and I were standing at a window of the ballroom last evening before dinner when the lake lights went on. He explained the arrangement and said also that there are a pair of electric lanterns over the gates and over the garage. It seems that the butler throws a switch that controls all the outside lights, turning them on at dark and off when he comes down in the morning. Moving about the grounds the murderer would not have been seen from the house last night, if anyone was looking out, but could have done his ghastly work in here, all right."

"I see. . . . Go on with your 'visualizing,'" Strawn commanded.

"Well, the rocks were placed inside the girl's skirt, but before that, I think, her little white apron was removed— "

"Apron?" Strawn repeated. "Part of her uniform, eh?" Maybe she took it off before she came out on a date—"

"No, I don't think she did," Dundee assured him. "When you send divers down into the lake I think you will find it wrapped about the pieces of the broken flask, for I feel sure the apron was dipped into the water and used to swab blood stains from the floor, and, possibly, from the clothes of the murderer. Also, to remove as much of the perfume as possible—but that was one task he found to hard for him!" he added, with grim satisfaction.

"Well, if he thinks it as easy as all that to get rid of blood stains, he's in for a surprise," Strawn promised. "Eh, doc? Takes more'n a little cold water to get rid of blood stains so that our chemist can't find a trace. What about the floor, doc?"

"I've already removed some of the blood-soaked dirt from the cracks between the boards, where the floor had been swabbed," Dr Price assured him complacently.

"Good man!" Strawn applauded generously. "Well, Dundee?"

"That's nearly all, I think. The stones were then placed inside the skirt and it was bound tightly about the girl's knees—"

"With Clorinda Berkeley's scarf!" Captain Strawn emphatically concluded the sentence for his subordinate.

"Which doesn't necessarily mean that Clorinda Berkeley did the tying," Dundee went on quietly. "Not that I'm saying she didn't, but we must not overlook the possibility that Clorinda left the house quite innocently for a walk about the grounds—headache, possibly— and that she rested here for a bit, leaving her scarf behind her, thus providing the murderer with another aid to his impromptu crime. We can't hang her with the scarf, you know—"

"Maybe not, but a rope will do just as well, if we find any of this perfume spattered on her dress," Strawn retorted triumphantly.

"If a spattering of this perfume were enough to get a conviction of murder, I'm afraid I'd be one of your first arrests, chief," Dundee grinned. "My dinner coat's reeking with the stuff."

"What!" Strawn gaped at him. "Say, you didn't happen to *see* this murder, did you?"

"No, I wasn't an eyewitness, any more than I was the murderer," Dundee assured him. "I should have told you before, but there's been so much to tell. . . . The truth is, chief, that every one who was in the drawing room last night—*hence, possibly every suspect that will turn up!—including Wickett, got splashed with Fleur d'Amour!*"

"To the devil with that kid!" Captain Strawn exclaimed disgustedly, when Dundee had told how Gigi Berkeley had seized upon the perfume flask, wrenched out the crystal stopper, and gone dancing madly from one to another in the drawing room the night before, lavishly sprinkling perfume upon the dinner coats and evening gowns. "If your crazy Gigi and that damned perfume don't quit bobbing into this case I'll go nuts. Now I suppose all we've got to go on is blood stains—if any! Would that wound have bled much, doc?" he turned to the coroner hopefully.

"Very little," Dr. Price answered. "There wouldn't have been any splashing of blood, if that's what you mean. Not from a scalp wound like that. As you can see from the remains of the stain—" and he pointed to the brownish spot on the floor—"there was a small pool of blood, which collected while the body lay there, during the time the murder was gathering the stones and binding the skirt. But I should say it is entirely possible that the murderer got none on his clothes. Probably the wound and the hair were swabbed off with the same cloth used to wipe up the floor."

"Damn!" Strawn growled. The he brightened: "Shoes! I don't suppose that little pest, Gigi, anointed every one's shoes, as well as dinner coats and gowns, did she? . . . Well, then, if I can find a pair of shoes stinking with this stuff, their owner's going to have a lot of explaining to do!"

"Of course, there is a bare possibility that the murderer is an outsider—some intruder who found the girl waiting here for her sweetheart, not knowing he couldn't meet her," Dundee offered dubiously. "Any evidence of an attack upon the girl, Dr. Price?"

"None whatever," the coroner answered.

"As I expected," Dundee nodded. "We couldn't hope that this case would be so simple as that. Furthermore, a chance intruder would scarcely have taken the time and the trouble to dispose of the body. He would simply have beat it as quickly as possible, fairly sure of many hours to escape before the hue and cry was raised. And still furthermore, such an explanation would entirely fail to account for the flask of perfume. . . . No, it seems to me that it's fairly obvious our murderer is a member of the Berkeley household, which includes all the servants and guests, of course. . . . By the way, where is Crosby?"

"I sent him to the house, along with two of the boys—Wilkins and Cain. Wilkins was to stand guard downstairs, to keep anyone from busting in on us down here, and Cain was to keep Crosby under strict surveillance. . . . Hey, boys!" he called to the three plainclothesmen and a uniformed policeman who still waited orders. "Which one of you can swim?"

The man in uniform stepped forward and saluted.

"All right, Collins. Come along with us. Detective Dundee will lend you his bathing suit. I want you to bring up a pile of five stones you'll find on the bottom of the lake about five or six feet from this summerhouse and then dive until you find a little white apron tied about some broken glass. . . . You can remove the body now, Dr. Price. I see the morgue ambulance has come. . . . And let me have your report as soon as possible, Carraway," he added to the fingerprint expert. "Be sure to include the fingerprints of the corpse, too."

The chief of the Homicide Squad hesitated for a moment, rubbing the grayish stubble on his massive jaw. Then: "Barnes, you and Peters are detailed to go over this section of the lawn and the lake's edge with a fine-toothed comb. Bring in anything and everything you find that shows people have been here—cigar or cigarette stubs, burnt matches, handkerchiefs, and so on. . . . You, Clemmons," and he addressed the only remaining plainclothesman, "come along to the house with us."

Strawn, Dundee, Collins, and Clemmons were setting off for the big stone mansion when a halloo stopped them. It was Detective Payne, followed at some distance by the two men he had chosen to help him search for Dick Berkeley.

"Sorry, chief!" he panted. "But no luck. We've been through every building on the estate, except the big house itself, and beat the shrubbery till a rabbit couldn't have escaped us."

Strawn frowned and shrugged. "Guess he's got away, all right, but he'll be a marked man, unless he's managed to change his clothes. . . . See anybody at all?"

"A deaf old man who said he was the gardener, and a boy of seventeen or eighteen who was helping him in the far east corner of the estate," Payne answered. "The boy told me they both live in town, and come to work at eight o'clock."

"All right! Come along!" Strawn growled. And the cortege was augmented by three somewhat disheveled and sweating detectives.

The chief halted it again, however, on the steps leading to the front veranda.

"Dundee," he ordered, "you bolt into the house and get your bathing suit for Collins. I'm going to study the lay of things from the outside a bit—get an idea of the plan of the house, that sort of thing," he explained lamely, and Dundee's heart swelled with gratitude. The "old man" wanted him by his side when the storm broke inside, wanted him to hear every word that was said, see the expression on every face when the hideous news was told.

Wickett, the butler, looking haggard and harassed, opened the big front door for him and Collins.

"Every one—that is, every one but Mr. Dick and Mrs. Berkeley, sir—is in what we call the 'little parlor,' sir, the first room on your right," he said in a low voice. "The other servants are in our own sitting room backstairs, sir. As I was instructed, sir, I have not given out any facts at all, but I am afraid Miss Gigi has told her father—"

"Mr. Crosby with them?" Dundee asked.

"Yes, sir. But I don't believe he has corrected Miss Gigi's statement that the poor little girl committed suicide. One of the detectives is with them."

"Thanks, Wickett! You've been a brick," the young detective whispered fervently, and ran upstairs, followed more sedately by the uniformed policeman.

When they returned, Dundee saw the butler's tired old eyes widen with dismay or horror at sight of the scanty new costume which Collins was wearing.

"Please, sir, you don't think Mr. Dick—?"

"We haven't found him yet," Dundee answered, pretending not to understand. But he was startled. Odd that the butler was the first to hit upon the idea that Dick Berkeley's disappearance might be explained as gruesomely as Doris Matthews'. Murder followed by suicide?

So it was that when Collins struck off for the lake, he was under orders to search it thoroughly, first for something much heavier than a little pile of stones or a small apron filled with bits of broken glass.

In the great front hall, Wickett quietly insisted upon the proper amenities. Preceding the invading group he opened the door of the "little parlor" and addressed Mr. Berkeley punctiliously:

"Captain Strawn of the police, sir."

Dundee, flushing in anticipation of the awkward explanation as to his own interest in the case, was at his chief's side when Strawn entered the room.

In the quivering silence which gripped the room George Berkeley advanced and held out his hand.

"I have been told something of what has happened here, Captain Strawn," he said, with grave courtesy, "and of course I am at your disposal, though I am afraid I know very little about police methods when suicide is concerned."

"Mr. Berkeley," Strawn answered, a little pompously, "I am very sorry to tell you that it is not suicide with which we have to deal, but—murder!"

The next minute was one of dreadful confusion. Dundee tried to see everything, hear everything, but his ears were ringing with Gigi's scream, and his eyes clung compassionately to the terror-stricken little face until it buried itself in Mrs. Lambert's lap.

"Don't my darling, don't!" the social secretary pleaded, her arms enfolding the child protectively. Her blue-gray eyes looked almost black with reproachful indignation as they blazed at Captain Strawn.

"Please remember sir, that this child has already suffered a terrible shock," she commanded, rather than pleaded.

"Sorry, ma'am, but this is no time to mince words," Strawn replied gruffly. "Doris Matthews has been murdered, and it is my duty to question every person who was in this house last night. But before the investigation gets under way I'll say to you, sir—" and he turned again to George Berkeley, "that you and me both can consider ourselves lucky that Mr. Dundee happens to be on the scene of the crime."

There was a slight movement of surprise on the part of every one in the room. Clorinda Berkeley gasped, then threw up her head, her black eyes measuring Bonnie Dundee with cool insolence. Seymour Crosby took a step forward, then halted, looking absurdly bewildered. Mrs. Lambert relaxed the fiercely protective pressure of her arms, made an effort to lend her usually charming smile to a puzzling moment. Even Gigi raised her tear-stained little brown face and stared. Dundee felt the hot blood of embarrassment burning in his cheeks.

VIII.

George Berkeley broke the silence. "Naturally, we're glad to have Mr. Dundee with us, though I am afraid his visit—" he began uncertainly.

"I'll explain, Mr. Berkeley," Captain Strawn assured him. "Mr. Dundee is what I'd call a might clever amateur detective, though I don't usually have much use for amateurs. Criminologist, I believe, is the word he uses. He's studied Scotland Yard methods and just this summer did me a good turn on the biggest murder case we've ever had in Hamilton. Getting material for books on the subject—that's his game. He writes shorthand, too, and he's going to take down what you folks have to tell me—"

"A *detective!* Are you *really* a detective, Bonnie Dundee?" Gigi cried, springing from Mrs. Lambert's embrace and running swiftly across the "little parlor" to seize Dundee's hands and swing them with frantic joy. "Oh, I'm glad! You won't let the police bully us and be horrid, will you? Of course, Captain Strawn looks like a gruff old darling bear—" and she whirled to pat the chief's cheek impudently. "Woof! You *do* need a shave!"

"I know it," Captain Strawn acknowledged ruefully. "Dundee hustled me out of bed and I didn't take time— But this is serious business, young woman!" he interrupted himself sternly, though he could not keep his eyes from twinkling at her. "Now, is everybody here? Are you Mrs. Berkeley, ma'am? He asked politely, turning to Mrs. Lambert.

Color swept over the still beautiful but tired face. "I am Mrs. Lambert, Mrs. Berkeley's secretary," she said, her voice low but very clear.

"My wife is still sleeping, I believe," George Berkeley explained stifle. "At any rate, she has not come down yet, and no one has been to her room to tell her that— anything is—wrong. It is—or was—her maid's duty to awaken her at half past eight, draw her bath and serve her breakfast in her room. Since—Doris—"

"I see," Strawn interrupted. "We'll go up and speak to her presently, but first, so we shan't be wasting time, I'd like for anybody that's got anything to tell me to speak up."

No one moved or spoke for a long minute, then Gigi, who had again returned to the shelter of Mrs. Lambert's arms, laughed hysterically.

"What! No confessions?" she cried, the burst into tears and hid her face against Mrs. Lambert's breast as her father pronounced her name sternly.

"Do you know where your son is, Mr. Berkeley?" Strawn asked.

"Dick?" The millionaire showed blank surprise. "In his room, I suppose. It is still rather early for him—"

"He's not in his room and his bed hasn't been slept in," Strawn cut in grimly, and as ruthlessly ignored the flurry of exclamations and half-uttered questions which followed upon his revelation. "Now, Mr. Berkeley, I'll ask you to show Mr. Dundee and me to your wife's room."

George Berkeley started to protest angrily, then checked himself abruptly, but his darkly handsome face was flushed and his nostrils flaring as he answered: "Certainly. This way—"

"Just a minute. . . . You folks stay right here—I don't know your names, but—"

"My daughters, Clorinda and Georgina, our guest, Mr. Seymour Crosby," Berkeley obliged, his lips tightening over the last name.

"Oh! So this is Mr. Seymour Crosby?" Strawn pretended vast surprise. "I've read a lot about you, Mr. Crosby—always thought I'd like to meet you." He added, his eyes narrowing significantly.

"Seymour Crosby flushed, but bowed without replying.

"Sorry you've got to run up against the police again, Mr. Crosby," Strawn went on wickedly, "but I hope you'll come out of this case with as clean a bill of health as you did out of the other one, sir."

Again Gigi sat up with a jerk and her round topaz eyes flashed excited, startled questions, but Strawn wheeled, grinning to follow the master of the house from the room. Dundee hurried, shamefaced, after him.

George Berkeley led the way up the broad, winding marble staircase to the second floor.

"You've certainly got a swell place here, Mr. Berkeley," Strawn told him appreciatively, his eyes roving over the thickly carpeted stairs, the carved oak panels of the walls.

"Thank you. . . . This is my wife's sitting room. If you don't mind waiting in here, I'll go and wake her—"

"Sorry, but we'll have to go along, Mr. Berkeley," Strawn interrupted genially, and pushed into the little foyer that separated the two rooms.

Mrs. Berkeley's rooms occupied the northeast corner of the house, her bedroom on the front and fitting into the tower which rose one story higher than the rest of the mansion. Between the enormous bedroom and the smaller sitting room, facing east, were the foyer and a large bathroom, all connecting, so that the mistress of the house could pass from sitting room to bathroom, thence to her bedroom, and from the bedroom to the hall by way of the foyer. In addition, the sitting room had a door of its own directly into the hall.

The detectives did not note all these details in those first moments, however. They were listening for an answer to George Berkeley's knock upon the bedroom door.

"She must be sleeping pretty sound," Strawn whispered, as Berkeley knocked again.

The little foyer was lighted, not brightly, but sufficiently, from the sun that poured into the sitting room from the four French windows that opened upon a stone and wrought-iron balcony overlooking the east lawn and the lake. The blinds had not been drawn, and the sun rioted through the curtains of finest gold lace, so that there was more than light enough for Dundee to see George Berkeley's face go gray with fear.

"Good Lord! Does he think *she's* dead, too?" he asked himself.

But at that moment a querulous voice called out: "Why are you knocking, Doris? For heaven's sake come on in! I can't *bear* any *hammering* this morning!"

Strawn and Dundee exchanged glances, as the millionaire called soothingly: "It's George, Abbie. May I come in?"

"Have you thought up a lot of new arguments, George Berkeley? . . . Well, so have I! But come on in, if you must! I'm still in bed and I've still got an awful headache—"

Rather hastily, as if to cut her short, Berkeley opened the door and the two detectives, the younger with a word of apology, followed him into the enormous and over-poweringly luxurious bedroom of the mistress of Hillcrest.

While Mrs. Berkeley squealed and protested and questioned futilely, Captain Strawn strode to the darkened windows which filled the semicircle formed by the tower of which the room was a part, and jerked up the shades.

Painfully embarrassed, Dundee halted just inside the door while George Berkeley, in a low voice, explained that Strawn was a captain of detectives and that their guest, an amateur criminologist, was there as an assistant.

"But what in the world are detectives doing here, George?" Mrs. Berkeley shrilled, drawing an orchid satin comforter up to her chin. "Has the house been robbed? Tell me—"

"I'll tell you, Mrs. Berkeley," Captain Strawn interrupted, marching to the bed and looking down grimly upon its disheveled, haggard occupant. "But first, I'd like to ask you when you last saw Doris Matthews, your maid."

"*Doris?*" Mrs. Berkeley squealed. "So that impertinent little snip is a thief, is she? I never trusted that girl, with her high and mighty airs and—"

Strawn shrugged as he glanced toward Dundee. Then: "And when did you last see the crystal flask of perfume which Mr. Crosby presented to you last night?"

"Oh!" the woman gasped. "So *that's* what became of my perfume! I thought it was awfully queer that Wickett should disobey me, when I told him to take it straight to my room last night! Quick, George! See if she took my jewels, too! Oh, the deceitful little wretch—"

"Another question, Mrs. Berkeley," Strawn interrupted harshly, "although you have not answered either of my other two: When did you last see your son?"

"Dick? Why—Oh, you don't mean—George, Dick hasn't *eloped* with that awful little thief, has he? . . . Oh, my God! And my head's splitting, too! George, why don't you *say* something? Tell me what all this means!"

"Abbie, my dear," her husband began sadly, "I am afraid this is all much more serious than stolen perfume and jewels. Please try to control yourself—"

"If you'll pardon me, Mr. Berkeley, I'll do the explaining," Captain Strawn cut in sharply. "Mrs. Berkeley, it is my unpleasant duty to inform you that Doris Matthews has been murdered."

"*Murdered!*" the woman gasped. The she whispered the word, her lips—like red crepe paper—quivering over the word. "Murdered!" then she lay back on her pillow, her disheveled, hennaed head rolling, the wrinkled lids falling over her faded, hard blue eyes.

"And I must inform you, Mrs. Berkeley," Captain Strawn went on implacably, unmercifully, "that your son is missing. He did not sleep in his room last night, and we know that he made an appointment to meet the girl after the family was in bed."

As he spoke, the woman began to lift herself in bed, her ravaged face with its terribly bleared eyes turned toward the detectives.

"You think—Dick—? Oh, you're a fool, a fool! My boy's not a murderer! He's dead, too! He killed them both, like he said he would! Oh, my God, my God!"

"*He?*" Strawn echoed, as George Berkeley forcibly held his wife in bed.

"Who do you mean, Mrs. Berkeley?" Captain Strawn asked again, when the hysterical woman had stopped screaming for a moment. "Remember, you are accusing someone of murder!"

"I mean Eugene Arnold, my chauffeur! That's who!" the woman panted, fighting off her husband's restraining hands. "Let me up! I'm going to find my boy! You can't hold me here, making me answer silly questions when my poor Dick—"

"Mrs. Berkeley, please try to control yourself!" Strawn commanded harshly, for he knew how to deal with hysterics. "I feel absolutely sure that your son is not dead, or we should have found his body where the girl's was hidden." He did not add that, at that very moment, Policeman Collins was diving into the lake on the slim chance that another body lay on its cement bottom.

"And where did you find—Doris?"

"In the lake, near the summerhouse," Strawn answered. "Your daughter, Georgina, got up a little swimming party early this morning and when she dived in she saw the body."

"Gigi? .. . . Oh, my poor baby!" Mrs. Berkeley sobbed, covering her face with plump, beringed fingers. "Where is she? Where's my baby now? She needs her mother—"

"Gigi is all right now, dear. She's with Mrs. Lambert," George Berkeley assured her, taking her hands to hold them tightly in his.

"Before Doris was rolled down the steps of the summerhouse into the lake," Captain Strawn went on, as if he had not been interrupted, "she had been hit upon the head with the crystal flask of perfume which Mr. Seymour Crosby gave you last night. The bottle broke and the perfume spilled on the floor. We've recovered part of the fragments and one of my men is searching the lake for the rest of the pieces now."

"Hit on the head with my perfume flask?" Mrs. Berkeley repeated blankly. Then horror twisted her oldish, ugly face. "But this is all too *silly!* Why should— Oh! She *had* stolen it, and it serves her right if she got killed with it!"

"Mrs. Berkeley," Dundee said gently, as he drew nearer the bed, "didn't I hear you say last night that Doris hated perfume, that it made her ill to smell it?"

"But she could have stolen it anyway, to sell!" Mrs. Berkeley cried angrily. "That's exactly what she did! The crystal flask must have been worth at least fifty dollars, and the perfume costs thirty-two dollars an ounce. I know, because I bought some myself on the Rue de la Paix—some of the very same kind—*Fleur d'Amour!* Doris had heard me say how wonderful it was, and how frightfully expensive. But why are you wasting time like this? Haven't I told you Eugene Arnold did it? Why, it was only yesterday—"

"Just a minute, Mrs. Berkeley," Strawn interrupted. "Mr. Dundee writes shorthand, and I want him to take down the statement you are about to make. Where will I find paper and pencil, please?"

"In my sitting room—but I don't want you taking down every word I say," Mrs. Berkeley sobbed. "I'll be frightened to death!"

At a nod from Strawn, Dundee left the stuffy, over-decorated bedroom, more suitable for a French courtesan than for the wife of an American business man, and went through the little foyer into the almost equally ornate sitting room. In the unlocked Sheraton desk he found a box of expensive notepaper, with a silver-embossed "Hillcrest." As he was leaving the sitting room there was a heavy knock and he opened the door leading into the hall, to confront one of the detectives who had been left on duty downstairs.

"Collins say there ain't no other body in the lake, sir, and that he's found the rocks and the bundle of glass."

"All right, Clemmons. Thanks! Tell the butler to take Collins up to my room by the backstairs, to change into his own clothes, then have him wait around downstairs until Captain Strawn has further orders for him."

When Dundee relayed the news to his chief, Strawn nodded. "Hear that, Mrs. Berkeley? Wherever your son is, he's not dead, for if he'd been killed with the girl, the murderer would have disposed of his body in the lake, too. . . . Now ma'am, I want you to get hold of yourself and answer my questions fully and truthfully. This is no time to hold back anything—*anything*, mind you!"

"George, don't let that awful policeman talk to me like that!" Mrs. Berkeley moaned. "If I've got to be asked all sorts of frightful questions, I want Mr. Dundee to ask them, not that awful old *bulldog!* At least Mr. Dundee is a gentleman, even if he is a—a—"

"Criminologist," her husband supplied, with a slight smile. "would you very much mind, Captain Strawn? My wife is a very—excitable person, and you must realize what an ordeal this is for her—"

"All right, Dundee! Go ahead!" Strawn commanded ungraciously. "It's not entirely regular, but anything to save time."

Dundee, with a rueful, apologetic glance toward his chief, drew up a chair and laid a sheaf of notepaper on his knees. With a pencil poised to take down the answer he asked his first question:

"Will you please tell us, Mrs. Berkeley, what happened yesterday to make you so sure that Eugene Arnold is Doris's murderer?"

Now that her son's safety seemed fairly certain, although his disappearance had not been explained, Mrs. Berkeley was far less hysterical. Indeed, as she plunged into her narrative, Dundee had a suspicion that she was rather enjoying it all.

"Well, you see, *dear* Mr. Dundee," she began, pushing the orchid satin comforter down and prinking the laces of her yellow silk nightgown, "my poor, darling Dick is so—how shall I say?—susceptible! Not that *I* think Doris is—or was—anything to get excited about. But of course if you like those skinny, washed-out little blondes—Well, anyway—" she floundered, flushing under the stern eyes of the men, "Dick thought she was awfully pretty and cute, and he flirted with her quite a lot, I'm afraid—"

"Pardon! Did Doris encourage your son?"

"We-ell, not exactly, at least when I happened to catch them together," she admitted. "You see, Dick got into the habit of dropping in when I was dressing, and I did suspect it was because he could see Doris. She acted as demure and shy as you please when I was around, but when I wasn't, goodness knows— Anyway, yesterday I had been out shopping and when I came home I had a lot of bundles in the car, so I had Arnold carry them up for me. I sent him on into my bedroom while I stopped to look at the mail on my sitting room desk. Then I heard voices—Dick's and Arnold's and the maid's—and I hurried in here, just as Arnold was shouting to Doris: 'If I find out you're double-crossing me with this—this young puppy, I'll kill you both, and I don't mean maybe!' . . . That's exactly what he said, Mr. Dundee!" she concluded triumphantly.

"And did you discharge Arnold for his insolence to your son?" Dundee asked quietly.

"N-no," she admitted reluctantly. "I bawled him out, all right, but—well, you see, with Mr. Crosby coming and the big party tonight and all, I simply couldn't fire my chauffeur and my maid. There wouldn't have been time to get others—"

"I see."

"I had a heart-to-heart talk with my poor Dick. He adores me, just as my other children do," she went on fatuously. "I made him promise to let Doris strictly alone—"

"Do you know what Arnold had seen, when he came into the room?"

"From what they all said, he saw—he saw Dick kissing Doris," Mrs. Berkeley admitted reluctantly. "Anyway, he told me he was sorry about it all, and promised faithfully not to have anything more to do with the girl. And I know he would have kept the promise if he hadn't drunk a little too much at dinner last night. . . . You needn't think, Captain Strawn," she added, "that you can arrest my husband for buying bootleg liquor. All our wines and whiskey and liqueurs are pre-war. I made George buy a big cellarful before prohibition went into effect."

"I'm on the Homicide Squad, Mrs. Berkeley," Strawn reminded her grimly.

"Oh! Well, then, you can simply arrest Eugene Arnold—if you can find him!" she cried. "Don't you see what happened? My poor Dick did forget his promise or maybe that deceitful girl led him on! Anyway, he met her, and Arnold caught them making love in the summerhouse, and he killed Doris and Dick escaped," she summed up triumphantly. "Don't you see it all? . . . Poor Dick was simply frightened out of his wits, for fear *he* would be accused of the crime, and—and he ran away! Please hurry up and arrest Arnold so it'll be in the papers and Dick will know he can come home!"

"You'd make a great detective, ma'am," Strawn told her sarcastically. "But there happens to be one or two little points your fine theory don't explain. First: how did the perfume flask get mixed up in the murder? If Doris was simply going to meet your son, why should she take a stolen bottle of perfume with her? She couldn't very well hide it from him during their love-making—"

He was interrupted by the sound of a door being flung open, followed by quick footsteps in the foyer. Then that door, too, was wrenched open.

"Dad! Mother! What the devil did you send for the police for? Can't a fellow spend a night out of his room without a swarm of detectives being called in to hunt for him?"

IX.

"Where did *you* come from?" Captain Strawn demanded. "I suppose you're Dick Berkeley?"

"In person, though I admit I don't feel quite all here. Terrible head, in fact," and the young man in the doorway to Mrs. Berkeley's bedroom bowed ironically. He was dressed in tennis flannels and a blue coat; he had just shaved, and his reddish-brown hair gleamed wetly. "As to where I came from, dear old sleuth—if you must know, I came from my room, descended to the front hall on my way to snatch a cup of much-needed coffee, and ran into old Wickett, who looked at me as if he'd seen a ghost; also collided with a covey of rare birds who said they were detectives. One of them said I was most urgently wanted up here—and here I am!"

"Well!" Strawn ejaculated, and was guilty of scratching his iron-gray head like any comic sleuth of fiction. He glanced at Dundee helplessly, then recovered sufficiently to bellow: "And how did you get to your room, I'd like to know, without any of my men seeing you? Where did you spend the night?"

"One question at a time, Sherlock," Dick Berkeley protested; then, laying hand to his brow: "And would you mind speaking more softly? You're hurting my head—and Mother's too, I see." Ignoring his mother's moaned "My darling boy! You're safe!" he answered Strawn's first question with apparent good humor: "You didn't happen to have one of your flatfeet stationed on the little stairs that lead to the top room of the tower otherwise I should probably have bumped into him, as I was none to steady on my pins then. But a cold shower and about a pint of ice water turned the trick nicely, thank you. Ice water on tap in all the bathrooms; every comfort of a first-class hotel, and we can now include house detectives, I see, Abbie," he added to his mother.

"Are you telling me you spent the night in the top room of the tower?" Strawn demanded sourly.

"Right you are, Sherlock!"

"And what were you doing there? . . . My name's Captain Strawn, by the way."

"And a devilish curious fellow you are, too, Captain, if you don't mind my saying so," Dick acknowledged the introduction cheerfully. "As a matter of fact, I was sleeping there—sleeping, that is, after about twelve o'clock, I should say."

"And why did you go there to sleep?"

"Well, to tell you the truth, Captain Strawn, I didn't go up there with the intention of sleeping," Dick answered, his cheerfulness suddenly giving way to angry annoyance. "Why I went is strictly my own affair. I happened to fall asleep, as I said, and did not wake up till about twenty minutes ago."

"You see?" Abbie Berkeley cried with hysterical joy. "The poor boy doesn't know a thing about it! Kiss me, George darling! I'm so happy!"

"I'm asking you—and I want you to give me a straight answer with no nonsense: did you go to the tower room to meet Doris Matthews?" Strawn asked sternly.

Dick Berkeley's weakly handsome young face flushed scarlet beneath the fine sprinkling of reddish freckles. Furiously he turned upon Dundee. "So you've been telling tales, have you? And I thought you were a friend of mine!"

"Mr. Dundee's a detective, too, Dick!" Mrs. Berkeley sobbed. "Oh, my poor boy! You don't know—"

"A detective!" Dick echoed blankly. Then his face, which had turned very pale, twisted into a grin. "I say, that's a great sell for me, isn't it? I invite a friend here for the week-end and he turns into a detective to spy on me. . . . Or, say, was it *Crosby* you had your eye on, and I just happened to tumble into your net?"

Strawn saved Dundee the embarrassment of answering. "I'm waiting for an answer, Berkeley. Did you go to the tower room to meet Doris Matthews?"

Dick glanced first at his father, then at his mother before answering. Then he flung his head back defiantly. "I did! And Mother knows why I wanted to see Doris so badly last night. I wanted to ask her to marry me!"

"Oh! Oh!" Mrs. Berkeley moaned, covering her face with her hands, but the father stared at the son as if he were looking upon a lunatic stranger.

"And did she consent to marry you?" Strawn pursued relentlessly.

"No! She—she didn't come," Dick admitted. "Say, Dundee, what the devil are you writing there? Am I being 'grilled' as the papers put it?"

Dundee glanced at Strawn, and the chief of the Homicide Squad nodded grimly. "Dick, I'm taking down what you say because this is an investigation into a—murder!"

The young man's body sagged as if he had been hit in the stomach. "*Murder!*"

"Doris Matthews' body was found in the lake this morning," Dundee explained quietly. "She had been either stunned or killed in the summerhouse and her body rolled down the steps into the water."

It was nearly five minutes before the questioning could continue, for Dick Berkeley turned so sick that Dundee had to abandon his notepaper and lead the retching boy to his mother's big, luxurious bathroom. At last, seated on the orchid-enamel bench before the low basin set in a big orchid-colored porcelain dressing table, Dick spoke to his friend.

"Ever been in love, Dundee? . . . And lose her? God, I'm sick! And I can't believe it yet. . . . Not lovely little Doris—"

When he was better Dundee helped him back into the bedroom, where his mother was holding out her arms. But Dick ignored them and slumped into one of the pale-

green satin boudoir chairs. Dundee took his own chair
again and very quietly began the unpleasant task of
dragging the boy's story from him.

With the questions deleted, and without the
numerous interruptions which marked the telling of it,
Dick Berkeley's story, in the form to which Dundee later
reduced it, follows:

"I have been in love with Doris Matthews ever since
the day I met her—Saturday, August 10, which was the
day Mother and Clorinda, accompanied by Wickett, Doris
and Mrs. Lambert, came home from New York. They had
been abroad for a year—Mother and Clorinda, I mean. I
think Doris liked me a lot, too, at first, though she never
said so. She was always talking about 'knowing her
place' and all that rot."

"But as soon as mother hired Eugene Arnold as a
chauffeur I knew I didn't have much chance. Since he
was a sort of servant, too, Doris felt all right about going
with him, and it wasn't a week before they were spending
most of their time off together. I saw her as much as I
could, but she never would go anywhere with me or even
take a walk about the grounds at night. And I was
getting crazier about her every day. At first, I admit, I
didn't think about marrying her, but when she and
Arnold got engaged last Sunday night and told the family
Monday, I went off my head, I guess. I knew then I'd
marry her in a minute if she'd have me, but she wouldn't
give me a chance to talk to her.

"Yesterday just before lunch I saw her go into
Mother's room, and followed her. I—I was telling her how
much I loved her, and—and I guess I tried to kiss her,
when Mother and Arnold came in from a shopping trip.
Arnold saw me trying to kiss her, and he went wild. He—
he said he'd kill us both if Doris was double-crossing him
with me. Mother heard the row from her sitting room
and came in. I was afraid she'd fire Doris, as well as
Arnold. Of course, I was sort of hoping she'd sack

Arnold—But no, I'm not that rotten! He had a right to be sore."

"Anyway, Mother got rid of both of them and tried to make me promise not to have anything more to do with Doris. I told her I was crazy about Doris, that I was going to ask her to marry me the first chance I got. She had a fit, of course, and swore she'd discharge Doris as soon as 'Lord' Crosby's visit was over. I told her if she did I'd walk out of the house myself.

"Well, you know the rest, Dundee. I got pretty tight at dinner and afterwards, and when Mother lit into Gigi I got so fed up I bolted. Doris was in the back hall, alone for the moment. The radio was playing, and I made her dance with me, and tried to get her to say she'd meet me in the tower room after the family was in bed. Told her I had something important to ask her. You heard her say she'd meet me. I didn't know whether she meant it or not, but I wasn't taking any chances of missing her in case she did. So I went upstairs before the party broke up, smoked awhile and drank the whiskey I'd sneaked from the sideboard after dinner. I knew she'd be sore if I met her drunk, but—Well, it was about five to eleven when I went up to the tower room. I listened at the stairhead and heard the Smiths saying good-night, so I beat it up quick, so as not to be seen. Doris had admitted she didn't have to wait up for Mother, and I thought she could get to the tower room, too, without anyone's being the wiser.

"Well, she didn't come. I smoked six or eight cigarettes and read an old detective story I'd left up there years ago—the tower room was my favorite hiding-out place when I was a kid—and then about midnight I must have fallen asleep, just as I said. It was nearly nine when I woke, and I beat it downstairs to my room, had a shower, shaved and dressed. You know the rest. . . . No, I didn't look out of the tower windows toward the lake, and I didn't hear a thing. It's pretty hard to hear anything up there."

When he had finished Captain Strawn beckoned to Dundee. "We'll check up on that tower room right now, Dundee. Then, Mrs. Berkeley, I'll come back to your story. In the meantime, I'll give orders to the butler to serve breakfast downstairs and to have a tray sent up to you. . . . Yes, *ma'am!*" he added emphatically, as Mrs. Berkeley began to swell with indignation, "*I'm* running this house now—till Doris Matthews' murder is cleared up!"

After Captain Strawn had given his orders to Wickett he joined Dundee in the third-floor hall.

"Before we take a look at that tower room, I'd like to have a sniff at the shoes young Dick was wearing last night," he said. "As I said before, the guy that crocked that perfume bottle over the girl's head is pretty sure to have got his shoes spattered with the stuff. Stepped in it, too, probably."

"Through here, chief," Dundee suggested, leading the way into his own room and thence into the connecting bath. "It was mighty decent of you to let me question Mrs. Berkeley and Dick, but I want you to know I'll be glad to play dumb any time you say the word."

"That's all right, boy," Strawn answered heartily. "You're doing a good job so far. George Berkeley is a mighty big man in this town and I don't want to antagonize him any more than I can help. If you forget anything I'll butt in. Don't worry! . . . Hmm. Swell room the kid's got! Wonder if he was lying when he said he wanted to marry the girl? His parents would have kicked him out, of course, and he knew it."

"I think he was really in love with her, though who knows what his love led him into?" Dundee answered thoughtfully. "Well, here's his dressing room. And these seem to be the shoes he was wearing last night."

Strawn took the fine, custom-made pair of black dress shoes and sniffed them, walking away from the dressing room to do so, for the odor of *Fleur d'Amour* was strong in there.

"Can't smell anything but shoe polish," he admitted. "Now let's see the suit he was wearing last night. . . . Tuxedo, huh? Plenty of the stuff on this, all right. Do you think the kid sister splashed much of the perfume on Dick?"

"She anointed us all pretty thoroughly," Dundee answered ruefully. "My own Tux will have to go to the cleaner before I can wear it again."

"Why did she do it? Pure cussedness?" Strawn wondered.

"I—don't know. She's a wild little colt, but—"

"Another mystery, eh? Well, I guess that'll wait. These trousers don't seem to have any of the perfume on them. . . . Let's get along to the tower room."

It was a circular room, two-thirds windows, which were draped with faded red velvet. The furniture seemed to be a collection of odds and ends, discarded perhaps, during one of Abbie Berkeley's orgies of redecoration. There were two ancient armchairs, a worn rug, a bookcase filled with juvenile and detective fiction, and a broken spring sofa, whose brown velvet cover lay in a huddle on the floor. A metal smoking stand stood at the head of the sofa, and in it lay the tamped-out butts of seven cigarettes.

"I'll have our chemist look these over and tell me approximately how old they are, though I don't suppose it matters a whale of a lot," Strawn said, as he emptied the ash tray into an old envelope from his own pocket. "The boy could have sneaked up here after the murder and done a furious lot of smoking then, to quiet his nerves. We have only his word for it that he was to meet the girl here. And even if he was, there was nothing to prevent his seeing her, from the window, as she went to the summerhouse to keep her appointment with Arnold—nor knowing he wasn't going to meet her. Afterwards, this room might have appealed to him as a good temporary hiding place. . . . What are you shaking your head about?"

"I still can't see, for the life of me, how the perfume flask fits in *anywhere!*" Dundee answered. "Besides, as I said, I think Dick was really in love with the girl."

"And he was drunk! Don't forget that! Many a man has liquored himself up to a state where he'd rather kill a girl than see any other man have her. But there's no use theorizing yet. Let's get back to the old lady. . . . Lord! What a woman!" he added, with profound disgust. "Now, if it was her that was murdered—"

Dundee grinned his full agreement, then, with an exclamation, bent to pick up a book that had fallen, open and face down, near the head of the couch. It was Sir Conan Doyle's *The Hound of the Baskervilles.*

"Looks as if Dick were telling the truth about his reading, at any rate," he observed, as he turned through the pages of the first third of the book. "At least, it seems that he made a stab at reading to pass the time, but his mind was pretty well occupied with something else. See?" and he pointed to page 54, on the margin of which was scribbled in pencil, "Doris. Doris Elaine Matthews. Doris Berkeley. Mrs. Richard Radcliffe Berkeley."

"Might be a plant," Strawn growled. "The kid had all the rest of the night to think up a story and ways to make it sound good."

"I hardly think Dick is quite that clever," Dundee objected. "And if this marginal scribbling can be taken at its face value, we have definite confirmation of his intention to ask her to marry him."

"All right. We'll take it along. . . . Nothing else? Then let's go."

When the two men reached the second-floor landing of the marble stairs they found Detective Clemmons awaiting them, a small wet bundle held gingerly in his cupped palms.

"The apron, eh? Good! Where did Collins find it?"

"In the lake, near the summerhouse, sir."

"Dropped off the bottom step, just as the body was, so it would make no splash that could be heard from the house," Strawn commented, as he accepted it. "That'll do now, Clemmons. How's everything downstairs?"

"Everything quiet now, sir, though Cain had to call for Harper a few minutes ago to help him keep Arnold from busting out of the servant's sitting room. He wanted to come up here and make you tell him what's wrong."

When Clemmons had departed Strawn took the wet bundle to a bench against the wall of the second floor hall and, regardless of the fine *petit point* upholstery, spread the contents. Among the fragments, large and small, of the broken crystal flask he found a little silver vanity case, marked with the initials "D.M."

"No letter," Strawn observed with satisfaction, as he looked into the tiny pocket of the lace and lawn apron. "Looks as if she didn't get Arnold's note, telling her he couldn't meet her, and went out to keep the appointment. It may be in her room, of course, but we'll let that slide till we've finished with Mrs. Berkeley. Can't do everything at once. I've got a man standing guard at the top of the backstairs in the third-floor hall, so her room's safe from meddlers."

"May I see that, chief?" Dundee asked, with strange excitement, and snatched up the vanity case.

"Want to see what kind of lipstick a blonde uses?" Strawn asked, grinning, as Dundee snapped open the mirrored lid.

"Yes!" And he evidently did, for he opened the little silver tube and squinted very thoughtfully at the bright red lipstick it contained.

They found that Mrs. Berkeley had taken advantage of their absence to rise, wrap her plump body in a marabou-trimmed negligee of orchid chiffon, and dispose herself in a nest of lace-trimmed silk pillows on the *chaise longue*. Her breakfast tray was beside her, and both she and her husband, who was seated at her feet, were drinking coffee. The toast, eggs and fruit seemed to have been untouched.

"You found that every word Dick said was true, didn't you?" she demanded triumphantly of Captain Strawn.

Without replying, the detective signaled to Dundee to get ready to continue questioning.

When he was seated near the woman, with pencil poised above the sheaf of notepaper, Dundee asked:

"Mrs. Berkeley, when did you last see Doris Matthews?"

"I did not see her at all after I went down for dinner," she stated positively. "Doris helped me dress, of course. Dinner was to be at half-past seven, and I left this room about seven-fifteen. I never saw her again."

George Berkeley looked at his wife as if surprised or startled, seemed about to speak, then clamped his lips firmly together.

Dundee saw, but was not yet ready to challenge Mrs. Berkeley's truthfulness. Her lie concerning Dick's promise not to press his attentions upon Doris had already given him ample indication of what to expect.

"Was it then that you told Doris she need not wait up to help you get ready for bed?" he asked.

"Why, yes. I am always careful to spare my servants as much as possible," she said virtuously. "Doris had been extremely busy yesterday and to-day was to be a heavy day for all of us, so I wanted her to get as much sleep as possible."

"And of course, since you were very much annoyed with Doris, because of Dick and Arnold, you were in no mood to see any more of her than necessary," Dundee agreed, disarmingly. "Now, Mrs. Berkeley, will you please tell me where you made up your face before dressing for dinner?"

She looked blank, then bridled indignantly. "Really, Mr. Dundee! . . . Well, if you must know, Doris gave me a quick facial massage at my dressing table in the bathroom, and applied cosmetics there, too. But I *really* can't see—"

"The mirror above the bathroom dressing table was spotless then?" he persisted, heedless of her anger.

"Why, certainly it was! My servants—"

"Mrs. Berkeley, did you by any chance so approve of your appearance after Doris had finished her work *that you leaned toward the mirror and kissed your own reflection?"*

X.

"Really, Mr. Dundee!" Mrs. Berkeley cried furiously. "This is too much! The very idea of asking me if I *kissed* myself in the mirror! I never did such a silly thing in my life—not even when I was a beautiful young girl, and I *was* beautiful at eighteen, wasn't I, George?"

"You are still beautiful to me, my dear," her husband replied with a dutiful gallantry, but his weary eyes did not meet his wife's.

"Then may I ask, Mrs. Berkeley, if, when you were using the mirror, you noticed upon its surface the print of rouged lips?" Dundee persisted.

"Certainly not! I've told you the mirror was spotless!"

"What are you driving at, Dundee?" Captain Strawn demanded, sorely puzzled.

"I'll show you! Step into the bathroom with me, sir?"

They left Mrs. Berkeley talking excitedly in a low tone to her husband.

"Looks like a movie set, don't it," Strawn chuckled. "Sunken tub, shower cabinet, towels big enough for blankets—Lord! What a dressing table! Enough cosmetics here to stock a shop," he added, his glance sweeping over the array of amethyst and pale green crystal jars and bottles lined about the wide top of the dressing table, in the center of which a basin was sunk.

"See that, chief?" And Dundee pointed to a Cupid's bow of bright-red rouge clearly defined near the bottom of the beveled, frameless mirror swung above the low dressing table. A nearly perfect Cupid's bow, except for the fact that the print was slightly smudged downward.

"Well, I'll be darned!" Strawn whispered, but Dundee was busy. He was unscrewing the cap of a tiny green crystal jar.

"Mrs. Berkeley's lip rouge," he explained, showing a dark-red salve. "And Doris's," he added, again opening the little silver tube of lipstick which the dead girl's compact had contained.

Not satisfied with comparing the color of the smudge on the glass with Doris's lipstick, he bent close to sniff the mirrored sample, then held the little tube to his nose.

"It's the same, chief. That print on the mirror was made by Doris Matthews."

"Well, now we're getting somewhere!" Captain Strawn ejaculated.

"Maybe," Dundee agreed, and they returned to the bedroom.

"Now, Mrs. Berkeley," he began, when he had resumed seat and notepaper, "will you please tell me whether Doris was permitted to use lipstick while on duty?"

"*Certainly* not!"

"And was Doris still in your room when you went down to dinner?"

She considered for a moment, then brightened. "No, I'd kept her longer than I expected, and just as I was nearly ready to go down Clorinda called on the house phone. We have an intercommunicating system, you know, so that we can telephone to almost any room in the house, just by pushing little buttons—"

"Yes? So Doris went to assist Miss Berkeley?"

"Yes, immediately, before I left my room."

"And would Doris have returned to this room later for any reason?"

"Why, of course! To lay out my night things and turn down the covers."

"She could have attended to those duties as early as she pleased?"

"Why, certainly, since I had told her I would not need her to help me get ready for bed," Mrs. Berkeley answered, casting an uneasy glance at her husband.

"Now, Mrs. Berkeley, may I ask when you came up to bed?"

"Let me see. . . . Hmm." Natural color mingled with and mottled the heavy coating of rouge on her plump, coarse-skinned cheeks. "I'd say it was about twenty minutes to twelve, wouldn't you, George?" she appealed to her husband.

He nodded, his lips tightening.

"On coming upstairs, Mrs. Berkeley, did you see anyone—hear anything?"

"Oh, no! Not a sound!" she assured him eagerly. "The house was as quiet as a grave!" Then she uttered a little scream as she realized what word she had used. "Oh! I simply can't realize—"

"And you, Mr. Berkeley?" Dundee turned to his host.

"Not a sound! I went directly to my room, saying good-night to my wife in the hall. My room occupies the northwest corner of the second floor. I went to bed immediately, I may add."

"And did either of you hear anything later? Any footsteps?"

"No!" husband and wife answered in unison.

"The sound of the limousine returning?" Dundee persisted.

And again they both answered "No!"

"Did you hear the car return before you went upstairs?"

"I didn't notice," Berkeley answered, and his wife: "Neither did I, but of course Arnold would have taken the car directly to the garage from the gates, not coming anywhere near the front of the house."

"Right!" Dundee agreed. Then, "You went immediately to bed, Mr. Berkeley?"

"I was very tired, and I had a terrific headache, so I just took two bromide tablets and went right to bed."

"Isn't it rather unusual for you to go to bed without removing you make-up and applying skin cream?" Dundee asked quietly.

"Oh!" Her hands flew to her heavily-coated cheeks. "I—yes, it *is* unusual, but I was very tired and—"

"And upset over your conference with your husband?" Dundee supplied, with deceptive gentleness.

"You forget yourself, Mr. Dundee," she rebuked him angrily. "That has nothing at all to do with—with poor little Doris's—death."

"But the subject of that conference—Mr. Seymour Crosby—knew Doris quite well, I believe. I heard him say last night that he was eager to see her again—"

"Stop, Mr. Dundee!" Mrs. Berkeley cried melodramatically. "I *will* not permit you to insinuate vile things against the man my daughter is going to marry!"

"The man our daughter is *not* going to marry!" George Berkeley cut in sternly. "Captain Strawn, the reporters will inevitably be swarming over the place, and I shall be greatly obliged if you will not refer to Mr. Seymour Crosby as my daughter's fiancé. . . . Mr. Dundee is right. My wife and I had a long—conference last night after bidding our good-night, and I made it quite clear then that no engagement would be announced at the party which was to have taken place this evening."

"I don't see why we can't have the party," Mrs. Berkeley protested angrily. "Just because a maid is dead—"

"Murdered, Mrs. Berkeley!" Captain Strawn reminded her grimly. "*Murdered!* And because of the peculiar nature of the case I must tell you now that every person who was in this house last night is a suspect until the murderer is under arrest."

"Oh, oh!" she moaned, rolling her head distractedly against the silly little silk and lace pillow. "Then will you please hurry and finish your horrid questions? I'll have to spend the whole day telephoning, calling off my poor party—"

"The newspapers will do that for you very effectively, Mrs. Berkeley," Captain Strawn assured her. "There will be extras before noon, and the regular afternoon sheets will be glad to carry a formal announcement from you. . . . Anything else, Dundee?"

"Just one or two things more. . . . Mrs. Berkeley, when you came to your room about twenty minutes to twelve, did you use your bathroom dressing table at all?

The shamed flush deepened on the woman's cheeks. "Why no. I don't think I did. There's a thermos bottle of ice water on my bedside table and I keep the bromide tablets in a little drawer in the table. In fact, I took the tablets after I got into bed."

"Then you had no occasion to look at the mirror?"

"No. I don't remember even glancing toward it."

"But you did miss the flask of perfume Mr. Crosby had given you?" Dundee asked quickly.

"I—yes, I did look about for it. Just glanced at the bathroom dressing table and at the vanity dresser in the rook, looking for it."

"And could not find it?"

"No. I was furious with Wickett for having disobeyed me. I gave it to him after—" she floundered and flushed, recalling the shameful scene which had ended in her slapping Gigi's face before her guests, "a few minutes after Mr. Crosby gave it to me, and told him to take it up to my room. That was when you were telephoning," she explained.

"You found that Doris had been in here to lay out your things and prepare the bed for the night.

"Oh, yes. Everything was exactly as usual," she assured him eagerly.

"Mrs. Berkely, I'll ask you again: was Doris Mathews in this room and or in any of your three rooms when you came up to bed?"

"No! How dare you doubt my word?" she cried furiously.

"And you did not see her or speak to her again after she left you to help your daughter dress?"

"No, I didn't!"

"Abbie, this is no time for—evasions or—lapses of memory," her husband cut in. "Please tell these gentlemen the truth."

"George Berkeley, don't you dare insinuate that I'm lying!" Mrs. Berkeley cried, furious tears filling her pale blue eyes. "Mr. Dundee asked me if I *saw* Doris again, or spoke to her, and I told the truth when I said I didn't. I can't *swear* it was Doris who answered when I called her on the house phone—"

"On the house phone? When?" Dundee demanded.

"While my husband I were talking in the library last night," the woman answered defiantly. "As I told you, I'd thought I shouldn't need her to wait up for me, and had given her permission to retire when she pleased. But my headache got to be so bad while George and I were talking that I decided I'd need a massage of my forehead and spine. Doris is—was—awfully good at that sort of thing. So I rang her room on the house phone and *someone* answered—"

"You did not recognize the voice as Doris's?" Dundee interrupted.

"We-ell, I thought I did. I—I was rather upset, and it never occurred to me at the time that it could be anyone but Doris. She had a room of her own, you know, in the servants' quarters on the third floor. I told her to go to my room and wait for me."

"At what time did you call her?"

"Oh, how do I know?" She burst out angrily, dabbing at her mascaraed tears. "I wasn't watching clocks! But it was something like fifteen minutes after George and I began to talk—"

"And I suppose you counted on your husband's feeling so sorry about your awful headache that he'd cut short the argument and let you have your own way?" Captain Strawn cut in, apparently distrustful of Dundee's more gentle methods.

"I refuse to answer such a question!" Mrs. Berkeley cried furiously.

With a slight smile Dundee put the next question: "Then how long was it before you went up to your room, after speaking with Doris—or someone!—on the house phone?"

"I don't know exactly. Half an hour, possibly. George simply wouldn't be reasonable— Anyway, when I got to my room, Doris wasn't here, so I got into bed as quickly as I could and took the bromide tablets, and went to sleep."

"Weren't you surprised and displeased to find your orders disobeyed?" Dundee asked quietly.

"We-ell, of course I was, but it was so late and I was feeling so wretched that I decided not to have a scene. Besides I had already made up my mind to discharge the girl as soon as Mr. Crosby's visit was ended. He is to be with us only a week—"

"You did not call her again on the house phone?"

"No, I didn't! Do I have to say so a dozen times?"

"You say you went to sleep very soon after you retired?"

"I didn't say so, but I did go to sleep very quickly, because of the bromide tablets, you know."

Without a word, Dundee rose, laid his notes on his chair, and strode quickly to the bed. He stooped to pick up something from the floor and when he returned he was holding, rather gingerly, a damp ball of handkerchief.

"Did you cry yourself to sleep, Mrs. Berkeley?" he asked gently.

The woman shrank for the handkerchief as if it had been soaked with blood, instead of tears. "No—no, no! I didn't! I cried this morning after I'd heard about Doris—"

"Pardon, Mrs. Berkeley, but the handkerchief you were using when Captain Strawn told you the news is the one you have in your hand now," Dundee corrected her courteously. "I remember the edging of the orchid linen. This one is all white, as you can see. And the condition of this handkerchief shows that the tears were not recently shed. You tucked it under the edge of your pillow when you had finished weeping last night, I think, and it fell out when you arose this morning."

The woman collapsed suddenly and began to cry into the orchid-bordered handkerchief which had betrayed her lie. "Yes, I—I did cry myself to sleep, but if you're thinking it had anything to do with Doris— If you must know, I was crying because George had been so—so cruel, so pig-headed, so *nasty* to me—"

"Abbie!" her husband broke in sternly.

"Mrs. Berkeley, forgive me, but there are a few more questions I am compelled to ask you," Dundee began again soothingly. "First, aside from the fact that you disapproved of your son's interest in the girl, what was your own feeling toward Doris? Was the relationship of mistress and maid a pleasant one?"

"Of course it was! I wouldn't stoop to quarreling with a servant!" she sobbed out indignantly.

"I am to infer, then, that you did not quarrel with the girl about Dick after the scene yesterday?"

"I—no, I didn't quarrel with her at all. I merely told her most emphatically that she was not to vamp Dick!"

"Was she sulky or impertinent as she helped you dress for dinner last night?"

The tear-reddened blue eyes looked startled, then roved wildly about the room as if seeking help. And when they encountered the stern gaze of George Berkeley they clung for a moment and grew wider.

"She—she wasn't like herself," Mrs. Berkeley admitted as if the words had been wrung from her. "She—she was clumsy—"

"So clumsy that you became disgusted with her, spoke to her sharply, and after she had retorted impertinently, you pushed her violently from you?" Dundee asked, his voice suddenly steely.

Captain Strawn hitched up his trousers and grinned approvingly. Now they were getting somewhere!

"I—you!—I—" Mrs. Berkeley gasped, her hand at her throat. The again she collapsed against the cushions. "I might have known she'd tell tales—make a mountain out of a molehill! I didn't push her! I—I just slapped her cheek, not very hard, either, but she *had* been grossly impudent—"

"Just when and where did this scene take place, Mrs. Berkeley?" Dundee asked.

"Why don't you ask Wickett, since he's already told you so much?" she cried angrily. "I'll discharge him, too! He and the girl were as thick as thieves, and both of them have acted, ever since they came, as if Mrs. Lambert and not I were the head of this house."

"Will you answer the question, please, Mrs. Berkeley?"

"Oh, can't you let me alone?" she wailed. Then capitulating suddenly: "It was while I was dressing for dinner. I—I told her to open a new bottle of perfume I'd bought in the city yesterday, and—and she said something impertinent—"

"Just what did she say, Mrs. Berkeley?" Dundee pressed, a strange excitement in his Irish-blue eyes.

"I—I don't remember!" the woman protested. "You don't expect me to remember every tiny thing, do you? . . . Well, it was just—just a word or two, like—" She knit her brows, and Dundee was absolutely sure she was concocting a lie. "Oh, yes! She said, 'You use too much perfume, Madame,' Of course I was furious at such impertinence, and I—I slapped her face!"

"And where did this scene take place, Mrs. Berkeley?"

"Why, in here! I was standing before the full-length mirror in my closet door, and Doris was adjusting the shoulder straps of my evening dress," she answered quickly and positively.

Dundee and Strawn exchanged glances, then the chief of the Homicide Squad decided to take a hand.

"In *here*, eh? You're sure it wasn't in the bathroom, ma'am?"

"Of course I am!" she shrilled. "I was standing right there—"

"Then when was it that you pushed the girl over against the bathroom mirror, Mrs. Berkeley?" Strawn went on, his eyebrows raised.

"The *bathroom* mirror? . . . Why, I—I don't know what you're talking about."

"Then let me show you, lady!" Strawn invited grimly.

She struck out at his hand furiously as he endeavored to help her rise from the *chaise longue,* and scrambled to her feet, clutching her orchid chiffon negligee about her fat body.

George Berkeley remained where he was, his chin propped broodingly upon a clenched fist, while the two detectives and his wife went into the luxurious bathroom.

"See that smudge, Mrs. Berkeley?" Strawn pointed to the mirror over the dressing table. "Doris's lipstick. And the print of her mouth is smudged downward, proving beyond the shadow of a doubt that Doris Matthews was *pushed* against that mirror!"

"I didn't do it! I don't know anything about it! I swear I don't!" Mrs. Berkeley's teeth were chattering as she backed away from the tell-tale mirror. "I didn't kill her, I tell you!"

"But she *was* waiting here for you, when you came upstairs last night?" Strawn persisted sternly.

"No, no! I swear she wasn't! I never laid eyes on Doris after seven-ten last night! I swear to God—" She was hysterical now, beating at the broad, uniformed chest of the chief of detectives.

"Don't take on so, ma'am," Strawn advised. "I'm not arresting you—yet. I want to have a talk with your daughter, Miss Clorinda, first."

"Clorinda?" Mrs. Berkeley whispered, the blood draining from her face.

"Yes, ma'am. Seeing as how it was her silk scarf with which the rocks were tied into the girl's skirt—"

But Mrs. Berkeley heard no more, for she had fainted.

XI.

It was Bonnie Dundee who mixed a dose of aromatic spirits of ammonia and George Berkeley who, staggering a little under her weight, carried the fainting woman to her unmade bed.

"Looks like a confession coming on, don't it?" Captain Strawn whispered as Dundee was hurrying past him to the bed.

But when Mrs. Berkeley opened her eyes and was jerked back to realization by the sight of Captain Strawn bending expectantly over her, she did nothing more illuminating than to scream, then close her eyes again, rolling her head distractedly on the mussed pillow.

They left her in her husband's charge shortly, but in the hall Strawn beckoned to a detective doing patrol duty and stationed him in the little foyer between sitting room and bedroom, with instruction to listen at the not quite closed door leading into the bedroom.

As Dundee and Strawn were walking down the broad stairs the latter whispered exultantly: "Pretty good case against her, eh? Wickett took the flask of perfume Crosby had given her to her room between ten and eleven. She says herself she told him to take it up, and I'd wager my shield he did. Perfume gone. Girl in struggle in the bathroom. And the old tartar admits she slapped the girl around seven o'clock. Tried to lie about ordering the girl to go to her room and wait till she came up. Thought her husband would back her up, and nobody else would know. But George Berkeley's a white man, and no fool, either. Wouldn't let her get away with it, would he?" and Strawn chuckled.

They had almost reached the last step, and Dundee halted before answering in a low voice.

"There's something—a lot—that hasn't come out yet, chief. Did you catch that about the other bottle of perfume? I'd give a good deal to know the truth about Doris's 'Impudence'—exactly what she said to make Mrs. Berkeley slap her. As it is now, I can't see Mrs. Berkeley chasing the girl out of the house, brandishing the flask of *Fleur d'Amour*, till she caught up with her in the summerhouse, and then crocking the poor thing over the head with it, no matter how impudent Doris had been or how serious the quarrel was, if she *was* there when Mrs. Berkeley went up for the night."

"Huh!" Strawn snorted. "You don't doubt for a minute that she was there, do you? You proved that yourself, with the mouthprint on the mirror. The struggle, too. And you saw what a spitfire the old dame is! Got fists like sledge hammers. My chest'll be sore for a week. No telling what a woman like that will do when she loses her temper. Not only was she sore at the girl for 'sassing' her, but she had it in for her plenty on account of Dick."

"Yes, I know," Dundee frowned. "But—well, what next? Clorinda?"

"Sure! If she gives us what sounds like a straight story as to how that scarf got into the summerhouse, I, for one, am pretty near ready to get out the bracelets for the old lady. Guess I ought to have checked up on the shoes she was wearing last night, to see if there was any of that perfume on the soles, but I didn't want to show my hand too soon. There'll be time for that later, when she's out of the way. The shoes are safe, all right. She can't dispose of them or souse them in benzene without being caught at it,"

They found the two girls, Mrs. Lambert and Crosby lingering at the breakfast table, though no one was eating. Lounging in the arched opening between drawing room and dining room was Detective Payne.

"Oh, hullo, Bonnie Dundee!" Gigi sang out. "Mr. Crosby has been telling us the most gorgeous story about a hunting trip in Africa. He bagged a lion and two tigers—" Suddenly her voice broke, and with it her pretense of gayety. "Have—have you found out who—who killed poor little Doris?" she pleaded.

"Not yet, Gigi," Dundee answered gravely.

"I'd like to have a little talk with you, Miss Clorinda," Strawn cut in. "Come along to the library. The rest of you will please go to the room you call 'the little parlor' and wait till you're called."

Calmly and disdainfully, Clorinda murmured "You'll pardon me?" to Mrs. Lambert, then walked across the dining room with the leisured self-possession of a queen or mannequin.

Gigi watched wide-eyed, a little brown fist pressed against her mouth. Then before her sister had reached the detectives she was on her feet and dashing after her.

"May I come with Clo?" she panted to Dundee, something much deeper than childish excitement and curiosity in her topaz eyes. Something oddly like panicky fear. . . .

"Go to the little parlor as you were told, Gigi!" Clorinda commanded sharply, her fine black brows drawing together in a frown. "I don't want—or need—your interference."

"It will be all right for Gigi to come along, won't it, chief?" Dundee asking, turning his head so that only the chief of the Homicide Squad could see the slow, significant dropping of his right eyelid.

"But no shenanigans, young woman!" Strawn agreed severely, and Gigi linked arms with him, rubbing her bright head against his uniform sleeve before matching step with him as the four moved through the drawing room.

In the big front hall they came upon Wickett about to ascend the marble staircase, with a silver tray laden with letters.

"Just a minute, Wickett!" Captain Strawn halted him. "Mrs. Berkeley says she gave you that flask of French perfume to take to her rooms last night. That right?"

"Yes, sir. I was just returning from the library, after showing Mr. Dundee to the telephone there, when Mrs. Berkeley called to me and gave me the flask. I took it upstairs immediately, sir."

"And where did you pit it?"

"On Mrs. Berkeley's bathroom dressing table, sir."

"Did you see anyone in your mistress's rooms?"

"No, sir. There was no one in the sitting room or in the bathroom, the only two rooms I had to enter to dispose as I did of the perfume, sir. I did not look into the bedroom, sir."

"And what time was this?"

"I can't say exactly, sir, but I believe it was between ten and half past."

After dismissing the butler, Strawn strode into the library, Gigi'd little legs stretching themselves ludicrously to keep in step.

"Will you be seated?" Clorinda asked coldly. Then added sharply: "Don't sprawl all over Captain—ah—Strawn, Gigi."

"Sitting on the arm of his chair isn't sprawling," Gig corrected her sister cheerfully. "I want to be where I can choke him if asks questions he shouldn't. Like this!" and she leaned over and encircled the austere detective's big neck with her little brown hands, then laid her flushed cheek against his and laughed wickedly. "You know, being only fifteen does have its advantages. Think of all the gorgeous men I can hug before I'm sixteen and grown up, if I work fast—"

"Shut up, Pest!" Captain Strawn roared, but Dundee saw that he was vastly pleased, so pleased that he was not suspicious—as a young subordinate—of the child's real motives. "Now, Miss Clorinda, I've got a good many questions to ask you, and I advise you to answer fully and truthfully, or—"

"Don't you have to tell her, 'And I warn you that anything you say may be used against you'?" Gigi interrupted.

"Your sister is not under arrest—yet," Captain Strawn reminded her, "so I don't have to warn her against incriminating herself."

"But Gigi has warned her, and—the haughty Miss Berkeley is on her guard!" Dundee told himself, sending an narrowed, newly respectful glance at the child, who returned it with wide-eyed innocence.

"Miss Clorinda, when did you last see Doris Matthews?" Captain Strawn began, and Dundee, seated in a big chair with conveniently broad, flat arms, waited with pencil poised over his sheaf of notepaper to take down the answer.

Clorinda Berkeley had seated herself on a dark-red leather couch, placed under the big double windows which looked out on the west lawn, so that her back was to the light. She seemed to be insolently at ease, her beautiful long legs crossed, her hands clasped behind her dark head. But Dundee suspected her of clever forethought in so disposing of her hands that they could not betray her in moments of surprise or tense emotions. The lids were drooping over her magnificent black eyes as she drawled:

"For about ten minutes just before eleven o'clock. I found her in my room when I went upstairs last night. She was laying out my night things, and waited to—to help me undress."

But Strawn was not yet ready to trap her in a lie. "How did she seem, Miss Clorinda? Unhappy? Worried about anything?"

"Not at all! In fact, she was in an unusually happy mood. She confided to me that she was going out to meet her *fiancé*, Arnold. The chauffeur, you know."

"You did not tell her that Arnold would not be waiting for her, that his services had been required by the Benjamin Smiths?"

"Certainly not, since I did not know that fact until this morning," Clorinda answered coolly. "I went upstairs before my aunt and uncle asked for the use of the car."

"But Doris also told you, didn't she, that your brother had made her promise to meet *him* last night when the family was in bed?"

The magnificent poise was broken. Clorinda Berkeley gasped, started to rise, then sank back against the couch, her eyes closing so that the fan-like fringe of her long lashes made a startling contrast with the sudden pallor of her cheeks.

"Does your silence mean yes," Miss Clorinda?" Captain Strawn prodded relentlessly. "Doris *did* tell you that she had promised to meet your brother, and even then you knew there would be—trouble?"

"No, no! Doris did not mention Dick! . . . Oh, please!" The tragic dark eyes flew wide, pleaded desperately. "Tell me whether that is true, or whether you are just trying to trap *me* into an admission damaging to myself?"

Dundee had an unprofessional impulse to tell her the truth, to relieve her strange suspense by telling her that her brother had spent the night in the tower room, waiting for the girl who never came.

But Captain Strawn was answering her with a cruel evasion: "She'd promised to meet Dick, all right! We have two witnesses to prove it. . . . Now, you've said you didn't know until this morning that Arnold couldn't keep his date with Doris, because of taking the Smiths home. Who told you that?"

With an obvious effort Clorinda got control of herself, and answered almost calmly: "Mrs. Lambert. She was wondering aloud at the breakfast table whether Arnold had got word to Doris that he could not keep his appointment with her, or whether he had asked her to meet him an hour later than they had planned.

"Did Mrs. Lambert also know last night that Doris was to meet Arnold?"

"No. I contributed that bit of news myself this morning," Clorinda answered lazily. "We were all threshing out the probabilities and possibilities—naturally."

"Naturally!" Strawn agreed, his voice heavy with sarcasm.

"Now, don't be nasty!" Gigi warned, pretending to be about to choke him as she had threatened. "And you mustn't mind Clo. She has a 'Lady Clara Vere de Vere' complex, though I must say the grand manner becomes her. I'd try to be just like her when I'm grown, except that dignity simply does not go with a pug nose," she added mournfully.

"I'll have to spank you yet," Strawn told her severely, but he shifted his arm so that she could snuggle more comfortably against him. "Well, Miss Clorinda, you two girls chatted together quite a lot last night, I suppose, as Doris helped you get ready for bed?"

"We talked—yes," Clorinda answered stiffly. "Doris and I are—were—very good friends," and her ripe, dark-red lips twisted as if with sudden pain.

"Talked about sweethearts and getting married, and things like that?" Strawn pressed genially.

Clorinda did not answer, but her black eyes were scornful.

"Doris bragged about her sweetie and you bragged about yours?" Strawn went on, with heavy good humor.

"Doris talked of Arnold—yes," Clorinda answered coldly.

"And just what did she say about Arnold?"

"A number of things. That she loved him with all her heart, that she wished he were not so 'jealous-natured'—"

"And even then she didn't say that it was Dick Berkeley her sweetie was so jealous of?"

"I've told you she didn't mention my brother."

"Did she tell you then, or when she was helping you dress shortly after sevem that your mother slapped her face?"

"What!" Clorinda was again startled out of her insolent calm.

"Oh, dear!" Gigi wailed. "Isn't it exactly like a detective story? . . . Poor old hot-tempered Abbie smacks

Doris for pulling her hair, or something, and the police
say, 'Aha! She moidered the goil!' I'll bet before the day
is over *I'll* be wearing steel bracelets, because Doris is
sure to have told somebody about my saying I could
simply murder her for being so darned pretty and cute
that Arnold couldn't see me at all. . . . You see," she
explained sadly to Strawn, "I was trying out my sex
appeal on Arnold, and for about a minute I thought that I
had him going—'Millionaire's Sub-deb Daughter Elopes
with Chauffeur,' you know, but I simply couldn't compete
with Doris, once he'd had a good look at her."

"Oh, so you threatened her life, did you?" Strawn
growled.   "Where   are   my   handcuffs?—Now,   Miss
Clorinda, answer the question please: Did Doris tell you
your mother had slapped her face?"

"She did not!" Clorinda retorted curtly.

"But she wasn't in such a happy mood when she came
from your mother's room about seven-fifteen to help you
dress, eh?"

"I—I was late, and rather in a hurry. I did not notice
Doris's mood particularly, but she was too well trained to
gossip   against   my   mother   to   me," she   answered
scornfully, after an instant of hesitation.

Strawn shrugged, then began on a new tack, his voice
suddenly portentous: "Miss Clorinda, I want you to
search your memory very carefully before you answer this
question, because it was important: Was Doris wearing
lip rouge when you saw her just before eleven o'clock last
night?"

"Lip rouge?" Clorinda repeated incredulously. Then,
as Strawn nodded grimly, she closed her eyes as if to
concentrate. At last she answered positively: "No, I am
quite sure she wasn't. Doris was a perfectly trained
maid. I never saw her with make-up on, when she was on
duty. If she had been wearing either face rouge or lip
rouge last night I am sure I should have noticed it. . . .
Wait a minute! She said she was going to her room to

make herself pretty for Arnold. I remember that
distinctly now."

"And did you notice whether she went directly toward
her room or not?"

"I—why, no. I—paid no attention."

"You don't know, then, whether she went from your
rooms to your mother's, to arrange the bed and night
things?" Strawn pressed.

"Oh, I'm sure she didn't," Clorinda answered more
readily. "You see, she had already been to Mother's room
before coming to mine. She remarked that she was all
through for the night, that Mother had said she would not
require her to wait up to help her get ready for bed."

Strawn and Dundee exchanged a quick, significant
glance. If Clorinda Berkeley was telling the truth, she
had definitely established the fact that Doris Matthews
had left the lip-rouge mouthprint on Mrs. Berkeley's
dressing-table mirror during a third visit to her
mistress's room, regardless of Mrs. Berkeley's
protestation that the girl was not there when she came
up. A visit made after the girl had gone to her own room
on the third floor to "pretty" herself for her sweetheart. . .

With deceptive casualness Strawn returned to the
attack. "Now, Miss Clorinda, I take it that you went to
bed right after Doris left your room?"

"I did," Clorinda lied coolly.

"And saw nothing, heard nothing to disturb your
rest?"

"Absolutely nothing!"

"Well, that's that, and you make a grand witness, old
thing!" Gigi cried blithely, hopping off Strawn's chair
arm. "My turn, now? I suppose I shouldn't continue to
rumple the hair of a gruff old Captain of Detectives who's
getting ready to g-r-rill me!"

"Not so fast, young woman!" Strawn commanded
sternly. "I have not finished with your sister yet, and
don't think I'm not on to the smoke screens you've been
putting up with!"

"Not so dumb!" Dundee grinned to himself.

"Oh!" Gigi subsided disconsolately upon an ottoman at Dundee's feet and laid her curly head against his knee.

"As a matter of fact, Miss Clorinda," Strawn began, "Doris did *not* help you undress did she!"

"I don't know what you mean!"

"I mean, my dear young lady, that you did not undress until quite a while later. I mean that you put on a gold metal cloth cape over your evening dress, and stole downstairs, unlocked the back door and slipped out into the night!" Strawn told her with terrible emphasis.

Clorinda caught her breath sharply, but did not change her pose of indolent ease. It was Gigi who cried out and pressed her hands to her cheeks.

"How do you know this?" Clorinda asked at last, in a cool, clear voice.

"You were seen," Strawn assured her. "I'm glad you see there's no use denying it. . . . Now tell us all about that little jaunt of yours, Miss Clorinda."

"I shall tell you nothing at all until you have told me who saw me!" she retorted imperiously. "Remember, I have admitted nothing. I do not believe you can bring forward any witness whatsoever who will dare stand before and—"

"There is my witness!" Strawn interrupted, pointing melodramatically to Dundee, whose face flushed scarlet with embarrassment.

"Forgive me, Miss Berkeley!" he begged, in all sincerity. "I assure you I was not spying on you. I was just about to leave the drawing room when I heard you cough slightly. I confess I peeped to see who it was, and I saw you descending the stairs. I waited until you had let yourself out the back door before going upstairs. I had been hunting for Dick. I knew he had forced Doris to agree to meet him last night, and I wanted to persuade him to abandon the adventure."

"I see," Clorinda said icily. "Dick seems to have been particularly—unfortunate in his choice of a week-end guest."

"Don't, Clo!" Gigi protested brokenly. Dundee could feel the trembling of her small body against his knees and involuntarily he laid his free left hand gently n the bright, bowed head. She reached up blindly and clung to his fingers with both hands—desperately, as if to a life-line. Poor kid, he thought, pityingly. She had fought hard to protect her sister, and she had lost. What had she known, or suspected? Oh, the scarf, of course! Probably her eyes would never forget a detail of that horrible picture which they had taken in under the water that morning.

"Very well, then!" Clorinda capitulated suddenly. "I—had a headache. I took a long walk about the grounds. I walked over the west part of the estate first, then to the south wall, and finally around the lake."

"And were you *alone* on this long walk, Miss Clorinda?" Strawn asked genially, now that his witness was tractable.

XII.

"Certainly I was alone!" Clorinda Berkeley answered emphatically.

Gigi's convulsive grip on Dundee's left hand loosened slightly.

"You didn't take advantage of the opportunity to enjoy a lovers' stroll with your future husband, Mr. Seymour Crosby?" Strawn suggested.

"I have told you I was alone, but allow me to correct you. Mr. Crosby is *not* my future husband!"

"Whoops, dearie!" Gigi shouted gleefully. "I was betting you wouldn't go through with it—"

"When was the engagement broken, Miss Clorinda?" Strawn asked suavely.

"This morning, when Mr. Crosby and I were walking together to the lake. I told him that since my father was violently opposed to the marriage it could not take place."

"And why is your father opposed to the marriage?"

"You must ask him," Clorinda retorted, and closed her eyes wearily.

"Did you want to marry Crosby, Miss Clorinda?"

The answer was in Clorinda's frostiest voice: "I fail to see how that concerns you or the case you are working on, Captain Strawn!"

"Darling, you *are* so haughty!" Gigi laughed hysterically.

"So you went walking alone, Miss Clorinda," Strawn resumed urbanely. "How long were you out?"

"Oh, I don't know!" irritably. "An hour, possibly."

"Did you see anyone—anyone at all—on this walk?"

"No one!"

"You say you walked around the lake. Just when was that part of the trip made?" Strawn pressed her.

"That was the conclusion of my walk. I crossed to the lake from the south part of the grounds, walked east first and then circled the lake on my way to the house."

"And stopped to rest in the summerhouse?" Strawn pounced.

The black eyes flew wide. "No! I—I didn't stop at the summerhouse at all!"

"Then, Miss Clorinda, can you explain how your batik silk scarf came to be there?" the detective asked softly.

"My scarf! In the summerhouse! Why, that's ridiculous! It wasn't there at all!"

"Then perhaps you have another explanation of how it came to be tied around Doris Matthews' knees when her body was taken from the lake," Strawn said with dreadful casualness.

"*Around her knees?*" Clorinda repeated blankly. Then she must have realized her danger for she sat bolt upright on the leather couch. "But that's impossible, I tell you! It must have been another scarf, somewhat similar to mine—"

"You admit, then, that you were carrying a silk scarf in your hands when you left the house?" Strawn caught her up triumphantly.

"No, because it is not true," Clorinda answered more calmly. "I was carrying a silk scarf until I reached the back hall, but I dropped it to the floor when I was slipping the chain and the bolt of the outside door. I did not miss it until I stepped outside and a slight breeze lifted my hair. I did not return for it, however, as the night was warmer than I had thought, and I liked the feeling of the wind in my hair."

"You see, she had no marcel to get mussed," Gigi struck in eagerly. "Her hair's naturally wavy—Oh!" she broke off, then rushed on with tremendous excitement: "Oh, Clo! How *terrible!* If you dropped your scarf *inside* the back hall, that means that the person who murdered poor Doris was somebody who was in this house last night!" She stared round-eyed for a minute, then, struck

with another thought: "Or maybe Doris *herself* picked it
up on her way out to see Arnold, not knowing he couldn't
meet her— Of course that's what happened!" she
concluded, and subsided against Dundee's knees again,
tremendously relieved.

Captain Strawn and Dundee exchanged glances of
admiration, before the chief resumed.

"How near to the summerhouse did you pass, Miss
Clorinda, on your way to the house?"

"Quite near. Within twenty feet of it, I should say,"
she answered cooly. "I walked across the grass almost to
the back door, since that was the shorter route than to go
clear to the summerhouse and strike the cement walk
there."

"Did you see or hear anything happening in the
summerhouse?"

"Nothing!"

"You heard no screams, at any time, during your
walk?"

"No! Nothing, I tell you!"

"No splash as of something being dumped into the
water?" Strawn persisted.

"I tell you I heard nothing!" Clorinda retorted angrily.

"But did you—*smell* something when you got near to
the summerhouse?"

"I presume you mean the perfume," Clorinda said
coldly. "You seem to know so much, I am sure you are
already aware that my sister sprinkled *Fleur d'Amour*
upon every person who was in the drawing room last
night. Since my dress was reeking with the stuff, of
course I smelled it, but I did not notice a stronger odor
near the summerhouse, if that is what you mean."

"Why did you splash that perfume around, young
woman?" Captain Strawn turned sternly to
Gigi.

"You may call me Gigi. Everyone does," she grinned
engagingly. "I don't like this 'young woman' stuff as
much as I thought I would. . . . But you *have* asked me an

embarrassing question. Guess you'll have to get out your old handcuffs, because—*I'm not going to tell you!"*

"Gigi did that foolish stunt for the same reason she does almost everything else," Clorinda enlightened them coldly. "She adores being noticed, and her chief sport is to annoy Mother."

"And I thought I was making the plot so thick it would curdle," Gigi mourned, but Dundee saw the smile she had flashed at her sister, and he knew there was gratitude in it. . . .

"Is there any way you could fix the time you returned to the house, Miss Clorinda?" Strawn persisted.

"I don't think so. . . . No, wait! I remember winding my watch when I was undressing for bed. At that time it was ten minutes after twelve. I had then been in the house about five or six minutes, I think."

"Did you see your scarf when you let yourself in by the back door?"

"No, but I had forgotten all about it. There is always a dim light in the back hall, however, as there is in the front hall, and I feel sure that I should have seen it if it had been there."

"Did you, on your way out or on your return, observe a letter or note lying on the back-hall table?" Strawn asked suddenly.

"A note? . . . No. I don't think I even glanced toward the table."

"No, Miss Clorinda, when you returned to your room, which stairs did you take?"

"The backstairs. When I reached the second floor landing I listened, heard nothing, and tiptoed to my room."

"Why did you tiptoe?"

"I was afraid Mother might have discovered my absence, and that she was listening for my return. On my way out, I heard her voice from the library, and knew she and Father were having another session over my engagement to Mr. Crosby. That was one reason I took the walk. I knew they would be quarreling about it again, and I was in no mood for another scene. I stayed out till I felt sure Mother would be asleep, unless she had discovered my absence and was watching for me."

"And did you see your mother after your return?"

"No. I saw no one, and heard not the faintest sound. I thought I was safe," she said wearily.

"You thought you had committed your murder and got away with it, eh?" Strawn asked softly.

"*I—?* You're being absurd!" she cried angrily. "Why should I, of all people, kill Doris Matthews, the most lovable, faithful, inoffensive—" Tears choked her voice for the first time during the grueling interview.

"Darling Clo?" Gigi sprang to her sister's side and dropped on her knees, cuddling the slim, white hands, against her tanned cheeks. "Haven't you ever read any detective stories, precious? They *always* accuse everybody, whether they think they think they are guilty or not. Don't mind, sweet! Gigi won't let them bother you any more!"

"Says you?" Strawn grinned.

"Yeah, says I!" Gigi blustered, shaking her fist at him.

"Nevertheless, and notwithstanding, Miss Clorinda, I am going to ask you to take us to your room now."

"Why?" Clorinda gasped, snatching her had from Gigi's to dab furiously at her eyes.

"Oh, just for a look around," Strawn assured her amiably.

"I'm coming, too!" Gigi cried passionately, springing to her feet and drawing Clorinda from the couch.

And go she did, flying ahead of the others on the stairs. When they caught up with her she was standing in the opened door of her sister's room, which was on the east side of the house, next to Mrs. Berkeley's sitting room. She backed in, to make way for the two detectives and her sister.

"Well?" Clorinda was almost calm again, and very haughty over the invasion of her beautiful, tastefully furnished bedroom.

"Your shoes, first," Strawn suggested amiably. "The ones you wore on you walk last night. Also the cape and dress."

Clorinda jerked open the door to an immense closet-dressing-room, snatched up the things he wanted and flung them at the chief of the Homicide Squad.

He caught one of the little gold slippers and held the sole of it to his nose, while his eyes watched the blood drain from Clorinda Berkeley's beautiful face.

"You see, Miss Clorinda, one can't think of everything—*every little thing!*" Captain Strawn sympathized, after he had sniffed the sole of each slipper. "You remembered to wipe off tell-tale traces of dew and earth from these little shoes of yours, but your nose was so accustomed by that time to the odor of *Fleur d'Amour*—"

"Maybe you'd better translate it and call it 'Flower of Love'—your French is terrible," Gigi interrupted with hard flippancy, her topaz eyes blazing like an angry cat's.

"—that you didn't smell it on the soles as you handled the shoes. But every criminal forgets something," Strawn went on, as if the child had not interrupted.

"I don't know what you're talking about," Clorinda told him tonelessly, but her face was very pale.

"These little shoes tell me a secret, Miss Clorinda. They tell me that you *were* in the summerhouse, that you stepped into the spilled perfume."

"I've told you already that Gigi splashed the stuff all over us last night," Clorinda countered wearily.

"But she didn't sprinkle the floor! A pretty keen eye-witness has already described that scene to me, young lady!"

"Our charming *guest,* no doubt!" Clorinda shrugged, and Dundee colored painfully. "Nevertheless, I was *not* in the summerhouse last night!"

"Well, let's have a look at the dress and the cape," Strawn said cheerfully. He lifted the long-skirted evening dress of red velvet and passed the front of it slowly through his hands, held close to his nose, sniffing so ludicrously that Gigi giggled hysterically.

Three times he found what he was looking for, but the spots were all on the bodice. The skirt yielded nothing until the hem itself was passing under his nose.

"Well, I guess that settles it!" he grunted with satisfaction. "The hem of this skirt has been in the summerhouse, Miss, if you haven't! Now for the cape!"

His nose was unrewarded, however, and he was about to toss the gold metal cloth garment aside when Dundee sprang forward.

"I think you've overlooked something, Captain Strawn," he said quietly, pointing to a thin, dark-brown horizontal line halfway down the back of the cape.

Strawn uttered a sharp exclamation, then scratched at the dark streak with a fingernail.

"Blood!" he announced triumphantly, his gray eyes boring into the girl who had retreated until she was leaning weakly against the foot of her bed.

"Blood?" she whispered. "I swear I didn't see any blood—I never dreamed—"

"You thought you'd got rid of every trace of Doris Matthews' blood, eh?" Strawn asked grimly. "Pretty hard thing to destroy—blood!"

"Stop! You're going to make her faint!" Gigi commanded. "And don't be an ass! Clorinda didn't kill Doris! Why should she? You have to have a motive to kill people— Oh, darling! Don't look so sick! Lean on Gigi!"

"I'm all right," Clorinda said dully, but she gripped her little sister's shoulder to steady herself. "Gigi is right. I didn't kill Doris—"

"Then maybe you'll tell us who did, since you were on the scene of the crime last night?" Strawn suggested. "Come now! Who was it? Your brother, Dick?"

"I saw no one kill Doris," Clorinda answered, her voice trembling. "I did not even know she had been killed until Gigi told me this morning. . . . Oh, please give me time! I'll tell you what little I do know. I did go into the summerhouse last night, because I passed near enough to it to get a terribly strong whiff of *Fleur d'Amour*. At first I thought it was just the perfume on my dress, but another gust of wind brought the smell with such sickening force that I decided to investigate. I walked toward the summerhouse, since the smell seemed to come from there. It was light enough for me to see—"

"How?" Strawn interrupted.

"The lights that encircle the lake, concealed among the rocks, were on, as usual," Clorinda explained tiredly, not realizing that she was telling the detectives something they already knew. "I entered the summerhouse and saw a big irregular wet spot on the floor, near the circular bench. I stooped, to make sure, and found that a lot of perfume had been spilled there. I also saw that whoever had spilled it had tried to wash it up, for the surrounding floor had been swabbed with water, but that was almost dry. I wondered who on earth could have done it, then I thought Mother had discovered my absence—"

"And had come looking for you with a flask of perfume in her hand?" Strawn interrupted, with a twisted smile of incredulity.

"Mother is excitable," Clorinda went on wearily. "I thought it possible that she had gone to my room, carrying the perfume, perhaps for me to admire again Mr. Crosby's thoughtfulness, had discovered my absence and had rushed out of the house to look for me about the grounds. I could imagine her stumbling in the summerhouse and breaking the flask. It was her perfume. I had heard her tell Wickett to take it to her rooms. Naturally I could think of no other explanation as to how the perfume got there."

Dundee and Strawn exchanged a long, questioning glance. Was it possible that Clorinda was telling the truth, that she had hit upon an explanation of the most puzzling factor of the case?

But another thought occurred to Dundee almost instantly. "Yet you went to your room, Miss Berkeley, without taking the trouble to go to your mother and reassure her?"

"Yes," she agreed, shrugging. "I don't expect you to believe me, but I simply could not bear the thought of talking with Mother. I knew there would be a row—"

"Why?"

"Because I should have had to tell her that I had made up my mind to break my engagement with Mr. Crosby."

"Why?"

"My father objected violently. Isn't that reason enough?"

"But," Dundee reasoned with her gently, "your engagement had withstood his objections for some weeks, I gather, and you mother, at least, was wholeheartedly in favor of the marriage."

"My father did not object to the marriage until yesterday, when it was too late to cancel Mr. Crosby's invitation to visit us."

"And why did he change his mind so abruptly?" Dundee pressed her.

"Until yesterday he knew nothing about Mr. Crosby except what Mother and Mrs. Lambert had told him. But he had, as a matter of precaution, asked his lawyer to get as complete a report on my *fiancé* as possible. It arrived yesterday, and Father immediately forbade the marriage."

"Do you know what was in that report, Miss Berkeley?"

"I—did not see it," she evaded.

"Look here! We're getting pretty far afield, it seems to me," Strawn interrupted ruthlessly. "Do you realize, young lady, that you've practically accused your mother of murdering her maid?"

"That's not true!" Clorinda flashed, while Gigi's eyes blazed with anger. "I have accused no one. I merely told you the truth, which included my own speculations when I found that the perfume had been spilled on the summerhouse floor."

"And pretty neat, too!" Strawn said, whit mock admiration. "Now, Miss Clorinda, let's get down to brass tacks! You either committed that murder or saw it done. Let *me* do a little speculating! You knew, before you left your room, that the family limousine and chauffeur were taking your uncle and aunt home to Westview, for you were standing at your window and saw the car driving out of the grounds. Your windows face east, I know, but I'll wager we find that the car, having been brought to the house from the west driveway, was heading east when the Smiths got in, and that Arnold circled the house before making for the gates. Right?"

"No. I did not see the car," she answered wearily.

"And I say you did. That you knew Arnold could not keep his appointment with his sweetheart, Doris Matthews. That she *had* told you your brother had forced her to promise to meet him last night," Strawn went on relentlessly. "I say, further, that you knew, somehow, that Dick was not in his room. Probably you went up to find out, to beg him not to get into trouble with the girl. Right?"

"No! Not one word of it is true!"

"And I say it's all true!" Strawn corrected her sternly. "I say you stole out of this house to find your brother—"

"Carrying the flask of perfume with me?" Clorinda interrupted scornfully.

"No. I think I lean toward your own 'speculations' regarding the perfume," Strawn corrected her. "But I'll tell you just how I see it all. Doris failed to tell you one thing: that her 'date' with Dick was to be in the tower room. You walked about the grounds, looking for him, or for him and Doris together, wondering why neither appeared. You finally saw Doris go to the summerhouse to meet Arnold, and soon saw Dick running to join her. He had seen her from the tower window, you know. You crept up to the summerhouse, listened, heard Dick propose marriage to the girl, heard her accept him, went in and quarreled passionately with them both. While the quarrel was going on, your mother came looking for *you*, heard voices in the summerhouse, flung herself in upon you all, perfume flask in hand, and insulted the girl. The girl answered insolently. Your mother—who had slapped this girl earlier in the evening for insolence, remember— retaliated by banging her over the head with the perfume bottle—"

Gigi interrupted the recital with a long, shrill peal of laughter.

XIII.

"Think it's funny, do you?" Captain Strawn asked savagely, as Gigi doubled up with hysterical laughter. "Well, you won't think it's so funny when I put your mother, your brother and your sister under arrest for murder!"

"Are you going to leave me out?" she mocked him, and laughed again, but her hysteria had been successfully conquered by Strawn's shocking threat. "Oh, don't be so silly!" she added passionately, her little brown fists clenched. "Women don't go around murdering maids because they are insolent! And I'll tell you something else, too; Doris was never really insolent in her life, and she was in love with Eugene Arnold with all her heart! She'd have snapped her fingers at Dick, if he'd asked her to marry him. Doris wasn't the kind of girl to marry one man for money when she was in love with another, and even if she was, she would have known that Dad and Mother would cut Dick off without a penny if he had married her! Now where's your fine theory?"

"Right where it was, young woman!" Strawn growled, but Dundee knew that his confidence was shaken. "However, I've got one little job to do before I've finished. Wait here, all of you!"

And he strode out of Clorinda's room, without a backward glance even for Dundee. But that young man was quite sure where he was going and why, and equally sure that he would return to report further.

"I'm very sorry, indeed, Miss Berkeley," he began hesitatingly, his face going red with embarrassment, "that I must appear a most ungrateful and obnoxious guest. Please believe me when I say—"

"Oh, don't bother! It's quite all right," Clorinda interrupted coldly, as she sank into a boudoir chair and closed her eyes.

"But you do keep dreadful company, Bonnie Dundee!" Gigi accused him. "I've always shivered ecstatically over the third-degree grilling in detective stories—but I never shall again! Ugh!" and she shuddered.

"I'm glad you're not so angry with me as you should be," he told her humbly.

"After all, murder *has* been committed," she justified her own tolerance. "And you're my friend."

She gave him her hand with a new shyness, which he found very sweet and very touching. They were still standing, with hands clasped, very close together in body and spirit, when Captain Strawn came striding back into the room, his face a thundercloud.

With that hot little hand in his, Dundee could not restrain the impulse to decrease her anxiety.

"Did you find any perfume on Mrs. Berkeley's skirt or on the soles of her shoes, chief?"

"No!" he admitted, his scowl deepening. "But I did make her acknowledge that she'd gone to Miss Clorinda's room and found it empty. Says she thought her daughter was taking a stroll with Crosby, and didn't worry. But that's the third lie we've caught her in," he added savagely.

"The third? Then look no further!" Gigi cut in flippantly. "Abbie has an iron rule never to tell more than three fibs in one day! She's funny that way—does everything by the rule of three."

"Well, let's see what's your limit, young woman!" Strawn addressed her sternly. "When did *you* last see Doris Matthews?"

"The spotlight at last!" Gigi seemed delighted. "Now let me think! . . . Ummm. What time would you say it was when I was talking to you in the third-floor hall, Mr. Dundee?"

"Five minutes to eleven," Dundee answered promptly, then turned to Strawn to explain. "It was when I was going up to my room, after the Smiths had left. Gigi was in the third-floor hall, waiting for a friendly word from some one before trotting off to bed. She had—"

"Let her tell it," Strawn commanded shortly.

"Delighted! You see it was this way," Gigi began eagerly. "I had gone to bed—but I couldn't sleep, and I thought I'd have a little powwow with Dick. I knew he'd gone up, because he'd stopped at my door while I was undressing to call 'Good-night, Honey!' He knew I was feeling pretty low, because Mother had slapped me—"

"Friday seems to be her day for slapping, doesn't it?" Strawn cut in.

"Oh, I deserved it! I'm an awful trial to Abbie, and I had been a little beast, wasting her perfume like that," Gigi defended her mother cheerfully. "Anyway, when I couldn't sleep, I slipped upstairs, in my pajamas, to see Dick, and I found he wasn't there, though there was smoke in the room and I knew he'd just left. Then Mr. Dundee came along, and we talked a little bit—"

"Gigi, what was that 'dreadful thing' you spoke about having done?" Dundee asked gently.

"Oh! That" . . . I shan't tell you!" and the puckish little face flamed red.

"So you confessed to doing something terrible, did you?" Strawn interrupted, smiling. Then the smile was wiped out by a new sternness. "I think I can tell you what you did, little woman! You'd been to your mother's room and stolen that flask of perfume, to get even with her for having slapped you for wasting it."

Gigi stared at him with apparently genuine admiration. "Haven't you got the most gorgeous imagination?" she marveled. "Say, Big Chief, you ought to write detective stories, instead of fiddling around with real murders, where you're so hobbled with facts! . . . Meaning, wrong again! And I'm not going to tell you what I did do! Arrest me, if you like!" and she laughed as she held out her little brown wrists invitingly.

"I asked you when you last saw Doris Matthews," Strawn reminded her, scowling prodigiously.

"And I'll tell you if you'll stop interrupting," she promised sweetly. "After I said good-night to Bonnie Dundee, I went downstairs to the second floor and almost bumped into Mr. Crosby and Doris. They were—"

"Crosby!" Strawn shouted.

"Sure! A brand-new suspect for you! Aren't you grateful?" Gigi laughed. "they were talking right outside Mr. Crosby's door, or rather, he was standing in the open door, and Doris was in the hall. Now, prepare to thrill! *Doris was crying!"*

"Gigi, are you making this up, because you don't like Crosby, and want to clear your own family from suspicion?" Dundee asked quietly.

"Of course I'm not! Ask Seymour Crosby, if you don't believe me!" she flamed.d "He was putting something into her hand, closing her fingers over something, and with her other hand she was dabbing at tears in her eyes. And I heard him say, 'I'm sorry it's not more—' and then he saw me and shut up quick. Doris said something and then started down the hall, without stopping to speak to me, if she saw me."

"Yes?" Strawn prodded, as she paused.

"That's all there is," she assured him. "I didn't hang around the hall in my pajamas. I went right to my room, which is next to Mr. Crosby's and went to bed. And I was asleep, too, in about five minutes."

"Did you hear your sister leave this room, which must be directly across the hall from yours?" Strawn asked.

"Mother taught us girls not to bang doors," Gigi answered virtuously. "No, I didn't hear anybody leave any room."

"Did you see Crosby go back down into his room and close the door as you were returning to your room?"

"Didn't look back. Didn't give a hoot what he did," Gigi retorted.

"You don't like Mr. Seymour Crosby?"

"I don't know whether I like him or not. . . . He's good-looking and has perfectly swell manners, but as soon as I saw him and Clo together I knew she wasn't in love with him, so I didn't want her to marry him. I'm a fool for romance, I am! And so is Clo, though you mightn't suspect it," she added, with a teasing grin at her sister.

"Shut up, Gigi!" Clorinda admonished her sister fiercely, but she blushed.

Something clicked in Dundee's brain, making him recall, with startling clearness, two apparently unrelated incidents of the night before.

"Miss Berkeley, was it John Maxwell, your old sweetheart, to whom you were talking on the library telephone just before dinner last night?" he asked quietly, his blue eyes taking in every change of expression on the beautiful proud face.

"The extent of your prying into our family affairs seems to have been unlimited," Clorinda answered contemptuously, but there was no doubt of the panic in her dark eyes. "The answer is—no!"

"Was it to meet John Maxwell that you stole out of the house last night?" he went on, despising himself and pitying her.

"No, and again—no!" she cried hoarsely. "I was alone, alone! How many times do I have to swear to that?"

"Please forgive me," Dundee pleaded, "but was it not your love for John Maxwell which made you decide on your walk last night to side with your father against your mother in the matter of your engagement to Mr. Crosby?"

"I—" Clorinda drew a sharp breath of pain. "I refuse to answer! And I fail to see how the state of my feelings toward any man concerns the murder of Doris Matthews."

"Miss Berkeley, Doris was murdered, we believe, during the hour you were walking about the grounds of Hillcrest. If John Maxwell was with you and if your story is otherwise true, he could do a great deal to corroborate that story, to furnish *you* with an alibi," he pointed out, very gently.

The black eyes were magnificent in their scorn. "I need no alibi, Mr. Dundee, for a crime I did not commit— a crime for which I had no conceivable motive. And— correct me if I am wrong!" she added icily, "I believe a motive is still considered necessary for a conviction!"

There was a loud knock on the door. Captain Strawn answered.

"Excuse me, sir, but a reporter has been talking to the servants through a window, and Arnold, the chauffeur, is pretty wild. Says he has something to tell you, sir," said Plainclothesman Harper.

XIV:

"Whew! I thought those reporters would tear my uniform off me!" Captain Strawn grunted disgustedly, as he let himself into the library, where Dundee and Arnold, the chauffeur, were waiting him. "Seemed to think I could pull a murderer out of my sleeve, like a magician's rabbit. I told 'em just enough to keep 'em from blackjacking me, and they're hot-footing it for their city rooms now. . . . Well, what have you got on your chest, Arnold? You've been giving a lot of trouble, my boys tell me."

The red-headed young chauffeur, who had been a huddled heap of misery, sprang from his chair and turned wild eyes on the chief of the Homicide Squad.

"Why didn't you tell me my poor girl was dead—*murdered!* He demanded hoarsely. "God knows I had a right to be told first, not kept stewing in agony in that damned sitting room backstairs, wondering what had happened, believing terrible things against her."

"Well, you know now!" Strawn jerked him up roughly. "What have you got to tell us?"

"*That I saw her murderer, sneaking out of these grounds last night!*" Arnold shouted, his whole body quivering.

"Wait—a—minute!" Strawn ordered sternly. "How do you know he was her murderer? If it *was* a he—"

"It was a man, all right! Or a beast wearing trousers!" Arnold interrupted violently.

"Keep your shirt on! . . . Now begin at the beginning and tell exactly what you know."

"I had a date to meet Doris at the summerhouse last night," Arnold began jerkily. "We were engaged to be married. Wickett, the butler, had been trying to make

things easy for us, and it was him that gave Doris
permission to see me for awhile last night. I was to watch
for her from my room over the garage, because she didn't
know exactly when she'd be free—"

"When was this date made?" Dundee interrupted the
chauffeur and his own rapid notes.

"While we—all of the servants, I mean—were eating
our dinner in our own sitting room," Arnold explained
impatiently. "Our dinner is from six to half past, an hour
before the family dines."

"Then all of the servants heard you make the date?"

"Sure! They all knew we were engaged. We asked
Wickett then and there, and he said it would be all right,
but he cautioned Doris to put the chain on the back-door
lock when she came in."

"Did she have a key?"

"Yes, because Wickett lent her his. Ordinarily, when
any of the servants are out after Wickett has gone to bed,
they have to ring the back-door bell, which connects with
his room. But he—he trusted Doris, and gave her his
key."

Strawn and Dundee exchanged glances. No key had
been found on the girl's body or in the pocket of her
apron.

"All right. Get along with your story," Strawn
ordered.

"Well, I'd been told that I wouldn't be needed during
the evening, but at about a quarter to eleven the phone in
my room rang. It's an extension of the house phone. It
was Wickett, saying that the Benjamin Smiths wanted
me to drive them home to Westview. I was pretty sore—
they're always mooching our car, to save gasoline, and
when Wickett told me that he'd heard Dick Berkeley
bully Doris into saying she'd meet *him*—well, I was ready
to throw up my job right then, but I thought I'd better
stick around as long as Doris was here, to protect her."
And he dropped his head on his crooked arm and sobbed
horribly.

"So Wickett told you, did he?" Strawn repeated thoughtfully. "Well, pull yourself together boy. . . . What then?"

"I took time to write Doris a note when I couldn't reach her on the house phone. I begged her, if she loved me, not to leave the house last night. You see, I didn't think she would meet Dick Berkeley, but I did fear she might figure how long it would take me to make the trip to Westview, and try to see me when I got back. I didn't want her to do that, sir, for fear that Berkeley puppy would be laying for her."

"And you gave the note to Wickett, to give to Doris?"

"Yes. When I brought the car around for him to announce. He said Doris had gone up to her room to write to her sister in England. He said he'd give it to her, but she never got it! If she had—Oh, my God!"

"How do you know she didn't get the note?" Strawn pounced.

"Here it is," Arnold answered, his voice dull and flat with grief. "Della, the upstairs maid, had it all the time. She gave it to me not more than ten minutes ago, right after the reporter, who had climbed up into a window from outside, asked us what we knew about 'the lady's maid murder,'" he quoted bitterly.

Strawn snatched at the note, but before he opened the envelope he asked: "How did Della get hold of it?"

She says she came down the backstairs about eleven last night to get a piece of fruit out of the ice box—they don't feed us any too heavy in this dump—and as she passed through the back hall she saw my note addressed to Doris lying on the table. She took it up to Doris's room, but Doris wasn't in, and instead of leaving it there for her, Della kept the note—curiosity, I guess, to see what kind of love letter I write. I could strangle her!" he added violently.

"One murder's enough for today," Strawn assured him cruelly. "Now, we'll have a look at this letter! . . . Hmm.

Hmm. . . . Here, Dundee!" and he tossed the letter to his subordinate.

The young detective read it quickly, for it was not long.

"My lovely little darling," it began. *"Just a line to tell you I can't keep our date to-night. Have to drive the Smiths home to Westview, damn 'em! Wickett has told me the latest about D. B. For God's sake, and mine, sweetheart, keep out of his way. Don't leave the house to-night on the chance of seeing me when I return from Westview. Go straight to bed, darling, and dream of the red-headed boy who loves you so much he goes crazy sometimes. Gene."*

"Get along with your story, Arnold," Strawn commanded curtly. "You drove the Smiths to Westview. When did you get back?"

"I didn't drive them to Westview," Arnold corrected him. "When we were passing the Riverside Country Club Mrs. Smith recognized a car that was turning in to the club, and hailed it. The folks in the car urged her and Mr. Smith to join them for an hour's dancing, saying they'd drive them home afterwards. So I let them out—"

"The Riverside Country Club?" Strawn repeated, startled, his eyes suddenly narrowing to slits. "That's only about eight miles from here, isn't it? If I'd known this, young man, you'd have been on the carpet long ago!"

"But I didn't come straight home, see?" Arnold retorted angrily. "I drove out the Hamilton Pike to Sheridan Road, parked the car and sat there for half an hour or more."

"Expect me to swallow that?" Strawn grinned. "Twiddling your thumbs and dreaming about getting married, eh?"

"Dreaming about getting married, yes! But instead of twiddling my thumbs I was counting cars, and here's the proof!" The hot-tempered young man drew two soiled envelopes from a breast pocket and passed them to the detective. "I made a mark for every car that passed that corner, and if you'll count the fives, you'll see that the total is 146. I've been planning to lease the southeast corner of those two crossroads and put up a filling station with my savings. I'd checked passing cars on a Sunday afternoon and on a week-day around six o'clock but I still wasn't satisfied, and wanted to see how heavy night traffic was, before I ventured my money. Doris and I had made up our minds not to work for anybody, man or woman, when we got married, but now—" and he groaned, hiding his eyes behind a crooked arm.

"Anybody to corroborate this neat little alibi?" Strawn asked.

"I suppose my car was noticed by at least a hundred people, but I don't know who any of them were. I didn't speak to anyone. But that's the truth—take it or leave it."

"And what time do you say you got back here, after using your employer's car on private business?"

"About five minutes after twelve. I remember looking at the clock on the dashboard when I was held up by a passing freight train just outside of Hamilton. It was twelve straight-up then, and it took me not more than five minutes to reach the gates of Hillcrest. It was when I was turning into our own driveway that I saw the man."

"What did he look like? What was he doing?" Strawn demanded skeptically.

"I didn't get a good look at him," Arnold admitted. "I just supposed it was a new sweetie that Della or Peggy, the downstairs maid, had picked up somewhere, and had been having a sneak date with. He was big and tall both, and was wearing a light-gray topcoat and a gray felt hat. When I swung my car in between the gates he was running away from them up the road. My headlights were on him just a second, and I only saw his back, but he ran like an athlete, I'm telling you! I thought at the time he was hurrying to catch the interurban trolley, which had just whistled at the stop about six blocks south of

Hillcrest. There's another station just north of here, you know, and he was headed in that direction."

"Big and tall—ran like an athlete, eh?" Strawn repeated thoughtfully. He reached for the telephone on the library desk and called Police headquarters.

"Round up John Maxwell, Sergeant Turner." He ordered crisply. "Yeah. That Maxwell. . . . He got into town yesterday. . . . Yeah. Maybe! . . . Not yet. . . . Sure! I'll be in at noon." He hung up the receiver and turned to the chauffeur.

"Now Arnold, come clean!" he snapped. "Why did you kill the girl and let Dick Berkeley get off scot-free?"

Fifteen minutes later Captain Strawn and Bonnie Dundee were strolling together from the garage toward the rear of the big stone house.

"What do you think, boy?" Strawn asked, scowling thoughtfully.

"I think Arnold has told the truth, chief. Aside from the fact that there isn't a trace of that confounded perfume on the uniform he was wearing yesterday, or on his shoes—"

"What about that half-empty bottle of cleaning fluid on his dresser?"

"I've got a bottle of the same stuff on my chiffonier at the Rhodes House," Dundee grinned. "Pretty good to remove spots, and a chauffeur must need it more than I do."

"And pretty good to cover up the stink of perfume, maybe," Strawn growled. "Hey, what the devil—?"

"Guess who!" a disguised voice demanded hoarsely from behind him, as two small brown hands were clapped over his eyes.

"The Pest again!" Strawn deduced, flinging up a hand to seize her arm. "Where did you come from? Didn't I give orders for all of you to stay in the house?"

"I've been *shadowing* you!" Gigi panted, laughing. "I trailed you to the garage, snuck up the stairs after you and saw you *quail with fear* when Arnold said he'd kill you if you said one more word about poor Doris stealing Abbie's perfume. And I must say I didn't blame him a bit! Of all the silly theories you've been reeling off today, that takes the prize!"

"I'll have to put you in jail to keep you from butting in," Strawn threatened.

"Oh, no! You need me around to laugh at you in the right places!" Gigi contradicted. Then, making her voice very deep and gruff, extraordinarily like Strawn's: "'Then let *me* tell *you* what happened, Eugene Arnold! Falling in with your plans to save every nickel you could get your hands on, honestly or crookedly, Doris Matthews *stole* that valuable crystal flask, filled with $32-an-ounce perfume, sneaked out of the house with it to meet you, not knowing you'd called the date off; went to the summerhouse to wait for you, was found there by Dick Berkeley, who proposed marriage to her; accepted him because he could give her more than you ever could, and was letting him make love to her when you came upon the, *And in a jealous rage you killed her, while Dick Berkeley ran away, like the coward he is!'* . . . I don't know," she added, in her normal voice, "whether to be an actress or a detective! But you'll admit you were a wow, Captain Strawn! I thought I'd choke to death, trying to keep from laughing out loud!"

"Yeah, damned funny!" Strawn growled, while Dundee laughed whole-heartedly.

"Listen, Captain Strawn!" Gigi commanded, suddenly very serious. "Anyone who knew Doris Matthews could tell you she wasn't the kind of girl who would have stolen a pin, much less a silly flask of perfume to help her sweetie build a filling station! And as I've told you before, she'd have laughed in Dick's face if he'd asked her to marry him, and then she'd have slapped him if he'd tried to kiss him. As a suspect, Eugene Arnold is a washout."

"How about *you* to take his place?" Strawn suggested.

"Ideal!" Gigi laughed. "Let me tell you all about it: I was sore at Abbie for having slapped me before company. I snuck into her room to get even with her by pouring out the rest of per precious *Fleur d'Amour*. Doris caught me in the act. Loyal maid protects mistress at all costs. Chases naughty child down the hall, down the backstairs and out into the night. Naughty child flies into a rage, bangs loyal maid over the head, and—" She broke off abruptly. "Oh, no!" she shuddered. "I can't go on, even as a joke! I—I was crazy about Doris. Anybody who knew her would have been!"

Without another word she tore her arm out of Strawn's grip and fled to the house, stumbling sometimes, for her eyes were blind with tears.

"Funny kid!" Dundee smiled. "But she's right, chief. This is a very devil of a case, and jumping to foolish conclusions will get us nowhere. . . . By the way, what about John Maxwell? Something Arnold said seemed to ring a bell in your brain. Do you know Maxwell?"

"Slightly," Strawn replied. "Son of one of Hamilton's former police chiefs. Old man's dead now. The boy's had pretty rough sledding; had to step in and be a daddy to his younger brothers and a sister. Paid his way through college and law school, after his mother married again. He's just passed his bar examination, according to the papers. . . . Ran into him on the street yesterday; told me he was going into the district attorney's office and try to work up into assistant district attorney."

"And he was wearing a light-gray topcoat and a gray felt hat when you saw him?" Dundee suggested.

"Right! But so were probably a thousand other young men on the streets of Hamilton. The point is, he's big and tall, and he was an all-round athletic star in college. If Arnold's telling the truth, it looks pretty certain that it was John Maxwell who strolled around these grounds with Clorinda Berkeley last night. If so, I want to know what he saw! That Berkeley girl has told so many lies—"

"Probably to keep John Maxwell's name out of the mess," Dundee pointed out. "Women in love do some might queer things. . . . Well, what next, chief?"

"Guess I'll have a go at the rest of the servants. No use keeping 'em tied up longer than necessary."

"Sort of—saving Crosby?" Dundee asked, and the two detectives looked at each other with significantly raised eyebrows.

Wickett met them in the back hall, his sad eyes asking questions he was too well trained to utter.

"The other servants? Of course, sir. Shall I come with you, sir? They are all in our sitting room."

"Yeah, and trip 'em up quick if you catch one of 'em in a lie," Strawn agreed.

They found two women, and two girls in the plainly furnished but pleasant sitting room.

"Mrs. Ryan, the cook, sir; her assistant, Mrs. Andrews; Della Blinn, the upstairs maid, and Peggy Harper, the downstairs maid, sir," the butler introduced them. "All except Mrs. Andrews live in."

"What time did you leave the house last night, Mrs. Andrews?" Strawn plunged immediately into the business of extracting information,

"At half-past nine, sir, after I'd washed up the dinner dishes," the drab little middle-aged woman answered eagerly. "And I come on at quarter-past seven this morning, jist as the young folks was goin' down to the lake."

"Know anything at all about Doris Matthews' murder?" Strawn shot at her.

"I swear to God I don't know nothing, sir!" she quavered.

"All right! Get back to your job," Strawn dismissed her curtly. "Now, Mrs. Ryan. . . . What about you? When did you go up to bed last night?"

"At nine o'clock, sir, after I'd set by bread to rise for breakfast rolls. I was in bed by half-past, and asleep in two shakes of a lamb's tail."

"Did you hear anything, or see anything at all out of the ordinary last night?"

"Oh, no, sir! I slept like a log, sir, as the old sayin' is—"

"Know anything about this murder?"

"As Holy Mary is my witness, sir, you coulda knocked me down with a feather, and I weigh 210 pounds!" Mrs. Ryan protested.

"All right, then! Back to the kitchen for you, too. . . . Now, Della, you're the girl who found Arnold's note to Doris and kept it, ain't you?"

"I didn't mean no harm, sir! Honest to God, I didn't!" the broad-faced, homely girl blubbered, new tears following the many she seemed to have shed already. "I meant to give it to her, but she wasn't in her room so I just took it to my room—me and Peggy room together, sir—and we got to giggling about it, and wondering what kind of a love letter—"

"It was you that opened it, not me!" pretty black-eyed, black-haired Peggy Harper cut in sharply. "Me—I wouldn't dream of opening anybody else's love letters—"

"Well, you read it, too, didn't you?" Della sobbed. "I—I tore the envelope a little bit, opening it with a hairpin, and then I was scared to take it to her, though me and Peggy heard her go into her room—"

"Wait a minute! What time was all this? First, what time was it when you took the letter to her room and found she wasn't there?"

"It was nearly eleven when I went downstairs to find me an apple, so it musta been just about eleven o'clock when I couldn't find her in her room. I don't know exactly, 'cause I didn't look at no clock nor nothing."

"And how long before you heard her going into her room?"

"I dunno! 'Bout five or ten minutes, I reckon," Della replied sulkily. "Then after a bit we heard her telephone ring, kinda faint-like, 'cause the door was closed, and right after that we heard her door open again, and we guessed she went downstairs, but we didn't look out, so we didn't see nothing."

"Did you hear her return again?" Strawn asked.

"No, but we wouldn't anyhow, 'cause me and Peggy was already in bed and pretty near asleep when her phone rang. And we didn't hear nothing else all night, did we, Peggy?"

"Not a sound!" Peggy corroborated eagerly. "Gee! It sure is too bad—a nice, pretty girl like Doris—"

"All right, girls. Get along with you work now, but don't leave the house without *my* permission. . . . Well?" and Strawn turned to Dundee, after the two girls had scurried out of the sitting room. "Doris's room next, eh? I'm getting pretty anxious to have a squint at that letter she was writing to her sister in England!"

XV.

"Anybody try to get into the girl's room, Wilkins?"
Captain Strawn asked the detective on duty in the third
floor hall.

"No, sir. All quiet up here. Haven't seen a soul except
a young man who said he was Dick Berkeley. He's in his
own room up front, now."

Dundee opened the unlocked door and stepped aside,
to let his chief precede him into the murdered girl's room.
It was very small, not much bigger than a closet, but
Doris Matthews had succeeded in making it homelike,
even pretty. There was a narrow wooden bed, a tiny
rocking chair, a flimsy bookrack, a table and a cheap
dresser, all freshly painted a soft green, undoubtedly
decorated by her own hand, for an almost empty quart
can of green enamel was tucked away on an upper shelf of
the miniature clothes closet.

"Guess she bought and made these curtains, too,"
Strawn said gruffly, fingering the pale yellow-and-green
flowered voile that fluttered at the narrow window.

Only the carpet on the floor was out of keeping with
the immaculate daintiness of the little cubicle. It was a
worn square of gaudily flowered carpeting, and Dundee,
with a sharp contraction of the heart, could visualize the
distress in Doris's blue eyes every time they rested upon
it.

In the closet they found four pretty but inexpensive
silk dresses, a very English-looking, jaunty little tweed
suit, and a lightweight fall coat. On a shelf was a hat
box, containing a saucy green beret and a close-fitting
cloche of silky, dark-blue felt.

"Good taste in clothes," Dundee said softly, almost as if he were speaking to the girl who could never flush with delight at another compliment; but his chief had turned to the table and was gathering up the closely written sheets of an unfinished letter.

"This ought to tell us a lot about Doris Matthews," Strawn said. "And—by George, it does?"

The iron-gray head and the black one bent together over the last letter Doris Matthews would ever write.

"Darling Kathy—" it began. *"I have been too miserable, too busy and too happy to write you as often as I should. I've destroyed your last letter, as you asked me to, but I think I can remember most of the questions, and I'll try to answer them.*

"First: Yes, I've been terribly homesick for England and for you, until—but that will come later.

"Second: Wickett is well, and the same old darling. I don't know how I could have lived the first two weeks here, if he hadn't been here, too, to buck me up. He sends you his love, and offers you my job when—But that comes later, too! I'm saving up for a grand climax.

"Third: Mrs. Berkeley is as impossible and tyrannical as ever. Poor thing! I can't blame her much, because of what I wrote you last time, and because she simply isn't a lady, and hasn't the ghost of an idea how real gentlefolk treat their servants."

Strawn chuckled. "Wonder how 'Abbie' is going to like *that*, when the papers get hold of this letter?" They went on reading.

"For instance, she slapped my face this evening when I was dressing her for dinner. I probably shouldn't have said what I did, but I simply couldn't hold my tongue any longer. Of course it had to do with what I wrote you about before, and I spoke for Gigi's sake. I've told you how adorable the child is, how crazy I am about her. We are the best of friends, and Miss Clorinda is still kindness itself to me. She will make a very great lady some day.

"And now for some real news for you, darling! Guess who arrived this afternoon. Mr. Crosby! I haven't seen him yet, but of course I shall. I dread it, in a way, because—Oh, well, you know all about that! He is engaged to Clorinda Berkeley. It's to be announced at a big party to-morrow night, and the old warhorse is simply on her head with excitement. Thinks that, with Mrs. Lambert's help, she's going to conquer Hamilton society, then march triumphantly upon New York, Paris and London! Mrs. Lambert is the same sweet, considerate 'great lady' always was. If only she were the mistress! But about Mr. Crosby. I can't see how he can possibly marry again so soon. It seems like only yesterday that that awful inquest—. I, for one, will never forget Miss Phyllis, the loveliest, sweetest, kindest person that ever lived. I shall never love any other mistress as I loved and adored her. If only— But it's too late now. My darling lady is in her grave, and the 'case' is closed forever, and maybe I did then what she would have wished me to do. At any rate, I thought so then. But I should die happy if I could live to see the one who broke her heart and killed her—yes, actually <u>killed</u> her!—suffer as she suffered. I know the law is powerless in a case like this, but there are <u>other ways!</u>"

The two detectives lifted their eyes from the underscored words and stared at each other for a long minute before they returned to the letter.

"But I can't wait any longer to tell you the biggest news of all. I am engaged to be married! Yes, I mean it this time, with all my heart! The man is Eugene Arnold, the Berkeley chauffeur. I think I mentioned him in my last letter. And, oh, Kathy, I do love him so! He's a red-headed, hot-tempered scalawag, but I could die of joy when he holds me in his arms. He's ambitious, too, even more so than I. He has saved up a lot of money to open what the Americans call a 'filling station,' where cars get their petrol and oil, you know,

*and after we're married I'm going to have a tiny
beauty shop of my own. I shall always be grateful to
my dear Miss Phyllis for having had me taught the
profession. It will take a bucket of money, of course,
but I know where I can get all or more than I need.
Yes, you've probably guessed right, but you mustn't get
the wind up. There's no danger of my—*

*"Later. Remembered it was getting late and
scuttled off to do my last-minute chores, and I've got to
dash now to keep a date with my Gene, but Kathy, I've
seen and talked with Mr. Crosby! I don't dare write
exactly what he said and what I said, even to you, but
he gave me—"*

The letter ended here, the pen having left a jagged,
sputter line, as if the writer had been startled from her
task.

"That's when Mrs. Berkeley called her over the house
telephone," Strawn deduced. He sat down heavily on the
immaculate little green bed and ejaculated "Well!"
helplessly.

Dundee shuffled the sheets, frowning at a line here
and a line there. "Like most letters, it's cryptic in spots,
darned cryptic, but—"

But it gives us what we've been looking for in this
confounded case—a motive," Strawn pointed out.

"A motive pointing to one person, and all our actual
facts toward others," Dundee retorted.

"Give me a good motive and I'll find facts to go with
it," Strawn promised grimly. "Let me see those
newspaper clippings on the Crosby case.

While the older detective studied the clippings with
painstaking thoroughness, Dundee wandered about the
murdered girl's room, prying reluctantly into table and
dresser drawers. "Kathy" must be notified of her sister's
death, of course, but he found not a single letter bearing
her signature. Possibly because she feared the curious
eyes of the other maids, Doris had destroyed any and all

letters she had received during her employment at Hillcrest, except a little bundle of love notes from Eugene Arnold, which Dundee found hidden beneath a pile of beautifully ironed and mended underwear. The dresser top, covered with a hand-embroidered towel, held only three objects—a pair of green glass candlesticks supporting primrose wax tapers, and, in the exact center, a squat flask of perfume. Probably a present from Eugene Arnold, in the early days of his courtship, before he knew that his sweetheart did not use scent. . . .

But in the table drawer Dundee found something which interested him mightily. It was an enlarged snapshot of a tea-table group in a garden. Slightly in the background, looking every inch the perfect butler, was Wickett. Seated at the little wicker table was Seymour Crosby and a very beautiful girl, whose dark curls were blown charmingly about a piquant, wistful face. Doris's adored "Miss Phyllis" doubtless. And standing by the tea-table, holding up a Pekinese dog to be fed by Mrs. Crosby, was Doris herself, in maid's uniform, the sun making an aureole about her lovely blond head. In very small "printing" was the inscription: "For my dear little Doris, with love. Phyllis Crosby, May 1, 1928.:

"What was the date of Phyllis Crosby's death?" Dundee asked.

"Sunday night, May 6."

"Is Wickett referred to in the newspaper story?"

"No, but there are several references to 'the butler.'" Strawn replied. "Why?"

"Because the butler was Wickett," Dundee obliged quietly. "And I'd rather like to ask him a few questions."

"That's easy!" and Strawn marched to the door, to give the order to Detective Wilkins, on duty in the third-floor hall.

Strawn returned to his clippings and Dundee continued his search of the room, his object now being the key to the back door which Wickett had lent to the girl. In her handkerchief box he found a savings bank book, crediting her with $357,42. Certainly not a very big nest egg with which to start a beauty shop, Dundee reflected. But her letter to "Kathy" had hinted at a way to augment the sum materially. *What way?*

"Here's the key, chief!" he cried at last. "In the pocket of her topcoat. Not the key to her own door, certainly, for that's on the inside of the lock now."

"In her coat, eh?" Strawn frowned. "That means she intended to wear the coat when she went to meet Arnold—'

"And that when she did go, she rushed out in too great a hurry to bother about coat or key, in spite of the fact that it was decidedly chilly last night," Dundee interrupted. "Here's something else, too!" And he untied a handkerchief, knotted about a pair of exquisitely mounted sapphire earrings. "Come in! . . . Oh, it's you, Wickett. Is this the key you lent Doris?"

"Yes, sir."

"Do you recognize these earrings, Wickett?"

The butler's eyes widened as they took in the expensive ornaments. "I—I can't say positively, sir. I have seen earrings which resemble them."

Dundee dropped them into his pocket. "Were you ever employed by the Crosbys, Wickett?"

"Yes, sir. From November, 1927 to May, 1928, sir."

"That is, until Mrs. Crosby's death?"

"Yes, sir. Before that I had been with Mr. and Mrs. Van Rensselaer Lambert, for nine years. When Mr. Lambert died in September, 1927, Mrs. Lambert found herself financially unable to keep up an establishment. Mr. Crosby, a very old friend of Mr. and Mrs. Lambert, was married to Miss Phyllis Benham in October, 1927, and he asked me to head their staff of servants."

"Miss Benham was a socially unknown but very rich girl at the time of her marriage, was she not?" Dundee asked.

"I believe she was so considered, sir, but later events proved that she did not control a fortune in her own name," the butler said stiffly.

"Doris was Mrs. Crosby's maid at the time you served as butler?"

"Yes, sir. Doris had been with Miss Phyllis, as we all called her, for three years before her marriage to Mr. Crosby. After the wedding, Mr. and Mrs. Crosby decided to spend a year in London, and took Doris and me with them."

"And Mrs. Lambert?"

"Oh, no, sir. Mrs. Lambert had gone abroad immediately after her husband's death, before the Crosby wedding," the butler answered.

"But the friendship between Mr. Crosby and Mrs. Lambert continued?"

"Certainly, sir. Mrs. Lambert and Miss Phyllis were the best of friends, too, if I may say so, sir. It was Mrs. Lambert who was largely responsible for launching Miss Phyllis Benham into New York society, and in London, Mrs. Lambert did as much as she could, considering the fact that she was in mourning, to guide her social career there."

"Being paid for her services?" Dundee asked.

"Certainly not, sir! Mrs. Lambert had a small but adequate income of her own at the time. This is the first time Mrs. Lambert has ever worked for money," the butler answered indignantly.

"Now, Wickett, will you please tell me if you were in Doris Matthews' confidence in regard to the secret causes behind Phyllis Crosby's death?"

The butler looked absolutely dumbfounded. "In her *confidence,* sir?" her repeated incredulously. "I am sure she knew nothing beyond what she told at the inquest, sir!"

Dundee shuffled through the pages of Doris's letter to her sister.

"Were you planning to advance Doris Matthews a sum of money with which to help her set up a beauty shop, Wickett?"

"I? Why, no sir! Doris knew that all my savings go regularly to my aged parents in England, sir. They are entirely dependent upon me."

So that too was a blind alley! Dundee shrugged. Then he asked abruptly:

"Wickett, what is you private opinion of Mr. Seymour Crosby?"

"I am glad to answer that, sir!" the butler replied emphatically. "Mr. Crosby is a gentleman in the finest sense of the word. I have never known him to do a dishonorable or discourteous act."

"Was he in love with his wife, Phyllis?"

"To the point of infatuation, sir! And Miss Phyllis adored him. It was the happiest marriage I have ever know personally."

"Wickett, do you yourself know anything at all, beyond what came out at the inquest, regarding Mrs. Crosby's death, or the causes leading to it?"

"Absolutely nothing, sir! I could only believe she had gone temporarily and suddenly insane. She was going to have a child, you know, and women in that—er— condition, sir—"

"That's all for the present, Wickett. . . . And thank you very much. Will you please tell Mr. Crosby to come to us here?"

The butler bowed and was departing when Dundee stopped him. "One thing more, Wickett. Can you give me the full name and address of Doris's sister, Kathy?"

"Certainly, sir. Miss Kathryn Matthews, lady's maid in the home of Sir Edward Moresby. No. —, —-Terrace, Mayfair, London."

"Sir Edward Moresby?" Dundee repeated joyfully. "You may go, Wickett. . . . Well, chief, we're in luck at last. Sir Edward Moresby is a personal friend of mine, was head of the records department of Scotland Yard during my six months there. We'll cable him to quiz Kathy. She knows a lot from Doris, if she'll only talk. And I think she will, *after Sir Edward hints to her that her sister was murdered for knowing too much!"*

The two detectives were framing the long cablegram when Mr. Seymour Crosby was announced by Detective Wilkins.

XVI.

"Oh, there you are, Crosby!" Captain Strawn greeted the man absently, without raising his eyes from the cablegram he and Dundee were concocting at the dead girl's table. "Have a seat, won't you?" and he waved vaguely toward the bed, since the room's only two chairs were in use. "Be with you in a minute. . . . Now, how's this Dundee? Does it cover the essentials?"

Dundee accepted the scribbled message, and to his chief's consternation began to read aloud, his eyes not so absorbed, however, that they missed a single change of expression on Seymour Crosby's face:

"Sir Edward Moresby, Scotland Yard, London. Doris Matthews, sister of Kathryn Matthews, murdered last night on Berkeley estate here. Please cable any information from Kathryn regarding confidences made her by Doris concerning Crosby case. Seymour Crosby guest here, engaged to Clorinda Berkeley. (Signed) James F. Dundee, Police Department."

His eyes still on Crosby's face, Dundee returned the sheet to Strawn. "O K, sir. We ought to have an answer by to-morrow morning."

If he had expected Seymour Crosby to betray himself by word or action, he was disappointed, for the man gave no sign, beyond a deepening pallor of his already pale and drawn face. Crosby had ignored Strawn's invitation to be seated. His tall, slim body very erect, his hands clasped behind his back, he stood near the door, awaiting the inquisition with admirable control.

"Well, Mr. Crosby!" Strawn shifted his chair to face his man, crossed his legs leisurely, filled a reeking old pipe and got it going with nerve-shattering deliberation.

"So you called Doris's bluff, did you? Or maybe you didn't think it *was* a bluff?"

Out of the sudden intense silence came the sound of knuckles cracking before Seymour Crosby answered: "Sorry, but I'm afraid I don't know what you mean!"

"Got sort of fed up, trying to meet her blackmailing demands, eh?" Strawn went on, grinning and raising his eyebrows.

That had its effect. Livid anger painted and distorted Crosby's handsome face. "You can call me any names you like, Strawn, but I can't permit you to label Doris Matthews a blackmailer. I have never known a finer, straighter, more loyal—"

"That so?" Strawn cut in lazily. "Well, well! The what would you call these, Crosby?" and he picked up the pair of sapphire earrings and rattled them on his broad palm.

"Those are earrings," Crosby began icily. "I made Doris a present of them last night."

"Friday seemed to be an early Christmas for you eh? A fine cut-crystal flask of perfume for you future mother-in-law and a pair of expensive earrings for you future mother-in-law's maid. What did you bring your *fiancée*, Miss Clorinda Berkeley?"

"That at least is my own affair, I believe!" Crosby retorted angrily. "As for the earrings, they were one of the last gifts I made to—my wife. I gave them to Doris last night because—"

"Because you were damned short of money, hadn't got your fingers into the Berkeley pile yet, and thought they'd hold Doris till—"

"No!" Crosby interrupted, his head upflung, his aristocratic nostrils flaring. "If you will kindly permit me, I shall tell you the truth concerning the earrings. I might add that I shall tell you the exact truth concerning any question you ask me, provided you have any right or authority to ask me the question."

Strawn's bushy eyebrows shot still higher. "Yeah? . . . Well, shoot!"

"My wife, who, as you doubtless know, is dead," Crosby began in his icy, well-controlled voice, "was a brunette. Her favorite stone was the ruby, which became her—enormously. I myself have a weakness for sapphires, and when I saw this pair of earrings in a London jeweler's I could not resist them. Phyllis—my wife—admired them and thanked me for them, but as soon as she had put them on I saw that I had made a mistake. Doris, who was her maid them was present at the time, and Phyllis took them off and laid them against her maid's cheeks. The effect was—enchanting, as the stones were almost exactly the color of Doris's eyes. I am sure Phyllis would have presented them to the girl then and there, if she had not been afraid of hurting my feelings. She did, however, laughingly remark that she would leave them to Doris in—in her will."

His voice broke here, and trembled slightly as it went on: "She—died suddenly—as you know, and without having made a will—"

"Which she would have done, if she had really contemplated suicide!" Strawn interrupted, with slow and terrible emphasis.

"I do not believe that my wife 'contemplated' suicide," Crosby retorted, very quietly. "I believed then, and I still believe, that she became suddenly deranged, a not uncommon symptom of her—condition."

"Yeah, she was going to have a baby, wasn't she?" Strawn interrupted callously. "Which makes it a double murder!"

With the agility of an athlete Crosby sprang for the detective captain's throat, but Dundee interposed, seizing the man's arm and forcing him backward, step by step.

"Please, Mr. Crosby!" he advised gently. "Violence can only make matters worse. You must believe that Captain Strawn has good reason for the conclusions he has reached, and—"

"I—beg your pardon!" Crosby bowed slightly, again in superb control of his anger. "Let me remind you, however, Captain Strawn, that a coroner's jury in London returned a verdict of 'suicide while temporarily insane' as the cause of my wife's death."

"A verdict which, you probably know, Crosby, failed to satisfy your wife's relatives and friends, and even some of your own friends!" Strawn pointed out sternly. "*A verdict which you owed to the testimony of a maid in your own employ—to Doris Matthew, in fact!*"

"Testimony which was absolutely true and accurate in every detail!" Crosby retorted coldly.

"And now Doris Matthews, the only eye-witness to your wife's 'suicide' lies on a marble slab in Hamilton's morgue, foully murdered within eight hours of Seymour Crosby's arrival at Hillcrest to celebrate his engagement to another rich girl!" Strawn pointed out, emphasizing each significant word with the tapping of his pipe bowl upon his palm. "Surely, Mr. Crosby, you did not expect the police department of Hamilton to overlook the obvious connection between the two facts?"

Crosby made no answer, but out of his white face his dark eyes blazed with a terrible scorn and anger.

"And what would you say, Mr. Seymour Crosby, if I told you that the Hamilton Homicide Squad did not wait until you murdered Doris Matthews to take a vital interest in 'The Crosby Case,' as the newspapers called it sixteen months ago?"

"I did not murder Doris Matthews," Crosby answered steadily.

"Yeah, we pricked up our ears when we heard who Clorinda Berkeley was going to marry," Captain Strawn went on, in the genial voice he could so suddenly assume. "You see, Crosby, Hamilton thinks a lot of its citizens, likes to protect 'em from fortune-hunters and wife-killers. So we sent Mr. Dundee, who happened to be one of the many not entirely soothed and satisfied by the coroner's verdict of suicide, to have a look at Phyllis Crosby's widower, who was consoling himself with another girl—"

Crosby interrupted with a sharp exclamation, then turned his blazing eyes upon Dundee, whose face was red with embarrassment.

"I am to gather then, Mr. Dundee, that it was your interference with Mr. Berkeley which resulted in Miss Berkeley's breaking the engagement this morning!" he said contemptuously.

"No, Mr. Crosby. I have not spoken one word privately with Mr. Berkeley," Dundee answered. "Until this morning I had not the slightest reason for discussing you with your future father-in-law. I came here partly out of curiosity, partly, as Captain Strawn has said, because I believed that the whole truth regarding your wife's death had not come to light. I wanted merely to study your face and your manner, to make up my own mind—"

"And did you conclude, sir, that I was a murderer?" Crosby asked icily.

"I came to the conclusion, Mr. Crosby, that you were a gentleman," Dundee answered quietly.

Crosby's "Thank you!" was genuine gratitude, not irony.

"The crime of murder is not confined to thugs and roughnecks, Crosby," Strawn reminded his victim genially. "Yes, sir, we were so interested in your visit to the home of Hamilton's richest citizen that we took the trouble to look up the famous Crosby case in our local newspaper files. Hamilton didn't give you quite as big a play as New York and London, but you weren't exactly slighted, you'll be glad to hear. . . . Now, Crosby, suppose you tell me exactly what happened on the night of Sunday, May 6, 1928, at your apartment hotel in London."

"Crosby's nostrils flared. "I shall have to refuse. The subject is a painful one to me, and it has been thoroughly threshed out before the coroner's jury and in the newspapers."

Strawn reached across the table and picked up the little sheaf of newspaper clippings. "Looks like I'll have to do most of the talking for a while then," he conceded genially. "I've just been looking over these clippings on the case, and it's pretty fresh in my mind."

"Please!" Crosby protested, his face very white and his mustached mouth twisting with pain. "That old story has nothing to do with Doris—"

"No? Why, her name's in headlines," Strawn pretended to misunderstand. "Listen to this: 'MAID CLEARS SOCIETY SCION IN SUICIDE OF WIFE' . . . Well, Crosby, I'll run over the story and—correct me if I am wrong!

"In October, 1927, you were married in New York City to Miss Phyllis Benham, daughter of a new-rich manufacturer, Cullen Benham. You had known her only a few weeks, having met her in the home of Mr. and Mrs. Van Rensselaer Lambert. Mrs. Lambert had taken the girl up quite suddenly and was acting as her social sponsor, until Mr. Lambert's sudden death, due to a polo accident, in September.

"After a honeymoon in Canada, you and your wife returned to New York, recruited the Lamberts' former butler, Wickett, to head your future staff of servants, and took Wickett and your wife's maid, Doris Matthews, with you to London, where you occupied a large apartment in Queen's Hall, a new and fashionable apartment hotel. Apparently, you and your new wife were ideally happy—"

"Not *apparently*—actually! In every sense of the word, my wife and I were ideally happy!" Seymour Crosby corrected the detective.

"Yeah?" Strawn grinned. "So ideally happy that, according to your own story, Phyllis Crosby committed suicide while still a bride—but according to *my* belief, supported by Doris Matthews herself, you and your wife were so 'ideally happy' that you murdered her!"

"That's a lie!" Crosby cried passionately. "Doris is dead. She cannot tell you herself that you lie, but I can, and do!"

"Yeah?" Strawn said again. "Look at this!" and he picked up the scattered sheets of Doris's letter to her sister.

"Well, what have you got to say now, Crosby?" Captain Strawn snapped, when Seymour Crosby had silently read the letter and was returning it with a trembling hand.

"All I can say is, that I wish to God Doris were still alive to tell me what she knew or suspected, so that I could avenge my wife's death," Crosby answered, his voice vibrating with what seemed to be passionate sincerity and grief. "As it is, I don't know what she meant—"

"'*If only—But it's too late now. My darling lady is in her grave, the 'case' is closed forever, and maybe I did what she would have wished me to do. At any rate, I thought so then. But I should die happy if I could live to see the one who broke her heart and KILLED her—yes, actually killed her!—suffer as she suffered. I know the law is powerless in a case like this, but there are OTHER WAYS!*'" Strawn interrupted, reading the damning passage with slow and terrible emphasis. "You don't know what she meant by those words, Crosby?"

"I do not!"

"Then let me tell you, Crosby!" Strawn commanded sternly. "For more than two weeks, according to your own admission at the inquest and according to the testimony of Mrs. Lambert, your wife had not been herself. She wept frequently, refused to see any of her friends except Mrs. Lambert, and even wrote to her father in New York that she had made a terrible mistake in marrying. In that letter she asked him to cable her twenty-five thousand dollars, and begged him to allow her to return home. Her father refused the first request, by cable, but told her to come home immediately. That's right, isn't it Crosby?"

"Those facts came out at the inquest, yes," Crosby admitted in a low, flat voice. "It was the first I knew of her letter to her father. I had no idea she—wished to leave me, and until this day I haven't the remotest idea why she wrote as she did. I repeat: I loved my wife with all my heart, and she loved me. During those two weeks you speak of she told me repeatedly that she loved me, but would give no explanation of her fits of weeping."

"Yeah?" Strawn sneered. "Can't you guess? By that time, Phyllis Crosby knew, beyond a shadow of a doubt, that you had married her for her money—"

"That's a foul lie!" Crosby flung at him furiously.

"Yeah? Well, lie or not, that's what Phyllis Crosby must have had good reason to believe; otherwise, why should she have written her father as she did?" Strawn gibed. "I believe, further, that your wife found that you were unfaithful to her, that you were keeping another woman on her father's money—"

"Strawn, I'll be damned if I let you—"

"How are you going to help yourself?" Strawn grinned. "I admit that's supposition on my part. But—how else could you break your wife's heart, as Doris Matthews charges you did?"

"Those words do not refer to me!"

"Who did she mean then?" Strawn demanded reasonably.

"I—don't'—know," Crosby admitted. "I wish to God I did!"

"Well, let's get along with the story. The climax came shortly after dinner on the night of Sunday, May 6. Your wife ate nothing, burst into tears at the table, and fled to her room in hysterics. You followed her and she refused to admit you. About ten o'clock that evening, Mrs. Lambert, who had been a guest in your home since the previous Sunday—summoned by you from Biarritz to cheer your wife up—discovered that Mrs. Crosby had left the bedroom. She traced her to the roof of the apartment hotel, found her weeping inconsolably, tried again to learn what was wrong, and finally, at your wife's request, returned to the apartment to tell you that Mrs. Crosby wished to see you.

"You left the drawing room instantly, and Mrs. Lambert summoned Mrs. Crosby's maid, Doris, asking her to take a wrap to the roof for you wife, since the night had turned cool and Mrs. Crosby was wearing a thin evening dress. Still correct, Crosby?"

"Yes," the tortured man admitted, and bowed his head upon his trembling hands.

"Now, according to your testimony at the inquest, you did not proceed immediately to the roof. Instead, you took time to go to the library to get a volume of poetry from which you say you intended to read to your wife."

"And that, too is the exact truth!" Crosby asserted passionately. "Phyllis was unusually fond of Swinburne, and I had a sudden inspiration to read to her. I believed then, as I have believed until to-day, that her hysteria was the result of her condition, and that the poetry she loved, and which we had read together during our honeymoon, would soothe her nerves and—and—"

"And convince your heiress-wife that it was she you loved, not the woman she was jealous of?" Strawn insinuated.

"For God's sake, stick to the facts!" Crosby moaned. "There was no other woman—"

"Suits me!" Strawn grinned. "The bare facts are that you had a volume of poetry in the pocket of your dinner jacket when your wife's body was found, and that you *walked* up the two flights of stairs to the roof, instead of taking the elevator. Consequently, no employee of the apartment hotel could say just how long you had been on the roof when your wife was killed. Right?"

"I rang for the lift, but as it was slow in coming, I ran up the stairs, to join my wife as quickly as possible," Crosby explained dully.

"Yeah? Well, your story is that when you got to the roof you saw your wife standing at the low railing which encloses the roof. You called to her, she raised her right hand to wave to you, then quickly climbed to the top of the railing and—jumped to her death in the court below!"

Only an agonized grown from the bowed head answered him.

"Now for Doris Matthews' story at the inquest," Strawn went on implacably. "She testified that she rang for the elevator, which opened for her almost immediately—"

"A point in Mr. Crosby's favor, Captain Strawn," Dundee interrupted quietly. "The elevator operator testified that he was ascending in answer to a previous ring, recorded when his car was on the first floor."

"Yeah?" Strawn grinned, in nowise nonplussed. "You didn't think Doris and her 'master' forgot to fix up that little point between them, did you? . . . Well, let's see what Doris testified now. She said she emerged from the 'lift' at the top floor, walked up the very short flight of stairs leading to the roof, and was just stepping foot upon the roof when she heard a shrill scream, followed by the sound of a man's voice calling, 'Phyllis, Phyllis! Oh, my God!' And, most providentially for Mr. Seymour Crosby, Doris testified that she saw him running across the roof to the spot from which the scream had come, the place from which his wife had leaped to her death. According to her story, Crosby, you were fully fifty feet from the railing when she heard the scream and caught a glimpse of fluttering white as the woman leaped."

"Yes," Crosby groaned, "that is all the exact truth. Doris reached the railing almost as soon as I did, and—restrained me from leaping after my wife."

"*So she said!*" Strawn nodded. "Now, let me tell you what really happened, as I reconstruct that tragedy. You were lying when you said you stopped for a book. It was already in your pocket. You went to the roof immediately, by the stairs, just as you said, because even then you were planning an alibi in case it became necessary to kill you wife. . . . Sit down, Crosby! And listen! You met your wife, she charged you with having married her for money, with having been unfaithful to her, *or with some serious crime.* The exposure of which would have ruined you socially. A crime, possibly, of which only Phyllis Crosby knew and for which she could have had you arrested!"

"That's a foul, lie, too!" Crosby groaned.

"Yeah? . . . Well, you became violently angry with her, and in your rage you lifted her small body and hurled it over the railing. *And you were caught in the act by Doris Matthews!"*

"You deserve to be killed, Captain Strawn," Crosby told him, in a dead, toneless voice.

"Yeah?" Strawn grinned, and lit his pipe again, striking the match upon the sole of his big shoe. "The unexpected appearance of the maid with your wife's wrap—you didn't know of course, that Mrs. Lambert had sent her, after speaking with you—threw you into a blue funk. Perhaps you did try to leap after your wife, and the girl restrained you. God knows what you said to her, for she seems to have been a pretty decent girl, on the whole. I don't say you offered her hush money then. I rather think you appealed to her lover for her mistress, urging her to believe that Phyllis Crosby would rather be listed as a suicide than that her husband should hang for her murder. At any rate, it is my firm conviction that you and Doris Matthews concocted your alibi between you, then and there. She had rung twice for the elevator. You made her agree to say that she had rung only once, so that your own story of having just come to the roof could be partially substantiated.

"Well, Crosby, it all worked out as planned. The girl stood by you at the inquest, and you were exonerated. Phyllis Crosby was listed as a suicide while temporarily deranged. But Doris Matthews had a conscience, and she loved her dead mistress very dearly. She confided to her sister, as this letter very clearly indicates, and Kathryn Matthews advised Doris, for her own sake, not to try to reopen the case, lest Doris be convicted of perjury. As Doris writes Kathryn *'The case is closed forever, and maybe I did then what she would have wished me to do.'"*

"But she hated you, Crosby! Doris wanted to make you suffer as Phyllis Crosby had suffered. And as she says here, *'there are other ways.'* One way was to expose you to the Berkeleys as a fortune-hunter, and, in strict confidence, as a wife-killer."

"No, I tell you! No!" Crosby denied hoarsely.

"You came here yesterday, not knowing that Doris Matthews was now Mrs. Berkeley's maid—"

"That's not true!" Crosby interrupted. "Mrs. Lambert had written me that she had hired Doris for the job."

It was Dundee who spoke now, with curious reluctance: "Pardon me, Captain Strawn. . . . Mr. Crosby, it is my duty to remind you that when Mrs. Berkeley mentioned Doris last night, you appeared surprised, even startled. You said, 'Surely you don't mean little Doris Matthews?' and Mrs. Lambert then told you she was quite sure she had written you of Doris being here."

"But Mrs. Lambert just *thought* she had written you," Strawn interrupted. "The truth is, you were in a panic. You knew you would have to see Doris Matthews immediately, and insure her continued silence by bribery or by murdering her!"

XVII.

"I'm sorry, Dundee," Seymour Crosby turned to the younger detective, ignoring Captain Strawn's damning charge for the moment. "I told you an untruth, the first I have uttered since this questioning began. I did not receive a letter from Mrs. Lambert, mentioning the fact that Doris had come here to be Mrs. Berkeley's maid. I *was* surprised—startled, if you will—at the news. But the surprise was a pleasant one, tinged only with pain that I should have so vivid a reminder of my dead wife's last moments. I had not seen or heard from Doris after the inquest, since my wife's death meant the breaking up of our—home."

"It is true, Captain Strawn," Dundee conceded willingly, "that Mr. Crosby added, immediately after Mrs. Lambert's news, that he would be delighted to see Doris."

"Hunh!" Strawn snorted, skeptically. "Well, the point is, Crosby, you lost no time in getting to Doris Matthews, and—"

"Pardon me! The meeting was entirely accidental," Crosby interrupted. "I happened to open the door of my room and saw Doris in the hall walking toward the backstairs. I called to her, and she came to me, standing just outside my door. We talked—"

"'*Kathy, I've seen and talked with Mr. Crosby!*'" Strawn began to quote solemnly. "'*I don't dare write exactly what he said and what I said, even to you, but he gave me—*' There, Crosby, you have the last words a murdered girl ever penned. I suppose you've had time to think up a nice, harmless explanation?"

Crosby flushed darkly. "My impulse is to refuse to answer, but I believe the truth will be less painful to—Miss Berkeley than the construction you are putting upon what Doris wrote. After we had exchanged the ordinary greetings and inquiries as to health, Doris said:

"'It brings it all back so, sir meeting you. It seems only yesterday—' Then she burst into tears, and whispered: 'Oh, sir, how can you marry again so soon, when you loved Miss Phyllis so much?'"

"So that's what Doris said!" Strawn sneered. "Strange talk from a well-trained maid!"

"Doris was rather more than a servant in our household," Crosby said quietly. "She had been with Phyllis for years; the two girls had been real friends, as mistress and maid frequently are. After our marriage, I became very fond of Doris myself."

"Well, now, that's interesting!" Strawn exclaimed triumphantly. "A little *too* fond, perhaps? As fond of her as Dick Berkeley was?"

"That's a vile thing to say, Strawn!" Crosby replied contemptuously. "It's absurd to have to deny such an insinuation, but I do—most emphatically!"

"Well, get along with your fairy tale," Strawn ordered curtly. "What did *you* say to Doris then?"

"I—" Crosby hesitated, the dark flush deepening. "I told her I could not live in the past, that, to save my reason, I must try to build a new life—"

"In other words. 'Gentlemen must live,' eh?" Strawn paraphrased contemptuously.

"I am not a penniless fortune-hunter, Captain Strawn!" Crosby returned with dignity. "When I married Phyllis Benham I was a man of a fair amount of means. Unfortunately, part of my small fortune was lost in unwise speculation after my marriage, in an endeavor on my part to more than equal my wife's income from her father. But I still have an income of approximately $10,000 a year, sufficient for a single man to live on comfortably—abroad, at least. I was not marrying Clorinda Berkeley for her money."

"All right, all right! Go on! What else do you claim was said between you and Doris Matthews?"

"Doris, still weeping, said she understood, and hoped I would be happy again, but she asked—as if jealous for Phyllis: 'But you don't love Miss Clorinda as you did Miss Phyllis, do you?' and I—please realize that these words are forced from me!—I replied:

"'My dear is in Phyllis's grave, Doris, but I am more fond of Miss Berkeley than of anyone I have ever known—except Phyllis.'" He paused, then explained defiantly: "I admit that I used a melodramatic, trite expression, but I did so because the sentiment was real and the words would appeal to Doris. And I believed Doris did not dare repeat them, lest somehow they come back to my future wife, and cause her pain. She told me then that she too was fond of Clorinda, and could understand. That was all, except that I asked her to wait a moment while I took those earrings from my wallet, where I have carried them since my wife's death."

"Carried them in your wallet, eh? Why?" Strawn prodded skeptically.

"Because Phyllis was wearing them the night she— died, and because they were the last gift of any importance I had made her. I gave them to Doris as an engagement present, and because I knew that Phyllis would have liked her to have them."

"And I say you gave them to her because Doris Matthews had made up her mind to expose you to the Berkeleys, partly because she was fond of Clorinda Berkeley, and partly because she wanted to make you suffer for your wife's murder!" Strawn told him sternly. "In you panic you promised her anything, everything, to bribe her to silence. The earrings would serve to hold her temporarily, but you were taking no chances. You made an appointment with her to meet her in the summer house, when the house was quiet for the night—"

"That is not true!" Crosby flashed. "I did not leave my room again last night, and you cannot possibly have any proof that I did so!"

"Yeah?" Strawn grinned, as if nursing secret knowledge.

But Dundee knew his chief had nothing more up his sleeve. During the lull the younger detective became aware that some forgotten fact was tapping at his memory. Suddenly he had it, and his tilted chair crashed to the floor as he asked"

"Mr. Crosby, was this conversation between you and Doris overheard by anyone at all?"

"Overheard?" Crosby puzzled. "Why, no, I don't think so. We spoke in low tones or whispers. Gigi passed us, but I can't think she overheard anything—"

"Where was the valet Mrs. Berkeley had hired especially for you?" Dundee asked tensely.

"Valet?" both Strawn and Crosby repeated blankly.

Then Crosby's somber eyes flashed with sudden comprehension. "By Jove, Dundee! In all the excitement I had completely forgotten about Johnson! The fact is, he was not on duty when I returned to my room last night— *and I have not seen him since!*"

"What's all this?" Strawn sputtered. "Who the devil is Johnson?"

Dundee explained: "Last night, when Mrs. Berkeley greeted Mr. Crosby, as he appeared in the drawing room before dinner, she hoped Mr. Crosby had not found Johnson 'too fearful' a valet, and remarked that he was the best she could do locally. She explained that Mr. Berkeley would not have a 'man' for himself—"

"Well, where is this bird now?" Strawn interrupted disgustedly.

"He unpacked my bags when I arrived yesterday afternoon," Crosby offered, "and helped me dress for dinner. There was nothing said about his waiting up for me, but I took it for granted that he would. However, when I went upstairs .about eleven last night he was not there, though my things had been laid out for the night. I have not seen him since."

"Is anything missing, Mr. Crosby?" Dundee asked.

"I can't say, since I have not taken the slightest interest in my own belongings since—since I went down for the swim this morning," Crosby answered. "I found my bathing suit hanging in the closet. . . ."

"Then we'd better, have a look around," Strawn decided abruptly, stuffing Doris's letter and the earrings into his coat pocket.

The three men left the dead girl's room, Strawn taking time however to lock the door and pocket the key, and descended to the second floor, which was being patrolled by a plainclothesman.

Seymour Crosby's room was a very large and very impressive chamber, with private bath and commodious dressing room.

"Did you have anything of value, Crosby?" Strawn asked, as the Berkeley guest plunged into the dressing room.

"My money was in my wallet, along with the earrings," Crosby replied. "This morning I transferred the wallet from my dinner clothes to the lounge suit I am wearing, now. . . Good Lord! My smallest bag is missing!" he ejaculated.

Within another five minutes he was enumerating his losses, while Dundee listed them on the almost exhausted sheaf of notepaper which had served him as a notebook since the investigation began:

"A pearl ring, which I had brought as a gift for Miss Berkeley; a necklace of seed pearls, intended for Gigi; a silver cigarette lighter, for Mrs. Lambert; a tooled leather billfold for Wickett, containing a new $50 gold certificate, and—a miniature of my wife, Phyllis, painted on ivory by a famous Parisian miniature painter."

Crosby's voice broke on the last words, and Dundee believed that he would willingly have sacrificed far more than he had lost, if the miniature could have been returned. . .

"Is that all, Crosby?" Strawn snapped. Then to Dundee: "Come along! We'll see if Mrs. Berkeley's jewels have been stolen, too!"

They left Crosby in his room, collapsed in a huge armchair, but whether from relief or weariness it was hard to say.

The detective who had been stationed in Mrs. Berkeley's foyer tried to report as his chief charged in, but Strawn brushed him aside and flung open the bedroom door, without knocking.

"Well! I must say—!" Mrs. Berkeley, still reclining on her *chaise longue*, began indignantly. She was alone.

"Sorry, lady!" Strawn cut her short impatiently. "Got a safe in you rooms?"

"A safe? For my jewels, you mean? . . . Certainly! It's hidden behind that Watteau painting. I thought of that all by myself—"

"Yeah? Well, can you open it?" Strawn demanded curtly. "Do it, then!"

"Why? Ooh! Do you think—?" Mrs. Berkeley bounded clumsily from the *chaise longue* and scurried to where the painting hung. "I told you this morning I bet Doris had stolen my jewels, too, and you didn't pay the slightest attention to me— Oh! Oh! Oh, my God! George!" she shrieked.

XVIII.

"HELLO! Sergeant Turner? Captain Strawn speaking. Listen now and get this straight: the Berkeley house was robbed before the murder last night. Yeah, looks like the same bird did both jobs. Now, take this down: Valet, giving name of Harvey Johnson, hired Friday through Hamilton Domestic Employment Bureau for work at Berkeley s home, Hillcrest. Description: About five feet ten inches tall, weight about 150; age, near 30; hair, light brown, rather thin, parted on left side; eyes brown or dark gray; features regular, strictly American type; considered handsome; fine, large white teeth, cleft chin. Wait a minute . . . Anything else, Dundee?"

The younger detective, seated opposite his chief at George Berkeley's desk in the library, consulted his notes. before replying:

'Was wearing dark blue serge suit, navy blue silk bow-tie with white polka dots, and white shirt with blue pin stripe. May be wearing pair of crepe-soled tennis shoes, size 8, missing from Crosby's effects."

Strawn repeated the information to Sergeant Turner at Police Headquarters as Dundee gave it to him, then added:

"Carried loot away in black pigskin bag of Gladstone shape. Bag was not initialed. Now here's what he took, Turner. Ready? . . . Necklace of matched pearls—49 of 'em—worth $35,000; diamond and platinum clasp. Necklace of seed pearls, worth about $50; pearl ring—large pink pearl, black enamel setting, worth $1200; five other rings—"

As Strawn's heavy voice ploughed on through the list of stolen articles, Dundee's attention wandered. A hundred thoughts flashed through his mind like minnows darting about a pool. And as be let his thoughts play he frowned, tapping his pencil thoughtfully upon the sheaf of notes he had made during the investigation which seemed to be practically over now.

When the long list was ended, Dundee heard his chief bark into the receiver: "Hop to it, Turner! Draw up a 'Wanted' placard, and rush it to the city printer. But first put every available man on the job to check railroad stations, hotels and every other likely place for a trace of the man. . . . Yeah, I'll be down in about fifteen minutes, but I wanted to start the ball a-rolling. Sure, I'll have his description broadcast over the radio every hour till he's caught. . . . By, the way, Turner, send somebody over to the employment bureau a get hold of his registration card. Best way to get his handwriting and fingerprints. O. K. Don't waste any time! Give the newspaper boys all you've got."

He was about to hang up when the officer at the other end of the wire detained him

"What's that?" Strawn snapped. "Oh—Maxwell! On his way here now, you say? Well, I'll give him ten minutes. He may have seen this bird Johnson leaving the grounds."

He hung up, wiped the perspiration from his heavy face and turned to Dundee.

"They've rounded up John Maxwell. Guess he'll clinch Clorinda Berkeley's alibi, all right, even if she did want to keep his name out of it . . . Heigh-ho! Pretty swift work, I'd say! Body discovered at seven-fifteen. Murderer's description in the noon editions of newspapers."

You feel sure the case is solved?" Dundee asked.

"In the bag!" Strawn exulted. "Why, lookee! Every single fact we had—outside of the old Crosby case, of course—clicks right into place! Even that pesky flask of perfume that we had such a devil of a time getting into the summerhouse. Here's how I see it now:

"This bird Johnson is a big-time crook, from the East probably, where it got too hot for him. He reads in the Hamilton papers that there's going to be big doings at the

Berkeley place, and registers with the employment bureau as a valet. Probably had a bunch of faked references and has used them before—plenty! As a matter of fact, I think he followed the Berkeleys out here from New York, after reading in the papers there how Mrs. Berkeley tried to smuggle in that rope of pearls and got caught by the customs.

"At any rate, the way he burgled that safe of the old dame's shows he was no amateur. As neat a job of safe cracking as I ever saw. Didn't leave a trace of a fingerprint, according to Carraway, either on the safe or in Crosby's room."

"Conceding that he stole the flask of perfume," Dundee interrupted, "we can definitely place the time of the robbery between half-past ten and a quarter to eleven. For it was half-past ten or thereabouts when Wickett took the perfume up to Mrs. Berkeley's bathroom, and about a quarter to eleven when Doris went to her mistress's bedroom to lay out her things for the night."

"And another fact clicks into place!" Strawn cut in triumphantly. "Doris caught him in the bathroom and *he* pushed her against the mirror—"

"Two objections to that conclusion, chief!" Dundee retorted. "In the first place, Doris was not wearing lipstick then. We have Clorinda Berkeley's word for that, and no reason to doubt it. In the second place, if Doris Matthews had caught a burglar at work in Mrs. Berkeley's rooms, she'd have given the alarm. Nothing will make me believe that girl was a crook, or even a potential crook."

"All right, then!" Strawn conceded. "Granted that Johnson did his job between half-past ten and a quarter to eleven. He stole the perfume and with the rest of the stuff in the Gladstone bag, he sneaked out of the house, while Wickett was busy in his pantry or in the drawing room, and was about to beat it when he saw the chauffeur, Arnold, bring the car around. We've got

Wickett's word for it that Johnson seemed to be badly smitten by Doris's beauty, while the servants were at their dinner last night."

"And that Doris turned a cold shoulder to him," Dundee reminded his chief.

"I believe you fell for the girl yourself," Strawn gibed good-naturedly. "Well, at any rate, Johnson, as well as the other servants, heard Doris and Arnold plan to meet at the summerhouse when the girl could get away. All right! He sees Arnold collect the Benjamin Smiths and drive off with them. It occurs to him that Doris may not know her sweetie can't meet her. He likes the girl's looks, wouldn't object to having a petting party—"

"Maybe!" Dundee cut in, frowning. "But if I had been Johnson, my first thought would have been a getaway, not a petting party with a girl I might not even be able to 'make.'"

"But what if Johnson didn't manage to sneak out of the house until just after or just before Clorinda did?" Strawn argued. "Either way he would have seen her before he could beat it, if she was on her way to the estate gates to meet John Maxwell, as I'd bet she was. Johnson would have run for cover, to the summerhouse, most likely, and was still hiding there, waiting for Clorinda to return to the house, when Doris, not knowing Arnold couldn't meet her, arrived and discovered him. She suspected what he was up to—stumbled upon the Gladstone bag full of loot, probably; started to run for the house to give the alarm. Johnson remembers the heavy flask of perfume in his bag, opens it in a flash—"

"And what is Doris doing all that time?" Dundee interrupted skeptically.

"Johnson's got her by the wrist," Strawn explained with satisfaction. "With his other hand he gets the bag open, gets out the flask and crocks her over the head with it."

"But he has no third hand with which to cover her mouth so she can't scream," Dundee objected.

"Hell! I wasn't there! I didn't see it happen, but we know damned well it did, and as far as I'm concerned, I'm satisfied!"

"Do you think he would go to as much trouble as he did to hide the body?"

"Sure! He knew Clorinda was walking about the grounds and might decide any minute to take a rest in the summerhouse. If she found the body, she'd give the alarm before Johnson had time to make his getaway. With the murder concealed, he could count on having till morning—"

"With the robbery likely to be discovered any minute, and the alarm given?" Dundee interrupted again.

"Well, Johnson looted the house and killed the girl! It's not up to me to go into his reasons for every step he took!" Strawn almost shouted in his anger. "Trouble with you is, this didn't turn out to be a fancy murder mystery and you're disappointed. Me—I take my crime neat, and glad to have it without trimmings. . . . Where the devil is Maxwell, anyway? I've got to get down to Headquarters." A knock at the door made him break off short, then shout: "Come in!"

"Peggy Harper, one of the maids, wants to speak to you, sir," Detective Payne announced, and withdrew as the girl sidled into the library.

"Well, Peggy, what's on your mind?" Strawn asked patiently.

"It's just something I thought maybe you ought to know," Peggy blurted. "Last night, at dinner, I happened to be looking at Doris when Wickett introduce Johnson all around, and I noticed that she acted some like she recognized him."

"Well?" Strawn snapped.

"After we'd finished dinner, there was just me and Doris in the sitting room for a while, and I said, 'Did you know Mr. Johnson before, Doris?' and she wrinkle up her forehead and said, 'I've been trying to place him. I know I've either seen him or his picture somewhere before, but

I simply can't remember where.' . . . And then I said, 'He sure is good-looking, ain't he? Look more like a gentleman than a valet, don't he?' And that's all, sir. I thought maybe—"

It was Dundee who asked the next question "Did Johnson act as if he recognized Doris?"

"I wasn't looking at him; I was looking at Doris; because of the funny expression on her face. But when I did look at him, he was saying something to Della and then when he was introduced to Doris, he didn't let on at all, if he did recognize her. But he didn't hardly look at anybody else all during dinner."

"All right, Peggy. Thanks!" Strawn dismissed her. When he and Dundee were alone again he rose, stretched and said, "Guess that clinches it, eh? The crook tumbles that the girl is wise to him, or he thinks she is. He planned to stay on here till the big doings to-night and make a clean-up, but the girl is something he hasn't counted on. So he does his job and then has the bad luck to run upon Doris in the summerhouse. Well, I'll be getting on to Headquarters. Hang around here till Maxwell comes, get what you can out of him, and then come on in after lunch. Nothing more to do here."

"Have you forgotten I'm taking the week-end off?" Dundee grinned. "I'm staying on till Monday, if you don't mind. . . . And say, chief, I wish you would have one of the boys get my parrot from the Rhodes House and send him to me. I'd rather like to have a session with my 'Watson.'"

For one uncomfortable minute Dundee was afraid his chief would turn nasty. But Captain Strawn contented himself with saying:

"Reminding me that you're the Police Commissioner's nephew, and therefore a privileged character, eh? All right! Have a good time with your society friends. And a nice litter o' kittens *they* turned out to be, even if Johnson is our bird!"

"I shan't be entirely idle," Dundee assured him cheerfully. "I'll ask Mrs. Lambert to lend me her

typewriter, and transcribe this bunch of notes I've taken.
. . . By the way, chief, since you're satisfied that Johnson
solves everything, there won't be any need of airing the
Berkeley family troubles in the newspapers, I suppose?"

"No—and you can bet that takes a load off my mind,"
Strawn grunted. "Lucky for me I soft-pedaled the whole
thing when the reporters mobbed me a couple of hours
ago! These multi-millionaires and society swells—Well,
I'm so grateful to Johnson for being the guy that croaked
the girl instead of Clorinda or Dick Berkeley that I'd
almost be willing to ask the grand jury to return a vote of
thanks, instead of an indictment.. . . So long, boy! You
know where to reach me if anything turns up, though it
won't. I'm taking all the boys back with me. We'll need
'em all for tracking down that crook."

Five minutes after his chief's departure, Dundee, who
was still frowning over his shorthand notes, was
interrupted by a gay tattoo upon the library door.

He chuckled, then called confidently: "Come in, Gigi!"

She flung herself into the room and upon the arm of
his chair, rumpling his crisp black hair ecstatically. "How
did you know it was me? Isn't it swell? Isn't it a gr-rand
and glorious feeling, when you've been saying *'Eenie,
meenie, minie, moe'* to find out which of your beloved
family or friends committed murder, to have it turn out to
be a common old burglar after, all?"

"Swell!" Dundee agreed, and retaliated by rumpling
her own short brown curls. "But how did the *'eenie,
meenie'* come out?"

"Wickett once, and me twice!' she laughed. "I was just
going to give myself up when Johnson was elected. Of
course, Abbie is having a grand time throwing hysterics
over her 'poils' and moaning that Doris was a heroine,
after all. . . . And she was, too, wasn't she?" she added
wistfully.

"I think she was," Dundee replied soberly.

"I'm afraid the rest of your week end is going to be
awfully dull", Gigi mourned. "How about tennis after

lunch? Oh, yes! I meant to tell you first of all that Abbie absolutely insists on your staying. You're her '*dear* Mr. Dundee' again. She thinks you're awfully, clever and *such* a gentleman."

"I want to stay, but I've got a couple of hours' work to do after lunch, honey-child," he answered regretfully. "Got to transcribe my notes, you know—"

"Better tear em up!" Gigi advised, and to his amazement she was in deadly earnest for the moment.

Before he could think of a reply, however, another knock at the door interrupted.

"Yes, Wickett?"

"Mr. John Maxwell, sir."

"Show him in, Wickett darling!" Gigi ordered. "And I'm going to stay, my bonnie lad!" she added emphatically to Dundee. "Oh, hello, Johnny Maxwell! Whoops! How you've grown!"

The detective felt a twinge of jealousy as the tall, broad-shouldered young man swung Gigi off her feet and kissed her soundly, to her evident relish.

"Brat," he apostrophized her, "you're a wow! Cuter'n a Scotch terrier!"

"Go on! Say it! If you weren't already wild over Clo, you'd give me a whirl! Lord, I'll be glad when that sister of mine gets married, so I can have a chance. 'Scuse it, please! This is Bonnie Dundee, Johnny —a detective! And if the police hadn't already picked out their criminal, you'd be in for the neatest third degree—"

"Have you really caught the murderer, Mr. Dundee?" Maxwell asked eagerly, relief lighting up his good-looking face.

"They haven't caught him, Johnny, but they know who he is," Gigi answered before Dundee could speak. "Oh, things have been happening at jolly old Hillcrest, let me tell you! Abbie hires a valet, to swank before Mr. Crosby, and Johnson—that's the valet's name—turns out to be a burglar and a murderer."

"Good Lord!" John. Maxwell ejaculated. "Of, course I saw the extras—"

"The point is, Mr. Maxwell," Dundee cut in quietly, "did you see this man Johnson on the grounds when you were here last night?"

Maxwell made no attempt to deny the truth which Dundee had guessed at. "No. I saw no one but Clorinda last night. I was afraid the poor girl might be having a rocky time of it with the police, when I saw by the papers that she was being 'quizzed.'"

"Then why didn't you barge right over?" Gigi demanded indignantly.

"Because I didn't see a paper until about twenty minutes ago," Maxwell answered. "After I left Clorinda last night I took the interurban to Mercyville, to see my uncle—"

"The old boy who struck oil on his farm?" Gigi demanded excitedly.

"The same," Maxwell grinned. "I put my pride in my pocket and asked him if he'd lend me enough money to set myself up in law practice, instead of taking a job as assistant district attorney at $3,000 a year. His answer was yes, obtained at half-past eleven this morning. When I stepped out of the downtown interurban station twenty minutes ago a cop told me I was wanted and showed me a paper with the news in it."

"And that's that!" Gigi cried. "So you can marry Clo and live happy ever after! I'll begin right now by giving the bride away. She has a rotten disposition before breakfast, is beatable by lunch, and an angel by dinner-time. She—"

"Shut up, Pest!" Dundee commanded. "Now, Mr. Maxwell, will you tell me exactly what happened last night, so far as you know?"

"Certainly!" Maxwell agreed eagerly, his gray eyes very friendly. "But I must go back a bit. I've been away for more than year, and before I left Clorinda and I had a—well; a tiff. We had been secretly engaged, and while we didn't actually break it off, the coolness continued in her letters until the letters themselves stopped, about six months ago. She was abroad with her mother by that time, and I wasn't much surprised but pretty badly knocked out when I got to town yesterday and read what the society columns had to say about Seymour Crosby and the party that was scheduled for tonight. But I took a chance on calling her up just before seven last night, and she agreed to meet me at the gates as soon as she could get away."

"And that was when?" Dundee prompted, as the young lawyer paused.

"About eleven fifteen. I was at the gates at eleven. We walked about the grounds, keeping as far away from the house as possible, for about an hour. It must have been a few minutes past twelve when I left the estate, for I caught the interurban at the nearest station at twelve eight."

"Oh!" Gigi said thoughtfully, disappointedly, and was about to say more when Dundee silenced her with a stern glance.

"Did you go to the summerhouse with Miss Berkeley?" he asked.

"To the summerhouse? Why, no!" Maxwell answered, surprised. "Our idea was to keep as far away from the house as possible. At Clorinda's request I left her sitting on a stone bench near the south wall, and struck out for the gates. She said she was going to walk around the lake to get back to the house, and protested she was not a bit afraid to go alone."

"I see," said Dundee thoughtfully. Then, "You are positive you saw no one at all during your walk or as you were leaving the grounds alone?"

"No one at all, until I was passing through the gates," Maxwell answered positively. "And I did not actually see anyone then. Just the Berkeley limousine. It was turning in toward the gates as I passed through them. I was running to make the interurban. I'd heard the whistle before I reached the gates, and thought I'd have time to get to the next station before the trolley did."

"Oh, well! What does it matter now?" Gigi challenged Dundee. "You've got your murderer—or at least you know who he is. You see, Johnny, Captain Strawn bullied poor Clo into admitting she'd been in the summerhouse, after he found a streak of blood on her cape and perfume on the soles of her shoes. Clo got there after poor Doris had been killed and rolled down the summerhouse steps into the lake. She thought Abbie had dashed out of the house, looking for her, with the perfume flask in her hand, and had broken the bottle. Captain Strawn got all het up and tried to make Clo confess she'd killed Doris, or had seen Abbie do it."

"What rot!" Maxwell was pardonably indignant and contemptuous. "Where is Clo now?"

"In Abbie's sitting room, with Mrs. Lambert. Dash on up! Abbie's busy having hysterics and will hardly notice you, even if she wanders in. . . . You did get engaged good and tight this time, didn't you?"

"Absolutely!" Maxwell exulted. "Was that all, Mr. Dundee?"

When he had gone, scarcely waiting for official permission, Gigi returned to the broad arm of Dundee's chair and leaned against his shoulder, sighing happily.

"All's swell that ends swell," she rejoiced. "Though I suppose Johnson will say he did it all for his aged mother, and wring my heart! . . . Say, why don't you smile, old Wet Blanket? Does it take all the joy out of your life for a case to be solved?"

"No," Dundee answered seriously; then he forced himself to smile.

"There! That's my Bonnie!" Gigi praised him tenderly. "You *are* the handsomest thing, with your 'smiling Irish eyes' and your crisp black hair. Believe I'll set the wave in it; Doris taught me how—

"Let my hair alone, Hellion!" he roared, then flushed as he looked up and saw Wickett's solemn face in the opening door.

"Luncheon is served, Miss Gigi."

"Attaboy, Wickett!" Gigi cried, springing from the arm of the chair and dragging at Dundee's hand. "I shouldn't admit it, but I'm starved."

In the hall they found Mrs. Lambert descending the stairs. At sight of the evident chumminess of the child and the detective, a faint, whimsical smile lightened the melancholy which had made her delicate and still beautiful face seem years older. Then she made a sudden decision:

"Mr. Dundee, may I speak with you after lunch—about—Doris?"

XIX.

GIGI was the only one who attacked the delicious meal with any enthusiasm. Dundee wondered, with some embarrassment, if it was his presence which prevented the relief the whole party must have been feeling from expressing itself more exuberantly.

"No, no, Wickett! Take it away! The very sight of food makes me ill!" Mrs. Berkeley protested, as the butler bent over her with a vegetable dish. "But do eat—all of you! . . . My beautiful, beautiful pearls! And my pigeon-blood ruby! If I could only get my hands on that vile man—and he seemed such a gentleman, too! I mean, for a valet—"

"Can't we talk of something else, Abbie," George Berkeley interrupted coldly. "Your jewels were insured They can be replaced—"

"But Doris can't!" Mrs. Berkeley wailed, dabbing at her eyes "Do you think you can get me another maid just as good, dear Mrs. Lambert?"

"I'm afraid not," Mrs. Lambert said coldly.

"Don't, Mother, for God's sake!" Dick Berkeley groaned, then, without excusing himself, he kicked back his chair and, bolted from the dining room.

"When I think the poor little darling died trying to defend my jewels from that wretched—" Mrs Berkeley went on, her voice quivering.

"You wish you hadn't slapped her, don't you?" Gigi cut in cruelly.

"George, are you going to let that child talk to me like that? Oh, sharper than a serpent's tooth—"

"Sorry, Abbie," Gigi apologized curtly, her topaz eyes blazing. "It's just that I can't *bear*—"

"That will do, Gigi!" Mr. Berkeley commanded sternly.

Throughout the meal Clorinda Berkeley and Seymour Crosby spoke not at all, except for murmured acknowledgments of Wickett's services. But Clorinda's silence was the stillness of deep happiness and peace—or so it seemed to Dundee. Her magnificent dark eyes were softly radiant, and an unsuspected gentleness and sweetness hovered over the beautiful mouth that had been so arrogant.

Crosby was silent out of weariness and profound depression—a silence which not even his exquisite courtesy could goad him to break.

Mrs.. Lambert dutifully sympathized with Mrs. Berkeley in her broken, semi-hysterical complaints against Johnson, the fact that the big party could not take place, and the unfairness of life in general. But only her lips sympathized, consoled, reasoned. Her blue-gray eyes, looking abnormally large now because of the purplish shadows, were infinitely remote, infinitely weary. But twice, when Mrs. Berkeley mentioned Doris s name, Mrs. Lambert glanced upward at Wickett, and each time their eyes held. And Dundee knew that, for a moment, butler and former mistress communed silently and sorrowfully as two friends who had loved a girl who was dead. And he treasured their grief jealously, wished he could catch the tears they would shed in private, bottle them in a priceless flask, and with them anoint the poor broken head. Sweeter, rarer than the perfume which her murderer had spilled upon her golden hair—

That was the Irish in him. The Scotch watched cannily for any tiny clue that might betray her murderer, if indeed he—or she—was in that room. A word, a facial expression; the hypocritical overstressing of a note of grief. . . .

But there was nothing, or if there was, he couldn't detect it. And he was glad when, the dessert served but not eaten, except by greedy Gigi, Mrs. Berkeley rose.

"I suppose," she sighed, "we must all try to get back to normal. Of course everything is at sixes and sevens. and I have so much to do I hardly know where to begin. Gigi, will you play tennis with dear Mr. Dundee or take him over the Country Club for golf? And Clorinda, darling, you must do your best to cheer poor, dear Mr. Crosby. I know this has been a sad blow to him, since it means the postponement of the announcement party—"

"Mother, please!" Clorinda interrupted. "I have already told you that Mr. Crosby and I have released each other from the engagement."

"Nonsense! But I haven't time to argue with you now," Mrs. Berkeley retorted. "Shall we go up and plunge into our tasks now, dear Mrs. Lambert?"

"Dear Mrs. Lambert" glanced uncertainly at Dundee and the detective answered for her:

"If you'll forgive me, Mrs. Berkeley, I'm going to borrow Mrs. Lambert for a few minutes."

"Oh!" Mrs. Berkeley looked startled, then indignant. "You mean you want to question her? I thought all the miserable third-degree business was over, since the police know who killed Doris."

"Won't you use the library, Mr. Dundee?" Mr. Berkeley suggested courteously. "I'm going to have a game of golf myself—if the police will permit me to leave the grounds."

Dundee flushed. He knew very well that Captain Strawn had no intention of keeping the Berkeley family or their guests under the slightest restraint, so he was lying, for purposes of his own, when he said:

"I believe Captain Strawn would like for all of us to be within instant reach. That is one reason why I am presuming upon your hospitality."

"I see!" George Berkeley agreed curtly. "How long do you think our liberty will be curtailed?"

"Probably only a day or two," Dundee answered uncomfortably. "Johnson may be caught any minute, you know. If he confesses or if any direct evidence of his having committed the murder is found—"

"What if he proves it wasn't him?" Gigi demanded. "Captain Strawn says Doris was—was murdered between half-past eleven and twelve o'clock. What if Johnson could prove he left here before then?"

"That is why I am not permitted to play golf this afternoon, Miss Sherlock Holmes!" her father answered for Dundee, a smile twitching at his stern mouth. "Use the library anyway, Dundee."

When Mrs. Lambert, slim and immaculate in the powder-blue sweater and pleated cream-colored flannel skirt of the tennis costume she had been wearing all morning, took her seat in one of the big leather armchairs in the library, Gigi snatched up an ottoman, planted it at the social secretary's feet and flopped down upon it.

"And I've always been told that adolescents were abnormally sensitive," Dundee grinned down at her. "Do you ever wait for an invitation, Miss Georgina Berkeley?"

"Never—if I think I shan't get it," she retorted cheerfully, pillowing her head comfortably against Mrs. Lambert's knees.

"Let her stay," Mrs. Lambert begged, laying a tender hand on the bright brown curls. "Gigi loved Doris too."

"You were very fond of Doris, Mrs. Lambert?" Dundee seized the opening.

"I loved her," Mrs. Lambert answered simply.

"How long had you know her?"

He was not making notes, for he wanted his "witness" to talk with the utmost freedom. Strawn had asked her two or three hurried questions after the discovery of Johnson's flight with the stolen valuables, but there had been no time then to go into past history.

"Since August, 1927, when I first met Phyllis Benham, who was Doris's mistress then," Mrs. Lambert answered. "The two girls were more like chums than mistress and lady's maid. I believe Doris had been with Phyllis about three years before Phyllis's marriage to Mr. Crosby. They were about the same age—twenty-two then, I think. I was instantly attracted to Doris, partly because of her sweetness and beauty, but largely because of her loyalty and devotion to Phyllis. And that, Mr. Dundee, is why I asked to speak to you."

"Yes?" Dundee prompted, when she paused because her voice broke.

"Oh, don't you see?" she cried, almost passionately. "Doris was not 'just a maid,' just an ordinary servant, if there is such a thing! She was a lovely girl, a beloved girl, a loyal friend. These truths about Doris must be recognized by you—by the police—when you are trying to solve her murder."

"The police think her murder is solved," Dundee reminded her gently.

"I know, but—"

"But *you* don't think so, Mrs. Lambert?" Dundee took her up eagerly.

"I—don't know," she confessed in a low, troubled voice. "I suppose Johnson, the valet, is guilty. But I've been afraid all sorts of insinuations might be made against Doris by the papers. Your Captain Strawn himself asked me if I had 'missed' anything since Doris has been here, and whether Phyllis Crosby had ever been robbed."

"That was because Doris seemed to recognize Johnson when they met at the servants' dinner table last night," Dundee explained. "The police naturally look for a confederate on the inside, as a matter of routine."

"You say Doris seemed to recognized Johnson?" Mrs. Lambert repeated, brushing aside his last words in her intense surprise.

"So Peggy Harper says. Doris did not say anything to you about having seen Johnson before?"

"Oh, no! If she had, I should have thought, naturally, that Johnson had been employed in New York or London, and, that Doris had seen him at the home of one of Phyllis's hostesses."

"That probably accounts for it," Dundee agreed. "did you see Johnson yourself, Mrs. Lambert?"

"Yes. It was I who engaged him," she answered readily. "His references were excellent, and his appearance good. In fact, as Mrs. Berkeley remarked at lunch, the man seemed to be almost a gentleman, in the narrow social sense of the word."

"With a gentleman's appreciation of art," Dundee said dryly. "One of the things he stole from Mr. Crosby was an ivory miniature of Phyllis Crosby. Something he could not sell—"

"A—miniature—of Phyllis?" Mrs. Lambert repeated, in a whisper.

She leaned weakly against the back of her chair, and the pupils of her blue-gray eyes dilated to an enormous size.

"Please tell me frankly what you are thinking, Mrs. Lambert," Dundee urged gently.

The social secretary got control of herself with an obvious effort. She even managed to smile slightly "You startled me," she confessed. "I know how Seymour—Mr. Crosby—treasured that miniature of Phyllis. It is an exquisite thing, a remarkable likeness of one of the most beautiful girls I ever saw. But as you said, it is a thing a burglar could not sell, without betraying himself. It seemed absurd, incongruous, to me that a burglar should steal it."

"To me, too," Dundee assured her quietly. "But, please, Mrs. Lambert. . . ."

"I know!" Gigi interrupted, striking her small brown hands together. "Everyone says Johnson looked like a gentleman, and I'm here to tell you he had S. A. plus—in a deadly, quiet sort of way, if you know, what I mean. Now, lookee! Doris halfway recognized him. Doris was Phyllis Crosby's maid. Johnson, or whatever his real name is, steals a miniature of Phyllis, which he can't sell, and which, therefore, *he wants for its own sake!* I'll bet my new golf clubs it was Johnson's showing up here as a servant that threw Doris off the track, so she couldn't remember where she'd seen him before—"

"Hush, Gigi! You're being ridiculous!" Mrs. Lambert commanded sternly, but Dundee saw that her face had gone ghastly pale.

"I'm not either being ridiculous!" Gigi protested. "I heard Dad and Abbie rowing about Mr. Crosby last night before dinner, and Dad said he was a wife-killer. Then this morning I asked Wickett how Mrs. Crosby died, and he said she committed suicide in London by jumping off a roof. He said Doris saw her do it, and that Mr. Crosby absolutely did not throw his wife over the railing, or push her, or anything like that. Now, *I* think this Johnson crook is back of it all! Don't you see! He—"

'Gigi, you *must* stop!" Mrs Lambert cried despairingly.

"If you don't mind too much, Mrs. Lambert, I'd rather hear Gigi's theory," Dundee interposed quietly but firmly.

'Wouldn't I make a swell detective, Bonnie Dundee?" Gigi exulted. "Well, this is the way I dope it out: Johnson was a 'gentleman crook,' playing the nightclubs in New York, or something like that. He meets Phyllis Crosby, or Phyllis Benham as she was then. She falls for him hard, doesn't dream he's a crook. They have a hectic love affair, and poor little Doris catches a glimpse of him—just once, maybe, because Phyllis is meeting him secretly. Then somehow she finds out he's a crook and ditches him, and he's sore, of course. Pretty soon she marries Mr. Crosby and Johnson keeps bobbing up to blackmail her. Probably he had letters or something proving they had been lovers—"

"Please make her stop, Mr. Dundee!" Mrs. Lambert implored. "She can't realize what she's saying. I was Phyllis Crosby's best friend—"

"That's enough, Gigi," Dundee agreed, but his smile at the excited girl had admiration and respect in it. Turning to Mrs. Lambert he asked gently: "Were you in Mrs. Crosby's confidence, Mrs. Lambert?"

"I was. We were devoted friends, in spite of the difference in our ages," Mrs. Lambert replied, her pale lips trembling.

"You were visiting her at the time of her death?"

"Yes. Seymour wrote me—I was at Biarritz—-that Phyllis was not well, and inclined to be morbid and hysterical."

"I bet she was going to have a baby!" Gigi cut in excitedly.

Mrs. Lambert flushed. "She was. I believed then and I still believe that her morbidness and her—her suicide were due to her condition. At Seymour's request, I went to London to stay with Phyllis as long as she needed me."

"Did she tell you why she was unhappy, Mrs. Lambert?" Dundee asked.

"I—I must refuse to answer."

Dundee and Gigi exchanged a significant glance, Gigi hugging her knees and shivering with excitement.

"Did she confide to you, Mrs. Lambert," Dundee persisted, "that she was being blackmailed?"

"She certainly did not!" the social secretary retort emphatically.

It was Gigi from whom the next question burst irrepressibly: "Was she sorry she was going to have baby, Tish?"

The flush deepened to scarlet. "You are becoming impossible, Gigi!"

"Now you're talking like Abbie, Tish darling," Gigi reproached her sadly. But she brightened as she added: "I bet I've hit on the truth!"

"Phyllis was very young, and her—her condition curtailed her honeymoon so much sooner than she had expected," Mrs. Lambert said stiffly. "Then, too, she was rather more ill than is usual, I believe. I have"—she caught her breath sharply, and her hand, again resting on Gigi's head, trembled noticeably—"I have never had a child; but it seemed to me that Phyllis suffered more physically and psychically, than most expectant mothers.

It seems to me only natural that; under the circumstances, she resented her condition."

"I see," Dundee agreed, very thoughtfully. "Now Mrs. Lambert, what was Doris's attitude toward her mistress at this time? I mean, was Doris obviously worried?"

Mrs. Lambert considered for a moment, her tired eyes closed. Then: "Yes, I think she was. She was even more tender and devoted than usual, I believe. The two girls spent a great deal of time together. Doris was with Phyllis even more than I was, Doris serving then more in the capacity of nurse than as lady's maid."

"It is quite possible then that Doris was wholly in Mrs. Crosby's confidence?" Dundee persisted.

"Quite possible, of course," Mrs. Lambert agreed stiffly, "though I feel sure there was nothing to confide."

"Mrs. Lambert, forgive me for what must seem like idle curiosity to you, but—would you say Mr. and Mrs. Crosby were happily married? That they loved each other?"

"Yes! With all my heart—yes! Seymour loved Phyllis deeply and truly and tenderly, and Phyllis adored her husband."

"And yet—Phyllis Crosby committed suicide, Dundee reminded her.

"I know!" Mrs Lambert sank back wearily again.

"She was temporarily insane. That is the only possible explanation."

"Will you please tell me all you can remember of Phyllis Crosby's last evening?"

"Mr. Dundee, I have been patient under this—this ordeal; I have tried to answer your questions as if you had a right to ask them, but I must protest—"

"Because you feel sure there is no connection between Doris's murder and Phyllis Crosby's suicide?" Dundee suggested quietly. "Please bear with me, Mrs. Lambert, for I honestly believe there *is* a connection, and that it is our duty to Doris—and to Phyllis Crosby—to bring that missing link to light."

Mrs. Lambert was silent for a long minute, her eyes closed, her trembling lower lip caught between her teeth. Impulsively, Gigi scrambled from the ottoman into the white-haired woman's lap and laid her head confidently, like a child, against her breast. Mrs. Lambert hesitated for a moment, then her arms went convulsively about the small body.

Her eyes were misty with tears when she lifted them to Dundee, and began to talk in a low, unsteady voice: "At dinner that Sunday evening—it was the sixth of May—Phyllis seemed more ill and hysterical than usual. She ate nothing, and finally went to her room, locking the door. Doris was with her, and I felt it would be useless to intrude until the poor child felt better. Seymour and I talked and read in the drawing room. He asked me again if I knew of any reason for Phyllis's unhappiness, if he had unconsciously hurt her in any way. I reassured him, and he spoke of how glad he would be when the child was born and Phyllis was her own happy self again."

"Was Mr. Crosby reading a book of poems?" Dundee interrupted.

"Why, no! He was reading a novel, or rather, trying to read. About ten o'clock I excused myself to go to bed, and on my way to my room I knocked at Phyllis's door to bid her good night. Doris answered, saying Phyllis was not there, that she thought she was in the drawing room with Mr. Crosby and me. I became slightly alarmed, then remembered that Phyllis was fond of walking on the roof of the apartment hotel where they lived. And there I found her."

"Alone?" Dundee asked quickly.

"Yes, quite alone. The roof could be used by any tenants of the building, of course, but there was no one at all but Phyllis when I found her."

"No one whom you saw, you mean?" Dundee corrected her.

"I saw no one," Mrs. Lambert amended coldly. "Naturally I did not search the roof. I was interested only in Phyllis. I found her seated on a stone bench near the coping which surrounded the roof. She was weeping quietly, and I soothed her as best I could—"

"You asked her what was wrong?"

"Of course, but she just shook her head. Finally she began to laugh hysterically at herself, called herself a little fool for behaving as she was doing, and asked me to go down and send Seymour up to her. She said she had something to tell him—"

"She did not tell you what it was?"

"No. There was no need. I knew what was wrong, or believed I did."

"Simply that she was ill and hysterical, because of her condition?"

There was the faintest hesitation; then: "Yes. I can give you no other reason whatsoever."

"Mrs. Lambert, did Phyllis threaten to commit suicide?"

"Certainly not, or I should not have left her alone for a moment!" Mrs. Lambert replied indignantly. "I went to give the message to Seymour and he was delighted. He believed the bad times were over. Then I immediately went to Phyllis's room and asked Doris to take up a wrap to her mistress, since it was turning quite cold. I then went to my own room and was undressing for bed when I became aware of a commotion in the street below. I was trying to see what the matter was, when Doris came running into my room, saying that—that—"

"Yes, Mrs. Lambert," Dundee said gently, as the woman began to weep silently, the tears running down her white cheeks. "Will you tell me now if Doris ever — then or later—confided her suspicions to you, regarding the real cause for Phyllis Crosby's suicide?"

XX.

MRS. LAMBERT'S eyes flew wide, to stare at detective incredulously. "Doris? Suspicions?" she repeated. "I don't know what you mean. I am sure Doris knew no more about Phyllis's suicide than I did!"

"Probably no more, but as much, Mrs. Lambert." Dundee retorted significantly.

"Don't mind him, Tish!" Gigi cried, stroking the cheek of her friend consolingly. Then to Dundee she blazed: "Can you blame her if she fibs a little to protect Phyllis Crosby's memory from scandal?"

"I have told nothing but the truth, Gigi," Mrs. Lambert said wearily.

"You were at the inquest, of course," Dundee insisted. "You heard her father's testimony. He was his way to see his daughter and to take her home when she died, I believe."

"Yes," Mrs. Lambert admitted, with sudden spirit. "But I believed then and I still believe that Cullen Benham was lying. He had consented to her marriage to Mr. Crosby, but he very mistakenly believed in Seymour, was marrying Phyllis for her father's money. Mr. Benham said he had received a letter from Phylis asking him to cable her $25,000 and to let her come home. But he could not produce the letter; said he had destroyed it. I don't believe—"

"Yet," Dundee interrupted, "Mr. Benham was on a ship hurrying to his daughter's side, when she killed."

"When she committed suicide," Mrs. Lambert corrected him.

"Pardon! And Mr. Benham had unquestionably cabled his daughter these words: 'Not another cent. Come home,'" he reminded her.

"If she had asked his permission to come home, I fail to see why he did not wait for her in New York," Mrs. Lambert pointed out.

"Possibly he wanted to deal personally with the man who had made her so unhappy," Dundee suggested. Then, as Mrs. Lambert expressed her scorn only with her blazing eyes: "Will you tell me whether to your knowledge Mrs. Crosby was jealous, or had cause to be jealous, of any other woman?"

"No! I can swear that such a thought never entered Phyllis's head!"

Dundee was silent for a while, his eyes narrowed in thought. Then: "Did you see Doris after the inquest, Mrs. Lambert?"

"No, not until she came to see me upon my return to New York," she answered. "Her mistress's death was a terrible blow to Doris, and after the strain of the inquest she collapsed. The papers said that she went to the home of an aunt, in a London suburb. I made a note of the aunt's name and address and sent flowers and delicacies to her there, but did not go to see her, since I myself was suffering from the strain and from grief. I went to a little village in the south of France and remained there, in seclusion, until I sailed for America early in August."

"Did you see Mr. Crosby during that time?"

"No, but I had several letters from him. He was traveling over the Continent, making a brave effort to conquer his despair. For several months I feared he would—follow Phyllis, and in my own letters to him I said everything I could to make him happier."

"And yet, just sixteen months after his wife's death, Seymour Crosby becomes engaged to be married to another girl," Dundee reminded her.

"No fair!" Gigi protested, making a face at the detective and burrowing deeper into Mrs. Lambert's embrace. "I've always heard that widowers who were crazy about their wives get married again quickly!"

Mrs. Lambert smiled, dropped a grateful kiss upon the tumbled brown curls, then explained to Dundee:

"It was I who introduced him to Clorinda, and I who encouraged him to try to find solace in a new life with a girl whom I esteem highly. When I wrote Seymour that I was returning to America, he replied that he too was homesick, and would join me on the *Mauretania*. On shipboard I became acquainted with Mrs. Berkeley and her daughter, and introduced them to Mr. Crosby. Seymour and Clorinda were obviously congenial from the first, though I should not say that either was tempestuously in love. Mrs. Berkeley encouraged the attraction—"

"I bet she did!" Gigi giggled.

Again Mrs. Lambert smiled, an expression which made her look almost like a girl again, and very beautiful. "When it became fairly obvious that an engagement would result, Mrs. Berkeley begged me to accept the post of social secretary. I had never worked for money in my life, and the prospect dismayed me, but—" She hesitated, then flung up her silver crowned head defiantly. "The small remnant of my dead husband's estate was almost completely exhausted, and it was necessary for me to earn money in some way."

"Why didn't you get married again yourself, Tish?" Gigi began eagerly. "You're so beautiful and such a lamb I should think every plutocrat that looked at you—"

Mrs. Lambert's cheeks flamed, and she stopped the rush of words by laying a hand over the child's mouth.

"I accepted the position and Mrs. Berkeley asked me to begin my duties by engaging a butler and a thoroughly competent lady's maid for herself and Clorinda. I had had a letter from Wickett while I was still in France, telling me that he was returning to America, and saying that he wanted to serve me if I should again set up an establishment. On my arrival in New York I located Wickett through an employment bureau and offered him this post, which he accepted. A day or, so later he sent

Doris to me. She was employed on a Long Island estate, but wished to be with Wickett again."

"She simply adored *you*!" Gigi cut in.

"And I loved Doris," Mrs. Lambert said quietly, for the second time during the interview. "I think that's all I can tell you, Mr. Dundee. As you probably know, Clorinda and Mr. Crosby became engaged on the last day of the voyage."

Dundee was silent again for a long minute. Then he asked abruptly: "Mrs. Lambert, was it from you that Doris expected to borrow sufficient money to set up a beauty shop of her own?"

"From *me*?" Mrs. Lambert was obviously surprised. "That is absurd. Doris knew quite well that I have nothing now except my salary as Mrs. Berkeley's secretary."

"Do you know whom she had in mind as her benefactor?" Dundee pressed.

"Why, no! I haven't the least idea."

"Mrs. Lambert, did Doris tell you last night that Mrs. Berkeley had slapped her face?"

The effect of the question was startling. The woman's tired eyes blazed with anger, and her lips were shaking as she repeated: "*Slapped* Doris? Oh!" Then, regaining a measure of control she answered: "No, Doris did not tell me that."

"Don't mind so, Tish," Gigi pleaded, stroking her friend's flushed cheek. "Abbie has a rotten temper, you know. She flies off the handle and goes banging around but she really doesn't mean any harm. I got biffed myself last night, remember, and I'm not harboring any bad feelings now against my peppery parent."

"I remember," Mrs. Lambert agreed quietly, but her arms tightened about the small body.

"Forgive what must seem like unwarranted prying, Mrs. Lambert," Dundee went on, "but last night I happened to overhear Mrs. Berkeley say to you, 'All right

I promise.' Will you tell me, please, what promise you extracted from Mrs. Berkeley?"

"Really, Mr. Dundee, I must refuse to answer the question," Mrs. Lambert retorted icily. "It was a pure personal matter, having nothing at all to do with—with the tragedy you are investigating."

Dundee shrugged slightly, then smiled at her disarmingly as he took a rather crumpled package cigarettes and a patent lighter from his coat pocket. He was snapping unsuccessfully at the flint when Gigi scrambled out of Mrs. Lambert's lap and snatched the lighter from his hands.

"Bet it needs filling!" she told him. "Let me do it. See this funny little fountain?" and she ran around the big desk to where an ornamental little keg with gleaning brass bands held a prominent position among writing accessories. "It's a filling station for starving lighters, but we feed 'em wood alcohol instead of gas. Watch!" and she jerked the lighter apart, then held the tiny reservoir directly under the miniature spigot, whose tap she turned. "Now see if it will light!"

Dundee accepted the re-filled lighter with thanks, then remarked admiringly: "That's neat. I never saw one before."

"Say that to Dad and he'll make you a present of one," Gigi assured him. "He patented the thing himself and one of his factories turns them out by the thousand. He's sinfully proud of it, too. Designs a new type of 'body' every week or so. The house is full of them. Abbie has a gorgeous one for her sitting room—a modernistic urn, the darlingest thing. But poor Dad has a besetting worry about them. He's afraid some thirsty and incautious member of his precious family will take a swig of the wood alcohol and fill an untimely grave. Therefore he delivers periodic lectures on the horrible effects—"

The ringing of the house telephone interrupted her torrent of words. Snatching up the receiver she cooed "Hullo!" and winked at Dundee. "Abbie—on the rampage!" she whispered after a moment. Aloud: "Yes, darling! She's, still being 'quizzed.' . . . Oh, me? Why, *Abbie*! How can you? I'm being my most charming self—your dear, little wide-eyed daughter. . . . Of course I'm not giving away family secrets! . . . All right, darling. Keep your shirt on. I think they're almost through."

"She wants you to hurry, because she needs Tish," she explained unnecessarily.

"I'll hurry," Dundee grinned at her. "Now, Mrs. Lambert, will you please tell me when you last saw Doris Matthews?"

"At exactly what time, you mean?" Mrs. Lambert asked. "Let me think. It was about eleven when I came upstairs. I went to my room first and was reading a long letter from one of my New York friends which I had been too busy to open when it came in the late afternoon post, when I suddenly remembered that I had neglected to enter an important engagement for this morning on Mrs. Berkeley's desk calendar. As I was opening my door to go to Mrs. Berkeley's sitting room I saw Doris hurrying past on her way to the back stairs. She looked as if she had been crying."

"Did you stop her—speak to her?" Dundee asked.

"Yes, I called to her. She stopped at my door and I asked her what was wrong. She said, 'Nothing. It's just that I've been talking with Mr. Crosby and—and remembering.' I saw that she was emotionally upset and did not detain her. She ran on up the back stairs to the servants' quarters and I went to Mrs. Berkeley's sitting room."

"You did!" Dundee exclaimed, startled. "We had no idea—How long, were you there, Mrs. Lambert?"

"Less than five minutes, I should say," she answered. "I made a note of the engagement on Mrs. Berkeley's calendar, glanced over two or three belated acceptances for the dance which was to follow the dinner to-night, and added the names to the list of guests."

"Did you go into Mrs. Berkeley's bathroom or bedroom for any reason whatever?" Dundee asked, only the glint of his blue eyes betraying his excitement.

"No. I was in the sitting room, only."

"Did you hear anything at all while you were at work there?"

"Nothing whatever," Mrs. Lambert answered positively.

"Was the door open into the foyer between the rooms?'

Mrs. Lambert knit her brows, then shook her head. "I'm sorry, but I can't remember. I was in rather a hurry, partly because I wanted to be finished with the work before Mrs. Berkeley came upstairs, and partly because I was very tired."

"You wanted to avoid Mrs. Berkeley?" Dundee suggested.

"'Avoid' is scarcely the word," Mrs. Lambert answered coldly. "I suspected that the interview in the library between Mr. and Mrs. Berkeley concerned Clorinda's engagement to Mr. Crosby, and I was too tired to hear a possibly hysterical account of it. I knew, too, that Mrs. Berkeley needed sleep more than she needed a confidante."

"Mrs. Lambert, have you been happy here at Hillcrest?" Dundee asked gently.

It was Gigi, climbing back into the social secretary's lap, who answered for her: "Don't be an idiot, Bonnie Dundee! Do you think a 'great lady' like my darling Tish would be happy working for another woman, when she'd never had to take orders before in her life?"

"I *have* been happy—on the whole," Mrs. Lambert answered for herself, her arms closing almost convulsively about the small body curling itself contentedly in her lap.

"You did not see Doris again? She did not come to Mrs. Berkeley's rooms while you were there?" Dundee went on.

"No. I saw no one as I left Mrs. Berkeley's rooms and returned to my own, but I did catch a glimpse of a silk batik scarf fluttering over the balustrade of the stairs when I opened Mrs. Berkeley's sitting-room door," Mrs. Lambert answered reluctantly. "I recognized the scarf as Clorinda's and told myself that she was going out for a walk. Since Clorinda has told me that you know all about it, I can't believe I have harmed her at all by mentioning the fact."

"Not in the least," Dundee agreed. "But please, Mrs. Lambert, don't let any such considerations keep you from telling anything and everything that may help us to learn the whole truth about Doris's murder. Did you see any one else at all, either as you returned to your room, or afterwards?"

"No one!" Mrs. Lambert answered firmly. "I finished reading the letter from my friend and went to bed, within ten minutes."

"You heard no one running down the hall?" Dundee persisted.

"Nothing of the sort. But the hall is very thickly carpeted."

"The servants' stairs are at the end of the hall, just beyond your room, are they not?" Dundee asked.

"Yes. The flight leading up to the third floor is very near my room, but the flight leading down to the back hall is nearer to the now untenanted guest room opposite my room. Those stairs are not carpeted, but the servants are all required to wear rubber heels while on duty."

"Then you did not hear Doris descending from the third floor a few minutes after you returned to your room?"

"No. But I was in my bathroom, taking a bath, with two or three minutes after my return. That is, I began to run the water immediately, and when the tub was full, finished reading my letter as I lay in the warm water. Even if I had been in my bedroom, I doubt if I should have heard footsteps in the hall, since the walls and doors are very thick—practically soundproof."

"I see," Dundee agreed, more disappointed than he wished her to know. "Have you nothing else to add Mrs. Lambert?"

"Nothing to add," she replied quietly. "But I would to emphasize what I said before: no solution of the tragedy which in any way reflects on Doris's character loyalty will be the true solution."

"I am sure of that, Mrs. Lambert,' Dundee answer sincerely. "You may go, and—thank you very much. You have been more courteous and patient, I am sure, than you think I deserve. But I want you to know that I have not been asking irrelevant questions out of vicious or idle curiosity."

Mrs. Lambert smiled at him suddenly out of a mist of tears, and held out her hand.

"One other thing," he detained her. "May I borrow your typewriter, to transcribe my notes?"

She flushed slightly. "I am afraid I shall need it, but Mr. Berkeley has a machine in his room which he seldom uses. I am sure he will be glad to lend it to you for as long as you need it."

"I'll show you where it is!" Gigi cried.

The three of them ascended the stairs together, Gigi in the middle, impartially swinging a hand of each.

"I thought you were never coming, Mrs. Lambert!" Mrs. Berkeley called reproachfully from her sitting-room door. "My telephone has been ringing constantly. Somehow those dreadful reporters have got hold of my private, unlisted number and they've been driving me crazy. Just to get rid of them, I've promised them all an interview, at four o'clock, and we must hurry to get up a written statement for them, listing my stolen jewels, and—"

Mrs. Lambert, murmuring apologies, joined her employer and the sitting-room door closed upon them.

Gigi ran up the hall to her father's door and knocked blithely. "Isn't in!" she announced to Dundee. "But come along! It'll be all right."

The detective obeyed, stepping into a spacious but rather severely furnished room. Two broad windows gave a view of the landscaped front lawn, and a third looked out upon the rolling, grass-carpeted slopes to the west of the house.

"Dad's a pretty good stenographer himself," Gigi bragged, beckoning Dundee to a large, old-fashioned secretary, upon the open leaf of which rested a portable typewriter. Rolled into the carriage of the machine were two pieces of blank white paper, with a sheet of purple carbon between.

"Here's a bunch of typewriter paper," Gigi offered, jerking open a drawer and appropriating at least fifty sheets of the good plain bond. "Need anything else? Carbon paper?"

"This sheet in the machine will be enough," Dundee assured her. "What's this? Another of your father's patent fountains?"

"Yes," Gigi laughed. "Funny Dad should choose in the shape of a whiskey barrel, isn't it? See the XXX? But see *also* the skull and crossbones below, to warn you that the liquor this little barrel holds is most awfully poisonous. . . . Ready? I'm going with you, and watch you work."

"No, you're not!" Dundee corrected her positively. "Go roll a hoop, infant!"

"I think you're mean!" Gigi sulked, but she was grinning cheerfully again when he firmly shut his door between them.

His room, which was really Dick Berkeley's study, was a pleasant place, with the afternoon sun flooding it, a crisp breeze stirring the wool embroidered pongee curtains. Although he was eager to get to work, Dundee stepped to one of the broad, low windows and looked out upon the beautifully kept front lawn, breathing deep of the tangy autumn air. Those were literally his first deep, lazy breaths since the body Doris Matthews had been discovered in the lake that morning.

Suddenly he leaned farther out of the window, surprised at the sight of two figures slowly approaching from the west side of the house. A big, splendidly built man and a slighter, younger one, both in tennis flannels, both swinging rackets as they walked and talked together in apparent good-fellowship. George Berkeley and his son, Dick!

"Well, if this tragedy has brought them closer together, that's something to the good anyway," Dundee commented to himself, as he prepared to set to work.

He opened Dick's desk, set Mr. Berkeley's portal typewriter upon it, arranged his sheaf of notes on one side of the machine and the pad of confiscated paper upon the other.

About to head the paper he had found in the machine with the words, MRS. BERKELEY'S STORY, he happened to look at the edge of the carbon paper projecting slightly from the edge of the two sheets of white paper. The carbon paper was turned wrong side up, so that if he had written, the second sheet would have been blank. Rolling the three sheets out of the machine, he was about to reverse the carbon when he noticed that it had been used but once, and that only the date, heading, and five lines of an unfinished letter had cut into its gleaming purple surface. He glanced at the reverse printing casually.

Suddenly he uttered a sharp exclamation, then dashed to the bathroom. Standing before the mirror above the basin he held the carbon paper so that it was easy to read what George Berkeley had written:

HILLCREST, September 27, 1929.
MR. C. E. ATWOOD, Attorney-at-Law, Greene
Building, Hamilton.
DEAR CHRIS:

> *There is a small matter which I wish you would*
> *handle for me personally, in strictest confidence. As*
> *if it were for yourself, I should like you to*
> *investigate the commercial possibilities of a small*
> *beauty shop or beauty parlor on a good block in*
> *Hamilton, getting an estimate of the cost of—*

Dundee whistled, long and low. Here was the answer to at least one of the perplexing questions which Doris's last letter had raised. It was *George Berkeley* she had meant when she wrote: "It will take buckets of money, of course, but I know where I can get all or more than I need."

Why should George Berkeley be willing to finance a beauty parlor for a girl who had been in his employ less than two months? A girl who had, innocent or not, captured the love of his only son?

And the date of Berkeley's letter to his. lawyer September 27, 1929—Friday. The day Doris Matthews murdered!

XXI

Why had George Berkeley not finished that letter?

That question had just crashed through Dundee's almost dazed brain when there came a knock upon the door. He opened it to find Wickett gingerly holding a large bird-cage, in which Cap'n crouched upon his perch, every feather ruffled indignantly.

"A policeman brought this, sir. He says you wanted it, sir."

"Right, Wickett," Dundee laughed. "Hello, Cap'n. I told you I might send for you," and he reached into the cage to stroke the yellow-and-green head soothingly.

"He nipped me, sir, when I tried to do that," Wickett offered sadly.

"I'm afraid he's a one-man bird," Dundee grinned. "By the way, Wickett, I'd rather you did not mention the parrot. I don't care to get a reputation for being eccentric."

"Yes, sir. Thank you, sir," Wickert said as he pocketed, with much dignity, the five-dollar bill which Dundee had slipped into his hand.

"One more thing, Wickett," Dundee detained him "Was Mr. Berkeley at home yesterday afternoon?"

"Oh, no, sir. He returned from his business at the usual time—half-past five."

"Do you know whether Mrs. Berkeley told him of the little scene between Arnold, Doris and Mr. Dick?" Dundee asked casually.

"I couldn't say, sir."

"Then, do you know whether Mr. Berkeley spent some time with Mrs. Berkeley before dinner?"

"Yes, sir. A messenger boy arrived about six with a large envelope for Mr. Berkeley. He was in the library then, sir. A few minutes after I took the package to him he went up to Mrs. Berkeley's rooms. He was there when Mrs. Berkeley rang me on the house telephone to ask me to come up for some instructions regarding dinner, sir."

"And they had been quarreling, Wickett?"

The butler hesitated, and instinctively looked over his shoulder. Then, lowering his voice, he confided: "Yes, sir. It seemed to be about Mr. Crosby, sir. I gathered that the envelope contained a report of some sort, concerning Mr. Crosby."

"Now, Wickett, tell me: did Mr. Berkeley send for Doris or see Doris after his return from his office yesterday?"

"Yes, sir A few minutes before the messenger arrived. He asked me to send her to him in the library, sir."

"Did he seem—well, angry?"

"No, sir. He seemed much as usual, sir, but Mr. Berkeley is always a stern man. She was with him for a few minutes only."

"Did you see her or talk with her after she left Mr. Berkeley?"

"I saw her, sir, as she was going upstairs to get Mrs. Berkeley dressed for dinner, but I did not detain her."

"Then Doris was with Mrs. Berkeley when your master and mistress were quarreling over Mr. Crosby's engagement to Miss Clorinda?"

"Yes, sir."

After a moment of reflection, Dundee asked abruptly: "Just when was it that Mr. Berkeley wrote letters on the typewriter in his room yesterday?"

"I can't say that he wrote letters at all, sir, but Mr. Berkeley was writing on his machine when I went to his room about a quarter to seven to ask for the key to the wine cellar, sir."

"Did he later give you any letters to send to the post office?"

"No, sir. Arnold went to the post office with some letters Mrs. Lambert gave me to have mailed, but they did not include one written by Mr. Berkeley."

Again Dundee considered for a long minute, frowningly. Then: "Wickett, tell me: did Doris tell you, or did you observe for yourself, that Mr. George Berkeley was—well, in love with her?"

Wickett looked profoundly shocked and indignant. "Certainly not, sir!"

Was that denial a shade too emphatic to be taken at its face value? Dundee asked himself, after the butler had been dismissed. And then he remembered that his "Watson" was with him, that it was no longer necessary to keep his thoughts to himself. And Cap'n had already proved, in the Rhodes House murders, that he was a stimulating audience.

"What do you think, my clever 'Watson'?" he addressed the parrot, poking him to attention. "Does it strike you as entirely absurd that a middle-aged, virile, handsome man, not at all in love with his impossible wife, should be more than a trifle indiscreet with his wife's lovely maid?"

Cap'n turned slowly on his perch and drooped a paperish-white lid.

"Exactly!" Dundee laughed. "But, 'my dear Watson,' Mrs. Lambert and Wickett are most anxious to have us think that Doris was not 'that kind of girl!' The kind of girl, for instance, who would let herself be kissed and then make the man pay and pay and pay. But what other explanation can there be for this letter which George Berkeley tore up before it was finished? What say you 'my dear Watson'? Did George Berkeley, multi-millionaire, suddenly decide to be damned before he'd pay blackmail, and—to insure the girl's silence in *another way*?"

Cap'n's sole answer was a throaty chuckle.

"Probably you're right, 'Watson,'" Dundee agree lugubriously.

"I should say he is!" a vigorously indignant young voice cried from the bathroom door.

"Gigi! You outrageous little snooper!" Dundee went to the girl, seized her by the arms and shook her. "You're a blight—and I ought to spank you."

"So many people feel that way about me," Gigi mourned. "But I wasn't eavesdropping intentionally. Dick sent me up to get him a package of his special cigarettes and I heard you talking through the open door into the bathroom. Thought you'd gone crazy and were talking to yourself. But why do you want to talk to a silly old parrot, when you could use me for a Watson? I at least could say, 'Marvellous, my dear Holmes'—"

"Oh, could you?" Dundee mocked. "You would laugh at every theory I trotted out."

"Yes, if they were all as silly as the ones I've hear so far," she agreed cheerfully. "Tell you what—I'll be the detective, and spin a theory myself. . . . *Sit down!*" she commanded suddenly, in an excellent imitation of Captain Strawn's most official and officious voice. "I'm going to put *you* through the third degree!"

Rather to his own surprise, Dundee obeyed.

"When did you last see Doris Matthews?" she began belligerently.

"Last night, at about half-past ten," Dundee answered promptly, grinning. "Your brother Dick was forcing her to dance with him in the back hall, as well as forcing her to promise to meet him later."

"When did you *first* see Doris Matthews?" Gigi went on sternly.

"At the same time," Dundee answered.

"Mr. Dundee, do you know an English gentleman named Sir Edward Moresby?" Gigi startled him by asking.

"Yes, I do. I was in his home several times when I worked in Scotland Yard. Of which he is a department head."

"And Kathryn Matthews, sister of Doris Matthews, works for Lady Moresby, does she not?" Gigi demanded, with lifted eyebrows.

"Yes. What of it?" Dundee asked, mystified.

"Just this, Mr. 'Bonnie' Dundee!" Gigi retorted, with exaggerated significance. "Doris herself told me that she sometimes called on her sister at Sir Edward's house in London. *Was that where you met, fell in love with, and led Doris Matthews astray?*"

"Don't be an idiot, Gigi!" Dundee commanded sternly.

"Every one seems to think that's a perfect retort to anything I say," Gigi complained in her natural voice. Then, becoming Captain Strawn again, she said slowly, heavily: "Mr. James Dundee, let me tell you the story of this murder as I see it:

"You *did* know Doris Matthews in England. You *did* fall in love with her. When Dick invited you to this house yesterday, you had no idea of course that you would see your old flame here. To your intense surprise and consternation, you come upon her in the back hall, *in another man's arms*! Jealous, or frightened at what she might tell on you, I can't say which—"

"I should think you couldn't!" Dundee laughed.

"That's right—laugh while the laughing's good!" Gigi retorted sternly. "You are in a panic. You telephone to Police Headquarters, cannily planting suspicion against Seymour Crosby, for a crime which has not been committed yet. When you go upstairs, it is not to sleep the sleep of the just, *but to plan a dastardly crime*! Your room is on the third floor. You waylay Doris, hear from her that she is to meet Arnold in the summerhouse.. She says she will tell her fiancé the truth about you, and that he will kill you! But you know that Arnold cannot meet her, that he is taking the Smiths home *And it is you who keep that tryst!*"

"That's good, all right," Dundee laughed admiringly.

"Good? Hell! That's perfect" Gigi corrected him "You have admitted that you stole downstairs, that you heard Clorinda unbolt the back door. And circumstance was playing into your hands! Here was another suspect made to order! On your way out, you pick up Clorinda's scarf which she has dropped while unbolting the door. A means of strangling the girl, if the flask of perfume which you have stolen from Abbie's room doesn't prove an effective weapon. That weapon you have chosen with the cunning of the devil. You know that any spilled perfume cannot betray you, since it has been sprinkled upon every one in the drawing room. You know, too, that it will implicate any one of three others—Crosby, who gave it to Abbie, Wickett who took it upstairs, or Abbie in whose room it had been left. Then there is the scarf to implicate poor Clorinda. . . . Well?" she snapped, as Strawn might have done.

"I can only say, 'Captain Strawn,'" Dundee protested with mock solemnity, "that it is all lies, lies! I did not kill Doris Matthews!"

"So *you* say!" she scoffed. Then, dropping suddenly into her own voice and manner, and seizing his hands, she cried: "I know you didn't kill her, Bonnie Dundee! I know that's an idiotic theory! But, oh, don't you see? It's so easy to build up theories against almost anyone who was in this house last night!"

"I grant you that, Gigi," Dundee answered soberly.

"Then you won't be an idiot?" Gigi begged. "You won't go off half-cocked and suspect Dad and Abbie, and Clorinda and Mrs. Lambert and Wickett, and—me?"

"I promise," Dundee answered with real solemnity. "Will you get out now and let me work?"

"What a fiercely loyal little thing she is!" Dundee reflected after Gigi had taken her leave, with surprising docility. "But—loyal to—whom? I'd give a month's pay to know who it is that adorable little pest is trying to shield. . . . Darned clever—her 'case' against me! Which reminds me that I must send that cablegram to Sir Edward Moresby."

He raced down to the library, dictated the cablegram to the Western Union office, directed that it be charged to the Police Department, then called Captain Strawn.

"No, nothing yet," the chief of the Homicide Squad answered disgustedly. "The earth seems to have opened, and swallowed Johnson, but we'll get him yet. Having a good time?" he added, rather sarcastically.

"Very amusing," Dundee answered cryptically.

On his way back to his third-floor room he stopped to get two fresh sheets of carbon paper from George Berkeley's desk. As he had expected, the waste basket had been emptied. Probably by this time the multimillionaire's unfinished letter to his lawyer had been fed to the furnace, but it did not matter. The beautifully clear record upon the otherwise virginal sheet of carbon paper would be ample evidence of George Berkeley's interest in a beauty shop for Doris Matthews—if such evidence were ever needed in a court of law.

It was nearly half-past three when the young detective began to transcribe his notes taken during the morning's investigation. He was a rapid typist. Within half an hour he held in his hands the complete transcript of Abigail Berkeley's story—that amazing tissue of lies, truths and half-truths. And as he read what he had typed automatically he felt again that queer surge of excitement which had tingled his nerves two or three times while the woman had babbled and evaded and admitted.

"Here," he said aloud to the parrot, "is the key to the puzzle, if I could only put my clumsy fingers on it."

His eyes fell again upon the passage which had puzzled and intrigued him:

MRS. BERKELEY: I—I told her to open a new bottle of perfume I'd bought in the city yesterday, and—and she said something impertinent—

Q. Just what did she say, Mrs. Berkeley?

A. I—I don't remember! You don't expect me to remember every tiny thing, do you? Well, it was just—just a word or two, like—Oh, yes! She said, "You use too much perfume Madame." Of course I was furious at such impertinence, and I—I slapped her face.

"A strange thing for a well-trained maid to say to mistress," Dundee mused aloud. "The question is: *does* Mrs. Berkeley use too much perfume? So much that fastidious girl like Doris forgets her station an protests?"

He wrinkled his forehead in an effort to remember. Had Mrs. Berkeley been wearing a disgusting amount of perfume when she greeted him the night before? He forced himself to reconstruct that scene with the sense of smell as well as those of sight and hearing. Mrs. Berkeley offering her hand, gushing at him—

"Good Lord!" he ejaculated so forcibly that Cap'n flapped his wings irritably and commanded: "Shut up, you old fool!"

"I've been a fool, but please heaven, the curse has been lifted!" Dundee exulted. "Perfume, Cap'n! *Perfume*! Did a poor struggling detective ever find such a weird stumbling-block in his path? Doris gets soundly slapped on account of *perfume*! Gigi gets her face smacked—by the same hand!—on account of *perfume*! And it is with *a flask of perfume* that Doris Matthews is stunned or killed!"

"Perfume!" Cap'n echoed tentatively. Then, exulting in the addition to his vocabulary, the parrot turned rapidly about on his perch, croaking the word repeatedly.

But Dundee was paying little attention to his useful pet. He was remembering another scene in all its tiniest details. Again he saw Seymour Crosby bending, with courtly grace, above Mrs. Berkeley as he presented the costly gift. Again he heard Mrs. Berkeley's squeal of delight, "Oh, you dear *man*!" as her plump fingers fastened greedily upon the crystal flask.

And into his mental picture came Gigi, skating across the floor, shrilling excitedly: "What is it?" Then that queer protest of hers: "Oh, *no!*"

As if it were just happening, Dundee saw that strange, significant side glance of Gigi's toward Mrs. Lambert, saw the child clap a restraining hand upon her own mouth.

With his eyes tightly closed, Dundee again saw Gigi seize the flask from her mother's convulsive grasp; saw the child dance madly about the room, wasting the precious scent prodigally.

He stopped short of picturing the shameful *dénouement*—the resounding contact of fat old palm with tanned young cheek. For that hurt too much.

Dundee sprang to his feet. "Work to be done, Cap'n — and light at last!" he exulted. A hasty glance at his wristwatch told him that it was five minutes past four. And at four o'clock Mrs. Berkeley was to grant an interview to the most importunate of the gentlemen of the press.

Delaying only long enough to lock his precious notes and the transcript of Mrs. Berkeley's story in Dick's desk and to pocket the key, he sped downstairs.

His knock upon Mrs. Berkeley's sitting-room door brought no response. Good! The reporters were received in the drawing room, probably, the better to impress them with the Berkeley grandeur, Dundee himself with a grin.

He did not tarry in the sitting-room, where a cluttered desk gave mute evidence that the social secretary was more than earning her salary that day. And with no doubt she was now further earning that salary by being introduced to the reporters by her proud employer as "*Dear* Mrs. Lambert—*the* Mrs. Van Rensselaer Lambert of New York and Newport, you know, who is now my social secretary."

He plunged through the little foyer and made straight for the over-luxurious dressing table, where twin orchid-shaded lamps glowed softly. And among the expected clutter of crystal and silver he found what he was looking for—a squat, modernistic bottle of fine perfume. It was the only one visible, but to satisfy any possible doubt he jerked open the narrow deep drawers and searched them thoroughly.

Still mindful of Gigi's admonition not to "go off cocked," Dundee raced to the bathroom and searched the dressing table and medicine chest.

There was no other bottle of perfume. And yet the one he held in his hand was only two-thirds full!

Before admitting the inevitable conclusion, however, Dundee took one more precaution. On the sitting-room telephone, which Mrs. Berkeley had said was a private, unlisted wire, he called the number of the department store whose name, on a tiny gold-embossed label, was affixed to the bottom of the perfume bottle.

"The manager, please," he requested in a low voice. "Hamilton Police Department calling. The Manager? . . . Oh, yes, Mr. Franklin. . . . Thank you. This is Detective Dundee speaking. Will you kindly look at the charge account of Mrs. George Berkeley, and get me the following information: First, the brand of perfume bought by Mrs. Berkeley yesterday; second, the number of bottles of perfume purchased by Mrs. Berkeley during the month of September. . . . Certainly, Mr. Franklin! The information is of real importance to the Police Department. . . . Thank you!"

The wait was a considerable one, but when the information came at last it did not surprise Detective Dundee, startling though it was.

When he had hung up the receiver he returned the modernistic bottle of perfume to Mrs. Berkeley's dressing table, saying very softly:

"Indeed you *do* use entirely too much perfume, my dear Abbie!"

Then he did a strange thing. He went to Mrs. Berkeley's commodious clothes closet, filled with enough frocks, cloaks, coats and ensembles to stock a small shop for 'The Stylish Stout." And he lifted each one of those gaudy, expensive garments to his nose and sniffed it. Oddly enough, however, the almost complete absence of perfume upon all of them except the evening dress which Gigi had anointed with *Fleur d'Amour* did not puzzle or disappoint him.

"Where do you keep your 'empties,' Abbie?" he inquired cheerfully of the room's absent mistress.

But he answered the question for himself, after a quick but very thorough search of every hiding place the big closet afforded.

"You have the ingenuity of a squirrel, Abbie!" Dundee laughed soundlessly, as he drew the fifth and last bottle from the tissue-paper stuffing of a smart French hat. "Wonder where the other two are. . . . But five are enough—oh, more than enough!"

Having deposited the five empty perfume bottles in a discarded shoe box, found on the top shelf of the closet, Dundee was about to return to his interrupted typing with his strange find under his arm, when he caught a glimpse of Gigi's brief yellow linen skirt disappearing into her own room down the hall.

The child must help him now, he decided; for at last he knew—or believed he knew—whom she was shielding. Poor Gigi! He felt like a cad when he thought of the questions he must ask her, but—duty was duty. And murder had been committed.

"Oh!" Gigi gasped, then her little brown face grew vividly joyous. "You've come to call on me? Another advantage of being only fifteen! I can receive a gentleman in my bedroom. . . . *Kommen Sie herein, mein lieber Herr!* . . . *Please* like my room. Abbie laughed at it until an interior decorator photographed it and wrote a grand piece for a magazine about it. Every single, solitary thing in it is real Early-American. The magazine lady said the whole room ought to be presented to the Metropolitan Museum—"

Dundee stared about him in amazement. "It's perfect, Gigi! I can't believe my eyes! Where on earth did you get these things?"

"You *do* like it!" she crowed, dapping her hands ecstatically. "I lifted this room right out of my Great-Grandmother Berkeley's old home in Vermont. She didn't die till I was twelve, and I made Dad—Why, you're not listening!" she reproached him. "What's—wrong?"

"Gigi," he began, very gently, "how long has your mother been a perfume addict?"

XXII

1

GIGI gasped, shrank away from Dundee, her topaz eyes widening to enormous size: Then suddenly she got control of herself; terror changed to blank innocence on her childish face.

"A—what?" she asked.

"Don't pretend innocence, Gigi!" Dundee commanded sternly, but his eyes were filled with pity for her. "I have more than enough evidence that your mother is addicted to drinking perfume for the alcohol it contains. Now will you please tell me how long she has had the habit?"

She crumpled suddenly, sinking upon the beautiful old four-poster bed covered with a patchwork quilt which her great-grandmother's fingers had "pieced."

"I—I don't know, exactly," she shivered. "Oh, why can't you let us all alone? We haven't done anything to you—"

"Doris Matthews has been murdered, Gigi," Dundee reminded her.

"But Abbie's drinking perfume hasn't got anything to do with that!" Gigi protested, with too passionate vehemence.

"I'm—afraid—it has, Gigi," the detective retorted Slowly. "Doris knew, didn't she?"

"I don't know," Gigi sobbed. "Oh, yes, I suppose she did, but if you're thinking Abbie would *kill* Doris, just because she knew— Doris wasn't the only one who knew!"

"Who else, Gigi?"

"Oh, shut up!" Gigi cried wildly.

"The whole family, and the other servants?" Dundee persisted.

"I—I suppose so," she sobbed. "We—we didn't talk about it—"

"Doris did," Dundee corrected her. "*For your sake, Doris begged your mother only last night not to drink the stuff any more; refused, in fact, to open a new bottle for her. And your mother slapped her for her impertinence!*"

"Was that why Abbie slapped her?" Gigi stopped crying and stared fearfully at the detective. "How do you know it was for *my* sake that Doris—?"

"Because Doris said so, in a letter she was writing last night to her sister," he explained gently. "Has—it been very bad, honey?"

"Awful!" Gigi began to sob again. "Abbie and I got along together pretty well before—before she went abroad for that year with Clorinda, but as soon as she got back I could tell something was wrong. She acted so *peculiar*! She was either awfully sentimental about me, or—or horribly cruel. Then—I found out. I found her that way one morning when I went in to kiss her before she'd got up, and I—I smelled perfume on her breath, and I—I knew what was wrong with her. I—well, I guess I wasn't very tactful. I'm—terribly frank, and I—I told her she was making a fool of herself. She—she's had it in for me ever since, and I guess I can't keep it out of my eyes when I look at her—what I think of her for—for—"

"I understand, Gigi. Have you talked with anyone about this?"

"Only Mrs. Lambert," Gigi confessed miserably. "I can tell her anything, because—because she loves me and I simply adore her. She said Abbie must have got the habit in Paris. It seems that a lot of people do it, and—and maybe Abbie thought it was the smart thing to do. You see, Abbie's father drank—a regular old town's drunkard, and—and I guess Abbie and—and Dick both inherited the craving from him. When Abbie quit high school she went to work in Dad's office, and he felt sorry for her because she'd had such a hard life, and—well, he married her."

"Did your father suspect?" Dundee hesitated.

"I guess he was always afraid for her, and for Dick, too," Gigi admitted tragically. "Not until I was a great big girl would Dad allow any wines or liqueurs to be served at dinner, unless it was a terribly formal one, and then he'd try to keep Abbie from having more than just a taste. Of course when she went abroad, there wasn't anyone to watch her and—"

"I see," he said gently. He could imagine with what avidity Abbie Berkeley had adopted the perfume habit, knowing that a supply would always be at hand; that neither prohibition nor her watchful husband could prevent her getting all she wanted.

"So that is why you wasted as much of Crosby's gift as possible?" he went on.

"Ye-es," she answered, dropping her eyes.

She was too transparent for Dundee to be deceived. "There's something else, Gigi . . . Did Seymour Crosby know that his gift would be particularly pleasing to your mother?"

"Yes!" she cried passionately. "Yes, he did! He wanted her to—to drink herself to death! That's why I hate him!"

"Gigi, my dear!" he checked her. He drew his chair close to the bed and took both her icy little hands. "Tell me quietly what you mean, what basis you have for such a charge."

A shamed red dyed her cheeks, but she met his eyes bravely. "I—you'll think I'm a nasty little sneak, but I didn't mean to pry— I was in Tish's room about a week ago, while she was taking a bath to dress for dinner. I was already dressed, and lots of times I go in to talk to her while she dresses. Well, I just happened to pick up a book on her bedside table and a—a letter fell out."

"Addressed to Mrs. Lambert?" Dundee cut in sternly.

"There wasn't any envelope, and when I was picking it up I saw a few words that—that made me perfectly furious! So I read it all. It was from Mr. Crosby!"

"What made you furious, Gigi?" Dundee asked softly, scarcely daring to breathe.

"Well, the letter was all about the visit he was going to make to Hillcrest, and—and about Clorinda. Oh, what he said about Clo was perfectly lovely; that wasn't what made me sore. The words that first caught my eye were: '—her perfectly impossible mother, but perhaps she will not long be a handicap.'"

"What!" Dundee ejaculated.

"Uh-huh!" Gigi sniffed, dabbing at her eyes. "So I read the whole letter, but first I read the rest of that paragraph. It said something like this: 'One can but hope that her vice, contracted so enthusiastically at so advanced an age, will not be slow in taking its toll. Otherwise a future which I had hoped would be a happy and peaceful one will present rather peculiar mother-in-law problems.' . . . Do you blame me for reading it?" she demanded piteously.

"No, Gigi," he answered, squeezing her hands tightly. But to himself he had to admit, in all fairness, that there was some excuse for Seymour Crosby. He tried to picture himself saddled with a mother-in-law like Abbie Berkeley, and involuntarily his hands loosened slightly their grip upon Gigi's. . . . After all, though it was a caddish thing to do, Crosby had written the words in strictest confidence to an old and trusted friend.

"So I simply couldn't bear it when I saw him giving her *perfume!*" Gigi told him vehemently. "I wanted to throw it all into his face, and tell him if he didn't like Abbie he could go straight to—"

"Did you tell Mrs. Lambert you had seen the letter?" Dundee asked.

"No," she admitted, flushing. "Tish would have been shocked at me. And it wasn't *her* fault! And she didn't feel that way at all! She did everything she could to make Abbie stop. I heard Abbie simply tearing into her just the other day for begging her to promise not to drink any more of the stuff."

So another mystery was cleared up. It was quite clear now what promise Mrs. Lambert had exacted from Abbie Berkeley the night before, so soon after Seymour Crosby had presented his shameful gift!

Suddenly a monstrous suspicion crashed through Dundee's mind, a suspicion which, if founded upon fact, would explain a great deal, probably everything.

"Gigi, tell me the truth: was that the only reason you tried to spill all that perfume last night?"

"What—do you mean?" she gasped, her eyes popping.

"You were afraid that Seymour Crosby had grown impatient!" he answered with slow emphasis. "You suspected there was poison in that bottle, intended for your mother!"

"No, no!" Gigi cried, shuddering. "I just thought he was helping her into a drunkard's grave." Suddenly she laughed shakily. "Don't I sound like a temperance pamphlet? You don't *really* think—?"

"I'm going to find out!" Dundee said grimly; as he rose.

"But—the perfume has all been spilled!" she reminded him.

"For a very good reason, probably: to destroy the evidence. But it is not so easy to be rid of traces of poison. The stuff is on our clothes, and they can be analyzed—"

"You shan't spoil my new dress!" she interrupted vigorously. "If a sample is all you need, I can give you the handkerchief with which I wiped off my hands after I sprinkled you all. . . . Wait!"

She dashed into her bathroom and was back in a moment. "Got it out of my clothes hamper," she announced triumphantly. "It still smells," and she thrust the little square of linen and lace against his nose. "Can they really tell from this whether the perfume was poisoned or not?"

"That will be no trick at all for the city chemist," Dundee assured her.

"But—where does Doris come in?" she objected, frowning.

"I don't know yet, but I can make a fair guess," Dundee retorted. "You saw that letter of Crosby's. Doris may have seen it, too."

"I know Doris wouldn't have read it," Gigi defended the dead girl loyally. "Besides, Della cleans Mrs. Lambert's room."

"But what if Della read it and told Doris, knowing that Doris was acquainted with Crosby?"

"But Doris didn't know that Mr. Crosby had given Abbie the perfume," she protested.

"Who can say now what Doris knew or did not know?"

He refused to say more to the child, for he knew how fatally loose her tongue was, but on his way to his room he reasoned to himself:

"Wickett could have mentioned the gift to Doris. Doris could have known about Crosby's letter. If our first suspicions of Crosby are correct, Doris could have known, from the past, that Seymour Crosby would not hesitate at murder. All that being so, Doris Matthews may have lost her life to save the life of the mistress who had slapped her! But why speculate until I know what the city chemist has to say?"

2

It was five o'clock that Saturday afternoon when Bonnie Dundee set out from Hillcrest to pay three calls in the city of Hamilton. Dick Berkeley, looking pale and ill, was acting as the detective's chauffeur.

Dick had wandered forlornly into Dundee's room just as his guest was getting into his topcoat.

"Going Out, Dundee? . . . You're lucky! I wish to God I could get away from this dump, even for an hour. I feel like prisoner."

"Then I'll make a trusty of you, and order you to drive me into the city," Dundee grinned.

They set out in the boy's roadster, with Dick pathetically grateful for the privilege, but strangely silent. Finally, however, Dundee asked him a question which galvanized his slumped body.

"Dick, can you think of any reason why your father should have been willing to install Doris Matthews in a beauty shop of her own?"

"*Dad*?" Dick echoed incredulously. "Don't be an ass, Dundee!"

"Doris was a very beautiful and appealing girl," the detective reminded him.. "Your father is in his prime, and at what the novelists call 'the dangerous age.' Almost every man of that age feels the urge for one more romantic fling."

"And you're hinting that my *father* planned to set Doris up in business, then make her pay and pay?" Dick snorted angrily. "Like any movie villain! Well, let me tell you this! if Dad could have made such a fool of himself, Doris would have laughed in his face—or slapped it! She was the straightest—" He choked, then went on doggedly: "Besides, she was in love with Arnold."

"Then do you think your father so feared an endangerment between you and Doris that he planned to bribe her to discourage your attentions?"

"Bribe her!" Dick snorted contemptuously. "She didn't need to be bribed to discourage my attention. What the devil put such an idea into your head anyway?

"Oh, nothing much," Dundee answered evasively. "Just something she wrote to her sister, Kathryn, in England. She said she knew where she could get all the money she needed to open a shop."

He did not add that he had documentary proof that George Berkeley was the "angel" that Doris had referred to.

"She didn't mean Dad," Dick retorted emphatically. "I suppose she meant she could borrow the money on business basis. . . . Now look here, Dundee! You'll save time and trouble for yourself if you'll take my word for it that Doris Matthews was straight as a string and a good dear through to the marrow of her bones. Any cockeyed theory of yours that makes her out otherwise is the bunk!"

"So Mrs. Lambert and Wickett have told me, to say nothing of Seymour Crosby," Dundee assured him cheerfully. "And Gigi is ready to scratch my eyes out if I dare question Doris's integrity. And yet Doris was murdered, Dick, by someone to whom her life was menace!"

Dick stared at the young detective, then slowly his weak face hardened into lines of character. "You've put your finger on it, Dundee," he said strangely. "Doris was killed because she knew something which would have ruined the person who murdered her. Doris couldn't be bribed, so she had to die!"

"Johnson?" Dundee suggested.

"Lord, I don't know!" Dick slumped again into a miserable huddle beneath the steering wheel. "If Johnson isn't the murderer, his bumbling into the case as a first-class suspect is the luckiest accident that ever happened to the fiend that *is* guilty. . . . Well, here's the City Hall. Want me to wait for you?"

"Please. I shan't be gone long," Dundee answered, as he swung his long legs over the door he did not trouble to open.

His destination was an office on the top floor of City Hall. He opened a door inscribed:

Dr. Abel C. Jennings
City Chemist and Toxicologist

When he emerged ten minutes later he was whistling blithely, for he had secured not only the doctor's promise to analyze Gigi's perfumed handkerchief for traces of poison, but also his promise to keep the job a strict secret. And the doctor was to telephone results on Sunday morning, though it meant he must work half the night, at least.

When he returned to the car parked at the curb he found Dick with his head bowed upon the steering wheel and for a moment he thought the boy was sleeping. But at the sound of his name Dick's head jerked up, and Dundee saw that he had been crying.

"To Police Headquarters now, Dick," he said gently.

They drove in silence, Dick gnawing at his trembling lips.

"Want to come in with me, Dick?" Dundee asked, when the car drew up before the big, ugly building.

"No!" the boy retorted with strange violence.

Captain Strawn was in the office on the first floor. Feet on his desk, uniform untidily open-at the neck, the chief of the Homicide Squad was glaring at the telephone when Dundee entered.

"Any news, chief?"

"News? Hell! That's what we ain't got nothin' else but!" Strawn growled. "Every nut in the state has phoned in that he's seen Johnson. But we haven't got Johnson, if that's what you mean. As slick a getaway as I ever saw. But what are you doing here? Why ain't you playing bridge or golf, or ping-pong with your swell friends?"

"I prefer to stay at Hillcrest, at least until Monday, Captain Strawn," Dundee said, without anger, "and for reasons not at all connected with bridge or golf. But if you need me here, naturally I'm at your service."

The chief's heavy face cleared. He even grinned shamefacedly. "Stay where you are, boy. The Johnson hunt is routine, and I don't really need you. Trying to run down the old Crosby case to your own satisfaction?" he added interestedly.

"Something like that," Dundee admitted evasively. "Thanks much, chief. And one more thing. If George Berkeley or anyone else at Hillcrest telephones to ask if he's at liberty to leave the grounds and go where he pleases, I wish you'd tactfully intimate that the police would much prefer all members of the household, except the 'help' which doesn't live in to remain on the estate, at least until Monday morning

"We've got no authority to do that, Dundee," Strawn objected, frowning. "I can say that's what we'd prefer, but if Berkeley or anyone else there wants to take issue—"

"Then will you arrange to have a plainclothes man with a motorcycle or unmarked car stationed near the gates on the main road, ready to follow anyone who does insist upon leaving? I'm not including the cook's assistant, Mrs. Andrews, of course, nor the two gardeners, all of whom live in Hamilton and will have to be permitted to return to their homes at night."

Captain Strawn's narrowed gray eyes studied the young man for a long minute. Perhaps he was reminding himself of the Rhodes House murders, for whose startling solution this imaginative and obstinate cub detective was largely responsible. Or he may only have been remembering that Bonnie Dundee was the favorite nephew of the Police Commissioner. At any rate he nodded, at last.

"O. K., Dundee. I've got nearly every man available tied up on the Johnson hunt, but I'll try to arrange it."

"Thanks, chief. By the way, what is Dr. Price's verdict?"

"Death by drowning," Strawn replied. "She was unconscious when the body was rolled into the lake, but she would not have died from the effect of the blow on the head. And his snap judgment was right: death took place between eleven and twelve o'clock last night."

"Was she—'in trouble,' by any chance?" Dundee asked.

"No. Virgin," Strawn replied brusquely.

Dundee's third call was a visit to the office of the fingerprint expert, Carraway.

"Yes," that busy young man answered Dundee's first question. "The mouthprint on the mirror was made by the dead girl, all right. But—a funny thing: I didn't find any of her fingerprints on the porcelain-topped dressing table below the mirror. Matter of fact, I didn't find any fingerprints there except yours and Dick Berkeley's, and you've told me that you were playing nurse to the kid this morning when he got sick to his stummick."

"Yes," Dundee agreed. "Then the dressing table and basin had been wiped clean?"

"Absolutely clean," Carraway shrugged. "By the way, here's young Berkeley's toothbrush I swiped this morning to get his fingerprints from, as you suggested. Better smuggle it back into his room before he accuses a maid of stealing it. Wonder if anybody ever stole a used toothbrush?" he ruminated, with a chuckle.

But Dundee had more weighty matters to occupy his mind. As he slowly descended the broad, dirty stairs to the first floor of Police Headquarters he was turning Carraway's two bits of information this way and that for all they were worth.

"Of course," he told himself, knitting his brows, "Doris, being the tidy and efficient little person she was, undoubtedly wiped off Mrs. Berkeley's dressing table and basin with a used towel when she had finished giving the 'facial.' But—how could Doris fall against the mirror without touching the dressing table? Whether she tripped and fell or was pushed, she *must* have tried instinctively to steady herself. Her fingerprints must have been on that dressing table! And not even the most efficient maid goes about wiping off fingerprints from an otherwise immaculate surface. The question is—*who wiped them off?* Answer: the person who pushed Doris Matthews so that her rouged mouth left its print upon the mirror. Second question: why didn't the same person remove the rouge spot from the mirror? . . . Answer: because he or she was in a great hurry; and did not notice the spot; or he or she was more concerned with removing his or her own fingerprints from that porcelain-topped table than in obliterating possible traces of Doris's presence there. Why? Because Doris had a right to be there, and the maid's attacker did not? Answer: possibly, or—quite probably!"

He was so absorbed in his speculations that his physical movements were almost automatic. Otherwise he must have realized before he reached it that the roadster was empty.

Dick Berkeley was gone.

Dundee was about to turn away from the car to search nearby cigar and drug stores for his missing "chauffeur" when he caught sight of a scrap of paper affixed to the steering wheel by means of a postage stamp. His hand shook as he reached for the note.

XXIII.

1

DICK BERKELEY had written in pencil upon the torn back of an old envelope:

"Dundee"—the note began—"Your 'trusty' has broken parole. For God's sake don't hunt me down and drag me back. I'll turn up soon enough, but by then it won't make much difference where I am. Sorry. Dick."

Dundee stared at the penciled scrawl until the words grew enormous.

"Suicide?" he whispered.

Fifteen minutes later, in the blue twilight of the late September day, the weary and shaken young detective turned the roadster's nose toward Hillcrest. Fortunately Dick had left the key in the ignition switch.

He had done all he could, Dundee argued with himself. It would have been foolish to conduct the search personally. The police department had the matter in hand, and could be relied upon to make a thorough job of it. And as Strawn had assured him callously, those who threaten to commit suicide seldom go through with it. Besides, the alarm had been given so quickly that the desperate boy had not more than fifteen minutes' start on his small band of uniformed pursuers.

Yes, he had done all he could, but it was hard to meet Gigi's eyes when that ubiquitous child sprang upon the running board of the car as it passed between the open gates of Hillcrest.

"Hello!" she greeted him blithely. "I've been lonesome. The reporters have just left, the last of 'em, I mean. They kept coming and coming, and Abbie gave 'em tea and let 'em take all the pictures they wanted. She wouldn't let *me* be interviewed. Afraid I'd spill something I shouldn't. . . . Where's Dick? I saw you and him drive off together."

"Dick deserted me," he said, as lightly as possible.

But Gigi was not deceived. She leaned over and stared into his eyes for a moment, then cried reproachfully: "Why didn't you keep an eye on him, for heaven's sake? If you hadn't rushed off without saying good-by I'd have warned you not to let him out of your sight."

"Why?" he asked, startled.

"Because all day he's been hellbent on getting drunk again," Gigi retorted, as if surprised at his obtuseness.

Dundee drew a sharp breath. He felt as if a hand clutching at his heart had loosened its grip. Stopping the car abruptly he drew Dick's note of apology from his pocket and passed it to the girl.

"It's too dark to read. Hop into the car and I'll turn the dashlight on for you."

To hold the scrap of paper under the weak little bulb she had to crouch close against him, and involuntarily he put his arm about her shoulders.

"Just as I thought! The pig!" Gigi snorted contemptuously when her quick eyes had taken in the scrawled lines. "I suppose it is worse for him than for the rest of us, because he was in love with Doris, or thought he was, but—oh, why can't he be a *man*!"

"You think that's what the note means?—that he's merely sneaked off to get drunk?" Dundee asked, as casually as possible.

"Of course! What did you think? . . . O-o-oh! I see!" and to Dundee's amazement she laughed. "You thought that this was a sort of cryptic confession and advance notice that Dick was going to commit suicide! If you knew Dick as well as I do! Nobody loves life better than that brother of mine, and nobody has less physical courage. A month from now he'll be crazy about another girl, and—say, did you sic the police onto him?" she broke off to demand with sudden amazing truculence.

"Yes," Dundee admitted curtly.

"Oh, dear! He'll probably be brought home dead drunk in the Black Maria, and what chance will we have then to keep Dad from knowing all about it?" she wailed. "A couple of weeks ago Dad put his foot down hard. Told Dick if he bought so much as one drink of bootleg liquor again he'd disinherit him, and he didn't mean maybe. Now—"

"Dick was drunk last night, and so far I've heard nothing about Dick's being kicked out," Dundee reminded her.

"Dad blames himself for that. The liquor was served at his own table, because Abbie insisted on the dinner being 'correct'," she explained impatiently. "Why couldn't you have believed Dick when he said he'd turn up soon enough? He could have sneaked in and I could have helped him to bed without any fuss. Detectives with vivid imaginations are an awful nuisance," she added mournfully.

Dundee was too indignant to frame a scathing enough retort, but beneath his ardent desire to spank her was an even more ardent desire to kiss her, in gratitude for the great relief she had given him. For he believed she was right in her interpretation of Dick's melodramatic note.

And she was. The summons to the library telephone came just as the young detective was about to enter the drawing room at the dinner hour.

"Hello! Dundee? . . . Captain Strawn. . . . We've got that fine young friend of yours. Yeah. Drunk. More than a little drunk. What had I better do with him? Book him on a charge of drunkenness, so we can keep an eye on him?"

Dundee chuckled with relief. "Do me a favor, chief. Have one of the boys escort him to a Turkish bath, boil the booze out of him, and then send him home. And I'd appreciate it if his escort left him at the gates, to toddle in alone. I'll try to keep his family from knowing what he's been up to—just to preserve the peace, you know."

But the skillful half-lies with which Dundee quieted George Berkeley's suspicions as to his son's absence were told for Gigi's sake, not for Dick Berkeley's.

As soon as possible after the serving of coffee in the drawing room Dundee made his escape. It lay heavy upon his conscience that he had not yet finished transcribing the thick sheaf of notes he had made during that long, gruelling day.

After typing steadily for an hour and a half he had finished his task, with the exception of making a summary of his discoveries leading up to the conclusion, clinched by Gigi's reluctant admissions, that Mrs. George Berkeley was a perfume addict.

Suddenly be sat back and stared at the last two condensed sentences he had typed:

"Mrs. B. purchased seven bottles perfume September. Found five empty perfume bottles concealed in Mrs. B.'s clothes closet."

Seven. Five. . . . Where were those other two bottles? Where, also, were the bottles, once filled with expensive perfume, which Mrs. Berkeley had undoubtedly brought with her from Europe?

"Maybe she drank it all before landing and chucked the bottles overboard," Dundee decided. "Her breath must have reeked with it or her fellow-passenger, Crosby, would not have got wise to her habit. But—those other two bottles. If she was afraid or ashamed to have the chambermaid see the five I found—" He did not finish the sentence, but drummed scowlingly on the desk. "Gigi knew. Others knew. Why not Dick? And Dick dared not buy bootleg liquor on pain of being disinherited!"

He sprang to his feet, overturning the chair. He let it lie and dashed through the bathroom to Dick Berkeley's bedroom. It took him less than five minutes to find what he was looking for. The boy was not so ingenious at concealment as was his mother.

But when his search was finished it had yielded him not two but four empty perfume bottles. The tiny, gold-embossed label of Mrs. Berkeley's favorite department store was pasted on the bottom of two of the flasks, but the other two bore no mark to identify their retail dealer. Obviously cheaper stuff, these last two. Dick had gone shopping for himself!

It was not surprise or shock at his discovery which made the young detective sink weakly into his own chair after he had added Dick's four bottles to Mrs. Berkeley's five and turned the key of the desk drawer. It was natural enough that Dick, learning somehow—probably in the same way that Gigi had—of his mother's strange vice, should succumb to the temptation of adopting that vice. Curiosity at first, perhaps. At any rate, Dick Berkeley was now a perfume addict.

It was the startling new vista which that discovery opened to the detective which made him dizzy.

Dick Berkeley had stolen perfume from his mother at least twice. Last night Dick had seen his mother receive a gift of at least five ounces of perfume from Seymour Crosby. . . .

Half-drunk at the time, had Dick tipsily made up his mind to appropriate the new supply before his mother could dispose of it herself? If she missed it, his mother would have good reason to suspect who the thief was and to shield him, as she must have shielded him for his two previous thefts—

"Well, here I am! And sober. Sober as hell after that damned Turkish bath," a sulky voice from the bathroom door interrupted the detective's cogitations. "I hope you're satisfied!"

"Your gratitude is overwhelming, Dick!" Dundee retorted dryly.

"Guess I ought to thank you," the pale, haggard young man mumbled. "Captain Strawn said you were pulling the wool over Dad's eyes. . . . But I risked a whale of a lot to get that jag on, and I'll be damned if I wanted to sweat it out in a Turkish bath."

"If you were in such a funk that you needed to get stewed, why didn't you play safe and swig a flask of perfume?" Dundee asked coldly.

"Too slow, and I can't stand the thought of the stuff now," Dick retorted. Then realization swept over his muddled brain. "Say! What the devil are you driving at, anyway?"

"No use, Dick!" Dundee's voice was like a whiplash. "And I don't doubt that you can't stand the thought of perfume—*now*!"

Dick Berkeley did not answer. His pale-brown eyes stared blankly at Dundee for a minute, then his body sagged and slowly crumpled to the floor.

There were several questions the detective longed to ask, when the boy, whom he had undressed and put to bed, came to his senses. But Dick Berkeley turned his face to the wall and pretended to be too exhausted, mentally and physically, to speak a word. And perhaps he was, Dundee decided, as he shrugged and turned away.

When he himself was ready for bed half an hour later, he laid his ear to the bathroom keyhole and listened intently. Yes, the boy was asleep and muttering brokenly.

Noiselessly Dundee entered his friend's room and tiptoed to the bed.

"Sorry, Doris," Dick Berkeley was murmuring. "Sorry, darling, didn't mean—"

There was nothing more, and Dundee crept to his own bed, so weary that he was asleep almost before he could jerk out the bedside light.

He overslept unpardonably, and was the last to appear for Sunday breakfast, which he had just sat down to when Wickett came from the butler's pantry to inform him:

"A Dr. Jennings on the wire for you, sir."

2

Dundee almost ran to the library, closed the door to insure privacy, and snatched up the telephone receiver without taking time to seat himself at the big desk on which the instrument stood.

"Dundee speaking, Dr. Jennings. You've completed the analysis?"

"I have," came the voice of the city chemist over the wire. "And my report is negative."

"*Negative!*" Dundee echoed.

"Yep," Dr. Jennings assured him. "1 tested for wood alcohol first—"

"Wood alcohol!" the detective exclaimed. "I never thought of that—had some quick-acting, subtle poison in mind."

"Strawn vows you're a story-book detective," the chemist chuckled, "If that bottle of perfume had been diluted half and half, say, with wood alcohol, the effect on the person who drank it would not have been swift, but it would have been very sure. Death probably, but blindness at least. Since that would have been the logical way to murder a person known to be a perfume addict—"

"Why, logical, doctor?" Dundee asked curiously.

"For the simple reason that the purchaser of the perfume could contend that if the stuff contained wood alcohol, it must have been placed there by an unscrupulous manufacturer," the chemist answered impatiently. "Another good reason is that bootleg liquor, not doctored perfume, would have been blamed. Perfume-drinking is a secret vice, and the addict, once dead, could not very well exonerate the bootleg fraternity and point to an innocent-looking perfume flask as the source of the poison."

"I see," Dundee admitted slowly, for his brain was whirling with new possibilities. "But since wood alcohol evaporates so quickly, how can you be sure that none was present?"

"I can't be absolutely certain," the chemist admitted. "If the perfume had contained perfectly pure wood alcohol, no trace would have remained. But that commodity is hard for the layman to obtain, and the purchase of it would be traceable. On the other hand, ordinary commercial wood alcohol, used for many purposes, is easily obtainable and has a strong odor due to the presence of small amounts of several impurities, including pyridine and furfurol. Furfurol is not very volatile, and hence would remain behind after the evaporation of the alcohol proper. It can readily be detected even in small amounts by sensitive color tests. I found none of these impurities in the scented handkerchief you gave me for analysis."

"But if the commercial wood alcohol has a strong odor, would not a perfume addict detect it and be repelled?" Dundee asked.

"Not necessarily," the doctor answered. "The odor of the very concentrated perfume would be the more powerful, and tend to conceal almost entirely the unpleasant odor of the impure alcohol."

"I see," Dundee assured him very thoughtfully. "An ingenious way to murder an enemy."

The chemist chuckled. "Unfortunately, few of us have enemies who are perfume addicts."

"That's true. . . . And you found no trace of any other kind of poison?"

"None whatever."

"Thank you very much, Dr. Jennings," Dundee said, and was a little surprised to hear the faint click of a receiver upon a hook. Odd that the genial chemist had not said good-by. He was about to hang up himself when he became aware that Dr. Jennings had not been rudely abrupt after all.

"You're entirely welcome, Dundee. Good-by."

A familiar, teasing voice cut into the detective's frown-lug concentration:

"Exit Mr. Seymour Crosby as a wicked old Borgia!"

"Gigi! Eavesdropping again! Now I *know* I'm going to spank you! I never saw such a girl—"

Gigi, on her knees in the big chair whose high back had hidden her from view until now, made a *gamine* "face" at him. "I guess this is my own father's library, and I've got a right to read a book in my own father's library, haven't I?"

"Are you reading 'Penrod' by any chance?" Dundee asked sourly.

"No. A detective story that Dad said was a corker. But I guessed the murderer in the very first chapter. Funny thing, too. He put wood alcohol in some bootleg liquor—"

"How many extensions has this telephone?" Dundee interrupted.

"Three," she answered promptly. "One in Wickett's pantry, one in Dad's bedroom, and one in Abbie's. She has a private unlisted phone in her sitting room, too. Why?"

"Merely that you are not the only eavesdropper in the house," Dundee said grimly. "Does this telephone ring on each extension?"

"No. Only here and in Wickett's pantry, but had it occurred to you that Dad or Mother might have taken off the receiver to call out, found that the line was busy, and hung up? Or that Wickett may have neglected to hang up the receiver in the pantry until you'd nearly finished your conversation? I suppose Wickett did answer the phone in his pantry and send you here to take the call, didn't he?"

"Yes," Dundee answered shortly. He was not satisfied, but there was clearly nothing to be gained now by trying to trace the eavesdropper.

"Poor old Sherlock!" Gigi sympathized. "Was he all hot and bothered because his grand, little hunch about poisoned perfume didn't pan out? Did he just yearn to clap nice Mr. Crosby on the shoulder and say, 'C-r-osby! The jig is up! I arrest you for the murders of Phyllis Crosby and Doris Matthews'?"

"Shut up, Hellion!" Dundee growled at her. What a capacity the little devil had for hitting the nail upon the head! "I confess I'm disappointed," he told her abruptly. "Not that I wish Crosby any harm. But my only ray of light on this confounded case proves to be merely a reflection cast by my own dazzling stupidity!"

"Very neat!" she applauded his simile. "But why not be content with dear old Johnson, the expert safecracker?"

The ringing of the telephone saved him the necessity of a lame reply.

"Western Union calling Mr. James F. Dundee," a voice droned in his ear.

"Dundee speaking. Have you a cablegram for me?"

"A prepaid radiogram from London, England, signed Sir Edward Moresby," the voice intoned with mechanical clearness. "I shall read the message: 'Kathryn Matthews unconscious following motor accident. Will question when possible.' . . . Shall I repeat the message?"

"No, thanks," Dundee said dully, and hung up receiver.

"Bad news?" Gigi asked quickly, with real concern.

Dundee grinned at her, and they were friends again. "If I don't tell you, you'll find it out yourself, you ferret! Kathryn Matthews, Doris's sister in London, is unconscious following a motor accident. It will be my luck to have her die before she can tell a few secrets regarding Phyllis Crosby's death, which Doris had confided to her."

"Mr. Crosby—or someone!—*is* playing in luck, he?" Gigi said soberly.

"Playing in luck or playing safe!" Dundee retorted, but he did not speak the words aloud, possibly because he had a strong hunch Gigi would have laughed at him.

"Come long!" Gigi cried, scrambling out of the chair. "I'll take you on as a partner for tennis, if Dad and Dick will play doubles. They're already on the court. Fancy Dick's being out so early after his bender last night. Maybe he's avoiding *you*!"

"I shouldn't be a bit surprised!" Dundee retorted. "Will you wait here till I go up and change my shoes and get my racket? I'll see you dressed with tennis mind."

"Yes. Tish was going to play with me, but Abbie had a sudden yen for spiritual consolation this morning and nothing would do but that Tish and Clorinda and Mr. Crosby should go with her to church. Oh, don't get a grouch on!" she commanded, as Dun frowned at her news. "Mrs. Lambert telephoned and asked Captain Strawn for permission."

As he ran upstairs Dundee wondered whether Abbie Berkeley's sudden and probably unusual need "spiritual consolation" was the real reason for her attendance at church this Sunday morning, or whether it was a more carnal need to show off her socially distinguished visitor, since she had been cheated of her big party in his honor.

In any event, Dundee wished fervently that he could read her mind as she bent her knees before an all-seeing God.

The tennis match proved to be an unexpectedly pleasant affair. The two couples offset each other evenly enough to make the game interesting. To make up for Dick's shakiness was his father's superb control and rather astonishing agility. And Dundee's excellence—he had once made the semi-finals in an intercollegiate tournament—counteracted Gigi's sometimes eccentric service.

As they were resting after a swift set, which had gone to Dundee and Gigi, George Berkeley took out his cigarette case and passed it.

"Here's a light, sir," Dundee offered quickly, snapping open his lighter. "Its performance is perfect since I filled it from that container in the library. Gigi tells me you invented the thing yourself. Very clever."

"I didn't invent the idea," George Berkeley denied, with surprising curtness. "I merely patented a gadget that simplifies the old cigar counter fountain."

"You use commercial wood alcohol to fill them, I believe?"

"That, or benzine," Berkeley answered brusquely.

"Wickett attends to the filling of the fountains here. . . Well, Dick, I think I've had enough tennis for one day. I'd like to go over that business proposition with you now, if Gigi and Mr. Dundee will excuse us."

As the detective watched father and son stroll together across the lawn he was remembering what Gigi had said: "Dad's afraid some thirsty and incautious member of his precious family will take a swig of the wood alcohol and fill an untimely grave. Therefore he delivers periodic lectures on the horrible effects." If that was true, then why had George Berkeley deliberately contrived to leave the impression that he did not know personally whether benzine or wood alcohol was used for the fountains in his own home?

Gigi was beating him rather badly at tennis, to her own delighted astonishment, when Wickett interrupted with:

'Police Headquarters on the telephone, sir. I asked them to hold the wire."

"Johnson!" Gigi cried, and pounded jubilantly after the running detective.

XXIV.

"I'VE brought Wickett along to identify Johnson," Dundee told his chief when he arrived at Police Headquarters. "You sounded a bit mysterious over the telephone. Where *is* Johnson.?"

"On his way here now, escorted by a couple of the finest," Captain Strawn grinned. "I told you that unless he staged the cleverest disappearing stunt of the century we'd have him here within twenty minutes."

"Where did you find him?" Dundee asked, still puzzled.

"Right here in Hamilton!" Strawn chuckled. "Wasn't in hiding at all. In fact, he was as conspicuous as a wart on a nose. He's been 'making' Hamilton regularly for six months as a traveling salesman for a Chicago silk hosiery manufacturer. Always stops at the Stuart House, which, if you don't happen to know, is Hamilton's most popular commercial hotel. A pretty good salesman, too!" Strawn added admiringly. "After the robbery and the murder Friday night he made his rounds Saturday morning, as usual, and booked a string of big orders from department stores, shoe stores and specialty shops."

"But if you found him at the Stuart House—" Dundee objected.

"We didn't," Strawn chuckled. "The boys picked him up ten minutes ago on the Municipal Golf Links. But I'll tell it from the beginning.

"About twelve o'clock today into this office walks a dame who says she's Hattie Schneider, chambermaid at the Stuart House. Wants to know if there's any reward for information about Harvey Johnson. I tell her to spill her story and let me see what it's worth. She opens a bundle and I'll be damned if she doesn't pull out a navy-blue polka-dot bow-tie and a white shirt with blue pin stripes. Says they belong to the 'gent' in 512, one of the rooms she cleans. Young man by the name of Cartwright—Hubert Cartwright. She describes Johnson to a T, except that this Cartwright wears horn-rimmed glasses and parts his hair in the middle instead of on the left side. But if you remember, Johnson's description would fit about four out of ten young men you see on the streets any day, and shirts and ties like the ones she showed me are pretty apt to be in every man's wardrobe."

"Yes," Dundee agreed.

"But I wasn't taking any chances," Strawn went on with immense satisfaction. "I went to the Stuart House myself, and had a talk with the manager. He gave Cartwright a swell send-off. Said he'd known him for six months, ever since Cartwright had taken over this territory for the hosiery manufacturer, and that, for a traveling salesman, Cartwright was a model character. Paid his bills promptly, didn't try to smuggle girls into his room, kept regular and decent hours. But as I said, I wasn't taking any chances. I made the manager take me up to Cartwright's room, and stay while I searched it. In the desk were a couple of wires and a letter from his sales manager, and everything looked jake for Cartwright. Nothing funny in his clothes closet or bureau drawers. No black pigskin bag, like the one Johnson stole from Crosby. But there was a big sample case, stamped with the name of the hosiery concern. It was locked. One of my skeleton keys opened it."

He paused provocatively, and leisurely lit his pipe.

"And there you found the loot, eh?" Dundee grinned.

"And how!" Strawn assured him grimly, as he opened a drawer of his desk and showed his subordinate a pile of silk stockings. "Look!" He lifted a pair of "sun-van" sheer silk hose and Dundee's fascinated eyes watched a gleaming snake writhe swiftly to the toe of a stocking

"Mrs. Berkeley's string of 49 matched pearls. Every piece stolen from Crosby, Clorinda and Mrs. Berkeley is here. Even the miniature of Phyllis Crosby. Each article was concealed in a separate pair of stockings, and the stockings folded so smoothly you'd never guess what Santa Claus had put into them."

"Pretty neat," Dundee commented admiringly. "And Johnson, or Cartwright, had left the loot there while he trustfully went out to play golf?"

"Yeah. The hotel manager says he plays every Sunday that he's in Hamilton. Went out this morning with a couple of friends he's made in the hotel. I had the manager put in a call to a soft drink and hot-dog stand near the links, and get a message to one of the two men he was playing with. This chap, name of Petty, has been living in the hotel for years and the manager could vouch for him. I spoke to Petty, told him who I was, warned him not to tip off Cartwright, and asked him to keep my man in sight until a police car could get there. . . . Come in!" he bawled.

Sergeant Turner stuck his head in. "Got him, chief. Want him in here?"

"Yes. What's he been told?" Captain Strawn replied. "Nothing, but that he's wanted at Headquarters for questioning," Sergeant Turner answered.

"Good! Bring him in."

Within two minutes the suspect was ushered into Captain Strawn's office. Wearing correct and rather expensive golf togs, the young man presented a surprisingly prepossessing appearance. Even his expression—mingled surprise and indignation—was eminently correct.

"Hello, Johnson!" Captain Strawn greeted him jovially, like an old friend.

"My name is Cartwright—Hubert D. Cartwright," the man answered with just the right amount vehemence. "I am a traveling representative of the Tru-Silk Hosiery Company of Chicago."

"Sergeant, there's a man out in the hall named Wickett. Will you bring him in?"

At the butler's name Cartwright's good-looking face paled, but he did not betray himself otherwise.

"Ever see this man before, Wickett?" Strawn asked genially, as the butler edged diffidently into the room.

"If he will kindly take off his glasses—"

Sergeant Turner cut short Cartwright's angry prow by jerking off the horn-rimmed spectacles himself.

Wickett studied the face conscientiously for a moment before replying. "Yes, sir," he said to Captain Strawn "I have seen him before. I know him as Johnson, the man Mrs. Lambert hired on Friday to serve as Mr. Crosby's valet."

"Thanks, Wickett. Sorry to have had to yank you away from your work like this," said the chief of detectives, "Payne, have one of the boys drive Wickett back to Hillcrest. Now, Johnson—or is it really Cartwright?—what have you got to say for yourself?"

"Am I under arrest?" the. man asked coolly.

"Arrest?   Oh, no. Not yet," Strawn retorted genially. "You're just here for a nice, quiet little chat. . . See here, Johnson!" he snapped, abandoning all pretense. "We've got you cold on the burglary business, and if you insist, I can put you under arrest right now; you can stand on your rights, demand a lawyer and refuse to talk. But I'm trying to be decent to you. I'm going to give you a chance to come clean on the whole rotten mess you got yourself into Friday night. I'm going to listen to your story with an open mind, then advise you honestly, as man to man, whether I think you have a Chinaman's chance, to get a minimum sentence for second degree murder or maybe just manslaughter, if you plead guilty.   Otherwise, Johnson, I'm going to book you right now for first-degree murder as well as grand larceny."

"You haven't got anything on me, except that I happen to look something like a man named Johnson," the man retorted, but his voice shook a little.

"Yeah?" Strawn grinned. "Life's just full of funny coincidences, ain't it? You 'happen' to look something like a man named Johnson; you 'happen' to sign the Stuart House register in a handwriting that 'happens' to look like Johnson's writing on his application for work filed Friday with the Hamilton Domestic Employment Bureau; you 'happen' to own a navy-blue silk bow-tie with white polka dots and a white shirt with blue pin stripes—just like Johnson's; and you 'happen' to have had in your possession about $75,000 worth of jewelry, just like the stuff Johnson stole from the Berkeley home Friday night."

As he spoke Strawn opened a drawer of his desk and pulled out the shirt and tie; then, still grinning at the white-faced young man, he opened another drawer and. exhibited the rumpled stack of silk stockings.

It was the last exhibit which completely shattered the nerve of the prisoner. He made no melodramatic lunge toward the chief of detectives; he did not curse or snarl. He merely collapsed so completely that Dundee, watching with keen but not unkind eyes, had a momentary fear that the man had died of a heart attack His eyes were closed, and cheeks and lips had, with amazing suddenness, taken on the grayish-lavender pallor of death.

Captain Strawn must have become alarmed, too, for, he jerked open the bottom drawer of his desk, seized a pint bottle of whiskey and, poured a stiff dose into a small glass.

"Lend a hand, Dundee!" he ordered. "Force his jaws apart. . . . That's right. . . . Ah—Well, my man!" he exulted, as Johnson's eyelids fluttered weakly. "Ready to talk now?"

"Give him time, chief," Dundee begged compassionately.

"I'll talk," Johnson whispered feebly. "Make—a statement—"

"You're darned tootin' you'll make a statement!" Strawn assured him. "Sergeant Turner, get Brede in here in a double-quick hurry."

Within five minutes the anemic stenographer attached to the Homicide Squad was seated across the desk from Captain Strawn, ready with notebook and pencil.

"All right, Johnson!" the chief of detectives snapped. "What's your real name? And what's your record?"

The calm of despair had settled upon the suspect. "My name is Harold Conway. I was convicted of burglary in Los Angeles in 1919, and served seven years of a ten-year sentence in San Quentin. I was released April 10, 1926."

"Any other convictions?" Strawn prodded him, as he paused.

"No. I've been going straight since I got out of San Quentin. This is the first job I've pulled. I—well, I needed some sudden money, and I didn't know how else to get it."

"May I ask a question, chief?" Dundee broke in. "Thanks. Conway, were you in New York City at any time during 1926 or 1927?"

"Say! What are you trying to pin on me now?" the suspect demanded, with a feeble spark of anger. "What if I was in New York?"

"You really do look amazingly like a gentleman, and it's quite possible," Dundee ruminated aloud. "Just where did you meet Phyllis Benham, Conway?" he demanded suddenly.

"Phyllis Benham?" the prisoner echoed blankly. "I've never known a girl named Phyllis Benham."

"Phyllis Crosby?" Dundee suggested.

"Never heard of her," Conway retorted. "Kin to that guy I was hired to work for?"

"His dead wife. You stole her miniature," Dundee replied quietly.

"I took everything that was in a jewel box, without bothering to open some of the cases," the prisoner explained frankly.

"Doris Matthews told one of the maids that she had seen you somewhere before," Dundee told him, trying a new tack.

"Yes. In the dining room of the Stuart House Thursday night," Conway answered promptly. "She was having dinner with a man. I met him Friday night at the servants' dinner. Arnold, the chauffeur, he was. He didn't see me Thursday night, because his back was toward me, but I nearly got the girl's goat staring at her. She was a peach. Of course I had on my glasses, and my hair was parted in the middle, not on the left side as it was Friday night. But I saw it had her bothered—where she'd seen me before."

"And you weren't taking any chances, were you, Conway?" Strawn cut in savagely. "You knew the girl might remember and give you away. That's why you killed her! Didn't I tell you so yesterday, Dundee?"

"I didn't kill her!" Conway retorted, with amazing calm. "And I can prove it!"

"Alibi, eh?" Strawn sneered. "It'll take a hell of an alibi to get your neck out of this noose, my man!"

"And I've got it," Conway assured him coolly. "Don't you think I know from the papers when she was last seen alive? Listen: I finished my job at the Berkeley house before ten o'clock. I could have stowed the junk in my pockets, but I took that black pigskin bag of Crosby's just to throw dust in your eyes."

"What did you do with it?"

"Chucked it on my way to the interurban stop," Conway grinned. "if you can find out who owns a Lincoln coupé parked at the curb in front of No. 4318 Fairview Road, and will tell him to lift up the back seat, he'll find the bag, unless he's found it already and has been afraid to turn it in. It's got Crosby's tennis shoes in it, as well as the velvet boxes that all the loot was kept in."

"Check it, Sergeant Turner!" Strawn flung at his subordinate, and Turner left the office on the run.

"That was about 10:15," Conway continued coolly. "By that time I'd put on my own shoes, which I'd carried out in the bag, buttoned up my topcoat about my collar, put on my glasses, and parted my hair in the middle, as I always wear it. I strolled on to the shed where passengers wait for the interurban and in about six minutes a car came along, just as I knew it would, because I've been catching the interurban at that stop off and on for six months, and I know the schedule."

"So you've been planning the haul that long, eh?' Strawn growled.

"No. This was a jumped-up affair. But I've got a girl friend that lives not a million miles from the Berkeley house. I take her home in a taxi, but I hop the interurban back to town."

"What's her name?"

"I'm not telling that," Conway retorted, and, meant it. "But the conductor and motorman who were on Friday night have seen me often enough the last six months to feel pretty well acquainted. Friday night, on the 10:22, there was only a handful of passengers and I stood up front, talking to the old boy who runs the car. Motorman No. 65," he supplied obligingly.

"Got it all down pat, haven't you?" Strawn commented sourly.

"Yes," Conway agreed. "He told me he had a fallen arch that was hurting like the devil, and he'd be glad to pull into Hamilton and turn the car over to the motorman that was to relieve him at 10:46. The old boy usually goes off duty at 11:56, but he'd arranged for relief an hour ahead of schedule Friday night, because of. his swollen foot."

"Check it, Payne!" Strawn flung over his shoulder at the detective lolling in the window. "Well, what's the rest of your yarn?" he snarled at his prisoner, and Dundee felt a surge of genuine sympathy toward his chief, who had counted so heavily upon "Johnson" to solve the murder.

"I left the interurban at the Stuart House corner at 10:42," Conway went on calmly. "I asked for my key, and chatted a while with the night clerk—"

"Get hold of the night clerk of the Stuart House," Strawn wearily ordered Detective Burns, who was also listening in on the confession.

"The night clerk looked at the clock, and asked me if my girl and I had had a row, since it was so early," Conway went on cheerfully. "Well, I went up to my room and stayed there till Saturday morning. I carried the jewelry in my pockets while I made my rounds of the shops Saturday, but this morning I stowed it away in my sample case, because I was afraid some of it might drop out of my pockets on the golf course. I was planning to call on the trade as usual all day Monday, then to leave Monday night for Chicago, per schedule. I aimed to get rid of the stuff there, through a fence who's been bothering me to go back to the old racket."

"Why didn't you get rid of the shirt and necktie?" Dundee asked.

"Just try to think up some way of getting rid of an incriminating bundle, and see if you wouldn't have done what I did," Conway retorted reasonably. "I thought of a dozen ways, each more dangerous than the last, and finally I just left 'em around, as if they didn't mean a thing in my young life."

"Good psychology, which didn't happen to work this time," Dundee sympathized. "The chambermaid brought them in this morning."

"You can't crack a safe without taking a chance," Conway shrugged. "But if I'd tried to sneak out and chuck 'em in an ash can, the chance would have been ten times bigger, and as it turns out later, if I'd left the hotel I wouldn't have had an airtight alibi on this murder business. I didn't even know a murder had been committed out there until I saw an extra Saturday morning, and at that time you didn't know there'd been a burglary, so we were quits!"

"And when you did learn of the murder?" Dundee prodded.

"God, I nearly lost my head" Conway admitted, with a shudder. "But I knew I had an alibi if worst came to worst and Hubert Cartwright was connected with Harvey Johnson, so I kept right on with my program of acting natural, and taking orders for silk stockings."

"You say this Berkeley job was a jumped-up affair," Strawn began sourly, after a long minute of silence. "What's the yarn?"

"Friday morning nothing was further from my mind than to try the old racket again," the prisoner answered earnestly. "But when I was showing my line to a buyer in a shop on Grand Avenue I heard Mrs. Berkeley talking to Mrs. Lambert. Shooting off her mouth to impress people, I guess. I heard her say, 'Dear Mrs. Lambert! Don't let me forget to go to the safe-deposit vault for my jewels, and right after we've had a bite of lunch, you must dash over to the employment bureau and try to get a valet for dear Mr. Crosby.'"

Even Strawn grinned appreciatively at the excellent imitation of Mrs. Berkeley's gushing speech and manner.

"Well, I needed sudden money, and it was me that 'dear Mrs. Lambert' hired as a valet," Conway continued. "I had some references, but there's no use asking me where I got 'em."

For nearly an hour Captain Strawn hammered away at his suspect, eliciting a very full and interesting confession of the burglary, but Dundee paid little attention. His mind was intensely occupied with more vital matters.

At the end of the hour every detail of Harold Conway's alibi had been checked and verified. The owner of the Lincoln coupé joined with the night clerk and with the interurban motorman in clinching the thing, for he promptly volunteered the information that he had left No. 4318 Fairview Road at five minutes to eleven. And Doris Matthews was alive at that time.

While Brede, the stenographer, was preparing a statement for Conway's signature, Dundee drew Captain Strawn aside and asked in a low voice:

"Well, what next, chief?"

"Right back there where we started from," Strawn admitted bitterly. "District Attorney Sherwood blew in here this morning, and told me he'd take a hand himself if Johnson proved a washout on the murder business. I'll have to call him now and tell him the bad news."

He put in the call, with such reluctance that Dundee felt sorry for him. When he hung up, he rejoined his young subordinate and told him gloomily:

"Sherwood wants to see the notes you took yesterday. Got 'em with you?"

"Yes," Dundee admitted, drawing the packet of folded sheets from his pocket. He removed the final page, however, and returned it to his pocket. "Nothing—just some stuff I jotted down," he hastily answered the suspicion in Strawn's eyes. "The stories are all complete, and I hope Sherwood has the grace to thank me."

"Catch him thanking a dick!" Strawn spat disgustedly. "I've got to wait here for that big bag of wind, then we'll go out to Hillcrest together, I suppose, to have another shot at digging up the truth."

"Telephone for you, Dundee," Payne interrupted.

"Hello, Bonnie Dundee!" Gigi's unmistakable voice shrilled over the wire "I'm dying for news. Has Johnson confessed?"

"To the burglary, yes," Dundee replied: "But he has an ironclad alibi for the murder. You're not to tell anyone though, and I mean that, young woman! Where is everybody?"

"Playing bridge," she answered promptly. "That is, Dad and Dick, Clarinda and Mrs. Lambert are playing. Abbie says she's too nervous to play, but she's kibitzing. As sure as Dad bids two spades—"

"I'll be right out," Dundee Cut her short. "Remember, you're honor bound not to spill the news till I get there."

"I'll keep out of sight of the bridge fiends till you get here," she promised.

"Can you spare me Payne and a car?" Dundee asked his thief. "We'll need him later anyway, and he might as well be on hand. . . . Thanks!"

Detective Payne liked and admired Detective Dundee, but on the ride out to Hillcrest he found his young associate very poor company.

"Park here, Payne," Dundee ordered, as they slowed down outside the gates of the estate. "Stop anybody that tries to leave the grounds."

He walked slowly to the house, wrestling with a new theory which began with the fact that Abbie Berkeley was a perfume addict, and led heaven alone knew where.

Fifteen feet from the southwest corner of the house, however, he stopped short, as his nostrils were assailed with the overpowering odor of benzine.

Who the devil could be cleaning clothes on a Sunday afternoon?

But before he tore down to the basement, from whose open window the fumes were pouring, Dundee was sure he knew the answer.

XXV.

"GIGI!" Dundee shouted, in a voice so harsh with anger that the girl, bending over a stationary laundry tub, withdrew reddened arms dripping with benzine and gaped at him incredulously.

"My! You scared me!" she laughed uncertainly as the detective strode toward her. "I'm doing my daily Girl Scout good deed, but I should have worn rubber gloves. This stuff burns like the devil!"

But he had no sympathy for her smarting arms. He seized them and shook her till her teeth rattled against each other. "You ought to have had on a strait jacket," he corrected her savagely. "Do you know what you've done?"

"I hope I've got rid of the stink of *Fleur d'Amour*," she retorted, when he had dropped her arms helplessly and a little ashamed. For she *did* look so innocent—"When the folks began to play bridge this afternoon, all sitting pretty close together, you know, the odor was sickeningly strong, because everybody's clothes are scented up with the stuff from hanging in closets with the evening clothes we were wearing Friday night."

"Who complained of the odor?" he asked quickly.

Seeing that she had his interest in spite of his anger, Gigi rushed on eagerly. "Abbie. She said it positively made her sick, and Mrs. Lambert said it did her, too, and she'd be glad when Monday came and the perfume-sprinkled things could be sent to the cleaners. And Dad said, 'If the police will let you send them!'"

"Did anybody suggest this stunt?" Dundee interrupted harshly.

"No. I thought of it all by myself!" she retorted proudly. "I told you over the phone they wouldn't let me play bridge, so I finally got tired of nothing to do, and sneaked upstairs and collected all the clothes that had

perfume on them, shot them down the laundry chute in
the bathrooms, and—there they are! I did the evening
dresses first, then doused all the tuxedoes,   even
Wickett's— Oh, don't look so peeved!" she protested. "I
didn't take yours. I was afraid you wouldn't like it;.
besides, I know you're not so squeamish about smelling it
as the rest of us are. Abbie was right for once; she said
the smell of *Fleur d'Amour* would always be the odor of
death to her, and I didn't see why all of us should be
reminded every time we open a closet door—"

"Just a minute, Gigi!" Dundee interrupted sternly. "At
exactly what time did this Good Samaritan complex
overtake you? *Before or after* you found from telephoning
me that Johnson did not kill Doris Matthews?"

Her eyes grew wide and innocent and injured as she
answered: "Why, it was after, but—".

"Gigi, you can't fool me! You have deliberately
destroyed evidence, which is a crime punishable by
imprisonment!"

Gigi laughed, a little shakily. "Which brings to light
still another advantage of being only fifteen! They'll only
send me to the reformatory—"

"You made a clean sweep of it, I suppose?" he cut in
disgustedly, gingerly lifting a soaked coat by a lapel.

"I'm afraid I did," Gigi confessed with an air of deep
humility, but Dundee saw a glint of triumph in her eyes
before she lowered them. "Every single thing but the
shoes we were wearing Friday night. I'd have doused
them, too, but there wasn't any perfume on anybody's
but Clorinda's. There *they* are, under the tub. I'm afraid
benzine isn't awfully good for gold slippers," added
ruefully.

"Clorinda's slippers, cape and evening dress were in
my room," he reminded her. "You at least knew they had
been confiscated by the police, as exhibits the grand jury.
And since the odor of perfume from them could not
possibly annoy your sister or anyone but me—"

"Why haven't you taken them to the police station then?" she challenged him.

"Because I was a fool!" he retorted bitterly. "There was a bare chance that Johnson was guilty of the murder and would confess; and that your sister need not be dragged into the case. I see now that chivalry does pay in this case. . . . Come clean, Gigi!" he commanded harshly. "Why did you do this? Why did you destroy evidence?"

"Why do you keep harping on 'destroying evidence.'" she cried angrily. "Clorinda *told* you she'd been in summerhouse after the murder was committed, you didn't need a cape with a streak of blood on it and a pair of slippers to prove it! As for the rest of the things, the only evidence I destroyed was that I sprinkled perfume on all of you Friday night, and you've still got your own Tuxedo to prove that!"

"You knew my coat was harmless," he accused. "As harmless as that handkerchief you gave me to analyzed for poison. . . . Quit stalling, Gigi! Why did you come to the conclusion that that flask of *Fleur d'Amour* was diluted with wood alcohol *after Wickett took it to your mother's room Friday night?*"

"You're crazy! I don't know what you're talk about!" she denied furiously.

"Oh, yes, you do, Gigi." He was grimly implacable. "This stunt of yours proves that! You were eavesdropping this morning when I was talking with Jennings, the city chemist. You heard me mention wood alcohol repeatedly. You knew wood alcohol was available in half a dozen of those patented fountains of your father's. . . . Now tell me whom you were trying to protect by this mad stunt of yours?"

"Not so mad!" Gigi retorted impudently, and turned back to the reeking laundry tub. "If anybody *did* put wood alcohol in Abbie's perfume, you're going to have a hard time proving it, darling!"

"Is that so?" he retorted savagely, and turned to stamp angrily out of the basement.

"Where are you going?" Gigi panted, flying after him.

"Go back to your washing!" he commanded.

"I shan't!" she sobbed, and followed him as stubbornly as a dog ignoring stones flung by his master, followed him as he strode across the lawn to the summerhouse.

In grim silence the thoroughly angry young detective knelt on the floor of the little arbor where Doris Matthews had been stunned to insensibility by the blow of a perfume flask in a murderer's hand.

"Oh!" Gigi gasped. "I never thought of that!"

With his penknife Dundee gouged the dirt from between the cracks of the floor, on the spot which had been saturated with the spilled perfume.

"I should have burned down the summerhouse," Gigi laughed hysterically, as Dundee transferred the loosened dirt from the floor to an envelope.

When the envelope was safe in his pocket, the detective faced the girl. "I'm going to take this to Dr. Jennings now, for analysis. But *like you*, Gigi, I haven't a doubt in the world that he will report the finding of wood alcohol impurities. And I'm going to give you one more chance to help me. Certainly you owe me a great deal for the damage you've done to-day. *Whom are you trying to protect?*"

"I refuse to answer!" she said steadily, but her face was very pale beneath the tan.

"You realize, of course, that you are shielding a person who plotted to murder your mother? Some person who knew your mother to be a perfume addict, and who confidently expected her death to follow the drinking of *Fleur d'Amour!*"

Gigi did not answer, but her topaz eyes were wide with horror and misery.

"Then I am to conclude that you are shielding yourself?" Dundee went on brutally.

"*Myself!*" she echoed incredulously.

"You confessed to me Friday night before the murder that you had done 'something dreadful,'" he reminded her. "You were very angry with your mother, for having slapped and humiliated you before guests. You knew your mother was a perfume addict. Her habit disgusted you. You have told me that she makes life miserable for you. You—"

"Oh, don't be an idiot!" she cried, stamping her foot. "I didn't put wood alcohol in her perfume, and *I don't know who did*!"

"But you know who hated her enough to plot her death," Dundee said almost gently. "And you love that person enough to wish for him—or her—to go free of a horrible murder that grew out of a crime which poor Doris Matthews prevented, by discovering the poisoner at work! Isn't that true?"

Gigi's horror-filled eyes stared at him for a long minute, then the girl turned and fled from the summerhouse.

It was past four o'clock that Sunday afternoon when Bonnie Dundee returned to Hillcrest after his visit to the home of Dr. Abel Jennings. The chemist had promised to forego a bridge game and rush the analysis, predicting a report by nine o'clock that evening.

Two sedans, which he recognized as belonging to District Attorney Sherwood and Captain Strawn of the Homicide Squad, warned Dundee that his superiors were again in charge of the case.

"Hello, boy!" Captain Strawn greeted him ruefully as soon as Wickett had admitted him. "Old Wind-bag's at it—hammer and tongs. Says you and me have been barking up a whole forest of wrong trees. Yeah, says it's plain as the nose on your face that the chauffeur killed the girl in a lovers' quarrel over Dick Berkeley, and that if he'd taken hold when the murder was first discovered he'd have had a confession by now."

"That so?" Dundee grinned. "I seem to remember that our Mr. Jerome Sherwood is up for re-election in November. One can quite sympathize with his determination not to antagonize so influential a vote-controller   as multi-millionaire Berkeley, by insulting him, his family or his guests with horrid old suspicions. . . . Well, I wish him luck!"

"Want to watch the show?" Strawn suggested, with malicious amusement. "It's being staged in the servants' sitting room.. The chances that Arnold would knock him cold looked pretty good five minutes ago."

"No, thanks. I might pitch in and help Arnold. Yes, Wickett?"

"Telephone for you, sir. Will you take it in the library?"

Two minutes later Dundee hung up the receiver and faced his chief, with a resigned shrug:

"Well, that's that! Kathryn Matthews died without regaining consciousness."

"Tough luck," Strawn admitted. "I guess that means the Crosby case is really 'closed forever,' as Doris said."

"Maybe yes, maybe no!" Dundee retorted with irritating cheerfulness..

"What are you up to?" Strawn demanded suspiciously, as Dundee rose to leave the library.

"Up to bed—for a nice long nap, until exactly nine o'clock!"

XXVI.

1

AT nine o'clock that Sunday evening Dundee descended to the library, put in a call to the laboratory of Dr. Abel Jennings, city chemist and toxicologist, and received the report that wood alcohol impurities had been found in the specimen of perfumed earth from the summerhouse flooring.

"Well, there's your case, Dundee," Dr. Jennings concluded cheerfully.

"And all I have to do is to prove it," Dundee retorted. "Thanks to certain interference, that will be an almost impossible task."

He lost no time, however, in setting to work.

"Wickett, I'm going to bother you again," he said to the butler whom he found at work in his pantry.

"You'd like some dinner, I expect, sir," the butler suggested.

"Not now. Later, if you'll be so kind, I'd like you to bring a plate of sandwiches and a large thermos bottle of strong black coffee to me in the tower room. I'm going to be working there several hours. It is the only place I know of where I can be sure of absolute privacy. By the way, there's a key to the door at the bottom of the stairs, isn't there?"

"Yes, sir," Wickett assured him, removing the key from a large ring. "The key to the room itself is in the door."

"Thanks, Wickett. Maybe two locked doors will keep Gigi out. . . . Now, Wickett, I've been told that it is your job to fill the lighter fountains, and that commercial wood alcohol is used."

"Yes, sir," Wickett agreed, with faint surprise but apparently no fear.

"Where do you keep your supply of wood alcohol? Has anyone access to it except yourself?"

"No one but myself, sir," Wickett answered promptly. "I keep it locked away in my pantry here, and the keys are never out of my possession, sir."

"Good! Mr. Berkeley told you to use wood alcohol instead of benzine, I suppose?"

"Yes, sir. Either fluid works in the lighters, but Mr. Berkeley asked me to use wood alcohol, because of the black, sooty smoke and the foul odor from benzine-burning cigarette lighters."

"Right, Wickett! When did you last fill up the fountains?"

"Friday morning, sir. None of them was completely empty, but I filled every fountain in the house, sir. There are six, all told: one in the drawing room, one in the library, one in Mrs. Berkeley's sitting room, one in the guest room which Mr. Crosby has now, one in Mr. Berkeley's room, and one in Mr. Dick's."

Dundee considered for a moment, then made a sudden decision. "Wickett, would it be possible for you to collect all these fountains without being observed?"

"The family is in the drawing room now, sir," Wickett demurred.

"That fountain is not important. But please get all the others, bring them here, and measure the amount of wood alcohol remaining in everyone of them. As soon as you have finished, report the results to me in the tower room."

"Very well, sir."

"Just a minute, Wickett," Dundee detained him, "Please send Peggy Harper and Della Blinn to me here. You need not come in with them, however."

When the two maids, looking very tired and frightened, entered the butler's pantry, the detective hastened to reassure them.

"I'll keep you only a minute, girls, and I'm not going to accuse either of you of murdering Doris Matthews. But I want to ask a question, and I want you both to think hard before answering it: While cleaning bathrooms and hand-basins yesterday and to-day, either downstairs or upstairs, has either of you noticed the odor of perfume about a drainpipe?"

The girls looked at each other blankly, then shook their heads decidedly in the negative.

"Would you have noticed such an odor if perfume had been poured down a drainpipe?" Dundee persisted.

"I'm sure I-I would, sir, since there's been so much talk about perfume, on account of poor Doris being hit over the head with a bottle of it," Della answered.. "But I didn't smell any perfume at all, yesterday or to-day. That is, in the bathrooms. All of the clothes closets smell of perfume because Miss Gigi sprinkled it on everybody before Doris was hit with the bottle. But I haven't smelled any at all anywhere else. Mrs. Berkeley uses violet bath salts, but she hasn't even used any of them since Doris was killed."

"I don't clean upstairs—just this floor, but I didn't smell any perfume in the lavatory down here," Peggy assured him.

"Then will you take particular notice to-morrow morning—both of you—and report to me if there is such an odor from a drainpipe?" Dundee asked, with his friendliest smile, reinforced by a five-dollar bill for each of the girls. "And don't mention to anyone—not even District Attorney Sherwood or Captain. Strawn—that we've had this little talk."

"A slim chance, but one that I couldn't afford to overlook," he said to himself as he left the butler's pantry and turned toward the drawing room.

Five minutes later he accompanied George Berkeley to the library and closed the door.

"Please forgive me, Mr. Berkeley, for calling you away from your bridge game," he began, "but there is a question I must ask you."

"I thought the district attorney had taken over the case," George Berkeley retorted stiffly.

"It is Mr. Sherwood's privilege to investigate any case for his own office, but he cannot ask the police to abandon their own lines of inquiry," Dundee explained courteously. He paused, groping for words with which to frame a question so that it would indicate the possession of knowledge which he did not possess at all. "Mr. Berkeley, when you went upstairs about half-past ten Friday night, to—say good-night to Gigi, and possibly to console her, did you see or encounter anyone at all on the second floor?"

The multi-millionaire fell into the trap. "I saw no one on my way to my daughter's room, but when I was leaving it I saw Wickett emerging from my wife's sitting room."

Dundee concealed his exultation. Not by the flicker of an eyelid must he betray to George Berkeley that not until this moment had he known of the visit to Gigi's room. The trap had been laid upon the flimsiest of foundations—merely a long-delayed recollection of the fact that when he—Dundee—had returned to the drawing room Friday night after his telephone call to Police Headquarters, Berkeley was not in the room and did not return until just before Clorinda Berkeley announced her intention of going up to bed.

"That was when Wickett took the perfume flask to Mrs. Berkeley's room," he said casually.

"I believe so," Mr. Berkeley answered coldly. "Though I did not know at the time what his errand was."

Dundee tried another shot in the dark. "When you went on into your wife's rooms yourself, did you notice the perfume flask?"

"I went no farther than the sitting room," Berkeley answered. Again the trap had sprung. 'I was there only five or six minutes, possibly less time

"What was your errand to your wife's sitting-room, Mr. Berkeley?" Dundee asked quietly.

His host flushed angrily, but he answered: "I was using my wife's telephone. I wanted to make a call, and her telephone was the nearest. I tried to reach my lawyer, but there was no answer."

For the third time, but very confidently now, Bonnie Dundee pretended knowledge he did not possess. "That call to your lawyer was a direct result of your few minutes' talk with Gigi, was it not, Mr. Berkeley?"

The millionaire shrugged, and the flush on his face deepened. "I am not surprised that Gigi has tattled. She has a very loose tongue. But I can assure you that I was not following her hysterical suggestion. I was not about to consult my lawyer in his professional capacity, but as a friend. He has a daughter, of Gigi's age, whom he has enrolled in a junior college in the East. After my talk with Gigi, I suddenly made up my mind to send her to this college, instead of permitting her to remain at home this winter as her mother had planned. Mrs. Berkeley's idea was that Gigi should be groomed for society by Mrs. Lambert. I wished to ask my lawyer's opinion of the college, for a girl of Gigi's temperament."

"I see," Dundee nodded. "Thank you very much, Mr. Berkeley. . . . You saw no one when you left Mrs. Berkeley's sitting room?"

"No one at all. It is likely that Doris went to Mrs. Berkeley's rooms soon after I left, to lay out my wife's things for the night, but I did not see her in the hall as I was returning to the drawing room."

"One thing more, Mr. Berkeley," Dundee detained him apologetically. "I understand that you had agreed to finance a beauty parlor venture for Doris."

"That is quite correct," the millionaire admitted coldly. "In fact, I began a letter to my lawyer Friday before dinner, but I was too upset over another matter to finish it. When Doris told me of her engagement to Arnold, she also confided her ambition to open a beauty shop. I reminded her that capital would be required. I admired the girl for her very evident good qualities, and particularly for her attitude toward my son. Another girl in her place might have leaped at the chance to marry the son of a rich man. I determined to help her financially, on a strictly business basis, of course. I am a silent partner in a number of small ventures in Hamilton, all of them handled through my lawyer, and I believed I should not lose money if I put it into a beauty shop. I might add that Doris had accepted the idea gratefully, on the condition that her *fiancé* did not object to my being her silent partner. She was going to tell him of my offer Friday night," he added frankly.

Dundee heard him through without interruption. "I am sorry Doris did not live to benefit by your kindness, Mr. Berkeley."

"So am I. If you'll pardon me, I'll get back to my bridge game," Berkeley answered stiffly.

Half an hour later Wickett was admitted to the tower room. He came bearing a tray of sandwiches and coffee, as well as information which seemed to puzzle him exceedingly. . . . .

"I have checked the contents of the fountains, sir," he said, depositing his tray as far from the parrot's cage as the length of the table allowed. "Here are the figures, sir. And I can't understand them at all. Mr. Berkeley's fountain was full, and less than an ounce of the wood alcohol had been removed from any of the others, except Mrs. Berkeley's. I can swear I filled it full on Friday, sir, but I found less than two ounces in it, and it holds five."

"That's our secret, Wickett," Dundee warned him, slipping a ten-dollar bill into his hand.

When the butler had left, the detective locked the door at the foot of the stairs, returned to the tower room and locked its door, then addressed his parrot:

"I'm afraid you're in for a long session, 'my dear Watson'!"

2

Bonnie Dundee had cheerfully endured a good deal of kidding from his uncle, Police Commissioner O'Brien, and from his chief, Captain Strawn, because of his use of a parrot as a "Watson," when he felt the need of an audience for the summing up of a case.

"I've tried talking aloud to myself, but I feel foolish. Cap'n is an ideal audience, for while he sometimes laughs at me, he can't waste my time by arguing or telling me I'm a fool," he answered them.

Now, after five hours of sleep, to clear his brain of all previous speculations and conclusions—worthless now, in the light of his new discoveries—he sat with the parrot's cage before him, his thick sheaf of typewritten notes ready for reference. He had been talking steadily for ten minutes, telling the parrot just how and when Doris Matthews had died. And Cap'n had listened, head cocked inquiringly, beady eye bright with interest—or so Dundee chose to believe.

"Now, 'my dear Watson,' that is the crime which you and I must try to solve," he summed up. "But behind that crime lies another, which did not come off. Our primary problem, therefore, is to find the person who plotted Mrs. Berkeley's death by wood-alcohol poisoning, but who was forced, by fear, to murder Doris Matthews instead. Is that clear?"

"Perfume!" Cap'n croaked suddenly, proud of the new addition to his vocabulary.

"Exactly!" Dundee grinned. "Some one transferred more than two ounces of deadly wood alcohol from the lighter fountain in Mrs. Berkeley's sitting room, to the flask of *Fleur d'Amour* which Seymour Crosby presented to his hostess Friday evening. And was caught in the act by Doris Matthews."

"Perfume!" Cap'n repeated and flapped his wings excitedly.

"Exactly—again!" his master applauded. "Where is the perfume which Mrs. Berkeley's would-be murderer removed from the flask to make way for the wood alcohol? Gigi had wasted about an ounce of the *Fleur d'Amour*. Mrs. Berkeley knew just how much was left in the bottle, for she took the flask from Gigi herself. Therefore, the would-be murderer had to remove about two and a half ounces of perfume before putting that amount of wood alcohol into the bottle.

"Now, it is not at all likely that the surplus perfume was poured down the drainpipe of Mrs. Berkeley's bathroom basin, for the very good reason that Mrs. Berkeley would have been almost sure to smell it when she came up to bed. Therefore it seems logical to suppose that the surplus perfume was poured into another, bottle—and what more logical than a perfume bottle to hold perfume?

"Mrs. Berkeley's would-be murderer probably counted on at least two days elapsing before the victim drank the *Fleur d'Amour*, since she had another large new bottle of perfume on hand, as the plotter could have seen by glancing at her dressing table—or, could have known already.

"Now—why the choice of *Fleur d'Amour* instead of the new bottle of department-store perfume? To incriminate Crosby, provided the would-be murderer was not Crosby himself? Or because the *Flour d'Amour* had come from abroad? You see, 'my dear Watson,' if the wood alcohol causing Mrs. Berkeley's death were traced to perfume she had drunk, it would be much safer for the poisoner if the perfume had come from France, rather than from a local department store, which could supply exactly similar perfume for analysis.

"If my reasoning is correct so far, the would-be poisoner expected to have ample leisure in which to dispose of that incriminating surplus of *Flour d'Amour* before Mrs. Berkeley's death. But consider the problem which confronted the poisoner when he—or she—but let's say 'he' for the sake of convenience—was caught in the act by Doris Matthews. We know there was a struggle, that Doris was pushed so violently against the bathroom mirror that the smudged print of her rouged mouth was left upon it—as one of our few clues to what took place.

"Then what happened? Doris succeeds in wresting the flask of poisoned perfume from the would-be murderer, flees with it—not taking time to get her coat or the key to the back door. Her goal is the summerhouse, where she believes she will find Arnold waiting for her.

"But the poisoner knows Arnold is not there, that he is driving the Benjamin Smiths home. So he pursues Doris. But he does not leave behind him, in Mrs. Berkeley's bathroom, the bottle containing the surplus *Fleur l'Amour,* And he does not take it with him when he follows Doris to the summerhouse. If he had, he would have cast it into the lake, along with the fragments of the crystal flask. Those fragments have been fitted together, Captain Strawn tells me, and they form one complete crystal flask. No other bottle was found on bottom of the lake.

"Therefore, 'my dear Watson,' he stopped long enough on his way out of the house in pursuit of Doris, to put the bottle away—most probably in his own room."

Dundee paused for a long minute, frowning. Then he cried triumphantly:

"Of course, 'Watson'! What an idiot I've bear! Shoes! No wonder we couldn't smell *Fleur d'Amour* when we sniffed at the shoes we knew had been worn Friday night! The poisoner was behind Doris. She fled first, and the poisoner had ample opportunity to observe how silent her flight was—in her rubber-soled, rubber-heeled shoes. Not even when she ran down the thin-carpeted back stairs did she make any noise. But in ordinary shoes the poisoner could not hope to be so noiseless. He stopped and changed to shoes as silent as the girl's. It would have taken less than a minute, and undoubtedly the poisoner knew, either from Doris herself or from deduction, what she meant to do. Doris would not find Arnold in the summerhouse, but she would wait, for a short time at least, expecting him to arrive any minute. Oh, yes, the poisoner had time to change his shoes—and he did!"

He was silent again for so long that Cap'n turned rapidly about on his perch three times, then croaked "Good-night! Good-night!"

"Good-night? Why, I've just begun," Dundee reproached the bird. "Be patient, 'my dear Watson'. Let's see where we stand now. Noiseless shoes. Bedroom slippers, or—tennis shoes? But I've stooped and snooped and sniffed in every clothes closet in the house, and I've not caught a single whiff of *Fleur d'Amour*, except from Clorinda's gold slippers.

"Let's follow the murderer back to the house from the summerhouse, after his ghastly work there had been done. It is almost certain that the perfume splashed upon his shoes when the bottle broke. Of course it splashed upon his clothes, too, but they didn't matter, since Gigi had helpfully anointed every one with perfume earlier in the evening. But perfume on soft shoes. . . . Now, how could he remove it most successfully? . . . By washing the shoes? Not so good. Perfume is devilishly persistent stuff."

Very earnestly he stared into the parrot's beady eye, then suddenly he smote the table with a triumphant fist.

"Tennis shoes—white shoe polish!" he cried. "Easy and quick. Freshly polished tennis shoes would cause no comment. . . . Well, that's that, unless I've been barking up the wrong tree— Now let's see what we know about this would-be poisoner.

"First: He knew that Mrs. Berkeley is a perfume addict.

"Second: He knew that Mrs. Berkeley had a lighter fountain, filled with wood alcohol in her sitting room.

"Third: He has what seems to him good cause to wish Mrs. Berkeley dead.

"Fourth: He knew Arnold could not meet Doris in the summerhouse; therefore he must have been present when Mrs. Berkeley ordered the car.

"Fifth: He was some one to whose appeal for mercy Doris Matthews, a kind-hearted girl, must have turned a deaf ear. Otherwise her murder would not have been necessary."

He was silent again, passing all possible suspects in review, putting them, one by one, to the test of his fifth conclusion. Finally he spoke aloud again, very gravely:

"So far as we know, Cap'n, there were only three persons in this house whom Doris could possibly have hated—judging from her letter to her sister, and from all the evidence we have in hand. Those three were Dick Berkeley, who had annoyed her with his love-making and made trouble between her and Arnold; Mrs. Berkeley, because she was a tyrannical mistress and an unfit mother to 'Gigi, of whom Doris was apparently very fond; and Seymour Crosby—provided it was Crosby whom Doris knew or suspected to be responsible, directly or indirectly, for Phyllis Crosby's death.

"Let's take Dick first. He was undoubtedly angry with his mother because of her interference in his unsuccessful pursuit of Doris. Is it likely, though, that he would plot to poison his mother, in order to remove that interference, when Doris herself would have nothing to do with him?"

Disconcertingly, the parrot chuckled, flapped his wings, and winked.

Dundee frowned and pressed his forefinger into his temples. "I suppose you're reminding me of Gigi's clever theory that Phyllis Crosby was being blackmailed by some man who had seduced her before her marriage. Of course she was being blackmailed! But—by whom? Somehow I can't fit Dick Berkeley into the picture. A seducer?—yes! But hardly a blackmailer, I think."

Again the parrot chuckled, but Dundee ignored the raucous interruption with great dignity.

"Next comes Mrs. Berkeley, on the list of Doris's hates. I suppose even you, you blasted croaker, will admit that Mrs. Berkeley did not put wood alcohol into the perfume to kill herself. And if she had, I rather think Doris would have stood by and let her do it.

"Now for Crosby. Let us say she only suspected that it was Crosby himself who was responsible for his wife's death, until she saw him plotting the death of another woman. But how was Crosby responsible? I'll never believe that Doris was not telling the truth at the inquest, when she said she saw Phyllis commit suicide while Crosby was fifty feet away from her on the roof. But—*Good Lord!*"

He was suddenly silent, his eyes widening to take in quite another picture. Finally he shook his head vigorously and began to speak again:

"There's no doubt of it, Cap'n! The would-be poisoner of Mrs. Berkeley and the person responsible for the death of Phyllis Crosby are one and the same person. And to that person Doris Matthews would have shown no mercy. If she had come upon anyone else than her beloved Miss Phyllis's 'killer,' preparing to poison a woman she herself hated, would she not have been easy to move with protestation's of repentance and promises not to repeat the attempt? I think so, 'my dear Watson!' I do indeed think so, if I am any judge at all of Doris Matthews' character."

Again the parrot uttered a raucous croak of mirth.

"Oh, I shan't go off half-cocked, if that's what you mean by your ribald laughter," Dundee retorted. "I'm going to consider every single possibility, every probable and improbable suspect. But before I forget! Doris's murderer returned to his room, and polished his tennis shoes, to cover up the perfume. But there was another problem confronting him: What to do with his bottle of *Fleur d'Amour?*"

He brooded for several minutes, while the parrot drooped sleepily on his perch. Putting himself in the murderer's place, Dundee asked himself, "What would I have done?" When at last the answer came he uttered so sharp a cry of triumph that the bird protested with one of the oaths he had learned from his mischievous old mistress, Mrs. Emma Hogarth.

It was nearly one o'clock when Dundee concluded his monologue to the parrot and covered the long-suffering bird's cage. Weary but triumphant, he unlocked the tower-room door, descended the steep stairs to the third floor, unlocked that door and was about to step down into the hall when he found that the door was pushing against something soft but unyielding.

"Gigi!" he whispered angrily. And then he saw that she was asleep, a woolly bathrobe wrapped about her gay silk pajamas, her curly brown head sunk upon her knees.

He stooped and gathered her up into his arms. She grunted, sighed, then the topaz eyes flew wide.

"I thought you'd never come out, Bonnie Dundee," she murmured. Then anger routed sleep. "I've been waiting here to tell you what a cad I think you are! Tricking Daddy into admitting that he came to my room Friday night and that I—I told him—" She hesitated, obviously not sure just how much Dundee knew.

"That you told him you hated your mother, and wanted him to divorce her?" Dundee finished the sentence for her, so confidently that she tumbled into the trap.

"I didn't mean it," Gigi whimpered. "I was just so awfully sore at Abbie because she slapped me. I guess he told you what else I said?"

"No, Gigi, but you're going to tell me now," Dundee said gently, holding her small body close against his heart. "And in exchange I'm going to tell you that you're not to worry any more—your father did not try to poison your mother, then kill poor Doris to keep her from telling."

XXVII.

THE Berkeley household had been notified on Sunday afternoon that the inquest into the death of Doris Matthews would be held Monday morning, at ten o'clock, in the funeral chapel of the city morgue.

When Dundee entered the dining room at half-past eight he found that he was the last to appear for breakfast and that every member of the party was decorously dressed for the coming solemn occasion.

"Hello, sluggard!" Gigi greeted him joyously, then broke into parodied song: *My Bonnie lies long past the hour, My Bonnie lies long in his bed!"*

"Gigi!" her mother reproved her. "Just when we were talking of a funeral, too. She turned explanatorily to Dundee: "George and I have decided to have the funeral here, dear Mr. Dundee. In the 'little parlor' not the servants' sitting room. I think we all looked upon poor, darling little Doris as a friend, rather than as a mere servant."

"Oh, Mother, for God's sake!" Dick groaned, and flung down his grapefruit spoon.

"Dick, I must say you're impossible!" his mother cried angrily. "I thought you'd be the most pleased of all, since you thought you were in love with her. Well, then, son, you *were* in love with her. Doris was Church of England, wasn't she, dear Mrs. Lambert? I'm sure that our own Episcopal minister would be delighted to conduct the services, both here and at the cemetery—"

"Mrs. Berkeley, Mr. Crosby and I have talked it over, and we'd like to take Doris to New York, and bury her beside Phyllis. We feel it is what they both would want—"

"Oh!" Mrs. Berkeley said uncertainly. Then, in a. rather strange voice: "You—won't be coming back, I suspect?"

Mrs. Lambert smiled faintly and shook her head. "I don't believe you will need me, now that—"

"Of course it was largely because of Clorinda's marriage to Mr. Crosby that I needed you," Mrs. Berkeley interrupted eagerly, "and now that she is going to marry John Maxwell instead—"

"I'm glad you admit it at last, Mother," Clorinda cut in quietly.

"Oh, I'm going to stop trying to manage other people," Mrs. Berkeley laughed, flushing brightly. "Your father and I had a long talk last night, children, and your old Abbie is going to settle down and be a model small town wife and mother."

Husband and wife exchanged the first frank, affectionate glance that Dundee had seen pass between them, and the young detective felt a sudden surge of something remotely akin to fondness for the woman he had disliked so heartily.

He looked swiftly toward Gigi. The child's eyes were downcast and her lips were trembling, but whether from grief at Mrs. Lambert's imminent departure, or from a painful joy over her mother's tacitly promised reformation he could not tell. But when he glanced at Mrs. Lambert he felt no doubt at all as to what had brought the tears to her blue-gray, shadowed eyes. For her eyes were upon Gigi.

At a quarter to ten Dick Berkeley knocked impatiently upon Dundee's door.

"I'll be down in five minutes, Dick," the detective promised. "Wait for me in the car. Have the others gone?"

"Everybody's gone—including the servants," Dick told him. "And you'd better make it snappy or we'll be late."

Carrying a suitcase Dundee moved swiftly from bedroom to bedroom, collecting white canvas tennis shoes and golf shoes. In one bedroom he paused before a dressing table, picked up a black-and-gold bottle of perfume, removed the stopper and sniffed. There came over his face a ludicrous expression of disappointment. Then he read the label again—*Nuit de joie*; he'd had a girl not so long ago who used that scent; he sniffed again, then smiled triumphantly. Very carefully he wrapped the bottle in his handkerchief and deposited it among the shoes.

"What are you doing with that suitcase?" Dick demanded. "I thought you were staying here until this murder business was cleared up."

"'I am," Dundee assured him. "I'm just taking some stuff into town to have it—cleaned."

They drove almost in silence, but when Dundee asked the boy to stop at City Hall, Dick commented dryly:

"I didn't know there was a laundry or a cleaner's shop here, though I suppose the politicians need one for their dirty linen."

Dundee was still smiling at Dick's brave attempt at a joke when he entered the laboratory of Dr. Abel Jennings, city chemist and toxicologist.

"Another job for you, doctor," he announced, as he opened the suitcase. "You may find it a poser. I want to know if there are any wood alcohol impurities lurking beneath the nice white polish on any of these shoes, but —particularly this pair."

"Then I'll analyze the cloth of these shoes first," Dr. Jennings promised matter-of-factly. "What's the poser?'

"I thought maybe the white shoe polish had queered our chances," Dundee admitted. "Then one other little thing, doctor. . . . Look! Can you tell me whether this perfume is a mixture of what the label claims it to be, and *Fleur d'Amour*, the scent on that handkerchief I gave you to analyze?"

"Each perfume is composed of its own essential oils," the doctor answered. "If there's any—what d'you call it?— *Fleur d'Amour*, I'll be able to tell you."

"When?"

"I'll try to have both reports for you by five o'clock," the doctor answered, then explained in some detail the need for so much time.

Dundee returned to Dick's car without his suitcase. "One more stop, please, Dick, and then for the inquest. Meredith's Department Store."

It took only five minutes for the detective to purchase a bottle of *Nuit de Joie*, identical in appearance with the one he had just left in Dr. Jennings' office, and three minutes more, when he reached the morgue, to give it into Detective Payne's hands, with explicit instructions. Before Dundee took his place among the witnesses to be called by the coroner, Payne was well on his way to Hillcrest. Coroner Price reproved the two inexcusably late arrivals with a fierce frown, which seemed to have no effect upon Detective Dundee's cheerfulness.

The inquest dragged along until past noon, bringing forth no new evidence, for of his own recent discoveries Dundee said nothing. Dr. Price called upon him to tell of the discovery of the body in the lake and of its removal to the summerhouse, then dismissed him. At one o'clock District Attorney Sherwood requested an adjournment of the inquest until Thursday, and the coroner readily agreed.

"Well! Where do we go from here?" Captain Strawn grinned at his young subordinate as they lingered in the cleared funeral chapel. I'll bet Sherwood would give his new silk topper not to have jumped into this Jonah of a case so cockily. Did you see the papers this morning? Promised the dear reporters he'd have the murderer behind bars within twenty four hours."

"I'm afraid his prophecy will come true chief—though no one will be more surprised than District Attorney Sherwood himself."

"Hey! What's that? Been holding out on me, have you, young feller me lad?" Strawn blustered.

"I *have* got a pot on to boil," Dundee confessed. "I can't tell you about it now, for I may be all wrong. But if

I'm right—and I think I am—you are now invited to attend a very private confession party this afternoon at six o clock—"

"And in the meantime what am I supposed to do?" Strawn demanded sarcastically. "I'm *only* the Homicide Squad chief. What are my orders?"

Dundee laughed. "I want you to telephone to Hillcrest this afternoon about four o'clock and officially request the presence of every member of the family and of Crosby, Lambert and Wickett in your office. I'll come along as a matter of course and to make sure there are no absentees. You can tell them anything you like, hammer away at them with as many questions as you can think up. I'll slip away at five, and telephone you whether the pot's boiling or not. If it is I'd like for you to duck out at about twenty minute to six, leaving word with Sergeant Turner, to dismiss the crowd ten minutes after you're gone. By then you'll be on your way to Hillcrest with a ten minutes start of the Berkeleys. I'll be waiting for you, and then—with luck the pot should boil over very promptly."

Probably if Dundee had not staged a confession in the Rhodes House murders in much the same secretive and dramatic fashion, Captain Strawn would not have lent his aid to the program outlined by his subordinate, without knowing what it was all about.

As it was, the chief of the Homicide Squad followed instructions to the letter. At five o'clock Dundee left Police Headquarters for Dr. Jennings' laboratory. At ten minutes past five he spoke four cryptic words to Captain Strawn: "The pot is boiling." In another five minutes he was in a police car, headed toward Hillcrest, his suitcase between his knees.

But he was not jubilant. So far as he was concerned, the show was over. With all his heart he wished he could leave the theater before the curtain rose on the third act —that terrible, necessary third act in which a human being, as life-loving as himself, would be crushed before his eyes. Dundee shuddered. He had solved the damned puzzle! That was all that mattered—the fun of solving riddles. He was no man-hunter, like Strawn. He had no joy in breaking men's nerves, 'looking at their naked' souls, leading them to jail by manacled wrists.

But he had to go on with it. With his heart like lead he set his stage. From the center of a dressing table in a bedroom at Hillcrest he removed the black-and-gold bottle of perfume he had purchased that day and put the original bottle in its place. But that flask had a new label now. In place of the gold seal bearing the name, *Nuit de Joie*, there was a large plain white sticker. And on the glaring white surface were the words, boldly lettered in black ink by Dundee himself:

FLEUR D'AMOUR.

On each side of the desecrated perfume bottle he placed the grayish white remains of a tennis oxford— shoes that had been so gleamingly immaculate when he had first seen them—on Saturday morning.

Ten minutes later Captain Strawn and Detective Dundee were crouching side by side in a clothes closet, whose door was open just enough for the two men to observe the entrance of the room's owner and any drama that might take place before that sinister, dressing table.

There were voices in the hall. Tired people coming up to dress for dinner. Faintly there came the sound of doors opening and closing. And it last the knob they were watching so intently turned quickly under an urgent hand.

"Coming!" Strawn whispered hoarsely, and his fingers closed hard upon Dundee's shoulder.

XXVIII.

INTO the twilight of the room stepped a woman's figure. The soft closing of the door was followed by the click of the electric switch beside it. In the dazzle of light from the four wall-brackets Letitia Lambert was revealed, leaning against the door, as if she were too exhausted to take another step.

From her lax left hand hung an afternoon paper, so folded that a two-column picture of George Berkeley was plainly visible to the detectives watching from the clothes closet.

Slowly she lifted the newspaper. Her closed eyes opened, fastened upon the picture with agonized intensity. With sudden fierceness she crushed the paper against her lips, low, dreadful moans throbbing in her throat, her usually serene face a mask of agony.

"Motive!" Captain Strawn breathed in Dundee's ear, and the younger detective pinched him to warn him to silence.

The woman could not have heard, but she lowered the paper, lifted her breast in a tearing sigh, and slowly, unsteadily started to cross the room. Her right hand, from whose wrist her handbag dangled, went up automatically to remove her close-fitting black hat.

Dundee held his breath. The supreme moment was upon them. For as he had known they would, those tortured eyes flew to the dressing table. Not once since Saturday morning—he felt sure—had Mrs. Lambert returned to her room without casting a terrified glance at her dressing table to make sure that the black-and-gold perfume bottle had not betrayed her, that it was still there. How many times she must have seized it, wildly casting about for a means to hide it or to destroy it's telltale contents, only to realize each time that it was safer with it in plain sight, in the plate where Della, the maid, had been accustomed to see it. In its rightful place, it looked supremely innocent, for the black glass concealed the fact that, once nearly empty, it was now full. Missing, destroyed, it might betray her."

Handbag, newspaper and hat slipped from her nerveless hands to the floor. Jerkily, as if she were paralyzed, Mrs. Lambert crept to the dressing table. The detectives saw her stare at the label, which Dundee printed and pasted upon the face of the bottle. A shaking hand went to touch it, then shuddered away, then, it seemed, did she see the grayish white remains of her tennis oxfords.

"Quick! She's going to faint!" Strawn whispered urgently.

Dundee was in time to catch her as she fell, but she was not unconscious. For a long minute she lay passive in his arms, her eyes still fixed in a blind trance of horror upon a vision of ruined shoes and a grotesquely labeled perfume bottle.

Finally the paralyzed lids relaxed and curtained the dawning agony of realization in her blue gray eyes.

Dundee was merciful to her. Motioning to Strawn to stay in the closet, he rose with his burden and carried it to the bed. She lay as dead until he had gone to the bathroom, mixed a dose of aromatic spirits of ammonia, and held it to her gray lips.

After she had drunk the dose she closed her eyes again and lay motionless, except for the rising and falling of her breast in quick, gasping sighs. Finally she spoke, her voice a gusty whisper.

"How long—have you known?"

"I wasn't sure until today," he answered gently; "At first I couldn't believe that you, who said you loved Doris, could kill her."

"I did love her!" the woman cried, beating her breast feebly with clenched hands. "That is what made it so—

horrible. . . . Oh, I'm glad it's over! Glad, glad! Do you hear? I couldn't have gone on much longer, trying to be natural, having to talk of—her. . . . I was going to kill myself to-night. Why couldn't you have given me time?"

"Wouldn't you feel better if you told me all about it?" Dundee suggested, very gently. "I am not trying to trap you, Mrs. Lambert. You realize that the evidence is conclusive, without your confession."

"Evidence? What do I care about evidence now?" she moaned, her hands still feebly beating her breast. "I warn you now that I'll not live to stand trial. I'll find a way somehow—soon! But you shan't go on thinking I lied about being fond of Doris!"

"You killed her in a frenzy of terror, Mrs. Lambert, because she was determined to expose you, not only as Mrs. Berkeley's would-be poisoner, but as Phyllis Crosby's blackmailer," Dundee told her quietly.

"Blackmailer?" she whispered, her eyes enormous. "I —never called myself that, but—I suppose it's true. We all lie to ourselves, justify ourselves, don't we, Mr. Dundee?" she asked pitifully.

She was silent for so long then that Dundee was afraid he had pushed her too far, that she would not confess. But at last she cried:

"Oh, what does it matter? It will hurt Seymour less to know the truth than to go on being tortured with doubts of Phyllis's love for him."

"I am sure of that, Mrs. Lambert," Dundee encouraged her.

"Please try to understand—not to judge me too harshly," she began, in a weary, flat voice. "All my life until my husband died I had more money than I needed —and all the pleasant things that go with money and high social position; When my husband's estate was settled, I found that nearly everything was gone. You see, a woman had been blackmailing him heavily for years. Disillusioned, sick at heart, for I had loved my husband, I faced the world almost penniless. Forty-four years old.

"The thought of marrying some old or middle-aged widower for his money was abhorrent to me, and I was not trained for any sort of work. The only position I could possibly fill was that of social secretary, and the idea was unthinkable—then. I was too proud.

"But to go back a little. A few weeks before my husband died—he was killed in a polo accident—I met and took a great fancy to Phyllis Benham. It amused and delighted me to force her upon society. My nephew, Tommy Cavendish, liked her immensely and I rather hoped he would fall in love with her. But Phyllis fell in love with Seymour Crosby. Seymour did not have much money; he hesitated to ask the child to marry him, for fear her father would regard him as a fortune-hunter.

"One Monday morning Mr. Benham telephoned me that his daughter was ill and hysterical, that she wanted to see me. I went. Phyllis told me a wild, almost incredible story. She had a friend who had joined the chorus of a musical comedy, opening in Atlantic City the previous Friday. As a lark, Phyllis accompanied her friend, staying backstage. When the show, was over, two young men, thinking both of them were chorus girls, invited them to go to a roadhouse. Phyllis thought it would be fun to accept. There was some drinking—not much, she insisted to me—but several hours later Phyllis awoke, to find herself in a hotel bedroom, her escort of the evening sleeping beside her. She began to scream. Guests reported the disturbance. The hotel detective came, and was about to take them both to the police station for disorderly conduct and false registration. The man in the case squared it with the detective, however; and left as soon as he could dress.

"Phyllis had not given him her right name the night before, and I tried to soothe her hysterical fears—told her she would hear no more about it, that it was not her fault, and that she must try to forget it. Then she showed me a letter she had received that morning from Seymour Crosby. It was a proposal of marriage. She protested that she could not accept, although she loved him with all her heart. The fear of blackmail, she said, would hang over her head for the rest of her life. May I—have, some water, please?" she gasped.

"So it was Phyllis herself who suggested blackmail to you," Dundee said thoughtfully, as he held the glass to her lips.

"Yes. But at the time I told her that it might be best for her or for me to tell Seymour the whole ugly story, trusting to his love for her. But that idea frightened her more than the other. The next day my husband was killed. I saw almost no one for weeks, and had nearly forgotten poor Phyllis's dilemma until I saw her picture and Seymour's on the society page of a New York paper, announcing their engagement and early marriage.

"Phyllis called on me just before the wedding, and confessed that she was in terror lest her companion of that dreadful night had seen her picture, and had recognized it; that he would blackmail her, knowing that her father was a very rich man. Again I advised her to tell Seymour, but she said she could not; that she was going to beg him to take her to England to live for a year, at least.

"As you know, that is what happened. I visited in their home in London, then went to Monte Carlo, where I lost almost my last penny in an effort to win enough to live on for a few months, at least. It was then, in January, that I conceived the idea of blackmail. Phyllis had told me the man's name, at least the name he had given her. I typed a letter to her, I signed the man's first name, and asked her to send a thousand pounds in banknotes to "W. L. Parker", care of the American Express Company in Paris. The money came. I asked for mail for Mr. and Mrs. W. L. Parker, representing myself to be Mrs. Parker, and received the package without difficulty. It was—so—easy—"

"That you tried it again and again," Dundee said softly.

"Yes, but the last time I was horribly frightened. I had asked for five thousand pounds in a letter written and mailed in Paris on my way to London. Seymour had sent for me, you know, to try to cheer her up." Tears forced themselves out of her closed eyes and down her pallid cheeks.

"It was to be my last demand. Please believe that when I saw Phyllis and realized the dreadful thing I had done to her, I was beside in self with remorse. I intended, if the money came, to return it to her with a note saying the persecution would be stopped—that she would never hear from W. L. Parker again. But when I went to the express company, I found there was nothing. I should have written her anyway, but as I was turning away from the window I saw Doris—"

"Doris!" Dundee exclaimed.

And Doris saw me," Mrs. Lambert went on wearily. "I am sure Phyllis had described the Atlantic City man, and had sent Doris to watch for him—perhaps to plead with him. I must have betrayed nervousness, but I was sure Doris believed me when I remarked casually that I was there to ask for my own mail. But you can realize that I was terrified, that I could not take the chance of writing again, even to reassure Phyllis—least of all to reassure her, for such a move might have aroused Doris's suspicions that it was I—her mistress's best friend—who had stooped so low."

"I see," Dundee agreed. "And I believe you."

"I tried to make up to her for the terrible thing I had done by being as kind and sympathetic as possible, but it was not until that Sunday night—the night she—she died, that Phyllis told me her worst fears had been confirmed; that she was being blackmailed, and that her father had refused to cable her any more money. I advised her—pleaded with her—to end it all by telling her husband the truth. I hated myself then for not having the courage to tell her that I was the 'man' she feared, and that she need fear no more."

"And Doris knew all about the night in Atlantic City and the blackmailer's letters?" Dundee prompted.

"Oh, yes. Doris knew as much as Phyllis herself knew. Mistress and maid were the closest of friends," Mrs. Lambert replied. "Phyllis and I were talking on the roof. At last she agreed to tell Seymour the whole truth, and I went down to give him the message. You know the rest— that she committed suicide rather than confess. She had agreed to do so only to get rid of me, that she might be alone when she leaped.

"At the inquest Doris exonerated Seymour, of course, but she confided to me that she would avenge her adored mistress if she had to devote the rest of her life to the cause. Her plan was to hire detectives to trace Phyllis's blackmailer, make him pay for his crime somehow, in some way that would not smirch her mistress's name. That is why she wanted the beauty shop—to make money more quickly. I don't think she ever suspected—me. She trusted me, was fond of me, until—"

"Until Friday night when she saw you pouring wood alcohol into Mr. Berkeley's perfume." Dundee finished the sentence for her.

"Yes," Mrs. Lambert agreed dully. "I did not hear her come into the bathroom, had no idea that Mrs. Berkeley had telephoned her to go to her rooms and wait for her. I thought I had plenty of time— She must have been watching me for minute or two, must have had time to think, for she said in a dreadful whisper: 'So you're a murderess! It was you—*you*—who killed Miss Phyllis!' I knew then that she would have no mercy, would not try to understand how I had been driven to—to murder—"

"I believe I do, Mrs. Lambert," Dundee interrupted. There were three reasons why you wanted Mrs. Berkeley, to die. First, you loved her husband and wanted him to be free to marry you—"

"But he didn't know! He never, by word or a look—"

"I know. But you hoped he would marry you for Gigi's sake, then come to love you for yourself. Gigi knows you love her father. Friday night, in a fit of hysterical resentment against her mother, she begged him to divorce her mother and marry you."

The drawn face softened, glowed. "Did she? My precious Gigi! Thank you for telling me that. But oh, what will she think of me now?"

"The second reason, of course, was that you adored Gigi, the child you told yourself you should have had."

"Yes," Mrs. Lambert whispered, and hid her face with her hands.

'Third: the same reason you blackmailed Phyllis Crosby. Money. You could not endure the thought of poverty, of working for your inferiors, of being humiliated daily by a woman like Mrs. Berkeley."

"She deserved to die!" Mrs. Lambert cried suddenly, rising in her elbow to stare at him with wild eyes. "A drunkard, a fool, a selfish and cruel mother, a nagging wife to the finest man in the world. . . . But I gave her her chance to live! Even after she had slapped my darling that night, I made her promise not to drink the perfume Seymour had given her. I told myself then: 'I shall poison it to-night. If she breaks her promise, she deserves to die."

"But it was Doris who died," Dundee reminded her.

"Don't!" she cried, sinking back upon the bed as if utterly exhausted. "Don't make me tell you all the horrible details! I can't bear it! . . . Don't you see— " she wailed despairingly, "that I can't bear any more?"

But Dundee had to be brutal. "Then let me tell you, Mrs. Lambert. You will correct me when I go astray. When you left your room shortly after eleven o'clock Friday night to go to Mrs. Berkeley's sitting room, you went prepared to poison the perfume Crosby had given her. You took a half-empty bottle of your own perfume with you, so that you might have a receptacle for the surplus *Fleur d'Amour*. Right?"

"Yes," she admitted dully. "But the plan only came to me that night, during that nightmare party—"

"First, you jotted down the forgotten engagement on Mrs. Berkeley's calendar. Then you took the lighter-fountain of wood alcohol to the bathroom dressing table, so that in case any of the alcohol was spilled, you could wash it away. Then, with a remarkably steady hand, you poured the perfume from Mrs. Berkeley's new flask into your own—"

"No, no! My hand was not steady enough for that!" the tormented woman denied. "I made a little funnel out of an envelope, then tore it to bits and washed them away."

"I see," Dundee accepted the correction quietly. "Then you held the crystal flask in the basin, under the spigot from the lighter fountain. I think you must have quite finished before you were aware that Doris had been watching you, else the fountain would have been overturned in your struggle with the girl. There *was* a struggle, of course since she left the print of her roughed mouth on the dressing table mirror."

"Yes. But I gave the flask up to her when she told me she'd scream if I didn't. I—I asked her what she was going to do, and she said she was going to tell Arnold, and get him to go with her to—to the police station, the taking the poisoned perfume as—evidence. I pleaded with her then, but she—she ran away—"

"And you followed her," Dundee took up the tale. "But you were in no hurry. You knew Arnold was not waiting for her in the summerhouse, as she believed. You had time to replace the fountain, return the bottle of perfume to your dressing table, and change from high heeled evening pumps to tennis shoes so that your footsteps might not be heard on the backstairs, anymore than hers—correct?"

"Oh, yes, yes!" the woman groaned. "But I didn't intend to kill her. I followed her to plead with her my knees. When, she wouldn't listen, I thought I could get the poisoned perfume away from her and throw it into the lake so she wouldn't have any evidence to go to the police with—that it would be only her word against mine. I—

got it at last, but—but suddenly she must have gone crazy with fear. *Because she knew it was I who had blackmailed Phyllis.* I knew Seymour would believe her when she told him everything. So I raised the flask and crashed it down on her head. I thought I'd killed her. Oh, if you have any pity, let me alone now!"

"I shant ask you any more questions now," Dundee assured her gently.

Hearing the pitying kindness in his voice reared her trembling body upon her elbow again and she began to plead in a frenzy of hope. "Then will you leave me alone here for five minutes? . . . Just five little minutes! Not for my sake! I don't deserve anything! But for Gigi's sake! She loves me. . . And you—oh, I've seen it!—you love Gigi, too! Five little minutes, Mr. Dundee—and then she can forget me, without having known the very worst about me. For Gigi's sake, not mine!"

Dundee rose, gently disengaging the frantic hands that clung to him. And there was no triumph at all in the gesture with which he signaled to Captain Strawn, chief of the Homicide Squad.

THE END

Other Resurrected Press Books in *The Chief Inspector Pointer Mystery* Series

More Mysteries by Anne Austin

Murder at Bridge

When an afternoon bridge party attended by some of Hamilton's leading citizens ends with the hostess being murdered in her boudoir, Special Investigator Dundee of the District Attorney's office is called in. But one of the attendees is guilty? There are plenty of suspects: the victim's former lover, her current suitor, the retired judge who is being blackmailed, the victim's maid who had been horribly disfigured accidentally by the murdered woman, or any of the women who's husbands had flirted with the victim. Or was she murdered by an outsider whose motive had nothing to do with the town of Hamilton. Find the answer in . . . Murder at Bridge

One Drop of Blood

When Dr. Koenig, head of Mayfield Sanitarium is murdered, the District Attorney's Special Investigator, "Bonnie" Dundee must go undercover to find the killer. Were any of the inmates of the asylum insane enough to have committed the crime? Or, was it one of the staff, motivated by jealousy? And what was is the secret in the murdered man's past. Find the answer in . . . One Drop of Blood

The Black Pigeon

There were plenty of reasons for "Handsome Harry" Borden to be murdered. After all, he had cost numerous investors their life savings with questionable securities.

And he had left his wife for a string of actresses and dancers, only to shed each in turn for a new flame. And the office boy that he had bullied. Not to mention the jealous boyfriend of his secretary to whom he had made unwanted advances. So there were plenty of suspects when was found dead of a gunshot wound in his office. The question is, which of them actually committed the crime?

AVAILABLE FROM RESURRECTED PRESS!

THE EDWARDIAN DETECTIVES
LITERARY SLEUTHS OF THE EDWARDIAN ERA

The exploits of the great Victorian Detectives, Poe's C. Auguste Dupin, Gaboriau's Lecoq, and most famously, Arthur Conan Doyle's Sherlock Holmes, are well known. But what of those fictional detectives that came after, those of the Edwardian Age? The period between the death of Queen Victoria and the First World War had been called the Golden Age of the detective short story, but how familiar is the modern reader with the sleuths of this era? And such an extraordinary group they were, including in their numbers an unassuming English priest, a blind man, a master of disguises, a lecturer in medical jurisprudence, a noble woman working for Scotland Yard, and a savant so brilliant he was known as "The Thinking Machine."

To introduce readers to these detectives, Resurrected Press has assembled a collection of stories featuring these and other remarkable sleuths in The Edwardian Detectives.

- The Case of Laker, Absconded by Arthur Morrison
- The Fenchurch Street Mystery by Baroness Orczy
- The Crime of the French Café by Nick Carter
- The Man with Nailed Shoes by R Austin Freeman
- The Blue Cross by G. K. Chesterton
- The Case of the Pocket Diary Found in the Snow by Augusta Groner
- The Ninescore Mystery by Baroness Orczy
- The Riddle of the Ninth Finger by Thomas W. Hanshew
- The Knight's Cross Signal Problem by Ernest Bramah

- The Problem of Cell 13 by Jacques Futrelle
- The Conundrum of the Golf Links by Percy James Brebner
- The Silkworms of Florence by Clifford Ashdown
- The Gateway of the Monster by William Hope Hodgson
- The Affair at the Semiramis Hotel by A. E. W. Mason
- The Affair of the Avalanche Bicycle & Tyre Co., LTD by Arthur Morrison

RESURRECTED PRESS CLASSIC MYSTERY CATALOGUE

Journeys into Mystery
Travel and Mystery in a More Elegant Time

The Edwardian Detectives
Literary Sleuths of the Edwardian Era

Gems of Mystery
Lost Jewels from a More Elegant Age

E. C. Bentley
Trent's Last Case: The Woman in Black

Ernest Bramah
Max Carrados Resurrected:
The Detective Stories of Max Carrados

Agatha Christie
The Secret Adversary
The Mysterious Affair at Styles

Octavus Roy Cohen
Midnight

Freeman Wills Croft
The Ponson Case
The Pit Prop Syndicate

J. S. Fletcher
The Herapath Property
The Rayner-Slade Amalgamation
The Chestermarke Instinct
The Paradise Mystery
Dead Men's Money

The Middle of Things
Ravensdene Court
Scarhaven Keep
The Orange-Yellow Diamond
The Middle Temple Murder
The Tallyrand Maxim
The Borough Treasurer
In the Mayor's Parlour
The Saftey Pin

R. Austin Freeman
The Mystery of 31 New Inn from the Dr. Thorndyke Series
John Thorndyke's Cases from the Dr. Thorndyke Series
The Red Thumb Mark from The Dr. Thorndyke Series
The Eye of Osiris from The Dr. Thorndyke Series
A Silent Witness from the Dr. John Thorndyke Series
The Cat's Eye from the Dr. John Thorndyke Series
Helen Vardon's Confession: A Dr. John Thorndyke Story
As a Thief in the Night: A Dr. John Thorndyke Story
Mr. Pottermack's Oversight: A Dr. John Thorndyke Story
Dr. Thorndyke Intervenes: A Dr. John Thorndyke Story
The Singing Bone: The Adventures of Dr. Thorndyke
The Stoneware Monkey: A Dr. John Thorndyke Story
The Great Portrait Mystery, and Other Stories: A Collection of Dr. John Thorndyke and Other Stories
The Penrose Mystery: A Dr. John Thorndyke Story
The Uttermost Farthing: A Savant's Vendetta

Arthur Griffiths
The Passenger From Calais
The Rome Express

Louis Tracy
The Strange Case of Mortimer Fenley
The Albert Gate Mystery
The Bartlett Mystery
The Postmaster's Daughter
The House of Peril
The Sandling Case: What Would You Have Done?
Charles Edmonds Walk
The Paternoster Ruby

John R. Watson
The Mystery of the Downs
The Hampstead Mystery

Edgar Wallace
The Daffodil Mystery
The Crimson Circle

Carolyn Wells
Vicky Van
The Man Who Fell Through the Earth
In the Onyx Lobby
Raspberry Jam
The Clue
The Room with the Tassels
The Vanishing of Betty Varian
The Mystery Girl
The White Alley
The Curved Blades
Anybody but Anne
The Bride of a Moment
Faulkner's Folly
The Diamond Pin
The Gold Bag
The Mystery of the Sycamore
The Come Backy

Raoul Whitfield
Death in a Bowl

And much more!
Visit ResurrectedPress.com
for our complete catalogue

About Resurrected Press

A division of Intrepid Ink, LLC, Resurrected Press is dedicated to bringing high quality, vintage books back into publication. See our entire catalogue and find out more at www.ResurrectedPress.com.

About Intrepid Ink, LLC

Intrepid Ink, LLC provides full publishing services to authors of fiction and non-fiction books, eBooks and websites. From editing to formatting, from publishing to marketing, Intrepid Ink gets your creative works into the hands of the people who want to read them. Find out more at www.IntrepidInk.com.